THE ROYAL HERETIC

....

SARAH MACKLIN

MVmedia, LLC
Fayetteville, Georgia

MVmedia, LLC
PO Box 143052
Fayetteville, GA 30214
www.mvmediaatl.com

Publisher's Note: This is a work of fiction. Names, characters, places, and incidents are a product of the author's imagination. Locales and public names are sometimes used for atmospheric purposes. Any resemblance to actual people, living or dead, or to businesses, companies, events, institutions, or locales is completely coincidental.

Book Layout ©2017 BookDesignTemplates.com

Ordering Information:
Quantity sales. Special discounts are available on quantity purchases by corporations, associations, and others. For details, contact the "Special Sales Department" at the address above.

The Royal Heretic/Sarah Macklin. -- 1st ed.
ISBN 978-1-7346279-2-3

Contents

CHAPTER ONE 9

CHAPTER TWO 19

CHAPTER THREE 29

CHAPTER FOUR 34

CHAPTER FIVE... 42

CHAPTER SIX.. 53

CHAPTER SEVEN 67

CHAPTER EIGHT.. 76

CHAPTER NINE 86

CHAPTER TEN 96

CHAPTER ELEVEN 108

CHAPTER TWELVE 123

CHAPTER THIRTEEN... 136

CHAPTER FOURTEEN 150

CHAPTER FIFTEEN.. 163

CHAPTER SIXTEEN 178

CHAPTER SEVENTEEN.. 187

CHAPTER EIGHTEEN 201

CHAPTER NINETEEN 214

CHAPTER TWENTY.. 228

CHAPTER TWENTY-ONE 240

CHAPTER TWENTY-TWO 252

CHAPTER TWENTY-THREE 266

CHAPTER TWENTY-FOUR 280

CHAPTER TWENTY-FIVE 293

CHAPTER TWENTY-SIX... 306

CHAPTER TWENTY-SEVEN 313

To my husband, Elgin, who supported my dreams no matter what.
Épée!

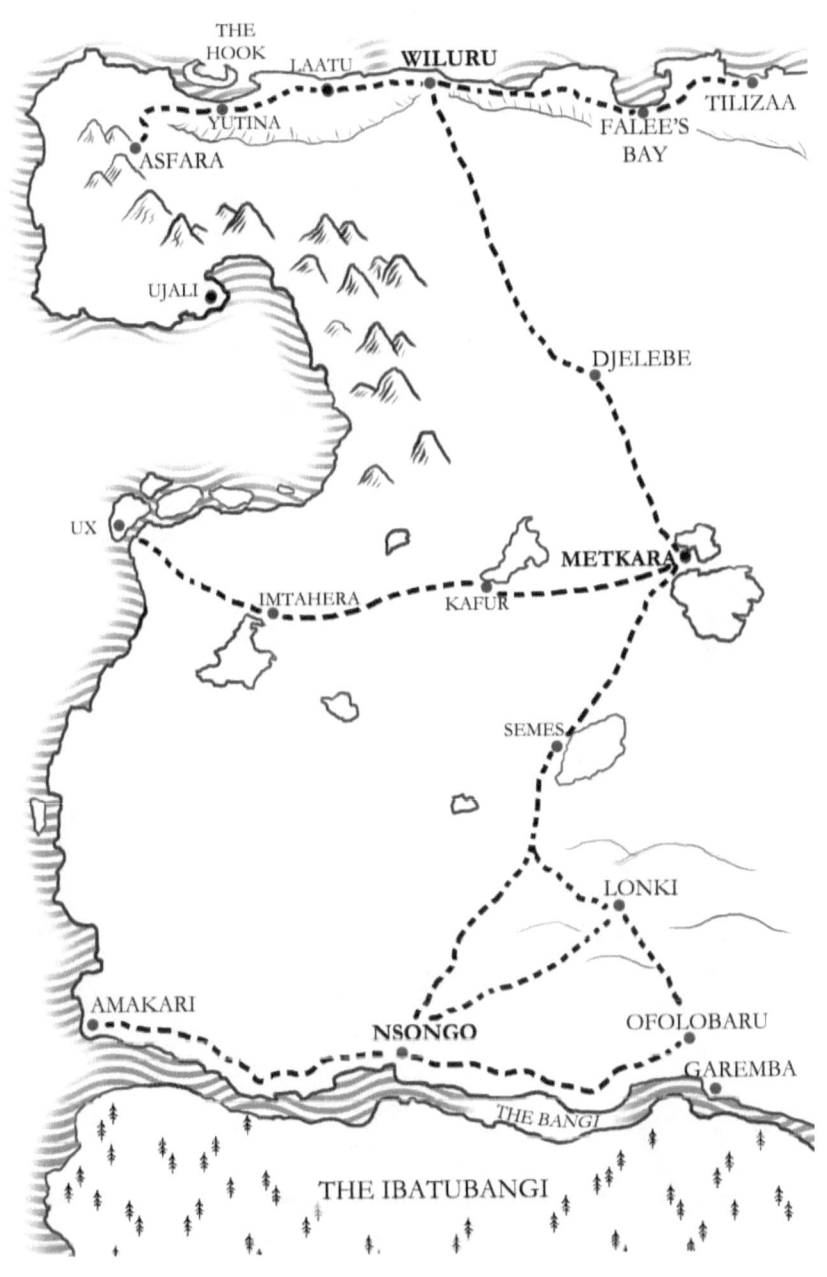

CHAPTER ONE

Over a thousand bulls, cows, goats, waterfowl, and crocodiles had been sacrificed on the Great Royal Son's behalf, but still the gods remained silent. The steps of the temple were slick with their blood, pooling in the inscriptions on the bricks. The air was hot and thick with the smell of their burnings on the funeral pyres from the previous day. Izriamat hoped the storm that was sure to come this afternoon would clear the air in the city. She didn't want to choke on the scent of smoke for the rest of the day.

She walked solemnly behind the netkoleh and his first wife, trying to keep her face from falling into the apathy she felt for the occasion. Behind her stretched the rest of the royal procession; the other wives and concubines, their children, the royal priests, courtiers, and servants. Each of them was garbed in the dull gray funeral clothes traditional in the capital, gray the color of ash. She stole a glance behind her, watching the long line of dullness trail down the steps of the god's hill and down to the Way of the Sky. Soon they would leave a trail of red behind them, marring the clean street. It was a shame.

They entered the shade of the temple, the air growing hotter and thicker. The vents in the stone ceiling weren't enough to purify the air here and Izriamat found her eyes beginning to water. The stinging was a blessing; now it would seem as if she were actually saddened by her stepson's passing. Indeed, it was a shame that one so young was joining his ancestors, but would she mourn any of the netkoleh's lineage? No. She prayed daily that their damned line would die out. But as she listened to the shuffling of hundreds of feet behind her, she knew her prayer was folly.

The sun suddenly shone again on them as they entered the open courtyard in the rear of the temple. The funeral pyre was erected in the center of the courtyard, the scent of the ola oil sweet and strong on the breeze. The rest of the procession filed in behind them, crowding into the space and filling the arcade around. Behind her, Izriamat heard the sniffles and sobbing of the princesses, the four of them standing with their nannies. Beside the netkoleh, his first wife finally broke down in tears. He put a tender arm around her shoulders. Izriamat had to resist crinkling her nose. She hated his hands. They were the hands of a defiler.

After a moment, the crowd parted behind them and the priests entered, carrying the body of the boy on an elaborate palanquin. It took twelve men to carry it, so laden was it with his possessions and items to carry him into the next life. The priests circled around the closest of the royal family, finally coming to a stop in front of the boy's parents. Sobbing, his mother took out the large white feather of purity and tucked it in the boy's crossed hands so that the gods would know his heart was clean. Izriamat kept her disdain locked down. If his heart was truly clean, the gods already knew that. No feather would save his spirit.

The netkoleh stepped before his eldest son and leaned down placing a kiss on the boy's lips. It would be his final blessing on his son and heir. Former heir. The boy would never inherit the title of netkoleh, the incarnation of Koleh on earth. That would fall on his next eligible son. Izriamat's nose did wrinkle then. It would be her son. To think that her blood would be forever mixed with his made her stomach twist. For the first time she wished that her counterpart would conceive again quickly.

When her husband stepped back from the body, the priests lifted it again making a slow, dignified approach to the pyre. Once the palanquin was secured on top, the high priest brought out the ceremonial torch. He bowed to the netkoleh, offering it to his sovereign. The netkoleh took it solemnly, staring at the unlit wood for some time. Izriamat leaned slightly, attempting to get a hint of his expression. He was supposed to begin the incantation to ignite the torch with a sacred fire. Even the first wife glanced over to him, unsure.

Another few awkward moments passed and he finally took a deep breath to begin. The torch burst into flame, the netkoleh's face still stoic. He passed it to the priest who in turn approached the pyre. The celestial flame eagerly took to the kindling. Flames leapt to the ceiling. The smell of a myriad of herbs filled the room. It was a nearly successful attempt at masking the smell of burning flesh.

The entire party stood there, watching the fire for nearly an hour. Wave after wave of heat washed over them, until everyone was covered in a fine layer of sweat. Izriamat resisted the urge to fan herself. What she would give to be near the sea again and feel its cooling breeze.

The last of the fire died out, its fuel crumbling at last into ashes. The ceremony was done and she held in her sigh of relief. The crowd parted again to let the netkoleh pass through. Izriamat stepped aside for her husband and the Great Royal Wife. Her counterpart wept heavily, but their husband didn't. One could think it was a sign of strength, but she could tell it was something else. There was a cold, empty look to his eyes. Unease stirred deep in her core. As she filed in line behind them, a chill ran up her entire body. Her husband was a deeply emotional man. This death had wounded him like no other. His sorrow would last for untold months, but there was something more to it. They passed from the temple and feeling wouldn't abate. There was more brewing in his heart and spirit than sadness.

* * *

Bakari looked out over the capital of Metkara and the lazy trails of smoke coming from the temple on the god's hill. Someone else's loved one would be burning to sever their ties to this plane and begin their journey to sail the heavens. The sky grew overcast as thick clouds moved in from the south. Any further funerals would be postponed until tomorrow. It was just as well. It wasn't as if there were any gods to send them to.

For weeks he'd pleaded with the gods to heal his son. The boy's illness had set in quickly, sending his heir and true son on a quick, downward spiral. It began as a simple cough, as if nothing more than dust was plaguing him. In a week it progressed to fits that let him gasping for breath. Just six days ago, he took to his bed, coughing up blood and barely keeping anything down.

Bakari leaned forward in his chair, resting his chin on his entwined fingers. He was the embodiment of Koleh himself, the power of a god wrapped in flesh. Yet nothing he could do, nothing he could say, no magics or rites he could perform healed his son. The gods kept their mouths shut and their power locked away from him as if he were some common mortal who wronged them. He was the netkoleh. They had chosen him and his line. This was a betrayal.

Tears welled in the corner of his eyes as he thought about his departed son. The boy was so strong, so clever. Now, the one left to replace him was the infant son of his second wife. He blinked the tears away. If only Arkoleh hadn't born so many daughters he wouldn't have to look to Izriamat for an heir. It was a miracle that his northern wife even conceived.

Talk ran about the palace of her being barren. How could she be a man's wife for seven years and not quicken even once? It wasn't for lack of attention. He dared think he desired her more than he loved Arkoleh. But last year the impossible happened and, early in the season of storms this year, she brought forth a son. The boy was strong with lungs like a bull, but Bakari now understood how fleeting strength could be.

"My husband."

He looked back at hearing the honeyed voice of the Great Royal Wife. She'd changed out of her mourning clothes, back into an everyday dress and makeup. He beckoned her closer, onto the palace balcony.

"What is it?" he asked, still looking at the smoke coming from the temple.

"I came to see if you were all right," she asked tim-

12

idly. It was so unlike her. "You did not seem yourself earlier."

"We'd watched our son burn, Arkoleh. You were not yourself either."

He felt her soft hand on his shoulder. "I was only concerned."

Bakari sighed. "I will be fine."

"Are you sure?"

"Yes!" he snapped. If she wanted someone to fuss and dote over why didn't she attend to the gaggle of daughters she'd given him.

Her hand slid from his shoulder, but she didn't leave. He could feel her hesitation.

"Will . . . will you come to my chambers tonight? I need you."

He didn't answer her.

"Bakari, my husband, we need each other. You . . . you must have an heir."

Bakari rose, turning on her. "You would replace our son, our beloved Koletun so quickly? My heart has been ripped from my chest and you only worry about having me between your legs."

"No, my husband, that's not what I . . ."

"Were your tears at the temple even real?"

Arkoleh burst into sobs, burying her face in her hands. "Of course, my tears are real. My heart has been broken too. I saw the son I birthed and nursed sent to the gods today. How could you think that I want to replace him?" She took deep breaths in an attempt to calm herself. "I was only thinking of your line."

Bakari's anger abated as he watched his first wife, his first lover, crying. He placed his hands at her shoulders.

"My line is secure. I have another son."

She looked up to him, wiping tears away. "Not from that woman."

Why was she trying to anger him again?

"That woman is my second wife."

"I'm sure she still stubbornly prays to her people's

gods. She'd poison the boy against us."

"That is my son regardless of her beliefs. He is my seed and chosen of Koleh. The netkoleh have taken a wife from her people since their kingdom was conquered."

"But none of their children have ever become the netkoleh. Will the gods be happy with someone with their blood as their body on earth?"

"Then the gods shouldn't have taken my son away from me!" he roared. Arkoleh took several steps back from him. "If you want someone to blame, then blame them. Go to the temple. Ask them why I couldn't heal my son. Ask them why they could create the world, separate the sky from the land, but they couldn't heal one small boy! Ask them!"

Arkoleh looked at him, mouth moving like a fresh fish. "You . . . can't mean what you're saying."

Bakari sat back down angrily. His right hand balled up tightly, pressing against his chair's armrest.

"All that I've done in my life, I've done in *their* name. I am supposed to be their speaker on earth, yet I've hardly felt their presence. Even when I've used their so-called power, I've felt no connection. If they've ever truly been listening to me, to my pleas, they've kept their answers to themselves." He rested his chin on his fingers again. "I am supposed to be both here and with the gods at the same time. In my life I've always felt solidly here."

He stopped himself before continued. He feared he might say something that would horrify his wife even further. There were thoughts beginning to brew in his mind that he wasn't sure he wanted fully formed. He scowled.

"Leave me," he commanded his wife. Out of the corner of his eye he saw her nod and quickly exit. He needed to be alone for some time. He had much to think about.

* * *

The morning sunshine was warm on her face as Izriamat nursed her young son. He was hungry this morning and eagerly latched on. It was strange, to feel nothing for one's own child. She'd grown more attached to him over his short four months of life, but still he felt like a stranger to her. It was as if she held someone else's child instead of her own. In a way, it was someone else's child. He already favored his father in looks. She didn't know how she would act towards him as he grew older.

She thought great Yutuu had mercifully closed her womb when she was brought here to be the netkoleh's queen. She couldn't understand why, after so many years, she would be given a child and, worse yet, a child with *that man*. That man who ripped her from her home and her calling under Yutuu. That man who selfishly threw aside tradition and refused to wait for her sister to come of age. That man who made her, a dedicated priestess, a symbol of the empire that her family had to bow down to. Her aunt had died under the weight of being the old netkoleh's second queen. She often wondered if that would be her fate as well.

Izriamat breathed in deeply, fighting back the sorrow. How she longed to return home, to see the beautiful northern ocean again. If she were to return home, somehow, she could no longer have her greatest joy, to serve in the temple. Her heart broke anew every time she thought of her vows, to be a faithful servant to the god of the sea and to only be wed to him, vows shattered on her wedding night. She remembered her father's controlled outrage at the idea of her marriage, yet there was nothing to be done about it. Going against the netkoleh's wishes and the treaty formed generations ago would be a declaration of war. Her father loved his people too much to set them against an entire kingdom. She was the price to pay for their continued peace, just as her aunt was before her, and her great-aunt before that. She knew her father understood that, but what she would give just to let him know that she was not completely crushed by her role.

The baby grew fussy and she held him up to burp him before giving him her other breast. As he still fed enthusiastically, she was suddenly glad for his wet nurse. She didn't know how she could have dealt with this both day and night.

She heard the shuffling sound of sandals and looked up to see her husband entering her room. When they were first married, it was a struggle to keep her scathing looks from showing. Now, it was habit. She lowered her head to him.

"My husband. To what do I owe this visit?"

He walked over to her, placing a hand on the baby's tiny head. "I came to check on my son."

His son. As if she had nothing to do with it! "He's fine, hungry but fine."

"Why is he so hungry? Is the nurse not feeding him enough?" He looked around the room at the servants waiting at the edges of the room.

"No. He's just growing." She was sick of his outbursts. "His body needs more. He is fine."

He ran his fingers across the boy's fine hair. "That's good. That's good."

She watched as his eyes moved from the child to her bare breasts. His hand moved to caress her chest and up to her neck.

"And, how are you? I know yesterday was a . . . difficult day."

Her skin crawled at his touch. "I'm fine. Death is a part of life. It has no care of age or station." She made a fuss of rearranging the baby, which her son didn't seem to appreciate.

Bakari didn't take the hint and ran the back of his hand along her jawline.

"As wise as you are beautiful."

"And how are you doing, my husband?" she asked casually.

"I've been doing a lot of . . . thinking. Trying to decide what I should do next, what steps I should take."

Izriamat didn't like the way he phrased that. It usually meant he was plotting something.

"I am sure that your infinite, celestial wisdom will guide you in whatever path you take." That should please his ego for now.

He suddenly looked to her. "I will need your help, Izriamat. Change is coming, great change. I only tell you because you are stronger in will than Arkoleh."

She was shocked. In the strict hierarchy of the palace, she'd become accustomed to being second to Arkoleh in everything.

"I see that I will need you to act in my stead many times in the near future," he continued. "You and she will become as my right and left hands. You two will be my voice in the places I cannot be. I'll need you to be ready."

Izriamat stared at him blankly. He'd never confided in her. He'd never referred to her as an equal to his first wife. It just wasn't done. In the few years she'd known him, he proved himself as a man who took everything to heart and lashed out from the heart. He was dangerous when he was emotional. Unfortunately, it wasn't he who suffered from his outbursts.

She chewed her lip. "How soon will you need me?"

"Soon," he answered with a determined smile.

She nodded, her mind racing. Deep within her heart, she felt that whatever his plan was it would trap her here even more. Her mind ran to the faces of her family the last time she'd seen them, full of helpless sorrow.

"My husband, may I make a request?"

"What is it?"

"May I travel to Wiluru to see my family?"

He looked to her, skeptical.

"It's been seven long years since I've seen their faces. I wish to see them again and then, after that, I will be forever at your side."

He seemed to be rolling the thought over in his mind. She begged Yutuu to move his heart.

"Please, my husband. I have done my duty and given you a son. Please grant me this one request."

"You may go," he said at long last. "But return soon. I need you more here and my son will need you as well." He leaned in to kiss her and she accepted it even though she wanted to wretch. He stroked the baby's head one more time and left her chamber.

Izriamat called for a servant. Her husband was a strange creature. She handed her now sleeping son over to the servant and rearranged her clothing to cover herself. She knew now that the rest of her life was to be filled with more misery, but at least now there would be some point of joy to look back on and remember. She began planning for the trip she thought she'd never be able to take.

CHAPTER TWO

Hetsaf arrived faster than Bakari expected, but his half-brother was always a punctual man. He strode in, the gold necklace of chancellor around his broad shoulders. It amused him. Hetsaf did favor Izriamat in many ways. They were first cousins, after all, but their demeanors couldn't be more different. His brother may have had a Wiluruan mother, but he was an Egan through and through. There was no one Bakari trusted more in this entire kingdom.

He smiled as the other man bowed to him.

"You called for me, netkoleh. How may I serve you?"

Bakari poured wine into his shallow dish, sipping thoughtfully.

"Do you love me, Hetsaf?"

His brother was clearly confused by the question

"Of course, I love you, netkoleh."

"No, no, no." He shook his head, setting the container of wine down. "Do you love me? Bakari, your brother?"

"Yes, I do."

"Would you follow me even if I weren't the netkoleh?"

He could see Hetsaf struggling for a proper answer, but he had to test him. He needed to know who was loyal.

"Yes, brother."

Bakari nodded, sipping again. "Do you remember how hard we tried to save Koletun? All of those offerings, bled and burned on the altar of Koleh."

His brother nodded.

"I tried everything to save him. Now I realize that this was just a lesson, the most important lesson that I've ever learned. There are no gods. There never were."

He found himself pacing back and forth in the small room. It felt liberating to finally say what had been on his heart this past day.

"Everything this kingdom has accomplished hasn't been the will or work of the gods. It has all been the work of our people, the work of our ancestors. Was it a god who came down from the heavens and finally conquered the warriors of the south? No. It was the work of me and my father. I am the hand that guides this land, because without a true leader it would fall into chaos."

Hetsaf simply stared at him, his face impassive. Bakari wondered if he'd said too much, if he'd pushed him too far. His brother finally lowered his head.

"What do you need me to do?"

Bakari's heart swelled. He put a hand on his brother's shoulder.

"I want the gods erased from every corner of this kingdom. I want every priesthood dissolved. Every shrine must be destroyed no matter how small. I want the texts burned. We won't live by their lies any longer."

Hetsaf sighed. "This won't go well with the priests. What will we do with them?"

"They can work for a change instead of getting fat off of the gold offered by the common folk."

"What of the Arakgu'un?"

Bakari paused, thinking of the sect of assassin priests. The high priest might seek to turn them on him and his family. They were a dangerous lot.

"We'll have to see if we can bring them to our side in this. I think they will be useful."

"Many of them are zealots."

"I think they will see the light."

Hetsaf folded his arms, staring intently at a spot on the floor. Bakari loved when his chancellor was deep in thought.

"Will you delay the Pilgrimage?"

Bakari released a breath between his teeth. Had it been five years already? He tapped a finger on his chin, pacing the room again. He hated that long trip and it would be even longer this time since they had to travel through the south. After a few months, he always grew tired of the monotony of grain and luxury tallies. He put his hands at his hips.

"We won't delay it. It will be a good way to spread the word of my decree."

Hetsaf frowned deeply. "The people may resist."

"And that is why we must move swiftly. Begin to have the palace walls cleaned today. I want this place rid of every picture and every inscription of the gods."

His brother bowed. "Yes, netko . . ." He paused, looking up. "What shall we call you?"

Bakari took a thoughtful sip of wine. He hadn't considered it.

"Call me emperor."

"Yes, my emperor."

* * *

Newa dangled the knife above the man's chest, the point dangerously close to his skin. His victim was tied down to the stone slab by his wrists and ankles without any slack to struggle. The man panted, panicking in the sort of way Newa delighted in. His apprentice stood in the corner, watching the confession. Newa knew the boy would be a bit squeamish about this, but he had to learn. An unrepentant sinner must be brought back to the right path and men like this could only be reined in by force. He moved the knife up to the hollow in the man's neck allowing the cold blade to rest lightly. The sooner his apprentice learned to enjoy shedding blood the better.

"Do you know why you're here?" he asked.

The man licked his lips nervously. They hadn't given him anything to eat and drink since they dragged him out of bed yesterday evening. Newa knew the man had to be nearly out of his mind with fear. They'd barely told him anything about his capture, but he knew he was in the clutches of the Arakgu'un.

"I'm a sinner," he croaked out. "I've sinned against the ways of the gods." His eyes flicked about the room in a panic. "Please," he said looking back at Newa, "I'm sorry. I'm sorry for all that I've done. I swear I will make amends."

Newa pressed the tip of his knife into the man's skin, coaxing a small drop of blood to well up.

"No, it's not so easy for someone like you. I know all about you. You are unrepentant, unashamed of your transgressions. You've flaunted them before man and before the gods who see all. There is only one true way to cleanse you." He waited a moment to leave the man in suspense. "You must confess your wrong doings. All of them. Every sorted detail."

"I'll tell you everything."

"Yes, you will." He pressed the knife in a bit more causing a trickle of blood to run down the man's shoulder. "I will get the truth out of you because I know every way to pull it out of a man. Don't even try to lie. I will know. If you do, I have been given the distinct permission by the gods themselves to punish you for a false confession." He withdrew the knife looking at the blood on the tip. "Such punishment is . . . an excruciating affair."

The man's eyes widened at the sight of his blood dripping from the knife. Immediately, he began divulging his deepest, darkest secrets. He had a penchant for very young women. He cheated on his yearly taxes. He beat his wife and children without reason. He drank to excess. All this Newa already knew. He'd observed the man for weeks. But to get it out of him was part of the fun of the experience. There was always something they didn't want to speak aloud. Always something they tried to hold back from him. Getting that last secret was where he found joy.

The man finally ran out of secrets to tell. He began to lick his lips again. Newa didn't miss the habit. He was still nervous. He was still hiding something. Newa smiled at the man.

"Do you not feel better?" The man nodded furiously.

Newa began walking around the room, stroking his
chin thoughtfully.

"So, you have confessed everything?"

The man nodded again.

"Are you sure?" Newa asked, enjoying the game of
cat and mouse. There was a minuscule pause but he nodded again. Newa stopped, just beyond the man's head, just
short of the edge of his field of vision.

"You're lying to me."

Horror lit up the man's face.

"No, no I'm not. I swear." He began to sweat, the
beads shining like jewels on his forehead. "I've told you
everything."

"No, you haven't. I can tell." He sighed dramatically. "Now, I have to punish you."

The man began to protest but Newa stabbed the
knife into his shoulder. The sudden scream made his
young apprentice jump. Newa chuckled. He remembered
when he was so young and inexperienced. However, at
witnessing his first confession he was thrilled when his
master began to torture their subject. The rush then was
the same for him now even after a decade.

He carved at the shoulder muscle carefully, using
the man's own struggling to cause the cut to go deeper. He
didn't plan on crippling the man, but he would leave
wounds that would take ages to heal and scars he would
never forget. Newa finished the crescent shaped incision
on the man, flicking the blood off of his knife. He gave his
victim a moment to get over the pain and focus. When the
man's eyes finally locked on him, tears running down his
cheeks, Newa smiled.

"Have you decided to tell me your last secret? Truly
you'll feel much better if you do."

"Please," the man begged. "I've told you everything."

"Lying again." Newa began running the knife along
the man's ribs, shaving off a thin layer of skin. With the

precision of a surgeon, he shaved off another layer, the blood running freely down his side. Newa waited a moment, seeing if the man would confess. The man took a deep breath and opened his mouth to speak, but Newa began shaving again. Each shaving he tossed to the floor. He took to his work like an artist, making sure each spot he shaved started precisely where the last ended.

By the end of half an hour the man's entire chest and stomach was raw and bleeding. Satisfied with his work, Newa flicked the blood from his knife. He looked to his subject with a kind smile. His grin was greeted with a look of pure pain and terror. After another suspenseful moment he bent back over the man, bringing his knife up to the man's thigh.

"All right!" the man croaked.

Newa stopped, looking up towards him. "Did you have something to say?"

The man swallowed and took a moment to pull himself together. "I'll confess."

Newa made a show of examining his knife. "I'm listening."

"When I was a young man, I slept with my stepmother while my father was away." He took a few more painful breaths. "She had my child. I never told my father what happened. He still believes his grandson is his son."

Newa was almost disappointed. That was all. He was expecting something truly blasphemous. He hid his feelings and regarded the raw, bleeding man with a grateful smile.

"It is good that you confessed." He made a gesture over the man, invoking the powers of the Judge of All. "Now that you have cleansed yourself, you can be forgiven by the gods. You have been given a second chance to live free and clean. Grasp onto it with all your might. There is no one alive who has been given a third chance."

The man nodded weakly and Newa could tell that he was succumbing to shock. He looked to his apprentice who stood slack jawed from his corner.

"Yanu," he called, snapping his fingers loudly. "Give

the man a healing potion, a sleeping drink, and bandage him up." The young man nodded and began gathering all he needed.

Newa smiled as he left the small room. Young Yanu would learn much from healing the man. Next week, they would work on a body or two to learn the intricacies of killing. Even in a city that burns their dead, fresh bodies were easy to find. He set out down the hallway that led back to the bed chambers wanting to change out of his robes that were splattered with blood. It just wouldn't do to be seen out like this. As he turned into the more common areas someone called his name. He looked over to see one of his brethren hurrying up to him. The other priest's face was a maze of worry.

"Is something the matter, Itakoleh?"

Itakoleh fell in step with him, leaning close before talking.

"Have you heard what's going on in the palace?"

Newa nearly rolled his eyes. He could care less about palace gossip but he indulged the faults of the closest thing he could call a friend.

"What's happening?" he asked echoing the man's whisper.

"The palace is being stripped of every statue and painting of the gods."

Newa's eyebrows shot up in surprise.

"They're even chiseling out the inscriptions on the walls. There's talk that the netkoleh wants to erase the gods from the land."

Newa sucked in a breath. Now this was troubling. This could lead to civil unrest. At least the proper priests wouldn't be happy about it. His own order might have to go underground. He didn't think he'd like the life of a fugitive. He'd already lived on the streets once. He wasn't thrilled at the prospect of returning there.

"Where did you hear this?" he asked after a moment.

"I overheard Gebun talking with his lover, you know, that maid from the palace. She was nearly frantic that she had to take all the statuettes from the lesser wives chambers."

Newa rubbed his chin. "Disturbing indeed."

"I don't like where this is may be headed."

"Then we'll have to look to our leader and the gods themselves for our help." He placed a hand on his compatriot's shoulder. "Thank you for bringing this to me." He looked around suddenly remembering that they were still in a public place. "I don't think you should let this get out too far. You know how some of us are."

"I'll heed your advice," Itakoleh said nodding and went on his way, giving a gracious smile as if they'd been talking about nothing more than the weather.

Newa hurried along, wanting to get back to his chambers to change but more over to talk to the leader of the order who'd been his teacher when he was brought into the Arakgu'un. Newa didn't care what happened to the proper priests. They were lazy charlatans who used half of the offerings left behind for their own gain. They were leeches of the state, every single one of them. They didn't believe in true justice like his order. The Arakgu'un were the ones who did the dirty work of turning around the worst of sinners. They were the ones who truly kept this land from descending into depravity.

Newa reached his chamber, stripping down from his old robes. His leader would have a plan. He trusted that old man with his life. He would have a way to preserve the order in the face of the upheaval this would cause. Newa smiled. Maybe they would even have to choose a new netkoleh. That could prove interesting.

* * *

It was late that night when the Hand of Gu'un had a chance to speak with Newa. Newa had waited patiently outside his office for an hour as the leader spoke with someone important. Finally, he heard his old mentor's voice beckoning him inside. Newa opened the door, not realizing who the company was in the room. He hid his surprise as he bowed before the netkoleh's chancellor. His suspicions were raised, but he kept his voice even.

"I am honored to be in your presence, great Hetsaf." He turned and bowed to his leader. "Honored Antakhan-an."

His leader and mentor beckoned him closer. "I'm actually glad you came, Newa. The chancellor has brought me some . . . interesting news and I want you to be a part of this."

He kept the frown from his face. "You know you have my utmost loyalty."

"That's good to know."

Newa looked at the two of them, standing in an almost conspiratory way at Antakhanan's desk, looking like old friends, or worse, like vultures waiting for the lions to finish at a carcass.

"What's going on?" he asked, feigning ignorance.

"What we are about to discuss must not go past this room. Am I clear?" Newa nodded to him. "Good."

Hetsaf shifted his stance. Newa noted that there was more authority to his posture now.

"The death of the Great Royal Son has affected the netkoleh greatly. He has come to realize that the gods have never truly been with us and it has always been up to man to determine his outcome."

Newa stared at the two men making a slow look of shock spread over his face. It was a shock to hear this blasphemy confirmed but he wanted to know more. A deluge of questions stormed in his head but he settled for one.

"Why have I been deemed worthy to hear such knowledge?"

"I trained you myself," Antakhanan answered. "I know your mind and I know you would be one of the ones least disturbed."

Hetsaf jumped in next. "My brother, the emperor, doesn't wish to disband your order. In fact, he wants to keep you all on as assassins on his behalf." He paused. "At least the ones that would be loyal to him. Are you one of those?"

Newa knew a trap when he saw one. "I am faithful to my leader. Where he goes, I shall follow."

Antakhanan nodded and looked to Hetsaf. "That is why I brought him in." He smiled. "I've chosen to follow our . . . emperor."

"Then I will follow him as well."

Hetsaf nodded with a satisfied smile. "That's good to know. The emperor will have orders for you all shortly, but for now, carry on as if nothing has changed." He nodded to Newa and his leader. Newa bowed deeply as the man exited.

He began to follow the chancellor, but his leader called to him.

"Newa, stay for a moment." The man motioned for him to close the door and come closer. "Are you sure that you're okay with this?" His mouth asked the benign question, but his hand was a flurry of motions. *Do not worry,* he signed in their secret hand language. *What did I teach you early in your studies?*

"You know that I'm loyal. I owe you everything." *That we're here to preserve the balance and peace of this city and beyond. It doesn't matter which of the gods we bow to.*

"So, I can trust you?" *Even if we have to go along with this blasphemy, we will still be able to serve Gu'un and through him Koleh.*

"Of course, you can trust me, master." *Understood. I will keep this to myself until you let me know it's time.*

"Very good, Newa. I'll call for you again when you're needed."

He bowed low to his leader and backed out of the room. His mind was working furiously as he walked down the hallway. Antakhanan was right. The state may have disavowed the gods, but that didn't mean he had to stop his righteous work. He would bring people to true and absolute justice until the day he rattled out his last breath. And he planned on that being ages from now.

CHAPTER THREE

The moon cast the cliffs in an odd shade of gray as Efah climbed. Each new handhold dislodged sand into her face. She cursed the soft rock, hating every moment of the dangerous climb but it would be worth it if she found something. Her foot slipped again on the sandy cliff face, her heart nearly stopping. She climbed well past where any of her partners dared go in the hopes of opening one of the higher, untouched tombs. She prayed to the new gods and the old not to let her fall. From this height she'd surely die.

Efah hadn't planned on the life of a graverobber. She just fell into it, but it was better than being poor. Kanta's band needed someone as small and thin as she and Kanta was a good *persuader*. The treasure they found and sold over the past year kept clothes on her back and her belly full. It was the longest she'd ever gone without being hungry. Sure, it wasn't luxury, but she was satisfied. Now if only she didn't have to climb so high.

Efah was relieved when she pulled herself up and found a small path cut into the soft limestone. As she rose to her feet, an eerie, chilling wind blew past, kicking up dust into her face. She coughed hard, forcing one stinging eye to stay open. Most people thought this vast burial site was haunted, that the spirits of old, Egan kings long gone still lingered. She didn't believe it, but there was always the feeling of being watched when they came. During the day it wasn't so bad, but at night it felt like someone breathing down your neck at times.

She shook the feeling and carefully made her way along the narrow path. Luckily, light poured back down when the moon finally emerged from a sheet of clouds. She ran her hand along the wall, pressing in every so often feeling for weak spots. There had to be a tomb here somewhere. There wouldn't be a path if there wasn't somewhere for the path to lead to.

Efah stopped when her fingers ran over a peculiar rough spot. She stopped, lightly running her fingertips over it again. She rubbed harder and sand began to fall. Soon an inscription emerged, then a name. She couldn't read it, it was in the language of the Ega, but she could tell it must be of an important person. She rubbed more and part of a detailed relief emerged. Her eyes widened. This was what they were looking for.

"Did you find something?" came the shout from the ground.

"Yes," she shouted back. "We may have found a hidden one."

She took out her knife and began tapping at the cliff with the butt of the hilt. A few taps and the knife sunk through a soft spot. She grinned, using the hilt to knock through the opening. Sand and shards of old brick began falling at her feet. Soon she had a hole large enough for her to shimmy through.

"I'm going in," she called down.

It was a tight fit. She scraped her arms on the rough sides, but it wasn't anything she hadn't endured before. At least in this tomb, she wouldn't have to worry about rats, owls, or snakes that had made their home. They weren't inclined to welcome such a large intruder into their spaces. She tumbled in, trying her best to roll to her feet. Feeling around her belt, she located the oil-soaked torch she'd been given. She set it on the ground, quickly taking out her flint stone. A couple of flicks later the hallway was filled with light.

Efah gawked at what she saw. Vibrantly painted paintings covered the walls. Elaborate pictures of kings, animals, wars, captives, and Egan gods stretched as far as she could see. A certain excitement welled up within her. This was the first untouched tomb she'd ever found. The best they'd done before was to come across a resealed one that hadn't been completely looted over the years. She continued down the narrow hallway carefully. They might finally be able to have a little bit of luxury after today. Perhaps she'd be able to buy a decent pair of sandals, maybe even a proper outfit and not the hand-me-downs of the rest of the band.

The entrance hallway led into a small room that had yet another hall beyond it. Efah's excitement grew. The size of it and how much effort went into carving this into the cliff told her that all of her efforts would be paid back ten times over. She stepped into the small room and was met with a loud, resounding crack. Efah jumped back, terrified, holding her torch out like a weapon.

She looked down to see what she'd stepped on and saw a broken bone on the floor. She held the torch out farther and saw that the entire floor of the room was covered in skeletons. Her breath caught. So, the old stories of servants being buried alive was true. Swallowing hard, she continued, picking a careful path across the room. She didn't exactly believe in ghosts, but she didn't exactly not believe in them either.

She let out the breath she didn't realize she'd been holding when she set foot in the next hallway. This one was short, only a few feet. As she moved along, torch trembling in her hand, she saw something shining in another room. She willed herself to hurry and came into the next open space. Efah held in her laughter. Every inch of the room was filled with treasure. There were statues of gold, urns painted with gold and trimmed in pearls. A huge mirror leaned against the wall. That would fetch an enormous price if they could figure a way to get it out of here. The large coffin in the middle of the room would surely hold a dizzying amount of jewelry.

Efah untied the cloth from around her waist, using it as a makeshift sack. She quickly grabbed several of the lighter gold items, leaving the rest for when her band made its way in. Her stash securely tied, she made her way back through the halls and outside. The moonlight was spotty, clouds shifting across the face of the moon. It was a relief to breath the fresh air again, even if it was dusty. Her sack clanked loudly on the ground.

"Efah, is that you?" she heard from the ground far below.

"I'll be down in a minute." She looked around for a better path down to the ground. She wasn't too keen on climbing back down the crumbling cliff that brought her here. She snapped her head to the right, sure she saw something moving in the shadows. There was nothing on the path ahead of her, but she knew better. Her hand went to her knife. There were wild dogs about in places like this, or worse, lions that had wandered from greener lands.

She waited for a few more moments, until she was sure nothing was there. Relieved, she took her hand away from her knife. Then she did see movement, a fluttering of feathers. She almost cursed as a trio of vultures hopped out into the moonlight. Was that all? Efah was tempted to throw a rock at them for terrifying her when a larger shape came into the light.

It was like the shadows birthed him forth. He was tall, taller than any man she'd ever met. Around him was a cloak of feathers, black as the night, leading up to the collar of stark white plumes just like the vultures that preceded him. His skin was a sickly color, the chalky brown of a man who'd died in a river. He moved closer to her, his steps not making a sound. Efah wanted to run, to get as far away from this man and this place as possible, but her legs refused to obey her. She was rooted to the spot.

His eyes rose to meet hers, two milky white spots in his bald head. Efah began trembling even though he stopped over ten feet from her. The vultures hopped about perching on the small rocks in the path. Her breath came raggedly. He looked like death itself. No, she realized a moment later, he was death itself. Tears began to form at the corners of her eyes. Why had death come for her? She was young. She was healthy. He had no reason.

"There is an upheaval in our lands." His voice was a whisper, but she heard him as clearly as if he stood beside her. "The old, true ways are being erased."

"I don't understand," she stammered, not even sure if she should be speaking to him.

"You, child of the south, must spread the news. There is going to be a rebirth. But in order for the land to rise anew, there must be a casting off of the old. There must be death." His eyes seemed to catch hold of her soul. "If they do not throw off these false ways, there will be even more death, more burning, more blood spilled. I name you, Efah Aboujale, my herald. You who have already known a lifetime of deaths will be my voice. Tell them."

She blinked and he was gone. She vaguely heard her band calling to her from below, but her body seemed still out of her control. All she could do was stand, trembling, as wetness spread down her legs.

CHAPTER FOUR

Seabirds called overhead and performed aerial feats as Yutuuan walked through the noble paths of Wiluru. The birds fought over fish stolen from the ships that had just pulled into port. He looked out toward the sea and his heart tugged. A sigh escaped him. What he would give to be out at sea right now.

"We'll set sail before you know it, your majesty," his bodyguard said behind him.

"Not soon enough," Yutuuan threw over his shoulder. He didn't miss the smirk on Naret's face. The man knew he grew antsy on land, but he didn't need to patronize him.

A group of noble women paused, bowing as he drew closer. Their braids, decorated with interwoven ribbons of blue and white, swung down into their faces. He greeted them, gifting a smile to the one who one who dared look up at him through her hair. Yutuuan chuckled as he heard them giggling behind him. She would probably be talking about the crown prince's smile for a week.

"If you are looking for a task, my prince, you do have the academy."

Yutuuan twisted his mouth. Leave it Naret to try to keep him responsible. He did need to take a day to visit the military school. While it was always good to show his face to his soon to be soldiers and sailors, it was the magicians he was most interested in. They had a number of magic users that would be retiring soon and if he could take a look at the students that might be filling the ranks all the better. He envied them and their powers. Magic was a subject that was beyond him. Not to mention that the rigorous training and religious study wasn't appealing to him in the least. No, he would stick to swordplay.

They passed under a great shadow and Yutuuan glanced up at the towering facade of Wiluru's temple to Koleh. The great statues flanking the entrance stuck out like sore thumbs among the surrounding buildings. Yutuuan scowled. Just like everything else they'd imposed on them. Most of the Egan people that lived in Wiluru had adapted to native ways, many of them residing here for generations. But the temples, built early in the days after their surrender, were stark reminders of their occupation.

"My prince," Naret whispered urgently, "your expression."

Yutuuan came out of his thoughts and realized a priest at the steps of the wide entrance was staring at him. He relaxed his face looking away. A thought brought his gaze back to the entrance.

"Come, Naret," he said with a sudden smile. "Let us pay our respects and look like loyal members of the empire."

He ignored Naret's over dramatic, long suffering sigh and began climbing the stairs. The priest who'd stared at him, lowered his head as Yutuuan approached. The prince made a note that he didn't lower it appropriately enough for his station, but it wasn't worth squabbling over.

"Welcome, Prince Yutuuan," he said with an accent that marked him a Wiluruan Ega. "May Koleh shine down on you."

"Thank you," Yutuuan replied with a smile that faded as soon as he entered the dark interior. Mindful of eyes on him, he kept his face pleasant but not too inviting. The temple was busy this morning. Egan worshipers and Wiluruan converts milled about. Yutuuan swept his eyes over the gaudy temple, looking about the priests and priestesses. He made his way to the main altar going through the motions of fervent worship. He reached in his belt for his money pouch, pulling a trio of gold coins and placing them on the altar.

"Thank you for your most generous offering, Prince

Yutuuan," said a priestess nearby.

Yutuuan smiled at the familiar voice. He subtly took in her curvy frame as he turned to her.

"Koleh has smiled down on me and my people for so long how can I not give generously?" He saw the little twitch at her nose that meant she wanted to laugh.

"I would hope to see you worshiping here more often. Koleh can work wonders in your life."

Yutuuan reined in his smile as the linen moved across her hips when she shifted her weight.

"I will consider it." He lowered his voice. "Perhaps you can show me how to worship him properly."

Coins were dropped on the altar noisily and Yutuuan looked back. Naret stared at him with a tired expression. The priestess cleared her throat to hide a chuckle. He lowered her head to him.

"If you will excuse me, Prince Yutuuan. I have work to do *in the back.*"

Yutuuan grinned brightly then brought it back down. "Of course." He nodded as she made her way out of the main room.

"My prince," came Naret's stern voice at his shoulder. "Let us go."

They left the temple in silence. Yutuuan was almost amused at how obviously annoyed his bodyguard was.

"What?" he asked once they were outside.

Naret didn't answer at first and the prince could tell the man was chewing back a response. They walked a little farther down the path before the answer finally came.

"You must be more careful. Can you imagine the scandal if your little . . . tryst with that priestess was discovered?"

"We won't get discovered. We're careful." He took in the scathing glance Naret gave him. "Fine, we could be more careful. But that's half the fun." He playfully shoved the servant who'd become his dearest friend. Naret sighed, rolling his eyes deeply.

"Now, if you'll excuse me," Yutuuan said stopping at an alleyway, "I've been invited to a meeting."

Naret's eyes widened. "You can't be serious."

The prince quickly made his way down the narrow path. "Just keep watch. I'll be back shortly." He chuckled. "Well, not too quickly."

He laughed at Naret's face and kept moving. He'd done this how many times and his bodyguard was shocked every single time. Yutuuan slipped from the side alley to the one running behind the buildings on this path. He kept his head down as laborers passed him. Luckily most of these people wouldn't have ever seen their prince up close so he was unlikely to be recognized. He hurried to the back of the temple, turning away as two priests came out into the alley. He ducked down the skinny side alley beside the temple, stopping below a small window. His heart thundered at the thrill of his recklessness. It was the middle of the day. He could get caught at any moment, but as he told Naret, that was half the fun.

Yutuuan pulled out the already loosened wooden bars from the window, pushing them inside. One last look around and he climbed in, rolling in and coming to his feet. He smiled as he looked up to his beautiful Talekh, waiting on the other side of the room. She rushed up to him, crushing him in a hug and pressing her lips to his. Yutuuan wrapped his arms around her tightly.

"You've been away too long," she whispered in the midst of their kisses.

He pressed his hands on her buttocks, grateful for more than enough to hold, bringing her hips flush with his.

"Then I'll have to make it up to you."

They stripped each other quickly, their kissing becoming more insistent. He picked her up, using the wall to support her as they began their lovemaking. Their session was rough and needy, each clinging onto the other when they'd finished. Yutuuan let her back down, Talekh still holding onto him for support. He took in the scent of her hair, the thick smell of temple incense mixed with her sweat. It was the smell of danger to him and he'd always liked danger.

"I have to find a way to get you into the palace so that I can have you all night," he said while he rubbed her back and bottom.

Talekh looked up to him drunkenly. "We have to." She licked his chest. "By the gods, I want more."

They moved in to kiss again when there was a sound in the hallway. They scrambled to dress, Talekh shaking her head at herself the whole time. He pulled her in for a quick kiss before she turned toward the door.

"I promise I won't be away as long."

She pushed him away. "You'd better not be. Koleh doesn't look kindly on oath breakers."

He made the sign of supplication, doing his best to look remorseful. A quick climb out of the window and he was back in the alley. Talekh blew a kiss at him as she set the bars back in place. Yutuuan sighed as she disappeared from sight and hurried back the way he came. Everything about this affair was wrong. He was a prince of Wiluru. She wasn't just a priestess but also one of the netkoleh's many lesser sisters. If word of it made it out it would be a disaster. Naret was right. He had to be more careful. He spared a glance back toward the temple. But the reward for such a risk was too great to give up.

He made his way back to Naret who'd waited patiently on the noble path.

"You see," Yutuuan whispered when he reached him, "that didn't take long."

Naret took a quick moment to straighten out his prince's clothes.

"Are you ready to head to the academy? I'm sure they'll be thrilled to have a visit from you as well."

Yutuuan rolled his eyes. "Very well. Back to duty." They passed back by the temple on their way. Yutuuan looked up to the ugly statues of the sun god again. While tacky, the temple did have its merits.

* * *

Izriamat looked out over the city of Djelebe, the infamous library and the wall built to protect it. The library
and surrounding university loomed higher than the surrounding buildings, dominating the skyline. Her ancestors
were sent to learn here for generations. Her younger
brother would have as well if he hadn't thrown himself into his duties as the commander of Wiluru's military and
navy. It would be a nice stop on her trip north. They'd
rested here on her first trip south and the governor had
been so kind and welcoming to her. She hoped he would
still give her a proper welcome despite the news she
brought.

The gates opened wide for her caravan's entrance.
The doors were as high as the walls, with ornate carvings
of scholars and other wise men traveling to the shining
star of knowledge that was Djelebe. Horns blew heralding
their arrival. People in the street, dressed in the customary
long robe of their people, parted, curious as to who the
important traveler was.

Izriamat shifted in her saddle, the horse's slow gate
becoming tiresome. She wanted to be inside and out of the
glaring sun already. For a week they'd been traveling
across the great plains of Ega. It was hot and growing hotter as the dry season approached. But she guessed that she
should be thankful. The rain they had encountered was
spotty and short. It could have been storming the whole
time.

They wound their way through the city to the governor's palace, a sprawling building decorated with bright
geometrics. It was constructed in the same, simple design
as the rest of the city, smooth walls with windows as the
only architectural feature. There were few representations
of life here in the city. It was as if everything was decorated
to not be a distraction to the scholars. She nodded in ad-
miration. It was a welcome change to the gaudy paintings
of the capital.

They were welcomed into the palace, their horses

and other animals taken away to stables well hidden from onlookers. Izriamat brushed the dirt from her dress. The doors ahead of their party opened and a group of people hurried out. She recognized the man at the head of them immediately. His balding spot had grown since their last meeting. Mgobe was an amicable man if not a bit on the nervous side. She was sure if she was able to get to know him more, she could count on him as a friend.

He and his party bowed to her deeply. "Queen Izriamat, we welcome you to Djelebe. I hope your trip was pleasant."

"It was, Governor Mgobe." She shielded her eyes from the sun. "I'm glad to see that you are still doing well."

"Perhaps a little older and a little slower, but well just the same." He gave an uneasy chuckle. "Please, come so that we may show our great queen the hospitality of our city."

Izriamat gave him a small smile and followed. The moment they entered the shade of the palace cool relief washed over her. She took down the scarf from over her braids, subtly dabbing the sweat from her face as she did so. Mgobe took her to a large, comfortable looking room. Low cushions were arranged around a large, low table. The table held drinks freshly prepared for her arrival. A pair of servants stood at the ready along the wall.

"How long will we have you here, my queen?" Mgobe asked as she sat. He lowered himself down with a grunt.

"Only for a night." She raised the cool liquid to her lips, forcing herself to not guzzle the entire glass. "I must make it to Wiluru."

"Ah, finally visiting family?"

"Yes." She debated on telling him the truth. It was disturbing news. But he was a king. He had a right to this knowledge. "I have news from the capital. It would be best if we spoke alone." She nodded her head at the servants. Mgobe was confused but gestured for them to leave. Izriamat waited another moment before continuing. "Official word will come soon, but the netkoleh has declared that there are no gods."

The scholar choked on his drink. "What?" he croaked out after calming his coughs.

"He's calling himself the emperor now. He had the palace wiped clean of anything with the gods' names or faces. I've never seen such blatant blasphemy."

Mgobe opened his mouth, then stopped and considered before speaking again. "Surely, he just means this for the gods of the Ega."

"All gods. He'll probably send people soon to cleanse your city too."

The governor quieted, deep in thought. "What of the books and scrolls?"

"I don't know. I don't know how deeply he's committed himself to this." Worry for the great library furrowed her brow. "Perhaps he'll overlook them."

Izriamat worried when a response didn't come immediately. Mgobe's gaze drifted upward to the high ceiling. He released a slow breath.

"We . . . thank you for the warning."

"What will you do?"

"I will obey the netkoleh."

She nodded. She wasn't sure how to feel about how easily he sided with her husband, but it was his decision to make. Not hers. She forced a pleasant smile onto her face.

"Let's speak on something far less troubling. Might I have a tour of the famous university? I wasn't able to see it the last time I rode through."

Mgobe's face lifted, relief obvious in his expression. "Of course, my queen. I will be happy to give you the tour myself."

CHAPTER FIVE

The forest closed in around the well-worn path. Efah shoved another branch aside, mindful of her band-mates behind her. Kanta led the way, slicing at the encroaching brush with his short sword. The rest of her band chatted before and behind her, speaking happily about their plans once they reached the city, but she couldn't bring herself to join in the conversation. She hadn't told anyone about her . . . encounter on the cliffs. She didn't half believe it herself.

The god of death, appeared to her not in the form from the Egan religion, but in the ancient ways. The dead man walking. The king of vultures. The thought of his presence brought goosebumps back to her skin despite the forest heat. His words rang true. She had seen more death than most. Her parents died of a sleeping sickness when she was eight. Her grandmother passed away soon afterward in the bed beside her. Her brother was found dead along the roadside from Nsongo. Talk began of her being cursed. It was then that she thought, at only twelve years old, that it would be better to set out on her own than to stay as a pariah.

Yes, she witnessed more than her share of death. Who hadn't during the wars against the Ega? But why her? Why couldn't he have appeared to someone, anyone else? All she wanted to think about was making a living. She didn't need this. Efah ducked a branch, frowning deeply. He chosen the wrong woman. He would just have to get someone else.

"Listen up," Kanta called over his shoulder. Efah snapped out of her thoughts. "You all need to hide as much as you can. We're not giving that bastard Ayodele more than we have to."

"You really think we can hide anything from him?" Efah muttered under her breath.

Kanta scowled at her. "We can if we're smart. Hide everything under your clothes, in tight places where it can't move. If I hear a single coin jingle, I'll gut you myself."

The other three bandmates grimaced, but she merely looked aside. She doubted Kanta's threat would be carried out to the letter. However, she knew she wouldn't be the one to get caught.

They trudged through the forest for hours, the undergrowth eventually giving way to a far more well-worn path. Other trails joined in from different directions constructing a wide road. Soon they spied the first high spires of Garemba. Thick vines clung to the ancient stones finding any purchase and piercing any crack. Large statues loomed over the parted foliage, birds making their nests at the shoulders, their excrement painting the heads of the fearsome warriors. This had once been the city-palace of some unknown king. Now, the forest viciously reclaimed its stolen property. The huge wooden doors that stood in the entrance lay in on each side of the road, nothing more than a broken, rotten heap. Efah often tried to imagine what this great palace was like in its height, tried to imagine its white walls clean and its halls full of people. She was sure that it was magnificent.

Now, it was a different sort that occupied the grand space. Now every sort of outcast crowded every corner in the palace. Thieves and murderers stalked the halls. Women cast out as witches washed clothes in the great pools. Children ran and played in overrun courtyards, relieving themselves in any hidden corner they could find. There were no riches left from the time before. It was all looted or horded long ago. Now, there were only people scraping by paying homage to a new king.

Efah and her crew walked past a group of smug looking men with wide, crude swords at their hips. One harassed a young woman on her way back from the forest. Another with a missing front tooth smiled at her and Efah pointedly ignored him. She had no time or interest for any of Ayodele's enforcers. Her crew continued on, deeper into the palace, heading up a wide staircase to the second floor. They passed more guards on their way through a long hallway and out onto another open courtyard. The courtyard ended at a natural cliff in the forest overlooking the Bangi river. Whoever planned this palace made use of every nuance of the forest.

On a great couch under the covered part of the courtyard sat the man they came to see. He was broad and tall with a wide mouth that often wore a cruel smile. A group of guards took their post around him, playing at bodyguard. His clothing was as fine as any lord, the fabric coming from as far away as Nsongo. Perhaps beyond. He wore but one piece of jewelry. It was a large necklace with broad engraved squares linked together befitting a man of his size. It didn't need to be said that the necklace marked him king of this forgotten palace. It was obvious.

A band of vagabonds knelt before him, spreading out money and trinkets on the ground, the "tax" for staying in the city. Their terror was evident and Efah was sure she saw them trembling even from this distance. Ayodele was a man of random moods. He could be a trickling stream at one moment and a raging storm the next. Just like the weather, you didn't know what you could get. He nodded his large head at the group and waved them away.

The guard nearest him looked to them sharply, beckoning them closer. Ayodele may be an imposing figure, but this woman Efah feared more. Iyola was a woman spoken of as if she stepped out of legend. Her skill with a sword was attributed to spirits, witchcraft, the old gods, or the new gods depending on the storyteller. Ayodele may be king but Iyola was his peacekeeper. Always suspicious, her punishments for any suspected crimes were harsh and swift. They needed to fool her even more than their self-styled king if they wanted to keep any of their gold.

Kanta came closest to Ayodele, going to his knees.

The rest of the band followed suit quickly. They'd done this enough times.

"My lord Ayodele," Kanta began as reverently as he knew how. "Here is our tribute to you for our stay in your city. We hope it pleases you." He emptied a palm sized bag of gold and trinkets on the floor, one large gem sliding to Ayodele's foot. The guards looked impressed and even Iyola raised an eyebrow as it was picked up.

"This is quite the bounty," the huge man on the couch said. He turned the gem around in his fingers, letting the sunlight filter through it. "Where did you find all of this?"

"We found a small unopened tomb. It had a few pieces of gold and some jewelry. They must not have been very rich."

Efah saw Iyola searching Kanta's face and prayed she wouldn't sense the half-truth. Ayodele was busy looking over the small pile of goods.

"You have been very generous today. Are you sure there isn't anything else you'd like to add? It may make sure your stay here is . . . safer."

Kanta hesitated uncomfortably, an act Efah was sure. He pulled out a small bag from deep in his shirt.

We were hoping to keep a bit more, my lord." Iyola's scowl deepened. "But we're happy to give it to our great and wise leader." He placed it down with the other gold items, a few of the coins inside spilling out.

Ayodele nodded like a proud father. "You have done well and pleased me. You may rest in the halls of Garemba."

Efah and her band scurried back from him, heads bowed all the way, muttering their gratitude. Kanta kept his face humble until they were far into the hall where it settled into a great frown.

"Old bastard," she heard him mutter deep under his breath.

"But we came out fine," Efah whispered to him.

"But we could have come out better."

She wanted to say that they should be thankful, that

they could have been searched, but she kept her mouth shut. It was no use. Kanta was as cheap as Ayodele was greedy. Even if they'd only had to give up one coin, he would have been angry. She sighed deeply and they began their long search for an empty room in the city.

It wouldn't be easy. The palace was steadily getting overcrowded. And they were never there for long. Any room they may have staked out before was long taken by now. It took them nearly two hours to find something both unoccupied and big enough for all of them. It was on the unstable third floor, but it seemed sturdy enough. They settled down, scrounging together a dinner for themselves. When Efah finally laid her head down to sleep, all thoughts of the god of death had been pushed aside. Only the concerns of what she was going to buy with all this gold filled her mind.

*   *   *

Efah awoke to sounds of struggle. She opened her eyes in the darkness and could just make out the silhouettes of people moving through the room. The sound of struggle suddenly stopped, replaced by rummaging noises. As her vision adjusted to the pale light coming in from the slitted windows, she saw a trail of blood on the floor leading to the still body of Kanta. They were being robbed. She tried to keep her breathing slow as panic tried to take over. Someone was coming closer to her. Looming over her, she knew they were going to kill her too. Closing her eyes tightly, she turned and kicked out for them.

With a heavy groan, the man stumbled away from her, but other hands were soon on her. Efah kicked and punched out, not caring what she made contact with as long as she struck with all her might. Fire blazed across her hand as she fended off their blades. If she could only get a moment to get to her knives, she would have a chance. Calling out for help wouldn't be of any use. No one would come. Not in a place like this. She was pinned down. A blade pressed against her throat.

That's when she heard the laughing. It was as clear as day to her and it drowned out whatever the robbers were saying to her. They, however, failed to notice. Until the first of them was snatched away. The moment her attackers turned their attention Efah lashed out, punching the one still holding her in the crotch. The man doubled over in pain just in time to be seized by the neck by a huge hyena. Efah heard the distinct crunch of bone as she scrambled against the wall. The first man was dead, his body torn open from his jaw to the top of his chest. The second man dangled from the jaws of the great beast. The third didn't have a chance to scream as he was quickly torn apart by another large hyena. She felt bile rise in her throat as it gave a final crunch on the man's twitching face.

Efah's knees began to shake. Her heart pounded against her chest as the beasts, bigger than any predator she'd ever seen, turned their attention to her. Tears ran down her face. Would they kill her too? Shouldn't they have had their fill from the others? She threw her hands up in front of her in a futile attempt to protect herself. The heat of their fetid breath warmed her cheeks as they sniffed around her. Then she felt a lick at her hands.

Efah opened her eyes, afraid of seeing her end coming. Instead she found both hyenas gently licking her wounds. One stopped to nuzzle against her, smearing blood across her cheek. She reached up for it, gently petting its neck. The beast made a pleased sound, leaning into the affection. The other leaned in, lowering its head. Efah scratched it, unsure what else to do. Her heart slowed as the fear of death slowly ebbed away from her. She forced herself to breathe deeply. They saved her. It was almost too much to believe. These animals that caused so much death . . .

She gasped. Had they been sent to protect her? One hyena settled down on the floor beside her, the other finding its place under her arm. She felt a small sense of comfort. She looked around at the six bodies spread about the small room. Death everywhere. He was right.

Efah willed herself to stand, willed strength into her

legs. She looked around the room one last time before turning her sight to her new companions.

"Come," she said softly. Immediately they fell in beside her. "We have to go." Carefully, she picked her way past the fallen attackers, past her fallen comrades and left the dark city.

* * *

Bakari closed his eyes and took a deep breath, taking in all of the smells of the day. The scent of the light rain outside. The smell of the sweat of hardworking servants. Most importantly, the dry scent of the dust formed as statues were destroyed and frescoes chiseled from the walls. He opened his eyes, a wide smile stretching his face. All around him in the great temple of Koleh workmen toiled to cleanse it of the taint of the gods. The cacophony of destruction was the most beautiful sound that had ever reached his ears. He jumped at the deafening boom caused by a statue falling. He almost wanted to cry. It was glorious.

He walked down the halls admiring his decree coming to life. The reaction was strong when he and his loyal guards came in this morning. There were a few dissenters, but they were quickly removed and dealt with. The slaves did as they were commanded by their ruler. Nothing had changed for them. The priests, however, were the group he'd been most worried about. The zealots certainly wouldn't want to give up their grip on such a lush position. But once he'd given his orders they stepped out of the way. They were curiously absent now. He was sure that they'd want to try to save what they could.

Bakari stopped in front of a ceiling tall painting that was just starting to be scrubbed away. The giant figure of Koleh, rendered in the brightest hues of gold, stood with his hand over the head of the first netkoleh, Kha. He studied the supposed figure of his ancestor. Strong featured with a menacing demeanor, his arm stretched out a whip as he beat back the early foes of the empire. Who these mysterious people were none were very sure. They could have been the Wiluruans or even the Djelebens. Even the scholars were said to have had an army at one time. Bakari sneered at the rays of Koleh's blessing radiating down on the scene. Even Kha's faithful spear bearer was Omet, daughter of Koleh and goddess of truth. Lies. All of it. Once this place was clean, he would have a new painting made commemorating a real battle, a real victory. The true names of heroes would be written down for all of time and all would see what greatness could be accomplished by the hand of man and man alone.

"Excuse us, my . . . emperor."

Bakari looked to his left to see a small group of priests gathered. He looked over each of them disdainfully. Shaved heads and simple clothes contrasted by their well-fed bellies. They were complicit in this grand lie. He looked to the head priest, a man that had taught him of his role, no his former role, as a Netkoleh.

"Yes?" he asked, voice dripping with scorn.

"We wished to speak with you about your decision." He hesitated. "We urge you to reconsider. This can only be step toward disaster."

"What could be disastrous about it?"

The head priest looked completely taken back. "My . . . emperor," he began in a way Bakari didn't like. The man had best get used to the title. "We have all witnessed the power of the gods, felt their essence coursing through us. You have as well, great Net . . . great emperor."

"Now you're going to tell me what I've felt." His face fell into a deep scowl. He was tired of these pampered, useless men. "All I have ever felt was my own power. It was my power. My father's power. His father's power. You all have even done are little tricks, little so called miracles to keep the people believing a lie."

Half of the priests took a step back from him, most of the rest making gestures of mercy. The head priest's mouth worked like a fresh caught fish.

"You surely can't believe this. Think of what you're saying, the effect it will have on your eternal soul!"

Workers glanced over at the crescendoing conversation.

"If you're so concerned about souls, *priest,*" Bakari started, "you should start with yours. When is the last time you've done something useful? When is the last time you've healed someone of an ailment that was more than just a mild sickness? Why is it that when your healing powers, your great faith driven healing powers, are needed the most there is nothing that can be done? Why is it always Koleh's will? Isn't that what you told me?" The priest sputtered for an answer. "Isn't that what you told me? Why would Koleh let his chosen die? Tell me, priest! Why would he? Because he is either a cruel and unjust god or he's not there!"

Bakari's breath came raggedly as he stared down the gaggle of priests before him.

The head priest stared back in disbelief. "You can't . . ."

"I do," Bakari snarled back. "Now, be gone. Never show your face to me again."

The priests scurried down the hallway. Bakari wiped the tears gathering at the corners of his eyes. How dare they question him. He quickly walked out of the temple, his guards falling in behind him. He may not be the Netkoleh anymore, but he was still the law. He frowned deeper. He should have had them beheaded immediately. They'll only be a source of dissent in his empire. He considered sending the Arakgu'un after them but decided against it. He didn't want any martyrs. He had to wait until they played their hand and then he would gladly have them beheaded in the street. Let their blood darken the steps of the temple for once.

As he came inside, Hetsaf waited for him along the hallway. He bowed dutifully.

"The last of the statues have been removed from the palace, my emperor. Unfortunately, some of the paintings are not finished yet. The older ones aren't responding to soap and are having to be scraped off."

"That's fine. As long as they're removed. Gather artists from around the empire to begin the redecoration."

"If I may ask, my emperor, what will we replacing the paintings with?"

"The truth," he answered. "We will replace it with the truth of this empire."

"Very well, my emperor." Hetsaf bowed again, quickly excusing himself.

If only he had more loyal servants like that. Bakari sighed, rubbing the bridge of his nose against the headache he felt coming. He retreated to his room ordering his servants to bring him a cup of wine. He lounged on a chaise, looking out toward his inner courtyard. The afternoon shower gave way to clear skies by that evening. A cool breeze began and that along with the peacefulness of the inner palace lulled him into sleep for a moment.

He was brought out of his dozing by the feeling that someone had entered the room. Bakari glanced over to the door, expecting his wife, but the room remained empty. He sat up in his seat. There was no one in the room but he still had the feeling that someone was with him. He frowned. One of his concubines had better not found her way to his rooms. He was not in the mood for any of their foolishness. He looked around one more time before laying back down in the cool evening breeze. He slowed his breathing, feigning sleep, and waited. He knew it wasn't just his imagination.

Soon his suspicions bore fruit. Someone was drawing closer to him. Bakari paused a moment more then grabbed the container of wine left beside his chaise, wielding it like a club. It hit the intruder's head, the pottery shattering. He took in the darkly clothed person in an instant. They carried a knife, a wicked blade with a toothed edge. Recovering from his attack, they lunged for him, aiming for his bare torso. Bakari jumped back and kicked out, his long legs closing the distance. The assassin took the blow and slashed for him again. He dodged then immediately lunged in for a punch to the side of the ribs. He blocked the backswing of his attacker with his free hand then punched them solidly in the stomach. When they doubled over, he twisted their knife arm, bringing his elbow down on the back of theirs.

Bakari looked to his assassin in disgust as they dropped the knife. He kicked it across the room then twisted their broken arm more, forcing them to their knees. What kind of second-rate assassin was this? He ripped off their mask to find some street thug.

"Who sent you?" he ground out. The man grunted in pain as Bakari pressed a knee on his back, but he didn't talk.

"Guards," he snapped. In moments, a group of six came into the room. They all looked in terror at the scene before them. "Gather this man and take him to the leader of the Arakgu'un. Tell him that this worm doesn't want to talk, and I wish to know who sent him."

The guards acted immediately, too afraid of a possible punishment to hesitate. Bakari walked over to the knife the man brought in with him. He turned it over in his hand. It was meant to cause a nasty wound. Even if it didn't kill him initially, the wound would fester causing him a lingering death. In a skilled assassin's hands, it could easily tangle the bowels. In this man's hands it was wasted. Now he had to know: who would hire an assassin to kill him, but only find one of such mediocrity? Bakari turned the blade in his hand. He would find out and they would die for it.

CHAPTER SIX

Hotemkhar waved his feather fan against the stench of the jungle people. The thick ostrich plumes did little but stir up their musky scent more. However, the fan did hide his slight sneer. His attendant walked quickly behind him as he surveyed the docks, expertly holding up the small canopy to block the rising sun. The people from across the Bangi River were just pulling their long canoes up to the piers. They worked deftly to unpack their wares. Large woven baskets of exotic foods and spices quickly filled the area, but this wasn't what he was interested in. He stopped as a sack was dropped heavily on the shore, its contents glittering in the morning light. Gold. His sneer turned to a smile.

Various other bits of glitter caught his attention as he looked down the docks. There were baskets and sacks of jewelry, odd statues, plates, and cups. But what Hotemkhar was truly interested in was the pure gold. These jungle people brought that as well in powder and nuggets. This was the source of Nsongo's wealth. This was why it was called the city of gold. Their special trading culture with their neighbors across the river had brought them great prosperity over the ages. It was precisely why the empire invaded their lands. Now the flow of gold had been rerouted directly to the heart of Egah.

He fanned again as one of these people passed far too close to him. He'd been told that their smell was a strange perfumed paste they rubbed on their bodies. He felt they should be taken to the north to learn what a real perfume was supposed to smell like. This seemed like a lie to excuse filthy lifestyles.

Hotemkhar continued along the length of the river-side, mentally cataloging what the cursory totals were for the jungle people. At thirty boats total, a light day for them, at least a good third of their cargo would be gold items. His sight trailed across the wide river. So how much did they keep for themselves, he wondered.

He looked around until he found one of them that looked like a talker.

"You there," he called, using his fan to point at them. "I need to speak to you."

The jungle man looked confused and a slightly older man stepped forward.

"What do you want?" he asked slowly.

Hotemkhar didn't hide his sneer this time. The man's accent was thick as mud in the trade language. Even a linguist like himself had a hard time understanding.

"Do your people keep much of the gold you mine?"

It took a moment for the man to process what he'd said before responding,

"I don't understand."

Hotemkhar nearly growled. "Do you keep most of the gold at home?" he asked choosing his words carefully.

"We keep some. We sell some."

He couldn't' tell if the man was being honest or eva-sive.

"Is there a lot at your home?"

The man shrugged. "There is enough."

Now he knew he was being evasive. He was in no mood to be toyed with by some jungle born animal who smelled of bull musk.

"Do you know who I am?" Hotemkhar asked slowly.

"You are the leader of the men from the far north."

"A very, very powerful man. You will answer me truthfully or I will make you pay."

"Your people hold no power over us," came a voice from behind him.

Hotemkhar turned to face another merchant, this one graying and balding. There was a shrewdness in his eyes that the northern man didn't like, but at least he didn't have to struggle to understand him.

"Oh, you think that we don't?"

"Our trade with the Nsongans has always been peaceful. We hoped that your people would honor that same tradition, but we see that you are filled with greed. Out of respect for the Nsongans we've continued to come to trade, but know this, if you mistreat any of our people we will pull back to our lands and never return."

Hotemkhar's face settled into a dangerous smile. "Then we'll just follow you into your precious jungle."

The man scowled back at him. "No one has ever crossed the Bangi. That . . . would not be wise."

"What is your name, jungle man?" he asked.

"Moteb."

"I will remember it."

"You should."

Hotemkhar's face settled into another scowl as the man turned his back on him and strode away. These jungle people thought too highly of themselves. He was the ambassador of the empire, a noble of Metkara, handpicked by the emperor's chancellor. He was higher than this little . . . jungle man could even conceive. He fiercely turned and walked away from the docks to far less fragrant areas of the riverside. How dare he make threats, veiled or otherwise, against him. Did he not understand the might of the Egah? Did he not understand how many troops he could easily call to take their precious lands?

He stopped, looking out across the great river again and the wall of vegetation on the other side. The Nsongans were a mighty people. It took over fifteen years to finally bring their lands and people to heel. With their might they could have easily stormed the jungle and taken these mysterious gold mines for themselves instead of waiting on the daily trickle from the merchants. Why were they content with this? Had they not crossed the river out of actual respect? This was a mystery he had to solve, and he knew who held the answers.

* * *

The early afternoon sun shone bright and warm on Ashaki's shoulders. Her servant brought her meal to her table, laying out each dish with a smile. Ashaki thanked the woman who had been in her service since she was a girl. It was nice to have a peaceful moment in her day. Her morning had been filled with hearing the concerns and disputes of the city folk. She was supposed to have all the answers. She was the wise Great Dara of Nsongo. Even after three years of rulership she still struggled. How did father do this day after day?

Ashaki sighed, slowly eating her lunch. Another servant, a plump older woman, entered the courtyard, approaching her table. She could tell by the look on the woman's face more trouble brewed. The servant bowed curtly before her. Ashaki sighed again.

"Yes, what is it?" she asked her.

"Great Dara, it is concerning your daughter." The woman paused and Ashaki had to wonder what mischief the girl had gotten herself into today. "I saw her at the market this morning. She was flirting with a young man."

Ashaki laughed. "Is that all? She's a girl of fourteen years. I should hope someone strikes her fancy."

"Great Dara, it is not so simple." The servant woman's serious face worried Ashaki. "He's the son of a wood-carver."

"What?" She shook her head in disbelief. "A craftsman's son?"

"Yes, great Dara."

"That . . . won't do." She tapped her fingers on the table. "I . . . I'll talk to her." Ashaki rose from her seat, a frown weighing down her face. "Has she returned to the compound?"

"Yes, great Dara."

"Thank you." She turned from her half-eaten lunch, her appetite failing her. Ashaki shook her head again as she left the courtyard. A craftsman. Her daughter was bold and headstrong, but she knew her place. She knew better than to be seen cavorting with such low-class people. Ashaki turned down corridor after corridor chewing her lip in thought. This was a time she truly wished for Lafosa's wisdom. That woman always knew just what to say to get through to their daughter. Ashaki took a deep, settling breath to steel herself against the pain. The last three years had done nothing to lessen it.

She turned another corner, nodding to bowing servants. Ahead, a tall man in pristine white robes walked toward her. His sandals made barely a whisper on the stone floor.

"Uncle," she called touching both her heart and her forehead.

"Great Dara," he replied with a nod. He was one of few people who didn't have to bow to her. "May I speak with you?"

Ashaki gave a wary smile. That was her uncle Erenemo, always to the point.

"Well, uncle, there was a matter that I needed to take care of presently."

"This won't take long. I'll walk with you."

She held in the frustrated sigh. "Very well. What is it?"

"I know that you are aware that the time of tribute is on us again."

Ashaki choked down another sigh. "I'm aware."

"Then you are aware that there may be interference this time." He turned his imposing gaze on her. "The Ega have imposed a myriad of sanctions on our people since our . . . surrender." His last word cut her like a sharp sword. "We don't know what they might do if they see so many goods leaving the city. And we have barely recovered from the initial penalties they saddled us with. Our economy may not be able to take another blow."

"Uncle Erenemo, you are wise as always and your concern for our people warms my heart." Her smile wasn't returned. She cleared her throat. "But I have taken this into account. I assure you; I'll make sure our allies across the river are properly compensated for all they give us. Was there anything else?"

"Yes, the newest Ega troops show no regard for our city. They've fouled their part of the city, defecating in alleyways, urinating in public. We can't go on like this."

"Uncle, what would you have me do?"

"*You* are the dara. Nsongo is yours to command."

"Not anymore, uncle. Even I have a master now." The disdain in his face was palatable. She sighed, under the weight of his frown. "I'll talk to their commander and see if they can be . . . controlled. Now, if you will excuse me."

He made the motions of reverence, stepping aside. "Great Dara."

Ashaki hurried on, not wanting to spend another moment discussing such unpleasant business. She turned down a colonnade that lead to her daughter's rooms. All she wanted to do was speak with her daughter. It was likely to dissolve into an argument, but at least they'd be talking. Masola had grown irritable since Lafosa's death. Their little girl had changed from a ball of love and joy to a brooding, bitter young woman. What she would give to see that carefree smile again instead of the annoyed frown. Ashaki sighed under the weight of her position. She would be grateful for enough time to see her daughter more than once a day. That would be nice.

"Great Dara."

Ashaki froze as the slimy voice slid down her back. She forced a smile on her face as she turned to the Egan envoy. Her hate for him threatened to show across her face, but she struggled and pushed it down. Everything about him disgusted her. His arrogance. His disdain for her people. The fact that with a word he could turn this city on its head. He eyed the forest of jewelry on her hands and arms, like a predator.

"Hotemkhar," she said with a curt nod of her head. He better take it. That was the most respectful she could be.

"Dara Ashaki," he said to her, his tone and smile

like poisoned honey. "I need to speak with you. I have a few questions for you."

"Is there any possible way we could meet later?"

He ran a hand over his feather fan, inspecting it. "I've already been waiting for some time. Your people told me that you were not available, so I decided to seek you out."

Ashaki fumed. *You arrogant piece of . . .* She forced a smile onto her face.

"Well, you've found me in a moment of freedom. What questions may I answer for you?"

"Those jungle people."

"The Batubangi."

"Yes, those people. Have any of you ever crossed the river to discover their homeland?"

Ashaki's mouth hung open. "Never."

"Why not?" He asked as if she gave a fool's answer.

"We respect their homeland. That's all they've asked of us. That was part of our bargain."

"Surely, at some time in your long history, at least one of the daras must have been curious about where all of this gold was coming from. Your city is rich, but you could have been even richer if you held the mines for yourself."

"Hotemkhar, Nsongo would never betray the very people that have made it the city of gold your people desired so much. But, unlike the Ega, we have no wish to spread our influence *everywhere*."

She realized she'd crossed a line, but she hated this man more than any of his people who'd descended on her people. A plague of locusts they were. Taking all their riches and eating all their food. She had to fight tooth and nail to get the city back to a functioning state.

The envoy stared at her, his eyes narrowing. "Then perhaps your people lack a vision for yourselves. It's a good thing we came to save you from your stagnant lifestyle." Ashaki let the slight roll off her shoulders. "I think we should work together to learn more about the jungle people. It may benefit the empire greatly."

"We have been warned against crossing the river.

You should heed their warnings."

He waved at her dismissively with his fan. She resisted the urge to snatch it out of his hands. He chuckled.

"Am I, an envoy of the Netkoleh, chosen directly by his chancellor, supposed to be put off by jungle superstitions? We'll find out what's over there. Your cooperation will be appreciated." He grinned. "As always."

His last words stabbed her. He held her, and thus her people, captive to his whims.

"We will . . . see what we can uncover."

"Wonderful," he replied with an energetic smile. "It is so nice to have these talks with you."

Without another word, not even a feigned show of respect to her position, he walked off down the hallway. Ashaki watched him, letting her true feelings settle on her face. *Horse's backside.* Walking around her compound like he owned whatever ground he put his feet upon. If she could kill him, she would. She sighed, defeated, and brushed the thoughts aside.

She could hear her daughter milling about in her room when she finally reached her area. Ashaki paused in the doorway, watching her daughter dancing to a song she was humming. She was a damn good dancer. Masola twirled, then stopped when she saw the doorway. Her smile melted.

"Hello, mother," she said, sitting down on one of the carved benches in the room.

Her daughter's greeting stung. She hadn't used 'mama' for her in years. Ashaki smiled.

"Good afternoon, Sola. Your dancing has gotten even better."

"Thank you," she said dispassionately.

Ashaki crossed the room to sit down by her daughter. She smiled sadly, admiring her. Sola wouldn't be her little girl much longer. She ran a hand over one of the two thick braids woven across her scalp.

"Have you been enjoying going to the market by yourself?" She knew Sola had been delighted to have the new freedom last year.

"I'm not really going alone. You have guards following me."

"I have to. The Egans are animals. They don't care about you or the fact that you're my daughter."

"They call you unnatural, you know." Masola drew her legs up to hug her knees

"I know. They think most of how we live is unnatural." She smirked. "But they're the ones who don't know how to relieve themselves like people and not beasts." She chuckled but Sola didn't join her. Ashaki cleared her throat. "Sola, my flower, the servants have been telling me than you've been talking to a boy in the market."

Her daughter almost looked at her. "Can't I talk to boys? The servants are so damn nosy!"

"Sola, you know you can talk to anyone you want. But you weren't just talking. They said you were flirting with him." She paused. "And he's a son of one of the wood-carvers." Her daughter stiffened and she knew it was the truth.

"Why can't I talk to him?" Masola asked launching to her feet and storming across the room. "Is this one of the new rules I have to follow since *you* surrendered to the enemy?"

"Sola, you *will not* speak to me like that. I am both your mother and your dara and you *will* remember it." She felt her face getting hot under her restrained anger. "Now sit down."

Masola turned to stared at her, then sat on a different bench. Ashaki would allow her that slight.

"Why can't I talk to him? We're just friends."

"You are the daughter of the dara. He's a craftsman son. There's a gulf between your stations. You know that. You should be glad I even let you have friends outside of our class. My father certainly didn't." Masola folded her arms, turning her head to look out of the window. Ashaki rose to go sit by her daughter. She remembered that pout from when she was a toddler. Always so headstrong.

"Sola," she said looking into those deep brown eyes. "My flower, there are some things that just can't be."

Her heart tore at the tears gathering in the corners of Masola's eyes. Her daughter scowled at her as she rose, then ran from the room. Ashaki rested her head in her hands, sighing heavily. Would any talk today end on a good note?

* * *

Wiluru baked under a relentless sun. The sea breeze did nothing to relieve the citizens as it blew half strength through the city streets. Umakaal wiped the sweat from her forehead with the back of a hand. She would give anything to not be in armor today. She would even take being positioned inside the palace instead of out. She released a breath, letting it vibrate between her lips. Even rotations, she told the guard when she'd taken command. Even she would take turns outside at the palace entrance. It seemed like such a good idea at the time.

Umakaal tugged at the top of her breastplate, feeling her clothing sliding and sticking to her skin. The other guards stood stock still, not wanting to disappoint their commander and princess. She didn't know how they did it. She had rivulets of sweat running down to places that never saw the sun. She was sure she would melt away before the day was over.

Umakaal looked around the nearby city for something to take her mind off this unusually hot day. The palace stairs faced the ocean and the main streets of Wiluru all wound their way here. The noise of the city would drift up on a regular day, but today was quiet. At least for the most part.

Faint shouting and cheers arrived on the weak breeze. Umakaal rose on her toes, hoping to catch some glimpse of the commotion. She met eyes with each of the guards on the stairway. She grasped her spear firmly, ready in case something had to be broken up. After a moment, a grand party turned onto the street leading parallel to the palace. A large group of travelers bearing all the trappings of the Ega approached. Umakaal wrinkled her nose. What the hell did they want here? But the people were cheering. Honest cheers of long life and blessings.

She came down a step as they stopped in front of the palace. A woman was helped down from her horse and led the way to the stairs. She was dressed in an elegant white dress, with all the gaudy jewelry the nobles of their kind favored. But her hair was braided in the fashion of Wiluru. Umakaal looked into her face, past the thick makeup. She gasped, dropping her spear.

"No," she breathed coming down another step. The woman looked up at the palace with a smile and Umakaal's suspicions were confirmed.

"Izriamat!" she shouted, running down the last few stairs. Tears streamed so freely she could barely see.

The woman looked over in confusion, then clasped her hands over her mouth.

"Umakaal?"

Umakaal collided with her sister, burying her face into her shoulder.

"I never thought I'd see you again." Her sobs rocked her to her soul. The feeling of the embrace was a gift from the gods.

Izriamat stroked the back of her head. "Oh, my sweet sister," she cried. "All praises to Yutuu for bringing me here safely."

Umakaal smiled as her forehead was plastered with kisses. "Look at how you've grown. I left and you were a girl. And are you in command already?"

Umakaal pulled her sister close again, not believing she was actually here.

"It's been a year. Father thought I was ready even though I was younger than Yutuuan was." Her sister stroked her hair again, taking her back to all those nights laying in her sister's lap getting her hair braided. She took her hand, wiping her tears away. "Did mother and father know you were coming?"

"No, no one." Izriamat looked up the stairs, started to take a step, then stopped. "I feel like it's been an eternity."

Umakaal gave her sister's hand a squeeze then gave a pleading look to her guards. Some of them looked to be teary eyed too. The most senior of them cleared his throat.

"Princess, I think you should escort your sister and her entourage into the palace."

She nodded her thanks, guiding her sister up the steps. She didn't want to let her go. It was unreal. It felt like a funeral the day Izriamat left. She remembered crying for days, her parents finding no possible way to lift her spirits. She took in her sister's clothing and makeup and felt a stab of guilt. That was supposed to be her instead. She turned her attention to the palace entrance, not wanting her sister to see her tears start anew. Her sister had taken her place in this. Izriamat should hate her. But . . .

Umakaal glanced at her sister who gave her hand a squeeze and smiled through her tears. It was a debt she'd never be able to repay.

The servants inside froze as they passed, making gestures of blessings, some coming to tears as well. Umakaal couldn't let go of her sister's hand. She led her through the halls of the palace, through places that they'd run through as children. Her sister was her second mother and playmate at the same time. She and Yutuuan had sat at her feet listening to stories just as much as they did with their parents. Umakaal took a moment to embrace her sister again.

They made their way to the rear of the palace to a small courtyard. The small flock of cranes strolled around, absently pecking at bugs they had no intention of eating. They knew to stay out of the way of the group assembled at the back. Umakaal led her sister in, not caring if she interrupted a council meeting. She sent smaller birds fluttering out of her way with her incessant pace. As they approached, their mother looked up from her place at the king's side. An ugly cry escaped her, and she struggled to her feet. Umakaal couldn't hold back her sobs.

"My child," the queen sobbed, running across the courtyard. "Yutuu has brought my child back to me!"

She threw her arms around her daughter, praising

their principal deity. The two women collapsed to their
knees, the elder princess falling against her mother.
Umakaal dropped down, throwing her arms around both
of them. Soon she felt her father's arms encompass the
group, his deep sobs vibrating through them. They show-
ered the lost member of their family with kisses, touching
her face in utter disbelief. Behind them, the council members quietly shuffled their way out.

Umakaal didn't know how long they stayed on the
ground, embraced, but it wasn't long enough. She pulled
back watching her sister laying against their mother's
chest, their mother stroking her hair. Izriamat's makeup
was a disaster after the weeping, but she smiled serenely
while their parents cried over her. Their father had his arm
protectively around his queen, his other hand holding Izriamat's. Umakaal leaned against her father feeling less like
the leader of the palace guard and more like the little girl
who'd watched her sister leave to become the second
queen of their conquerors.

"Where is Yutuuan?" Izriamat asked weakly.

"At the docks," their father answered. "We will send
for him."

Their mother hugged her tighter. Umakaal reached
out to touch her sister again.

"How were you able to come back?"

"The Netkoleh allowed me." Izriamat sat up, stroking her mother's cheek. "We have much to talk about."

The king shook his head. "It can wait. We have to
celebrate your return."

Umakaal helped her father to his feet, her mother
helping Izriamat. Tears came to his eyes again.

"Praise be to Yutuu." He embraced her, kissing her
forehead. "My sweet child."

"I love you, baba."

"You have my heart, daughter."

"For as long as the sun shines," their mother added.

Izriamat was wracked with sobs once again, her
knees giving. Umakaal moved swiftly to her sister's side
putting her arm around her waist to give her support.

"I have you, sister." She tried her best to give her a smile. "I'm much stronger than when you last saw me."

The three of them took Izriamat to her old rooms. Servants stopped to revere the royal family as they passed, some breaking down in tears as they realized who was being escorted through the halls. Several dropped to their knees, heads bowed to the floor. Umakaal was pleased to see her sister start to smile and make motions of blessings over the servants as they passed.

Izriamat's rooms were kept in immaculate condition since the day she left. Their mother made sure of it. The heat of the day hadn't reached the back of the palace yet, so her room was still at a comfortable temperature. Izriamat let her go, taking slow steps around the bedroom. She gave a deep sigh, her shoulders slumping completely. Their mother walked over and led her to sit on the bed.

Umakaal suddenly felt the weight of her armor again. "I . . . need to return to my post," she said sadly.

Her father put a hand on her shoulder. "No, you can be relieved of duty for the day. Stay with your sister and mother. I need to apologize to the council, and I'll return."

As her father left, Umakaal took a moment to wipe her face on the back of her sleeve. Izriamat looked up, beckoning her to come over. Umakaal came and knelt by her sister, placing her head in her lap. The feel of her sister's hand stroking her head was better than anything this world could give her.

CHAPTER SEVEN

Izriamat passed away the afternoon in her mother's embrace, her hand on her sister's braids. She could find no better expression of peace in her normally dismal life. A contented silence filled the room. She sighed deeply, happy for the first time in years.

The sound of running broke through the silence. Izriamat looked up just as her brother rushed through the doorway. His eyes saucered at the sight of her.

"Yutuuan," she said rising from her bed. She chuckled as he stood there, his mouth moving.

"Sister," he finally breathed, coming forward to embrace her.

Izriamat chuckled as he crushed her, lifting her off the ground. "It's so good to see you, little brother." She kissed his cheek when he set her down. Their father entered behind him.

"I couldn't believe it when father told me you were here. Did you run away?"

"How would I run away?"

He gave an embarrassed laugh. "That . . . wasn't a very smart question, was it?"

"No, but it's all right. I'm just glad to see you again."

"I . . . still can't believe it's you." He scooped her up into another hug.

Their father chuckled. "Put her down before you break her."

The family sat back down on her bed, Izriamat in the center of their love. She took her brother's hand.

"Mother tells me that you have yet to find a wife." She laughed at his uncomfortable squirm.

"I am being careful in my selection. Besides, I'm far too busy with the military at the moment to concern myself with such a search."

"I'm sure."

"How long will you be with us?" he asked quickly.

"I'm . . . not sure," Izriamat answered, looking at the floor. "For as long as I can manage. I'm afraid that there may not be another chance for me to visit ever again after this."

Her family looked to her in shock and she hated to snatch their happiness away from them. "There is something I have to tell you all about the Netkoleh. He hasn't made it official beyond the capital, but I think he will very soon." She swallowed with difficulty, the words piling in her throat. "He's declared that there are no gods."

Her family stared at her in silence, her mother gasping.

"He's styling himself as the emperor now, taking down statues, scrubbing paintings from the palace walls. I heard before I left that he wanted the whole city 'cleansed' of the gods' influence."

"Has he lost his mind?" Yutuuan said.

She looked to her brother in all seriousness. "I don't know. When his son, his first son, died it affected him. He was broody. I think since he wasn't able to save the boy it's made him think that the gods have failed him. I couldn't believe it when I heard."

Her father spoke up carefully. "He doesn't mean to spread this . . . this heresy to the rest of the empire, does he?"

"Yes, father. And I'm sure he wants me to be one of his emissaries to spread the word. He said that he wants Arkoleh, his first wife, and I to be his left and right hands."

Yutuuan shot to his feet. "We can't abide this. They've done enough to our people and now they want to take away our gods as well. May his soul turn to dust."

Her father put a hand on her shoulder. "Do you feel he can be reasoned with? Perhaps we can persuade him to allow us to carry on with our religion and leave his ideals to his people."

"No, father. You don't know him."

"Surely, we can speak to him on -."

"You don't know him like I do!" She regretted raising her voice to him immediately. "I'm sorry, baba. I'm sorry. But you don't know him like I know him. He's rash and vengeful. He can be calm at one moment and a slave to his emotions the next. He's selfish and brutish and . . . and . . ." She burst into sobs that wouldn't cease.

Izriamat struggled to stop her crying. She heard her mother shoo everyone from the room and pull her to her shoulder. Izriamat clutched onto her mother, all the pain from the past seven years flowing out of her. Her mother said nothing, smoothing her hair until her sobbing came under control.

"Oh, my daughter, I can't imagine all that you've gone through. But you are home now. You are home now, and we are with you." Izriamat didn't respond but let her mother rock her gently. "We heard that you had a son," she began softly. "Surely that brought you some joy."

"None." Izriamat wiped her tears and runny nose with her hand. "Mama," she said quietly. "Mama, I hate him. I have tried and tried to love that babe but not a shred of emotion will rise for him but hate for him and his father. Isn't a mother supposed to love their child? Have I become a monster?"

There was a moment of silence from her mother and Izriamat felt all the shame and pain descend on her again.

"I don't know if I could muster a mother's love if I were in your place, my heart." She felt a tear fall onto her forehead. "If I could have saved you from everything I would have. You feel however you feel. Our lot in life may not be fair, but it is our life and you can feel however you want about it."

"Mama, what will I do when I get back?"

"I-." Her mother's voice broke with tears. "I don't know, my heart. But may Yutuu give you the strength to endure it, may Abasha give you the clarity to see your way through, and may Uaani keep your enemies at bay." A sob escaped her mother. "But you are here now, in my arms. Don't give another thought to that life. You are here."

Izriamat nodded and let her mother hold her.

*　*　*

The rains reflected Bakari's mood. A torrential downpour assaulted the capital, collecting in minuscule grooves in the arcade before running into the courtyard's pool. Bakari paced the dry side of the space, his sandals slapping against the tile. It had been days since that clumsy assassin tried to take his life. Guards were questioned and tortured. Some he'd outright executed for being inept at their jobs. Even if there was a person bold enough to attempt assassination, his guard should have caught it. He needed better men. He needed an assassin to catch one.

His path turned abruptly, taking him away from the courtyard. A servant appeared from a side hallway, bowing.

"Shall we accompany you, my n . . ., my emperor?"

"We are going to the Arakgu'un."

"Yes, my emperor."

As Bakari walked, a handful of servants emerged from the sides of the hall, falling in line behind him. He noted their obedience, satisfied. At least they understood that their place hadn't changed. An awning was produced for him, a thick leather hide supported on four poles. His servants quickly moved it over him before his foot touched the ground outside the palace, not even interrupting his gait.

The Way of the Sky was nearly empty. Only a few people ran along it, obviously on errands that even a storm couldn't halt. A few looked to him as he made his way by. There were the usual looks of fear in their eyes, but there was something else there. Each person turned their heads when he looked their way. No, there was the look of disgust and revulsion hiding in their eyes. Bakari frowned deeply. It seemed more than the priests were unhappy with his decision. That he would have to take care of later.

The stronghold of the Arakgu'un was quiet as usual, the men near the front scrambling to show their respects. This building had no guards to stop or question anyone coming by. Who would want to pay a visit to the workers sanctioned by the god of wrath? Bakari strode down the hall looking about. He had never been in the assassin priests' temple before. It was sparse without a single painting or carving of their patron deity. Inscriptions ran along the wall at waist level, speaking poetically on justice and truth. Verses waxed on about the ever-seeing eye of Gu'un and their place as his blades on this world. Bakari continued to read, curious. The actual mentions of Gu'un were few and he had to wonder exactly how religious these priests were in the first place.

He reached a large room where priests hurried back and forth, the fact that their leader was present spreading through the crowd slowly. Some passed by him without even a glance his way.

"You," he called to a man looking over a scroll as he walked.

The man looked up, annoyance skewing his expression. His face fell once he realized who stood before him.

"Netko-," he stopped himself as he bowed. "Emperor, how may I serve you?"

"Take me to your order's leader. I have tasks for him."

"Yes, emperor."

The dark clad man led him along, weaving through the hallways without a sound. Bakari realized that it was deathly quiet in this building. The Arakgu'un that did speak did so in hushed tones. They were a strange bunch, so unlike their other priestly brethren. The priest took him to a room where a group were gathered in formation. Rain poured down from the large skylight in the middle, so the group was forced to gather at the side. They each stood in front of a crudely made dummy, talon-like knives in hand. An older man walked along the group, instructing them as they performed a quick series of strikes about the dummy's neck. He corrected some as he walked, talking aloud so the entire group could hear. He spoke in measured even tones but there was a deep level of punishment promised in his words about failure.

The priest that led him in rushed to the instructor, speaking to him quickly. Bakari looked over the older man as he excused himself from the class and approached. He looked to be nearing sixty years old but moved with the same fluidity of a man half his age. His unadorned hands were worn, and a pair of fingers bore the signs of an old, bad break. This man was nothing like the priests of the other temple. He liked him already.

The Arakgu'un leader bowed low when he reached him.

"To what do I owe this honor, my emperor?"

Bakari smiled. There was no hesitation when he said emperor.

"I need you to catch an assassin. Your name?"

"Antakhanan, my emperor. I have heard about the attempt on your life." The leader began walking away from his class, taking Bakari to the other side of the room.

"You have?"

"We keep our eye on many developments in the empire."

Bakari wasn't sure what to make of that statement. "Well, my men have tortured the assassin, but he hasn't given any names. He's either fiercely loyal or truly doesn't know who he was working for. I need to know who is working against me."

"My emperor give him to us. Matters such as these are what we excel in. We will have your answer although I already have an idea of who could be behind this . . . travesty."

The man didn't continue and Bakari scowled.

"Well?"

"From what my men have told me and from my own observances the priests of the other orders have been struggling with their newfound unemployment. Especially those of Koleh's sect. It seems the prospect of having to find a new calling frightens their delicate sensibilities. I could have them infiltrated and investigated." He bowed his head slightly. "If that is your wish, my emperor."

Bakari was pleasantly surprised. This man may prove to be just as invaluable as Hetsaf.

"Can you have one of your men placed in my personal guard? I'm shorthanded as several have been . . . relieved of their posts."

"Of course, my emperor. I will have that done as soon as possible."

"Very good. And let me know what you find from the assassin. I may wish to punish him myself."

Antakhanan gave a small bow and Bakari walked away and out of the room. His servants were waiting for him when he reached the front of the compound. He was right to keep the Arakgu'un in his fold. He felt in his gut that they would be a necessity in the coming times. The servants raised his canopy again and he set back out in the rain.

*   *   *

The military barracks were a mess to put it lightly. Soldiers lounged here and there, paying Hotemkhar not an ounce of attention or respect. He waved his fan against the heavy smell of unwashed bodies. He thought he'd find some sort of reprieve from savagery amongst his own people, but he realized these were common foot soldiers. He should have known better.

He wound his way through the occupied building, ignoring the unashamed debauchery going on inside rooms until he came to the outside arcade. The man he was looking for sat at a table, going over papers while he ate from a nearby bowl. A serving woman from the Nsongans stood beside the table holding an elaborately sculpted jug. Her long, twisted hair told of a noble heritage. Hotemkhar had to wonder. Was this the lady of the house before their forces settled in? How far their people had fallen, he thought with a chuckle.

"Commander Tutamen," he called coming near.

The tall, thick man glanced up from his work. Hotemkhar didn't miss the eye roll.

"Can I help you?"

The commander would have to be reminded of his place. "I would remind you to whom you speak. You do not speak to some mere footman."

"Can I help you?"

Hotemkhar scowled at the man. "Commander, I have been thinking of the Bangi and what lies across it."

"The jungle. Anything else?"

"Commander," the nobleman began a warning in his tone.

"Hotemkhar, I have a lot to do in keeping this region's men in order. If you've come here to talk about your daydreams, I suggest you find one of the servants. They're obligated to listen."

Hotemkhar breathed out the comments bubbling within him. Unfortunately, while he was the envoy, he had no direct command of the troops stationed here. He needed Tutamen in order to bring his plans to fruition.

"Commander, at the docks this morning I took the time to observe the jungle people and the vast amounts of gold brought over on their boats." The soldier made no reaction but continued to write. "They bring much here but they admitted that they keep more at their homes. If we were to push into the jungle, we could capture the source of the gold for the empire and not have to work through these people at all." Tutamen stopped his writing. "Imagine how much could be held beyond the river. And imagine how much glory that would bring you and your men."

"I would need more troops."

Hotemkhar waved his fan at the man. "Use the Nsongans. They still have enough fighters, especially if you count their so-called women warriors."

"We would have to be sure of their loyalty. They're still rebellious."

"Then we will have to remind them of the might of the Ega."

The commander finally looked at him. "No one has set foot on the other side of the river."

"Oh, don't tell me you've fallen prey to their superstitions."

The look he received from the commander shrunk him.

"We have no map and no idea of the layout of the land. We have no idea what sort of dangers may lay on that side of the river. I've only seen the jungle people simply disappear into the forest, somehow with their boats in tow."

"Then capture one of the jungle people. Make them talk. Surely they can't be that hard to beat secrets out of."

"I will see about gathering intelligence first, then I will construct a plan for crossing the Bangi. Does that satisfy your musings?"

Hotemkhar jutted his chin out, defiantly. "Very well, commander. When *you* are ready, *I'll* assure you get the troops you need for our little excursion." He turned without another word, leaving the courtyard.

That bastard thought he could talk down to him. He thought he could act like his better. Tutamen was lucky he was in such high regard back in the capital. But he was still just a brutish soldier. One day he would learn to come to heel and Hotemkhar would relish that day.

CHAPTER EIGHT

Newa admired all the activity in the compound to-day. In the past few days, several members who weren't on board with the empire's new direction were rooted out and taken care of. He'd gotten to send a few on to their final judgment himself. That had been a most satisfying day. Now the Arakgu'un moved swiftly to reorganize and see to the vacuum made by the dissolving of the other priest-hoods. In his patrols in the city, he was amused to see so many confused when they went to pay homage at the temples only to be turned away or to find them empty. He had the pleasure of seeing to a few priests who'd tried to steal some of the treasures stored in the temples. There were reports of some priests and priestesses making off with sacred artifacts and scrolls. It was of no matter. They would be found and dealt with accordingly. That's what his sect was here for.

Newa straightened his robes as he walked down the hallway to their leader's chamber. A pleased smile stretched his lips. He knew he was favored in his master's sight but to have confirmation of such did things to a man's confidence. He knocked on the door ready for what-ever orders his leader had summoned him to give.

"Come," came the reply from inside.

Newa entered, making the gesture of respect when he stood before the Hand of Gu'un.

"You called for me, master."

"Yes, I have a very important task for you to per-form." His old teacher looked up to him warily. "But I fear it may put a bad taste in your mouth."

"I am ready for whatever you ask of me. I live to serve the order."

His leader assessed him for a moment before finally nodding.

"Newa, I need you to go to the south."

Newa nearly choked. His master was right. "And what would you have me do . . . in the south?"

"The emperor's official decree will be sent soon, and we need to make sure that our brethren in the south are prepared for the change. There will be some who will disagree with it and I need one of the best there to make sure they are ushered on. I'll be sending another brother to the north soon enough." His leader looked him over again, but Newa couldn't keep some of his displeasure from showing in his posture. "I know that you were born and bred in the capital. You have little need for the countryside, but I need someone I can trust and who better than you?"

Newa bowed. "You honor me, master," he said even though it felt like a punishment. "How long will I be away?"

"It may be some time. I need you to visit the major cities in the south and the towns and villages in between."

"What if I'm outnumbered in one of the cities? Perhaps the majority don't want to bow down."

"Then return and we will send a force. We cannot let any rogue agents roam loose against the emperor and his wishes."

"Of course, master. When shall I leave?"

"As soon as you're ready."

"Yes, master." Newa bowed and his leader dismissed him with a wave.

The distaste he had for his new mission flooded his face as soon as he left the leader's room. He was not looking forward to this journey. The south was an empty expanse, full of nothing but backward cities until you reached Nsongo's sphere of influence. He wasn't looking forward to being out in the elements either. It was heading toward the dry season and the temperature would be climbing steadily.

Newa chided himself. Was he some neophyte, complaining about a little bit of hardship? Had it been so long from his childhood on the streets that he'd grown soft in his comforts? His mind flashed back to nights spent in alleyways rooting through trash heaps before he was brought into the priesthood. No, a simple trip to spread the news to the south would be nothing.

He headed back to his rooms, his apprentice waiting on him.

"Help me pack," he ordered the young man. "I'll be heading to the south."

"And what of me, master?"

Newa paused. Normally, his apprentice would be left in the charge of another member until his return. However, he wasn't sure he wanted anyone else's influence on the boy. Not until they could be sure of everyone's loyalty.

"You will be coming with me just as I accompanied my master everywhere."

The young man eagerly leapt to action, fetching everything Newa would need for the trip and packing it carefully. The boy already took impeccable care of his instruments; however, he still needed the push to use them. He still had the squeamishness of newness about him and none of the bloodthirstiness he had when he came in. But this boy didn't have his hard upbringing. He took a moment to watch his charge. Perhaps, this trip had been a godsend. Hopefully, it would harden the boy further. He was the future of the Arakgu'un.

* * *

Efah awoke in the warm bundle her hyenas made around her. Their journey from the hidden city was peaceful and without note. People tended to shy away from a girl flanked by two huge beasts. Her wandering eventually led her to the road to Ofolabaru and she wished she had wandered elsewhere. Ofolabaru was the city most of the people

in Gerembe had fled. They said it was ruled by a harsh dara who was more inclined to the Ega than Nsongo. Her
laws were strict and her justice swift. Unlike most other
daras she kept a host of lovers to show her opulence, many
of them functioning as her personal guard. Those that fell
under her steely gaze met a harsh end.

Efah shuddered trying to shake off the stories as
much as from her fear of them. One of her hyenas, the one
she'd named Usa, nuzzled up to her. She scratched behind
its ears, touching her forehead to its. The other, Nesi,
stretched lazily and plopped its head in her lap. Efah
laughed at her unusual companions. The familiars of death
were such loving creatures.

The trio arose, taking to the road again. She could
see the city in the far distance, the gold roofed compound
of the dara shining in the early morning sun. Travelers had
already started their journeys and she heard the sounds of
wagons and animals behind her, probably heading to the
city's market for the day. A wagon pulled by a thick ox gave
her a wide berth, nearly pulling off the road to avoid getting close to Nesi. While Efah hated the looks of fear that
people gave her she was glad that no one would trouble
her anymore.

She stopped her trek as the walls of the city grew
ever closer. She looked to her companions warily. It was
one thing to quickly avoid them on the road, but she was-
n't sure how people in the city would react to them. It
would probably start a panic.

"Nesi, Usa, you'll have to stay out here. Stay in the
forest until I call you."

The two hyenas rubbed their huge heads against her
chest, then padded into the forest disappearing at once.
Efah took a deep breath. The god's mission to her still felt
like a dream. What was she supposed to tell them? If she
even got their attention, would they listen to some strange
woman from who knew where? Would they label her a crazy woman and go about their day? Would they throw her
in a pit to never escape? She heard the whine-cry of her
hyenas from the forest and felt encouraged. She was sent

on a mission from the god of death. She was his messenger. They had to listen to her.

Efah approached the gate with the rest of the traffic. The guards barely moved, but she watched their eyes surveying everything. One of the guards locked onto her for a moment and her heart jumped. His eyes moved on to the next traveler. Efah breathed in relief as she walked down the main road. The hoard of travelers dispersed, taking side roads to their destinations. Efah wandered, lost in the sheer enormity of the city. Is this what Gerembe would have looked like in its heyday? No. She shook her head. The city of thieves could have never looked so splendid.

Her feet took her to side roads and eventually to the marketplace. This was nothing like the markets in the towns and cities where her group sold their stolen trinkets. She walked past stalls selling some of those same, obviously stolen, ancient treasures. Others peddled fabrics of southern and Egan makes. Jewelry of both cultures glittered in the sun, calling the well off to further adorn themselves. Efah shook her head. This was only the early morning crowd. She hated to see what the rest of the day looked like.

Her eyes took in more of the dizzying displays of the city's market, her gaze finally trailing up to the tall towers of the dara's compound and its golden domes. The bright reflection blinded her for a moment, and she blinked heavily. The glow morphed as she stared, and she couldn't tear her eyes away from it. The light pulled and stretched settling into flames. More flames lit up the compound extending from the towers to the walls and beyond. Efah turned to yell to the other marketgoers but when she turned the market washed in a red hue. The world slowed as people went about their shopping and chatting, oblivious to the destruction in the heart of their city. Efah yelled at the top of her lungs, desperate for someone to listen but it was as if she were no longer there. People walked past her without even a sideways glance.

She reached out in panic to catch a shopper walking past. Her fingers grabbed onto the man just as he crumbled to dust. Efah gasped, taking in smoke and ash. She looked back to the compound and the fire had spread to the rest of the city. Flames painted the sky red and orange. She looked around the market, desperate for someone to cry to but every person she laid eyes on crumbled to dust before she could open her mouth. She ran around the market desperately trying to find someone, but everyone had fallen away. She looked around alone with flames closing in on her. She let out a scream of terror as the city crumbled down around her.

The world came back to her in a rush and she realized she was surrounded. Her hands clutched her hair in an iron grip, her breathing ragged and quick. She heard questions of her sanity floating over her. She looked up suddenly at the crowd. A layer of ash covered them, on some thicker than others, the ash of their destruction.

"You have to listen to me," she said finding her voice. "You must turn from the ways of the Ega and return to the old ways. The true ways. If you don't . . ." Her mind returned to her vision. "If you don't death and destruction will visit this city." Around her people groaned, a mixture of annoyance and disbelief.

"You have to believe me!" she cried louder as the crowd began to disperse. "You must save yourselves. Please save yourselves." She breathed harder. "I am the messenger of the death god," she proclaimed. She hesitated, not wanted to name him. "I am the messenger of Usharabi." She felt authority pass through her the moment she spoke his name aloud. "I am the messenger of Usharabi, and you must turn from these false ways and find your way to the true path."

She was suddenly shoved from behind. She looked to see a gruff older man.

"You're scaring people away from my wares. Get out of here." She started to speak but he shoved her again.

A woman came from her other side, a cane in her hand.

"You heard him. Go on. We don't cater to crazy people here."

Before she knew it, she had a small mob forming around her, crying for her to leave. Efah tried to shout them down but her cries were drowned out. They had to listen. Their lives were in danger. She pleaded and cried for their belief. Just when she was about to give up a loud growl sounded over the crowd. The people jumped back as Usa and Nesi leapt down from on top of a nearby building. The crowd stood, unsure of what to do. Their eyes drifted up in fear and Efah noticed the large flock of vultures lining the rooftops. The birds looked down on them, judgment in their stares.

A woman clasped her hand to her mouth. "She is the messenger of death."

"I am," Efah responded placing her hands on her beasts. "Now will you listen?"

Before anyone answered, a man made his way through the crowd. He came forward without fear, even at the sight of the pair of beasts making a point of staring him down. He made a small bow to her, his handsome face betraying no emotion.

"I would like to listen and I'm very sure my dara would as well."

Efah scratched the back of her hyenas' necks to calm them. "Then I would like to speak with her." The vultures dispersed as they made their way on, the crowd pulling to the sides of the market for her. She looked around at the expressions as she passed. She was very sure that the message was received.

* * *

Erenemo paced the private chamber of his home, his mind churning. Egan soldiers had tried to camp out in the temple of Bamii. After a night of revelry, they found themselves too drunk to make it back to their makeshift barracks so the temple happened to be the first structure they set their eyes on. A few even tried to accost the priestess attending the temple. Luckily, a few of Nsongo's guard happened to be walking by and ousted them. He let go of a grunt of frustration. This is why he told his niece to increase the guard, but for some reason she refused to heed his advice.

"Father, good afternoon."

Erenemo looked to the door to see his son entering. His scowl dissipated at his son's cheerful greeting.

"Ofemu, greetings and blessings be on you." He embraced him, kissing him on each cheek. "What brings you here?"

Ofemu shrugged. "I've been too busy to visit for days so I thought I'd take the first chance I had."

"Have you greeted your mother?"

"I did," he chuckled. "Now I'm obligated to stay for dinner."

Erenemo laughed. "I don't think there's a higher authority in our lives than her."

Ofemu looked into his eyes, his smile shrinking. "Something's troubling you, father."

"Just the same troubles," Erenemo replied, waving dismissively. "Nothing to worry yourself about."

His son folded his muscular arms, his head tilted to the side. "What has she done now? Or, rather, what hasn't our *great dara* done?"

Erenemo's scowl returned. "It's nothing of note."

"Her rule will be nothing of note." His son sighed harshly. "It's been three years, father. Three. Years. And she still turns over and shows her belly to those northern bastards. Imalu's tits, is she even showing any backbone after all this time or is she still mourning over her beloved Lafosa?"

"Lower your voice." He watched his son carefully until he was satisfied with his obedience. "Your cousin is still the unsure, youngest child that should have never taken the golden seat."

"It should have been me," Ofemu grumbled.

Erenemo struggled not to roll his eyes. He was not having this discussion again, but it was inevitable when Ashaki was brought up.

"Ashaki may be unsure and too compliant for my tastes, but it was she who took up leadership when her last brother fell. The council saw merit in that."

"I bet they rue their decision now."

"You sound like a petulant child."

Ofemu sucked his teeth. "Father, we both know she's unfit for true leadership. We need someone with a firm hand. Not a weakling who surrendered when things got tough."

"We can't change what's happened," Erenemo replied, speaking as much to his son as to himself.

His son opened his mouth to speak, then paused. "What if we take steps to change it?"

The old priest eyed his son warily. He wasn't sure if he liked this look in his eyes. "What are you talking about?"

"What if we *do* change our circumstances?" Ofemu took a step closer to him, lowering his voice. "What if we can find a way to replace her?"

"I will not entertain this."

"But father, if we can somehow have her . . . removed, then I could take her place. Not only would we have a stronger Great Dara, but we would keep leadership in the family."

"Not another word." He paused again, trying to use his will to push back this idea in his son. "Dara's have only been removed by death."

"And?"

"Not another word! I will not entertain such talk. Now leave me. I have work to do. I'll see you at dinner."

Ofemu kissed his father on the cheek then left the room. Erenemo sighed, deflating. A growl escaped him as he slammed his fist against a table. His son had too many lofty ideas about himself. It was laughable to think that the council would ever name him Great Dara. While a fierce warrior, his cousin was a far better strategist and leader on the battlefield. Ashaki was more comfortable on the battlefield than under the mantle of dara, that was certain. But if there was anyone better suited for the position . . .

Erenemo struggled to shake the feelings of bitterness he felt toward his niece. It was unbecoming of a man of his station. Yet, surely, he, as the highest priest and brother of the late Great Dara, would have been a far better choice. He was more experienced in the day to day running of the city. He had the respect of the populace. He wasn't a traitor.

She said she'd surrendered to protect the people. He grunted. She surrendered out of fear and grief. As if she were the only one who had lost someone in the wars. Had her courage been so fleeting? And that damned council was more interested in preserving what was left of a long bloodline than what was best for the city. Ofemu was right. He was sure the council rued their decision to approve her ascension.

Erenemo stroked his thick beard. He took to the shelves of his study, pulling out books on the history of their city. He knew that no dara had been removed by anything but death or assassination, but was there any provision for removing an unfit dara? Even if there wasn't, they were living in unprecedented times. Perhaps if there were a way to convince the council Ashaki was woefully unfit they would have to name a new dara. And then he . . . while he was a priest, these were unprecedented times. Erenemo frantically began reading, searching for some way to save his city.

CHAPTER NINE

Ashaki drowned in the minutiae of the day. She fanned the front of her shirt against the stickiness already beginning in the morning air. The city storehouses were being reorganized and tallied for the tribute in just a few days. She took a deep calming breath. It would be her first tribute without her family and the first the city had done since the occupation. She was glad this was only every ten years.

She stepped out of the way of a hand wagon coming by to be piled up with sacks of spices. Her spirits sank a bit as she walked by the dome shaped buildings. Under her father's reign they would have been near bursting with goods, waiting to be traded or waiting for the next tribute. She took in the sparseness with a pang of guilt. The Ega came like vultures, picking at what they'd so carefully saved. Many things they'd reserved purely for the batu-bangi, the soldiers had taken upon themselves to use, eat, or just destroy.

A swaggering trio of their soldiers sauntered by on a side street. She had to resist the urge to grab her sword. She hated them. People didn't understand how much she hated them. They only saw her as the one who surren-dered. The one who delivered their people into foreign hands. But what was she supposed to do? Her father and all six of her brothers had fallen in battle. Lafosa had fall-en. She had to surrender to preserve what was left of her people. She had to do it. She couldn't leave her little girl without either of her mothers. Ashaki shook her head, clearing her mind lest she begin to tear up. She focused on her tallies of the goods in the storehouses instead.

A sound ahead caught her attention and she looked up to see an Egan soldier cornering a merchant against a wall. The woman was trying to slip away, but he would quickly block her passage. Ashaki glowered, marching her way over. She heard the foul things he was saying to her and her blood began to boil.

"You there," she called loudly.

The soldier and the merchant looked up, the merchant in utter relief. The soldier looked her up and down his face settling on annoyance.

"What do you want?" he asked as she stepped closer.

"Let her be on her way. I'm sure she has work to do and I'm very sure you do too."

"And who the hell are you?" he slurred in that odd northern accent.

"I am Ashaki, the Great Dara of Nsongo. And who the hell are you?"

"I don't listen to you, woman."

Ashaki placed a hand, casually, on her sword handle. "You are in my city, on my lands, and you will do as commanded. I'm sure your commander wouldn't like to see you acting in such a manner."

"What about his commander?" came a voice from behind her. Ashaki turned, facing the man she hated almost as much as the Egan ambassador. The tall man looked over her head, as he liked to do, to his soldier.

"Let the woman go," he said as if she weren't there.

The man stepped back from the merchant, sneering at Ashaki as he did so. The woman muttered a quick thanks to her and hurried on. Ashaki turned her anger on the Egan commander.

"Your soldiers need to learn how to behave."

He dismissed his man, before committing his attention to her.

"My soldiers are under my command. They will behave however they see fit. If I haven't reprimanded them, then their behavior is fine."

Ashaki took a breath. "I've been meaning to talk to you about this for some time, Commander Tutamen. Your men have been steadily running amok in *my* city."

"Your city?" he chuckled.

"*My* city. Acting like animals with no respect to my people. They have taken their pleasures with any women they can force themselves on, especially those who have no desire for men."

"Taking it personally I see."

Ashaki ignored the attempt at a slight. "Your empire is supposed to be so great; I thought the soldiers of it would know how to conduct themselves accordingly. And especially now. We have the tribute coming in just two days. If the batubangi are insulted it will affect trade with them for the next ten years. Can you get them to behave for at least two days?"

His expression turned dangerous and she had to stop herself from grabbing her sword.

"Are you implying that I don't have control over my forces?"

"Obviously, my ideas of a tight leash and yours are very different."

"Our ideas of winning a war appear to be vastly different as well." Ashaki scowled, the sting of his words duly noted.

"Great Dara," he began with exaggerated sarcasm, "if my men wish to go about and show how relations should go between a man and a woman then we are doing your people a service. You should be glad I haven't allowed any of them to just slaughter any of the unnatural men you have here. And now I hear reports that there are some among you that enjoy both?" His lip twisted in disgust. "We could not have conquered you fast enough. If for nothing else than to bring you back to rights.

"Besides, you are a conquered people, defeated, beneath us. You are a horse, freshly broken in and ready to be ridden. You should be thankful for my mercy thus far. I could have really let my men have their way with your city."

Ashaki closed her eyes, taking another long breath. She pushed down the frustration building.

"Can you give me at least two days without incident? If the tribute doesn't go well, our supply of gold could dwindle meaning your people's supply of gold will shrink to a trickle. I just need two days from your men."

She watched as he thought. His face took on its usual arrogant frown.

"I will tell them to keep it to a minimum."

She bowed, the act almost causing physical pain. "Thank you." She had to force the words from her lips.

Ashaki released a breath as he walked off. She wanted to cry. She wanted to fight. She wanted to take her sword and ram it through his back, force his head back so she could watch the life drain from his eyes. But then she would die and who would be there for 'Sola.

"Great Dara," came a voice from her side.

A group of the batubangi stood patiently to the side of the small road. She forced herself to regain her composure, praying that they hadn't witnessed the exchange.

"Yes," she said with a small smile. "What can I do for you?"

The elder of the group came before her, his face a whirlwind of emotions. "Great Dara, we have a problem. One of our kind is missing. We have looked everywhere we could, even staying here for the past three nights in search of him. We do not know what else we can do."

"That's horrible. I will have my city guards on it immediately. We'll look in every corner of the city until we find them. You have my word."

The group bowed their heads at once. "Thank you, Great Dara." They made signs of respect and continued on their way.

Ashaki sighed again, informing the nearest tally keeper that she'd return soon. Egan soldiers that wouldn't behave civilly, a missing batubangi, and the tribute weighing down on her. There was so much to do today.

* * *

Efah looked around in amazement at the grand hallway leading into the dara's inner compound. Stone columns supporting the highest ceiling she'd ever seen rose up, covered in gold gilded reliefs. Servants and other nobles stepped to the walls to give her and her companions space. Usa and Nesi didn't growl at anyone, but their heads moved about constantly, surveying the room. While she felt completely safe flanked by them, a little spark of nervousness wouldn't go away. This dara was said to be such a harsh woman. What if she didn't believe her? What if she had her thrown out after telling her story? What was she to do? She sent up a quick prayer to her new god for guidance.

The man who'd led her here was no help either. He hadn't spoken a word since they began their walk and his expression hadn't changed a bit. She had no idea what kind of reception she was walking into. As if sensing her nervousness, Nesi rubbed her head against Efah's cheek. She smiled. At least she would have the best protectors in the world at her side.

The hallway opened into a circular courtyard that ringed around the inner compound. Soldiers trained in rectangular groups, fighting each other in pairs. Nobles took leisurely walks trying to behave as if they weren't watching. Soon Efah and her hyenas were the new center of attention. She was grateful when their walk across the courtyard was over. The inside of the inner compound was cool and a slight breeze blew through. They took to a couple of hallways, then finally reached the audience chamber of the dara of Ofolabaru.

Efah's breath caught at the sight of her. This woman didn't sit on a stool like the great dara but an ornate chair with elephant tusks making up the back. She rested on cushions made from delicate Egan cloth. Her skin was of the darkest brown and smoother than any she'd seen. Sharp eyes rested on her and her pack and Efah felt her fear grow. A woman with sword and shield stood at one side, her muscles telling of readiness.

The man who'd led her here came to one knee before the dara. The woman greeted him with a small, knowing smile.

"And what have you brought before me, Ala?"

"A stranger from the market, my dara. She was pleading with the people to turn back to the old ways. I thought her mad until her curious beasts leapt in to protect her and vultures gathered as if to witness the scene."

The woman raised an eyebrow as she looked back to Efah. "I am Dara Ngoli and you are, girl?"

"I am Efah Aboujale." She paused, unsure. "I am the messenger of death."

The guard standing by the dara snapped her head towards her, making a sound of disapproval. The dara chuckled.

"Are you now? And is that why you made such a spectacle in the market?"

"He has given me a message to spread."

She leaned forward, resting her chin on her hand. "And what is that message?"

"You must turn from the false ways, the way of the Ega." Dara Ngoli sat back. "You must throw off the worship of their false gods and go back to our people's true ways." She paused, not wanting to finish but the message compelled her. "If you do not, there will be death. There will be death from the lowest hovels to the highest houses. This land will be cleansed and the trash burned away." The words flowed through her as if someone else were speaking. "I saw your city burn and it started here, in your compound. The towers burned and bled their gold away. Your people fell away in ash and there was nothing left of ruin. That is what awaits you if you and your city do not turn to the old, the true ways."

Efah released a breath. She suddenly felt as if she'd run from the outer gates to here. Silence hung over the room. Ngoli changed her sitting position again, chin to hand.

"You saw Ofolabaru? Burning?" The eyebrow raised again. "In your mind?"

"Yes, Dara Ngoli."

"So, you claim to be a seer?"

Efah blinked at the question. "I'm just a messenger."

"But you saw visions of the city burning?"

"Yes, dara."

"How long have you had these visions?"

Efah felt ten times smaller under this woman's gaze. Her companions moved closer to her.

"This was the first one."

Silence fell again. The dara's gaze didn't move from her.

"You'll have to understand that I will have to think on this. So, please, stay a night here while I talk to my council. It is the least I can do for the messenger of the god of death." The dara looked to the man who'd led her in. "Ala," she began with a smile. "Would you find our new seer a room? A nice one please."

"Right away, my dara."

"And Efah, please rest yourself. I assure you; your message has not been brushed aside."

Efah showed her respect to the dara and followed the man out. The meeting hadn't been as hard as she thought it would be. Yet, that feeling of nervousness wouldn't fall away. She placed a hand on Nesi and Usa's back for support and followed the guard to a room.

* * *

Yutuuan couldn't bring himself to go to sleep. He took to the hallways of the palace, agitated. He was happy, elated, that his sister was back in Wiluru. Yet, her news from the netkoleh was disturbing. It was bad enough that the Ega had come and shoved aside the Wiluruan pantheon, dropping their temples across the kingdom like so much dung. They had endured their humiliations for generations but this was a step too far. They would not, could

not abandon the very gods that had sustained them and
brought them to this very blessed spot.

Before he knew it, he was walking through the main
hallways. Ahead of his he saw his parents strolling along,
talking happily as they headed to their rooms. Yutuuan
schooled his expression, forcing a smile onto his face.

"Mother, father," he said as he drew near.

His mother smiled, happier than he thought he'd
ever seen her. "My son, do you not have an early morning
tomorrow?"

"I . . . can't sleep."

His parents looked to each other, concerned. His father kissed his mother on the forehead.

"Go on without me. I'm going to walk with Yutuuan."

His mother nodded, coming over to kiss him on the
cheek before going on. "I hope you can find rest tonight."

He returned her kiss. "I will."

Once she had walked on a good distance, his father
motioned for them to continue walking.

"What troubles you, my son? You looked disturbed
as we came up."

"Izriamat's news is disturbing. How can the
netkoleh declare such heresy? This is beyond anything his
people have ever done." Bakari paused as a pair of servants
passed. "I've never liked him. I know we only met him
briefly, but I knew he was unfit to rule back then. He'll
lead us into ruin with this."

His father took in all of his words with a studious
face. "This will not go over well with our people."

"Or the priests!"

"Or the priests," his father concurred.

"What will become of all of the priests and priestesses? Are they supposed to just give up their calling as if
they're a carpenter retiring?" His mind briefly brought his
favorite priestess to the front. "We'll have scores of people
suddenly without occupation or purpose in their lives.
How will they live? How will we live?"

"Wiluru will survive," his father said with finality.

"We have weathered their occupation and we will weather this as well. We won't abandon our creators and sustainers."

"Then what will we do when his decree comes?"

His father was silent, with an expression he'd never seen before.

"I'm not sure as of yet. We will be diplomatic about the situation. Surely, he will see the folly in this."

"Father, you can't believe that." He looked in his father's face for some sign of unsurety. "Father, you really can't believe that. There is no reasoning with them. He and his line have always looked to Wiluru as their plaything. We're nothing to them. They know that we'll roll over."

"We're not going to 'roll over'." His father sighed.

"Then we have to *do* something. Fight back somehow."

"No." His father looked to him with all seriousness in his eyes. "We will not fight. You know as well as I do the might of their forces. What could our small area do if they decide to bring down the might of the Egah upon us?"

"Our warriors are fierce."

"But their numbers are finite. And the Egah now have the ability to call troops from all the way to the southern lands. What would you do?" Yutuuan struggled for an answer. "We would be slaughtered. Our people slaughtered along with our warriors. My son, as a king you must think beyond your slighted honor. Yutuu has placed us as the keepers of our people. How would he look on us if we let our sheep be devoured by wolves?"

"But father, we can't just sit here and do nothing as they turn us into heretics."

His father sighed heavily. "We will come through this. But until the official decree comes, we will think and consult Yutuu as to our path forward." He looked into his eyes deeply. "We cannot act rashly."

It was Yutuuan's turn to sigh. He would get nowhere with his father tonight.

"Yes, father. I will await your wise decision."

"Good." His father patted his shoulder. "Have faith,

son. Yutuu will guide us through."

Yutuuan nodded continuing his walk. His frustration wouldn't leave him even when he returned to his rooms. He undressed and dropped down on his bed. Doing nothing was not an option. Sitting and waiting was not an option. The penalty for such blasphemous actions needed to be swift and decisive. There had to be some kind of retaliation to make their point.

He turned over, his restlessness easing some. He had to make sure he was there when the emissaries made the announcement. If father wouldn't make it clear that this was a demand too far then the responsibility fell on him. He didn't want to disobey his father and king but his hand was being pushed. Father thought he was just thinking about the honor of their people, but he was thinking of their people. They could not turn away from their gods. That was out of the question. If the emissaries wouldn't take a firm no for an answer, then they had to go a step further. Yutuuan closed his eyes, resigning himself. He was fully prepared to take that next step.

CHAPTER TEN

Nsongo was alive with music and song. The market along the docks had been cleared out, making way for tables and mats for people to feast. A band of musicians occupied the farthest end of the market, the music drifting all throughout the city. Dancers made their way down the length of it, brightening this most auspicious day.

Ashaki smiled, clapping along with the music. She wanted to take her turn dancing, but as the Great Dara her place was where she could oversee the festivities. The platform she and the other officials sat on vibrated from the foot stomping along with the rhythm. She smiled down to Sola who smiled back for just a moment before returning to looking disinterested. Ashaki smirked. Her daughter couldn't fool her. This would be the first tribute since she was barely out of babehood. She knew her girl was enjoying herself. Ashaki leaned over, whispering, "Perhaps, I can let you dance later."

Masola's posture changed. "That sounds . . . all right."

Ashaki shook her head and returned to watching. The batubangi they were honoring seemed to be having a great time. It appeared many of them hadn't been to a tribute either. Ashaki smiled. Her people were behaving as great hosts despite everything that rested on their shoulders. At every other street that led down to the market, she could see curious Egan soldiers watching the gathering. Some sneered, some laughed, but at least they were conducting themselves in a respectable manner.

Now if others would do the same. She looked out of the corner of her eye at Hotemkhar sitting at her left. That space was supposed to be reserved for her uncle but the northern peacock inserted himself at the last moment. He waved his fan against the heat and looked on with mild disapproval. Ashaki resisted scowling at him. If he didn't like the festivities, then he could always leave. She was sure he was due to reapply that ridiculous eye makeup their people wore.

As if he could sense her loathing, he looked to her with his usual haughty smile.

"It seems your people can provide adequate entertainment," he shouted over the noise. "I wish that we could bring a troop of dancers from the capital to show you true skill. Not all of this," he waved at the dancers with his feather fan, "wild convulsing."

"We enjoy our dancers well enough," she responded pushing a saccharine smile on her face. "I see it as less convulsing and more of full usage of the body. We enjoy working in the south." Before he could respond, she leaned across her daughter to the leader of the batubangi delegation on their right. "Are you enjoying yourself, elder T'kosu?"

The balding man smiled brightly at her. "We are, Great Dara. The food is very, very good and the music is most good. This is very wonderful."

"I'm glad you're enjoying yourselves." Her smile faltered when she felt Hotemkhar looking over her shoulder.

The northerner chuckled. "Yes, they did put together a meager little festival, didn't they?" he said, over exaggerating every word.

"Do you not like it?" T'kosu asked him.

"Our festivals are much grander in the capitol and they spread out over the whole city. You see, our festivals are holy days. Dedicated to our gods. We wouldn't have a celebration for just any occasion."

Ashaki ignored him. "Elder T'kosu, we will bring out the tribute in an hour. I wish to apologize in advance. It is not to the same standards that my father provided in his day, but I hope it will please you and the other elders here."

"We know that things are different for you now," he responded and she could see one of the other elders nod to her relief. "We will take this into consideration when we inspect the tribute."

"Thank you," Ashaki said lowering her head, yet feeling butterflies in her stomach. That last comment felt a bit non-committal. She could only hope they would be merciful at the amount included in her tribute. They'd done the best they could. With most of their gold rerouted to the north, they hadn't been able to purchase as many of the pearls the batubangi were crazy for. The Ega had raided their spices as well, sending those back to their cities. She'd gathered as much as possible, making various promises to the other cities that she prayed she wouldn't have to go back on.

She glanced over her shoulder to her uncle and aunt who sat, unhappily, behind Hotemkhar. If he found out about her deal making, he'd be furious. What was she to do instead? The tribute had to go on without a hitch and if she had to be a little . . . creative to accomplish it, then so be it.

Her thoughts were interrupted by a scream farther down the docks. She stood trying to see where the disturbance was. She knew in her heart that one of the Egan soldiers had done something but she saw a group of batubangi gathered at the far end of the market. Ashaki hopped down from the platform. Sola hopped down behind her, ready to go.

"Stay here," she commanded.

"But mother," she whined.

"Stay with Aunt Patya."

Ashaki rushed along the market. She glanced back at the sound of the footsteps behind her and saw her uncle, T'kosu, and Hotemkhar rushing too. She called loudly for people to clear the way as they whole of the festivities had stopped at the scream. People gathered thickly about the scene and she had to forcefully part the crowd to reach the source.

Five batubangi gathered along the side of a boat, pulling something out of the water. It took Ashaki a moment to realize it was a body. She gasped and heard the reactions behind her. T'kosu rushed past her to his people, helping them with the body. Ashaki grimaced at the sight of it. Fish had been at it, the dead man's eyes already eaten out and part of a cheek. She ran her eyes down his body. He couldn't have been in the water for too long. Crocodiles would have gotten to it. His throat was slit cleanly, but there were bruises and other cuts along his body.

Murders weren't uncommon in Nsongo. Every now and then a body would be fished out of the river, but how could someone have the gall to do this now? She neared the group, kneeling.

"Elder T'kosu, I'm so, so sorry this has happened. I will find the murderer and they will pay for this wrong."

"You people promise our safety in this city," he responded, not even looking at her.

"I know, I know."

Her uncle took a step forward. "We will invoke the ancestors to speak to the gods on his behalf. We would see his soul safely move to the other side as well."

Hotemkhar snorted derisively and Ashaki wanted her sword.

"Why are you all groveling so? There's nothing to apologize for."

Ashaki turned her hot gaze on him. For the first time, he avoided her gaze. Her anger quelled out of shock. That was guilt.

"You know something," she growled.

"What are you talking about?" he said dismissively, still avoiding her gaze.

She stood, closing in on him. "What did you do?" she hissed lowly.

Hotemkhar turned his nose up switching to proper nsongan. "It's just one dead jungle man. There's nothing we need to apologize about. I knew nothing about it anyway."

"Your people did this. Hogalo's fury, it was you people." She took a step away from him in revulsion.

The northerner made a face, looking more like her daughter caught in a lie than a grown man.

"And if we did?" he whispered back harshly. "Just

make a show of investigating and declare it the work of
thugs. Execute them and be done with it."

Even her uncle looked at the man in disgust. T'kosu
came over to them.

"Your people killed one of my people?" he asked,
rage hiding behind his eyes. Hotemkhar looked to the man
in shock. "I understand the language of these people very
well even if I do not speak it very well." He looked to
Ashaki. "The tribute will not go on." She felt her knees
buckle. "You are too . . . in debt to these people who are
jackals. We will think about this again in ten years." He
turned to his people, calling in his own language loudly.

Ashaki watched as the batubangi around immediately started to pack up to leave.

"What about trade?" she asked desperately.

"We will think about that in ten years as well." He
began to walk away from her. Ashaki felt her heart stop. If
there was no trade, there was no gold. Her city would fall
into poverty. Nsongo would fall.

Hotemkhar stormed past her. "You listen to me, little man," he said gesturing with his fan dangerously. "You
can think you will stop the gold trade with this little show,
but we will have your riches. You can either continue your
trade here or we can come into your little jungle and take
it."

T'kosu turned in his tracks, fixing a deadly stare on
the northern man. "If you value your people, you will stay
on this side of the Bangi. If you come to our home, you will
find nothing but misery." He turned and continued to
gather his people.

Hotemkhar continued throwing threats at the batubangi, but Ashaki couldn't hear them. The only sound
coming to her was her blood pounding in her ears.

"You diseased piece of shit!" she roared, taking a
step toward him. A firm hand caught her arm, stopping
her from raising her clenched fist.

The northerner looked to her, surprised. "You can
let her go, priest," he said looking to her as if she were a
puppy trying to bite him. "She knows what would happen

to her and your beloved city."

"You have ruined everything," she shrieked.

He snorted at her. "You speak to your better, *Great Dara*. You should remember that."

"If they will not trade with us, then how will we survive?"

"Don't you worry about that. That is a concern for those who actually rule this city. Just keep it in order until our warriors arrive and you all can make a living off of servicing them."

She watched him as he sauntered off, scowling at any batubangi that dared come near him.

"Get yourself together," she heard her uncle hiss at her. Ashaki took a deep breath then let loose a scream, because it was all she could do.

* * *

Umakaal approached the small courtyard apprehensively. She wasn't sure of what her brother wanted in this private setting but she was sure it would be an odd request. Yutuuan wasn't one for secrecy unless he was up to something and it was usually a rash decision. She saw him pacing by the rain collecting pots, his hand in his chin. She raised an eyebrow, smirking. This was probably going to be something ridiculous.

"Yutuuan," she called walking over. "You wanted me?"

He smiled slightly, beckoning her closer. "I need to talk to you about what Izriamat told us."

Her smirk melted. "About disavowing the gods?"

"Yes. What do you think we should do about it?"

Umakaal blinked. This wasn't something that she thought would ever be brought to her.

"What do you mean?"

"I'm asking you honestly. What do you think we should do about it?"

"I think we should see what father will do." His annoyed growl pricked her. "What? That's my honest answer.

I mean, it's not my place to consider what the country will do. I run the palace guard."

"But you do have your own personal opinion."

She bit her lip, thinking. It hadn't really come to her. As her brother waited, she thought back to her sister saying those words, those filthy words. It made her angry beyond belief.

"We can't allow it," she said at last. "But I don't know how we'll disobey the netkoleh."

"Disobey," he spat, leaning against one of the large pots. "This is a blasphemy we can't allow."

Umakaal looked down, reading her own feelings. "You're right. We have to fight back. Should we bar the netkoleh's people from delivering the message?"

"We can't. I know father wouldn't let us."

"Then we have to find some other way to make it clear that we won't go along with this."

There was a moment of silence, broken by the sound of nearby birds taking flight. Yutuuan looked to her.

"Once we make it clear we're not cooperating, you know he'll retaliate."

Umakaal bit at her lip. "Then we have to fight."

"Father's afraid he'll bring the might of the rest of the empire on us. And he's kind of right."

"But even the netkoleh can't take that many troops from around the country. It would leave so many places without peacekeepers and defenders." She stared at her brother. Surely the netkoleh wasn't that type of man. No man could be that reckless.

"I don't know. When we met, before they took Izriamat away, he was spoiled and petulant. He tried to get me to speak on her body and what I thought of it as a man. I wanted to punch him. I can't imagine him changing much now."

He looked up past her shoulder and Umakaal looked back to see their sister entering the courtyard. She had to resist the urge to run and hug her again. Izriamat smiled serenely at the both of them. She looked majestic out of her Egan clothes, the vision of her sister that she kept in her head all these years.

"I was wondering where you two were. Why such a secret meeting?" she asked lowering her voice dramatically.

Their brother hesitated and she bit her lip again. "We were talking about the netkoleh's decree." It pained her to see her sister's face fall.

"Father is stalling and we need to make a decision quickly," Yutuuan added.

Izriamat frowned. "Father is taking his time, deciding what's best. You know he isn't one for quick decisions."

"But this isn't the time for hesitation."

Umakaal jumped in as her sister walked to them. "We feel that a strong message needs to be sent."

"You're talking about war," Izriamat breathed out. She looked aside, her eyes resting to the reflections in the collected rainwater. "I don't know if that's best."

"What other choice do we have?" Yutuuan asked emphatically. "You said yourself that he can't be reasoned with. If we *politely* tell him that we'll be keeping our gods what do you think he'll do?"

Izriamat looked pained. "He would attack us. He would try to wipe out everyone who opposed him."

Umakaal winced. She looked to her sister, trying not to imagine losing her again.

"But," she began, a thought hitting her like a lightning bolt, "what if there were a reason why he couldn't attack us?" Her siblings looked to her in askance. "You," she said looking to her sister.

Yutuuan's eyes widened. "We have you."

"What are you two talking about?" Izriamat asked looking between the both of them.

Their brother laughed. "We hold you hostage. If we threaten your life, he can't attack."

"I . . . don't know. I don't know if he won't attack anyway."

"How does he feel about you?" Umakaal asked, not sure if she wanted the answer.

Izriamat looked aside again, rubbing an arm. "He is

very fond of me."

Her tone made Umakaal want to wretch. Yutuuan grimaced. "Then he will be hesitant to attack if we have his beloved wife," he said softly.

"I don't know. You don't know him. He can be unpredictable."

Umakaal took her sister's hand. "If he holds you to be so precious, he won't be able to risk your harm."

Yutuuan suddenly frowned. He softened his tone.

"What of your son?"

"What of him?"

The coldness in her voice chilled Umakaal. "Will he try to use him as a hostage as well?"

Her sister's face hardened. "He may. It doesn't matter to me. That is his child, not mine."

"Sister," Yutuuan began, "surely you can't -."

Umakaal shushed her brother. She couldn't imagine the pain and sorrow her sister had gone through on her behalf and she wouldn't let her be judged for anything she felt.

"Then the child is of no concern," Umakaal concluded. "Good. That makes things a little cleaner."

"This is still foolish," Izriamat said evenly.

"What choice do we have?" Yutuuan asked. "Will you abandon Yutuu and the rest of the gods?"

Their sister's answer was swift. "Never."

"Then we must prepare for war."

Yutuuan's words weighed heavily in the air between the siblings. He looked to Umakaal and she nodded. They both turned to Izriamat who looked conflicted. Finally, she nodded.

"How are our forces?" she asked.

Yutuuan smirked. "Loyal and ready for another conflict. Peace has made for boring times."

Umakaal shook her head at her brother. "We need to speak to the other city leaders and get their commitment to this."

"I'll travel and speak to them."

Umakaal nodded. "Then we're ready for what's

coming." She looked to her siblings who nodded in grim agreement.

* * *

It was beautiful. Every inch of the palace was clean, fresh, and without a trace of the lies of the past. Bakari took a deep breath, enjoying the moment. From here on, he would fill these halls with the truth of the world and all that man had done. This palace would be full of the tales of his family and their greatness for all time. He already had plans of what he wanted to start with but where he wanted it painted shifted in his mind daily. He chuckled. There was plenty of time to decide.

"You called for me, my husband?" Arkoleh stopped near him, smiling.

Bakari reached his hand out to her and she coyly placed her hand in his.

"My wife, I am sorry I haven't seen you much over these past days. I will make it up to you."

She smiled even wider as he pulled her to him. "I know you have been busy, my husband. You are reshaping the nation."

"Oh no, I am reshaping the world." He began to walk with her down the hallway. "My dearest love, what do you see around you?"

She tilted her head, confused. "I'm not sure what you mean. I see the empty hallway. I have to say it's a bit strange to see nothing on the walls and columns."

"It is a bit strange, isn't it? We've spent all of our lives studying them, learning what we thought was the history of the world." He gestured about him. "This hallway isn't empty, my love. It is full of possibilities." He stopped, looking her in the eyes. "I have so much that needs to be done and I only have but one lifetime to do it. That's why I need you."

She dipped her head. "Whatever you need of me I will do it."

"Do you believe me when I say there are no gods?"

"If you decree it then I believe it, my love."

He sighed, stroking her cheek. "You are one of the most important women in the world. Your words have weight and from here on they will have as much weight as mine. From now on I need you to be as my right hand, by my side in all things. Izriamat, when she returns, will be as my left. You two, my two proper wives, will be my voice in places I cannot be. Your words will have the weight of the empire behind it."

Arkoleh shook her head. "Are . . . are you sure?"

"Surer than of anything in my life. Can you be this for me?" He ran his thumb gently across her bottom lip.

"Yes, my husband."

"Thank you."

She looked aside and he had to wonder what was going through her head.

"My husband," she began quietly. "Are you sure you want that woman as an equal to me?"

He frowned. "Yes, I do. You are my proper wives." She looked down nodding. He would let his annoyance at her question pass. It didn't matter if she didn't like Izriamat. It was his choice to raise her up. He smiled to assuage her fears and continued their walk.

"Tell me, where do you think we should begin the repainting?"

"I'm not sure. Perhaps something in the main hallway?"

"I like that idea." The pair strolled along, servants stepping to the side. Torches were beginning to be lit, the smell of their smoke faintly wafting through the air. He stopped before a large column near the back of one of the main halls.

"How about this, my love? People will see it as they enter the inner courtyard."

"It will be fine, my husband."

He cupped her chin. "No, no for my first love something even more grand must be found."

They strolled through the grand hall, Bakari inspecting each column with exaggerated care. He was enjoying himself. It was like the days of their early liaisons, searching for a hidden spot to speak without prying eyes. He stopped, looking past the columns to the vast expanse of wall before them. There was enough space to paint an impressive tableau.

"Here," he said pulling her close. "Here we shall have an incredible scene painted. You will be larger than life, my love, as large as they once painted the goddesses. You will be remembered for all of history as a mother of this country. They will remember the name of Arkoleh until the end of time."

She put a hand on his chest. "Will I be painted as large as you?" she chuckled.

"As large as me for you are as important to me as air, water, and food." He slid his arms around her waist and kissed her neck.

"And what shall we be doing in this painting?"

"Casting down gods and our enemies." She turned around in his arms, pulling him into a kiss. He smiled through it.

"We will be remaking this world as we see fit. We will bring all we see to heel." He turned her to face the wall, his hands working to lift her skirts. Her hands reached back to raise his kilt.

"We will create a new world," he said as he entered her. "And this world will be in our hands."

CHAPTER ELEVEN

Hotemkhar threw his feathered fan down on a cushion and stalked his room. He would not be threatened by little men from the jungle. They couldn't even speak a proper language and they dared threaten him. He was a noble from the capital of Metkarah. He kicked a stool over, suddenly dissatisfied at his surroundings. To think that he would be treated so badly in a place where he should be revered as the voice of the netkoleh. It was maddening. It was infuriating.

They would pay for this insult. It didn't matter that they lost one of their little men. Their soldiers had gone a bit too far, yes, but it was just a worthless jungle man. And that ridiculous, unnatural woman ruler of theirs had the audacity to raise her voice at him. He would deal with her in time but this was beyond insulting. Those people would pay and their jungle fall under the heel of the netkoleh's rule. Even if every inch of forest had to be burned to the ground, those people would pay for their insult. Then their gold would flow freely.

Hotemkhar smoothed his clothing, trying to calm himself. He should be completely in control of any situation that came up. He took a few deep breaths. Chancellor Hetsaf had chosen him personally. His family was amongst the most powerful in the city. It was believed that they may even be distantly related to the netkoleh's line. He took another breath. He was too good to be riled up by some jungle man's threat. But they would pay. They would pay dearly.

Hotemkhar took to the streets of Nsongo, his attendant struggling to keep up. People scrambled to clear him a path as he passed. He was sure his face looked like death and that was fine by him. Those little people would see more of them dead for this great insult. His path led him back to the compound the commander used as his headquarters.

"Is your commander in?" he snapped at the soldier standing guard.

The man snapped to attention, jerked out of his lazy daydreams. "Yes, he is." He stepped aside hastily, barely in enough time for Hotemkhar to pass.

The noble didn't mind the shambles of the men here today. This was a rather easy assignment and they'd grown accustom to having their way with the city, its riches, and inhabitants. However, they had best ready themselves for war quickly. He didn't care what plans, or lack thereof, the netkoleh had for the people across the Bangi. He would have his gold and make those people pay.

After a quick questioning of the servants, he found the commander coming out of one of the private rooms of the compound. Through the slightly open door, he could see the woman that had been serving him before sitting on a bed, readjusting her clothes. Tutahmen looked up, surprised at his approach. He pulled his belt tighter, his face settling into his normal, impassive expression.

"I've heard that there was some commotion at their festival today. Is that what brings you here?"

"Commander, your men need to ready themselves for war."

The soldier raised an eyebrow. "What happened?"

Hotemkhar felt his temper rise. "The body of the jungle man you captured was found at the docks. How incompetent could your men be? Can they not even dispose of a body properly?" The nobleman shrank slightly at the light in Tutahmen's eyes, but he refused to be cowed. "Did you at least get usable information from him?"

"We did," Tutahmen said, turning to walk away.

Hotemkhar followed him. "Well? Did you think it

might be important enough to inform the overseer of this city?"

The commander glanced over his shoulder. "Their people live a few days journey into the jungle and their mines are even deeper still. The man we kidnapped didn't know where the mines were. He'd never been there. He said they keep sundown to the right so they must head roughly south to their lands. And he spoke of other superstitious nonsense."

"What nonsense?"

"He said that their jungle had protectors and they would consume any outsiders who came." He made a little surprised sound. "He sounded quite confident of it. Now, are you going to tell me what happened at the festival that would lead us to war?"

Hotemkhar scowled at the man. Why was everyone trying him today?

"They realized that it was us who killed that man."

"How the hell would they have realized that?" Tutahmen looked back at him, his face melting into disgust. "By the gods, you looked guilty, didn't you?"

The nobleman felt a stab to his pride. "I was . . . surprised. I thought you were going to keep him alive! I was just as shocked as they were that he turned up dead. And now they've pulled back to their jungle, saying they will think about trading with the Nsongans again in ten years. The unmitigated gall! As if they have a choice in this matter."

Tutahmen stopped in his tracks. "They've cut off trade to the city?"

"Immediately. They pulled their people away and returned to their precious little jungle. And that is why we must ready for war. They will pay for this slight."

The commander turned on him. "You're concerned for your pride. If there's no trade, there's no gold. If there's no gold, the prosperity of the land will wither. Gods curse you. How thick are you?"

"How dare you?" Hotemkhar hissed. "You had just best get your men ready to take their skills across the

Bangi. I want those mines as quickly as possible."

"Who, in the deepest parts of the shadow lands, do you think you are talking to?" Tutahmen growled back at him.

Hotemkhar pulled himself to his full height, still only coming to the bridge of the commander's nose.

"I am the overseer of this city. Perhaps even one day, its governor. All aspects of it fall under my jurisdiction, even the soldiers placed in it as peacekeepers. Even you."

"You have officially overstepped your bounds, little man."

"With one letter, I could have you easily replaced."

"Careful, before you're the next body found in the river."

Hotemkhar seethed under the threat. "And if I am, then you would be executed for failing to ensure my safety. Are you prepared for your afterlife? Is your family prepared to live without the prestige and protection of your station?"

In the deadly silence that filled the hallway, the two men stared each other down. Hotemkhar was pleased when the commander deflated and turned to walk again.

"I will have scouts ready to enter the jungle soon."

"By the end of the week."

There was a pause in Tutahmen's gait. "By the end of the week."

"And I will have soldiers brought from the nearest garrison to bolster our invasion forces." The commander didn't respond and Hotemkhar smiled as he watched him turn a corner. It was time he learned who truly ruled this city. His smile melted by the time he turned to leave. It was time they all learned. He left the compound, envisioning the jungle across the Bangi burning with flames as hot as his anger.

* * *

The sun filtered in rich and pink through the high windows of the room. Efah looked about the ceilings of her new surroundings for the hundredth time. Hours had passed since her audience with the dara. Her hyenas grew restless. She sighed. She was growing restless. What could be going on? Efah leaned back on the large bed, Nesi coming to rest her head in her lap. Usi patrolled the edge of the room as if ready for the chance to run out. Efah ran a hand absently over the comforting fur. This was taking too long. She had more cities to visit although she wasn't so sure she was looking forward to it.

The vision in the market still chilled her veins. Would she be granted a new vision in each city she visited? She wasn't sure she could take it. To watch the violent destruction of people over and over again seemed like a curse. But behind her uncertainty lurked a glimmer of determination. She remembered how clear her vision had been. There was no question in her mind of the validity of it. This city would burn if there wasn't a change. Efah stood, not wanting to sit around and wait any longer. She had a mission to fulfill.

Just as she was about to take a step toward the door, it opened. Efah looked up in surprise as the woman she'd seen at the dara's side earlier came in. She raised her eyebrows slightly at Efah's posture.

"Were you planning on going somewhere?" she asked nonchalantly.

Efah sat back down in this woman's presence. It weighed on the room much like her master.

"I needed to speak to the dara again. I can't stay."

"We understand that your calling is very important. But you must understand that it's very unusual to have some girl speaking of being the voice of death causing a ruckus in the market."

Efah felt unease growing in her chest, but pushed it down. "I can see how that would be . . . strange."

The woman took a small stool from the side of the room, setting it across from her.

"Now," she began sitting down, "may I ask you a few questions?"

Nesi turned her head to look at the woman and Usi

stopped her patrolling to come by Efah's side. Efah felt a
calm come over her.

"Yes."

"Well, first allow me to introduce myself. I am
Afami, Dara Ngoli's most trusted peacekeeper. I often
work as her second in command. You are . . . Efah, am I
right?" Efah nodded. "Very good. Seer Efah, exactly how
long ago was it that you came to realize that you were the
messenger of death?"

"It has been . . . only a week."

Afami raised an eyebrow again. "And was there
some sort of incident that happened to lead you to such an
important revelation?"

Efah hesitated. "I was in the barren lands when I
saw the god of death, not like the Ega paint him, but how
our people see him. He told me that I was to be his messenger."

"What were you doing in the barren lands? There's
nothing out there but old Egan tombs." The peacekeeper
crossed her legs, leaning on them. "But I suppose that is a
fitting place to see the god of death."

"I was grave robbing," Efah answered slowly. She
shifted uncomfortably in her seat.

"What could have possibly led you to such a filthy
position? Surely you had family you could rely on?"

"My family is dead. All of them."

A silence passed. It was obvious that Afami wanted
her to go further, but that was all Efah was going to give.

"I'm sorry that you've been left alone in this world.
But I suppose the god of death chose the right person."

Efah bristled at the lack of belief in her tone.

"Now, when you say you saw death was it in your
mind, like in the market?"

"It wasn't in my mind and neither was the vision in
the market." Efah frowned at her but she blinked slowly,
patiently. "I saw the god of death as clearly as you are sitting across from me. His skin was a sickly brown, his eyes
white and without any color. His cloak was like a vulture's
feathers. The vultures stood at his side like he was one of

them. No, like he was their great lord."

"Did anyone else see him?"

"Well, no."

That eyebrow raised again. "Really?"

"I was high in the cliffs. My group was back on the ground. They couldn't have seen anything so late at night."

"I see."

"And the vision in the market wasn't in my mind. I saw the city burn as I looked around. I saw your people fall away in ash. You may not believe me but it *will* happen unless you and your city turn back to the old ways."

Afami made a small, pensive sound that Efah didn't like. "And what makes you think that we are not observing the 'old ways' as you call them? Have you been to our city before?"

Efah squirmed again. "No, I've never been here. But I'm sure of my vision."

"Such surety is admirable, but who is it that needs to turn from the Egan ways? Do you mean the dara? Her court? The people of the city?"

"All of you," Efah responded forcefully.

"And what do we need to do to come back to the 'old ways'?"

Efah was at a loss for a moment. She didn't know. Her mind hadn't gotten this far in her thinking. Then her lips began to move.

"Abandon the temples to their false and perverted gods," she began with an authority in her voice she didn't know she had. "Cleanse your cities from their manners and customs. Return to true worship and follow the teachings that were handed down to your ancestors. Come back to purity."

Efah slumped at the last sentence, her hyenas drawing in close to support her. After a moment to clear her head, she turned her eyes back to the peacekeeper sitting across from her. The woman stared, confusion playing across her face.

"Are you well, Seer Efah?"

Efah started to speak when the room changed. She

114

found herself in a courtyard watching Afami talking to the dara. No, a younger version of the peacekeeper and her ruler. She watched Afami kneel down, the dara cupping her chin to bring it up.

"Do you love me, Afami?" the dara asked.

"More than my own life," Afami responded, utter devotion in her eyes.

"Would you do anything for me?"

"Of course."

"Then I need you to kill someone for me. A priest. He thinks himself higher than his future ruler. Kill him for me, Afami."

The younger peacekeeper hesitated. "But, my abodara, a priest?"

The future dara jerked her chin roughly. "I thought you loved me."

"I do, my abodara." Tears started to form at the corners of her eyes. "I love you with all my heart and spirit."

"Then kill him."

"Yes, my abodara."

Then scene changed, suddenly inside the innermost rooms of a temple. Efah could tell that this was the room where the main priest communed with the ancestors and gods. She saw the middle-aged man meticulously cleaning the room, taking great care with each artifact and idol. Then, she saw Afami step into the room silently. The priest didn't notice the young woman approaching so consumed was he with his routine. Afami slid a knife from beneath her clothes, a curved blade, gleaming with cruelty. The priest didn't even notice her until she stood directly behind him and then it was too late. Afami clasped a hand around the priest's mouth, the man immediately starting to struggle. Quickly, she slashed the knife across his neck, a clean gash opening his throat. Blood was flung against the altar and smeared the relics as the priest flailed in his death.

Afami stepped back, breathing harder than her exertion required. A wild look stirred in her eyes, a mix between confusion and horror. She looked to the bloody knife in her hand, then to the dying priest. In death, his lifeless eyes stared at her. Afami shook her head, stepping back again, then fled from the room.

The present came to Efah in a rush. She felt a wetness on her chin. She reached up to wipe it away and realized it was blood from her biting her lip. The urgent call of the peacekeeper floated back to her and she looked to the woman in disbelief. Afami's face was an angry frown as she called her name repeatedly.

"You," Efah began and her own voice cut through her malaise. "You have blood on your hands. Innocent blood." The peacekeeper's frown melted away. "You have murdered a servant of the god of the rivers, a good servant, a just man. You murdered him for your dara's whims and arrogance."

Afami's hand went to her side and Efah knew she had a weapon on her somewhere. "How did . . . I don't know . . . You can't possibly know that," she stammered.

Efah stood to her feet. "Such a crime. Who do you think will be the first to burn when the cleansing comes?"

Afami struggled to her feet, nearly tripping over the stool. She stared at Efah, a bit of fear behind her angry expression. She left the room quickly, keeping her eyes on Efah until the door was closed. Efah sat back down on the bed, suddenly exhausted. She stroked Usi and Nesi's heads. Unease settled in her stomach. Somehow, she knew she'd just made her situation infinitely worse.

* * *

Dust flew into Yutuuan's face as he crested another hill. He coughed and spat as his horse plodded down the dry road. Behind him Naret and the royal caravan stretched out, servants, guards, and advisors barely bothered by the land's assault. The landscape around them grew constantly more arid as they headed away from the sea and towards Wiluru's western mountains. He could just see the peaks ahead and Asfara emerging from the rock. The city blended in with the mountain so seamlessly you could only distinguish it by its shadows from afar. He could understand how this was Wiluru's greatest rival in times before. It would have been perfectly defensible against every threat.

"Have you ever been to Asfara?" he asked the nearest guard to him, an older man Umakaal handpicked.

"No, my prince."

"Then this should be interesting. Half the city is underground, carved from the mountain itself by their old king, Teiida." He laughed at the uncertain twist in the guard's lip. "It's not as depressing as you'd think."

"I trust your word, my prince."

Yutuuan laughed again. It would be amusing seeing the faces of his people that hadn't traveled so far as they entered the infamous city. He would enjoy it too. As long as she wasn't here.

It was afternoon by the time they arrived at the path up the mountain. Children herding their families' goats forgot their duties and stood watching as the procession passed. Yutuuan gifted them with a small smile and motioned for one of his soldiers to toss the children a few coins. He chuckled to himself at the delighted squeals as they scrambled for the money. The procession passed under the great arch of Asfara, a sculpted entrance of two warriors holding each other's arm (hands), swords held in the other. People of the city quickly moved aside to allow them passage.

They wound through the wide street until they reached the entrance to the estate of the governor. The main street stopped at a small courtyard that jutted out from solid sandstone. The face of the mountain reflected the colors of the rest of the city, bold stripes of peach, red, and orange. A host of servants emerged from hidden side entrances, coming to attend to their horses. Yutuuan dismounted, thanking the servant who looked puzzled by his gratitude. His frown tempered. He forgot what city he was in. Governor Begarmen was not the most genteel man. Fair, but not one for unnecessary pleasantries. He had to remember that for his talk with the man.

He and his personal guard were swiftly escorted into the estate, the temperature immediately cooling when they passed the threshold. The carved halls were lavishly decorated, more carvings and statues serving as reinforcements and columns for the passageways. Highly polished stones were set into the mosaics on the wall and floor to reflect what little light was in the halls. In high sconces, carved from the hands of support statues, a lazy fire added more illumination. Yutuuan watched the flames as they moved slowly, as if the fire had been robbed of its urgency. It reached up in tones of rich greens but the light it emitted was like pure sunlight. He had always wanted to bring some of Asfara's infamous inakrafire home, but they were protective of their secrets and rightfully so. One didn't stay a bastion of power without keeping some things hidden.

Their escorts brought them along to a pair of heavy doors, a set the prince had been fascinated by the first time he'd visited the city. He smiled at the scene of their great founder fighting off some ancient, other worldly enemies and the men who'd allied with them. The servants tugged on the handles and the doors swung open, a cool breeze wafting out. Inside was a large room, lit by a skylight carved through the lengths of mountain overhead. A pool sat in the middle of the room to catch any rainfall from the skylight. Large fish swirled around it, hiding behind plants growing in it as his party approached. Many potted plants sprung up around the room, giving a calmer feel to the area than the bare stone halls.

From an opposite hall, a man in a long flowing robe with a richly embroidered vest strode toward the room, his attendants struggling to keep up. Yutuuan smiled at his favorite former commander.

"Governor Begarmen," he called approaching him.

Begarmen gave the tight smile the prince remembered from his childhood. The governor had been high commander of Wiluru's navy when Yutuuan was just coming into manhood and was humored at his prince's eagerness to ascend to the role. Begarmen bowed, then embraced him.

"It is good to see you, prince."

"You as well."

Begarmen led him to a pair of seats in the room, motioning for a servant to bring drinks.

"I was surprised by the news of your visit. Is there any particular reason you're here?" He raised his gray eyebrows knowingly.

Yutuuan shifted in his seat. Not this again.

"I do wish I could have come to pay my respects to Luunja, but I come with graver concerns." He shifted again. "She's not here, is she?"

"No, she decided to stay in port until the Iskraana is due to set sail again. Now what concerns are you talking about?"

Yutuuan nodded his head at the servants and Begarmen waved them out of the room.

"My sister has returned from the capital."

The governor stared at him for a moment before taking a sip from his drink.

"Has he sent her back?"

"No, the netkoleh allowed her to visit us. But it's the news she brings with her that prompted my visit."

He paused, not wanting to say the blasphemy. Begarmen raised an eyebrow. Yutuuan leaned in, lowering his voice.

"The netkoleh has decided that we aren't to follow the gods any longer."

Begarmen grunted. "They've been trying to strangle our religion since they came here. They should know by now that our faith won't die so easily."

"No, he has declared that there are no gods. None. She told us that he wants temples destroyed, their images stricken down. He wants us, all of us to be a godless people."

Begarmen didn't respond at first, his face settling into a deep frown. "How did your father take such news?"

"Not well. He wants to appeal to the netkoleh's better senses."

"Ha. Appealing to our master's better senses. That will go well."

Yutuuan paused again. His next statement had played out so smoothly in his head, but now he found the words hesitant to emerge.

"I and my siblings disagree with him. We know this will not go over well with the people and we refuse to turn our backs on the deities. We know this will lead to war."

"You go behind your father's back." The look on the old commander's face dripped with disappointment and shock. "My prince," he began using a tone he reserved for lectures, "you forget your place."

"My place is preserving my people. Do you remember the netkoleh when he came to 'fetch' my sister? She tells me he's even worse now. The mention of him reduces her to tears. What better nature can we appeal to in such a man? My father wants peace, but we only see war as the outcome to this. Even Izriamat agrees. The netkoleh can't be reasoned with.

"And when we refuse to concede to his outrageous demands? Do you think he'll be content to leave us be? Or do you think a man like him will take steps to *convince* us to go along with his blasphemy?"

Begarmen placed his cup on the table with barely a sound. "Then may I ask exactly why you're here?"

"I'm going to the governors to secure their commitment to the war that's coming."

Silence fell on the room. Time could have stopped in this secluded room and they wouldn't have noticed. "You... are working behind your father and your king's back to form a war committee. Prince Yutuuan, this is unsettling to say the least."

Yutuuan couldn't help the small sigh that escaped him. "We had no choice."

"Your father is a reasonable man. You had but to talk to him."

"We have." His voice echoed around the room to his regret. "We have spoken to him," he repeated, softer this time. "He still believes Netkoleh Bakari to have matured since our meeting. I don't think he wants to believe that my sister's words are true. We have to be prepared if... when the peace talks fail." He stopped to see what affect his words had on the governor. "And, we have a hostage."

"Who?"

"Izriamat. The netkoleh has grown fond of her over the years. She knows he wouldn't see her hurt and she refuses to return to Metkara. It would be beneficial to our cause."

Begarmen frowned deeper. "You say our cause as if you have something else in mind than just defending our faith."

He played with his cup on the table. "On my trip here, I had much time to think about the predicament the netkoleh's announcement puts us in. And if war is coming inevitably, then perhaps this is our time to break from the empire. We could become Wiluru again."

The old commander sat back in his chair. He stroked the coarse hairs of his beard for a moment, looking across the room.

"That is a dream even my father and his fathers before could not have imagined."

"So, can I count on you to help defend our people and our faith?"

Yutuuan shrunk when the governor turned his steely gaze his way. Begarmen kept his eyes on him for moments more before speaking.

"And what if Asfara wants to regain her independence?"

"What can we do to persuade you to not break away?"

"You've never made your stance on a marriage alliance clear. Perhaps you'd like to now?"

Yutuuan winced. There was nothing wrong with his eldest daughter Luunja, but . . . His mind wandered to his lovely, shapely Talekh. "I would be honored to have Luunja as my wife and my future queen."

"Then you will have my support in your endeavors as we will be family."

Yutuuan lowered his head to his old commander. "I will be honored to call you father."

Begarmen gifted the prince with one of his rare, small smiles. He called for the servants to return.

"Bring something stronger to drink," he told the tall woman who rushed forward to her lord. "We have a stronger alliance to celebrate."

"Indeed." Yutuuan brought his cup to his lips to hide his wavering smile.

CHAPTER TWELVE

Newa wiped the sweat from his brow and cursed under his breath. The merchants that surrounded him and his apprentice seemed happy enough in this heat but he thought he'd die. He slapped at a bug that landed on his cheek with more vehemence than he intended, more than likely leaving a mark on his face. He was trying to keep his mind on his mission but it was hard. He chided himself. He was not a soft city dweller. He spent his childhood on the streets, digging through garbage to get his next meal and fighting off rats that tried to sample his flesh when he slept. He would endure this with the strength he'd learned since those times.

He slapped at another bug and frowned. His trip so far had been without note. After leaving Metkara, he'd found a merchant caravan and persuaded them to allow them to travel along. He told them they were good with a sword and could offer protection if they were attacked by bandits along the way. A charming act later and he was their newest bodyguard until their destination. It amazed him how well feigned humility could disarm a person so quickly. A smile at the right time. The right compliment at the other. A carefully constructed conversation and they had no idea that they traveled with an assassin priest of Gu'un.

He made friendly conversation with the other travelers as they progressed. Yanu was never much of a talker and Newa took it on himself to entertain their traveling companions. So far, they liked them, but he was glad when he saw the next city come into view. While he wasn't looking forward to spending the night in a little town in the middle of nowhere, it was all for the mission and the order. Newa thanked his traveling companions when they arrived, the merchants asking if they wanted to continue with them. He made a great deal of needing to visit a sick relative and bid them goodbye.

He schooled his face, forcing it into an amicable smile as he walked into town. People stared as they passed by. It was understandable. He was sure this place didn't get many people who actually stopped in town. He greeted a pair of women in front of what had to serve as the local travel house. They in turn smiled back. Newa had to resist a scowl. Vapid creatures. Useless.

"Yanu," he called back to his apprentice. "Get us a room in the travel house while I speak to the town priest. This shouldn't take long."

"Yes, master," the young man said quickly and rushed to his task.

Newa walked through town until he found what served as the temple of Gu'un. This town was fortunate to have a few temples and, while they were very small, much of the pantheon was represented. Newa dropped his overly cheery facade when he moved the curtain aside to step in. He failed to keep the look of confusion from his face when he saw that it was only one room. He looked around, shocked, taking in the weapons on the wall and the sparse furnishings. The weapons were arranged ornamentally, all of them with their blades pointing toward the altar. His attention was caught by the ever-familiar sound of someone sharpening a weapon nearby. He looked about and realized there must be another room.

"Hello," he called loudly. "I'm here to speak to the priest."

The sound of sharpening stopped and then there was an extended silence. After some time, he heard a voice.

"And what brings you to the temple of Gu'un?"

"I'm sent from the capital with a message from the Hand of Gu'un."

Newa heard the sounds of items quickly being put

down and a shuffling coming closer. A door opened behind the altar itself and a small man entered the temple. He was balding early, his hair curling in a ring around the shining patch in the back. His robes were faded, but at least they were clean and Newa could tell from the heavy draping of them that the man was armed, as he should be. He had a slouched walk, eager and unsure at the same time. Newa kept his eyebrow from raising. This was the priest?

"A message from the Hand? I'm honored and I am most honored to see one of my brothers from the main temple." He lowered his head. "How may I further serve Gu'un?"

Newa looked around the temple, at its simplistic design and the door, open to all who may enter or wait outside, listening.

"Do you have another place we can speak? What I'm about to tell you cannot go beyond us. Perhaps the room you were in?"

The man looked excited but kept it in. "Of course. This way."

Newa followed him behind the altar to the second, hidden room. This one was the same size as the temple, but held far more. There was a small kitchen to one side, the wall and ceiling holding several ventilation openings. A large box was to another side, beside it the simple bed palette. He looked around a second time. There was only one bed. Was this man the only priest?

"Your name, brother?"

"Tekhamun."

The single priest brought a stool forward for Newa to sit on. Newa refused with a gesture. "Are you . . . alone here?"

"Yes," he answered, nodding. "It may be a lonely life to some, but I enjoy my solitude. I have more time to focus on my worship without the distraction of people." There was a bit of disdain in the way the man said 'people' that Newa caught. "What was the message that you've traveled so far to give me?"

"I've been sent to the south to tell this to all of our

brothers." He noted the slight deflation in the man at finding out this wasn't a personal message. "The netkoleh has declared that there are no gods."

Tekhamun gasped so hard Newa thought he would fall over.

"He can't do that."

"He can and he has."

"What will become of us?"

Annoyance speared Newa. If this little man would let him continue.

"We are to now call him the emperor and he has decided to allow our priesthood to continue. We will still serve Gu'un even if the emperor doesn't believe in the deities anymore."

Tekhamun stared at him with wide eyes. "And the Hand of Gu'un is fine with this blasphemy?"

Newa drew himself up. "Our leader will guide us to what's best for our brethren. Do you not trust his Gu'un given wisdom?"

"I do." The short priest nodded, thoughtfully. "So, do I continue on as always, even when the other temples are no more?"

"Yes, and if you find the other priests resentful and that they want to come against you, well . . ." Newa made the hand gesture for a righteous death.

"I see. Then I will keep bringing the unredeemed to Gu'un."

"Good. The official word will arrive from Metkara in a few days."

The two made gestures of farewell and Newa left the tiny temple. Something in his gut gnawed at him about this meeting as he walked down the main road to the travel house. It weighed on him for the rest of the day. The man had accepted the news easily but he wasn't sure if he like how easily the acceptance had come. Newa shook his head. He was letting his distaste for his surroundings affect his judgment. Besides, if the man caused any trouble then he would send him on to Gu'un like any other sinner.

* * *

The words of that capital priest stayed with Tekhamun all night. It plagued him as he slept and into the next morning. How could the netkoleh so easily throw off the gods? He was their avatar, the most blessed person to walk to earth. And to hear that his order was going along with it without protest. He wanted to think that the Hand of Gu'un was plotting something, but from the capital priest's words, it didn't seem so. It truly seemed as if he was being instructed to become a heretic.

Tekhamun felt the bile rise in his throat at the thought. Joining the sect of Gu'un was the best event of his life. He was a sixth son, not destined for anything great. Not even destined to inherit anything from his father. He was sure his father didn't even like him. His mother either. He was the smallest, the weakest, and as they often reminded him, not the smartest. He was very sure after some time that his arrival into the family had been an unwelcome surprise. A chance at the priesthood of assassins was his only chance at becoming something. It was a profession that few chose and fewer made it through. Now, they wanted him to cast off all that he held dear and live a farce.

The thoughts swirled through his head as he attended to his tasks for the day. It consumed him so much that he didn't even notice the uneasiness of the people he traded within his town's tiny market. He couldn't even focus on his communion with Gu'un and took to sharpening the temple's many weapons for the rest of the afternoon. How could he be faithful to both Gu'un and his leader under such instructions?

Tekhamun laid down after a light dinner, his mind still a tempest. Somehow, he found sleep and it was deeper than the night before. He found himself dreaming, falling gently until he landed into a pile of bones. Skulls, ribs, and spines fell in on him. Tekhamun struggled in the pile, clawing and dragging himself back to the top. He was surrounded by darkness, the only light from a distant moon shining down on the skeletal pile. He turned in a panic, calling out despite a fear that he shouldn't.

In response to his calls a glimmer pulsed through the darkness. He shielded his eyes against the strong light. A figure cut through the darkness, heavy arms moving it aside like black curtains. Tekhamun gasped, too shocked to bow. Gu'un towered over him. His god's piercing eyes bored into his soul, two points of fire in a face devoid of emotion. Thick, sinewy arms hung down heavily, the near black skin transitioning to bright silver metal. They ended near his feet in two bladed hands that reflected the moonlight.

Tekhamun threw himself down. "Praise unto Gu'un," he cried out, face buried in a pelvis. "May the unjust find their way to righteousness with the help of your blade."

"Priest Tekhamun," rumbled the voice far above his head. "Rise." The little village priest struggled to his feet as his legs shook. "You have been in my service for nearly 20 years."

"Yes, great one."

"And why did you come to me and not one of the other gods?"

Tekhamun licked his lips. "I . . . I wanted power. I wanted authority. I wanted no one to treat me like I was useless ever again."

He chanced a glance up and saw Gu'un lean closer. "You speak the truth when others would lie to lay pleasant words on my ears. I see your worship and service has been true. Despite your reasons for first joining the priesthood, I see in your heart that you've become married to your calling. Few others have done so. You should feel proud." The god paused. "But I also see your spirit troubled."

"Great one," he began, tasting the bile at even mentioning the news. "The netkoleh has thrown you all aside. I can't do that. I have dedicated my life and my soul to the gods and to your mission on earth. How will I continue on?"

Gu'un ran his bladed hands against each other, the sound echoing into the darkness. "It has angered us all and

Koleh himself has declared that the netkoleh should be dealt with and all that side with him."

"I will do whatever is necessary. Even if it means killing the netkoleh myself."

"No," Gu'un said firmly, his voice shaking in Tekhamun's chest. "He will have too many on his side, including those of your brethren that have been corrupted. You will need allies."

Tekhamun forgot all protocol and looked up to his god. "Allies?"

"Go. Go and find those who wish to hold to the true path. Find those who are unsure. Convince those who try to leave the protection of the gods. Convince them by the blade if speaking will not. Through them you will find an army, an army of the faithful and you will crush the netkoleh and his blasphemous followers."

"But, great one, I am no leader."

"You are not now, but you will become one." Gu'un brought one of his blades to Tekhamun's chest. "I will give you everything you need and cleave away the rest." He gasped as his god pushed his blade into his chest.

Tekhamun jerked in bed, halfway falling out of it. He pushed himself back up, starting again at the sound of a rooster crowing. Sweat beaded on his forehead and rolled down his spine. He swallowed hard; his mouth dry. His hand shot to his chest feeling for the wound from Gu'un's blade. His chest was smooth and unmarred. Gu'un spoke to him. Gave him a vision. He swallowed again. And gave him a mission.

An army of the faithful, Gu'un said. He would lead them. Tekhamun worked to breathe normally. How would he accomplish such a thing? He was just a forgotten son in a temple of a forgettable village in the middle of nowhere. A nobody. His mind shifted to Gu'un's blade pushing into his chest like it was paper. His god told him he would have everything he needed. The rest would be cleaved away. Tekhamun felt his doubt begin to leave him. If Gu'un said it would be so then it would be. He would follow his deity's word until his last breath. If he were to the be leader of an army, a righteous army, then he would lead them with a fervent belief in their cause and unwavering determination.

Tekhamun steadied himself and placed his feet on the floor. The ground beneath him felt different. There was a new energy in the earth. It rose up his legs, filling his body with purpose. For the first time in ages, Tekhamun smiled with his whole being. The people would hear Gu'un's message. They would come back to the true path. Or they would be cut down.

He washed off and dressed quickly. He began taking down weapons from the temple walls, choosing the ones that would work best in his hands and could be given to others along his journey. He stepped out into the street, a beaming smile stretching his face.

People stared as he made his way to the center of his little town.

"My people," he shouted. People stopped, startled by the normally quiet priest. "Gu'un, great and mighty, swift in justice and retribution, has given me a vision! Our netkoleh," he spat on the ground, "wishes to take us away from our gods. Our gods who sustain us every day. We cannot let that be. Join me! Join me and we will rise to cut away the nonbelievers like a scythe through wheat. Join me and we will renew this empire and make it acceptable in the eyes of the gods!" He raised his weapons in the sky, waiting for people to come to him.

"Crazy, old fool!" a woman yelled from a stand in the market. The town erupted in laughter.

A priest of Koleh approached him, a small smile on his face. Tekhamun recognized it for what it was immediately, pity.

"Brother, let's get you back to your temple. Perhaps you need rest."

Tekhamun closed his eyes, concentrating on his vision from Gu'un. His path was true and righteous. His message was blessed. Tekhamun opened his eyes, looking about the laughing villagers. If they refused to hear his mandate from the god of justice and wrath, then he would begin the cleaving here.

* * *

Bakari stood still, arms outstretched, as his attendants dressed him in his regalia. The murmur of the crowd outside floated in through the balcony curtains reverberating through him, fueling his excitement. This balcony hadn't been used in a decade, since his father declared the conquest in the south over. He tried to keep from tapping his foot as the servants looked over every detail, but to have an official proclamation of his own, one not connected to any sort of religious significance, thrilled him.

Hetsaf circled him slowly, overlooking the servants work. Bakari smiled wryly. If the look on his brother's face wasn't motivation enough for excellence, the thick reed he held behind his back was an exceptional back up.

"Is the whole city attending?"

"Yes, my emperor," Hetsaf answered, never taking his eyes off the servants. "Save those who are bedridden."

"How many do you think that is? I can't remember the numbers from the last census."

"Probably at least ten thousand."

He grinned widely. "And the ex-priests are ready to work to assure my word carries?"

"Yes, my emperor. They will obey or die."

"Excellent." Bakari turned his attention to Arkoleh who blessed him with a smile.

"You look like a true ruler as always," she said.

As always. Something about her phrasing struck him. The servants brought him his crown, bowing low as he took it. Bakari frowned and placed it slowly on his head. No, this wasn't right. His brother motioned for them to bring the large bronze mirror for him to take a look at himself before he addressed the crowd.

"No," he said at taking in his jewelry. "No, no, this isn't right. Take it all off."

"My . . . emperor?" stammered the head attendant.

"No," he began, sliding off rings and dropping them on the floor. "No, I won't speak of a new day dripping in

131

the trappings of the old."

The attendants rushed forward to undo all of their hard work. Bakari helped them, suddenly disgusted by the rings, cuffs, and the heavy, multilayered necklaces passed down through his family for generations. These items were covered in symbols of the gods. He would not wear them. Never again. He stopped as he took off his crown, a tall, flat cylinder dyed red. A gold sun disk stood out, centered in the front with the wings of Koleh spreading out from each side. By placing this on his head he showed his place as the embodiment of the firebird who lit their sky and led them to the second life. Bakari grabbed onto it, struggling with the emblem. With a final grunt he ripped it free.

"My emperor," Arkoleh called to him.

Bakari considered the emblem in his hand. Relief spread through him as he dropped it to the floor. He placed the crown back on his head, adjusting it as he looked himself over in the mirror. There was a slight mar in the red where he tore off the sun disk but it wasn't all that noticeable. He looked to Hetsaf and Arkoleh.

"Come, let us address the people."

He threw aside the gauzy curtains and stepped out into the sunshine. Throngs filled the street before him. Their cheering was half-hearted, uncertainty hiding in their accolades. Bakari breathed in the air of the scene, this moment in history. It felt thick in his lungs like he was holding the weight of his proclamation. He looked to the former priests, nodding for them to amplify his voice.

"My people," he began, holding his arms stretched wide. His voice carried across the great square, bouncing off the surrounding buildings. "I am sure you are concerned about all of the happenings in the city. You have seen priests ousted from their positions; temples scoured of every sign of the gods. But do not let your hearts be troubled. You are witnesses to the start of a new day, a new era in history.

"I have suffered much and contemplated much. On the death of the Great Royal Son, *my* son, I cried out to the gods for understanding, for some sign that this was part of a greater plan. I beseeched them to return him to me, to us, so that the line of the netkoleh would remain unbroken." He stopped, his voice catching at the thought of his son. "And the gods have shown me that they are not there!"

The crowd broke into cries of shock. Bakari took a moment to let them settle before he continued.

"We have been lied to. For generations, we have struggled and shed our blood for gods that were not there. We have given up our riches hoping for favor and all we have succeeded in doing was making the priests fat and lazy. We have been told to be patient, be faithful only for our prayers to be met with dust and silence.

"We will live under these lies no more." He smiled brightly on his people, taking them in. These were the vessels that would carry out his vision. "Truly, it is a new day. This country, this empire will live under its own will. No longer will we be shackled by the 'will of the gods.' We will each be responsible for our own future. We will carve out our destinies. We will be our own masters." He threw his arms wide. "Rejoice, for you have entered into the age of man!"

"Blasphemy!"

The crowd gasped in near unison. Bakari's eyes shot over in the direction of the shout.

"Who dares?" he roared. "Find who said that." Guards entered the square, pushing their way through the throng. The people protested their rough treatment.

Arkoleh touched him gently on the back of the hand. Bakari took hold of her delicate fingers, giving them a light squeeze. He took a deep breath to disperse his anger. He turned his attention back to the crowd at large.

"Some of you," he began, "may be frightened of a new era. Some of you may have never thought on your own. To face uncertainty can be terrifying. But with our empire's new direction, which I, your emperor will lead you through, we will see glory like we have never seen before."

He stopped waiting for his people's response. There

were cheers but not the boisterous applause he was hoping for. Bakari kept his feeling from his face and turned to enter the palace. Once he was inside, his face dissolved into the darkest frown.

"Find whoever it was that shouted blasphemy. They have given up their life for their outburst." He took off his crown, shoving it to the nearest servant.

Hetsaf came to his side immediately. "My emperor, may I suggest using the Arakgu'un?"

"Yes. Tell their leader that I want them to patrol the streets looking for other dissenters as well. I will not have this new day be ruined because of a few peasants who want to stick to the old ways."

Hetsaf bowed and quickly excused himself. Bakari was brought out of his anger when Arkoleh took his hand. Her sweet smile smothered the fires of his rage. He smiled as she brought his hand up to kiss it.

"My emperor, let me take you to your rooms so that I may ease your mind." She stroked his cheek. "You shouldn't have to endure such disrespect from your people so let me adore you."

"Yes, my Great Royal Wife." He let her lead him through the halls of the palace back to his apartments. She dismissed the servants, pouring him a cup of wine herself.

"My husband," she began, sitting him down on one of the plush couches, "it has come to my thoughts that, perhaps, you will have to help the common people along in your vision."

Bakari took a sip of the cool liquid. "What do you mean?"

"Well, the commoners live simpler lives than us." She knelt behind him and began massaging his shoulders. "Maybe it's beyond their thinking that we could have a life without the gods." Bakari nodded, leaning back to her. "You may have to force them. The temples have been closed but you know they have trinkets and idols in their homes. We should ban them. The less interaction they have with the old faith, the more they will bend to the new."

Bakari turned to look at his first wife. He never thought such brilliance was behind that beautiful face. He pulled her into a passionate kiss that left her breathless.

"You are a woman beyond my expectations. I was more than right to place you as my right hand. We will forbid any religious items in the city and then move onto the rest of the empire."

Arkoleh stroked his cheek. "And . . . may we think about the future of the empire now, my love?"

Bakari caught the look in her eye. "Do you not still mourn?" he asked her tenderly.

"I do." She looked aside, sitting back on her folded legs. "I still expect to see him running around the palace, playing ball with his lesser brothers." He watched in adoration as she straightened herself back up. "But it is more important now than ever that you have an heir. We must continue your line, my emperor."

Bakari studied the sad determination in her eyes and nodded. "Then so be it."

CHAPTER THIRTEEN

Three days.

Efah relaxed on the bed, Usa's head across her stomach. She'd been captive here for three days. Efah assumed that the dara might have a change of mind after hearing about her last exchange with her beloved peacekeeper. She was trying to be patient with the woman, give her the benefit of the doubt, but it seemed nothing was going to change.

She ran her fingers through Usa's fur and watched Nesi chase a butterfly that had flown in through one of the high windows. They'd provided her meals, food better than she'd eaten in her life but had only let her out of the room to use the rest areas. They'd forbidden her familiars to accompany her and she was glad that they were sent by death himself or else this room would have become far more unpleasant.

This was becoming more and more of a prison with each day. She had to leave and spread the word. She was beginning to feel the urgency of her message. There was something coming. It played just at the edge of her being. A darkness was coming, something worse than the occupation and returning to their true calling was the only way they were going to weather it. She had to get out of this room.

Efah raised her head to look at her familiars.

"I think it's time to leave, girls." Usa raised and tilted her head as if in question. Nesi stopped her playful chase and padded her way over.

"We have work to do." The hyenas nuzzled her and Efah got the sense that they were happy at her decision.

Efah patted their heads and went to the doors. There were guards placed on the other side, several more since that peacekeeper fled out three days ago.

"I need to use the rest areas," Efah called, her familiars close behind her.

"Very well," one responded. "Tell your animals to stay back."

"They're already back." Nesi and Usa moved so that they couldn't be seen when the door was opened. Efah stood to the side where she was supposed to. The guards would only open the door a sliver.

After a moment, the door cracked and swung open slowly. "Come on," he said, eyes darting around.

Nesi immediately grabbed the door with her teeth, pulling it nearly off its hinges, and Usa charged down the narrow hall. Efah followed, Nesi closing in behind her. Efah felt sorry as she heard the cries of pain from the guards being run over or thrown aside by Usa. She didn't want to have any unnecessary bloodshed but the dara and her people were in the way of a greater mission. Nesi nudged her in the back as they ran. She was doing the right thing.

The trio turned down hall after hall, many times having to backtrack after finding a dead end. Her hyenas were growing frustrated. So was she. They could hear more guards assembling and she knew it was only a matter of time before they had a real fight on their hands. That was something she was looking to avoid at all costs. She petted her familiars as they had to turn around again. Even if they had to eventually break down a wall, they'd find their way out.

Another hall finally took them to another part of the palace, away from the personal rooms. Servants screamed as they ran out of the way of the huge beasts that suddenly appeared. The hallway opened up on both sides to court-yards. Efah recognized one from the memory she'd seen from the peacekeeper.

"This way," she yelled to her girls and they bounded to the right, frightening more of the palace's inhabitants.

The courtyard was vast with a great number of winding pools and flower beds. Efah stopped, looking around. There were also a number of ways out. The walls were far too high for the hyenas to jump so their exit had to be through one of the doors but which one. Cursing her hesitation, Efah chose a direction. Ahead was a massive archway leading into what looked like a major walkway of the palace. More screams announced their arrival. They ran around another corner, Nesi and Usa knocking a small group of guards down. There was a large room at the end of the hallway and Efah prayed that from there they could find an exit.

The trio burst into the room to find it filled with guards and more of the dara's peacekeepers. The man who'd escorted her to the palace was in front of them, sword already out. Apparently, they'd interrupted him giving out orders. Efah, her familiars, and the guards froze, staring at each other. Efah heard shouts behind her and another group of guards were coming up the hallway they just left.

The peacekeeper in charge eyed her hyenas warily. "Seer Efah," he began in his smooth baritone, "I think you and your beasts need to give up this escape attempt. The dara hasn't decided if it's safe for you to be out on the streets."

Nesi and Usa began to growl, the hairs on their backs standing up. They formed a perfect shield around her, one facing the group in front of her, the other facing behind. Efah could feel the fear of the guards crawl across her skin.

"I think it would be best for you and your warriors to remove yourselves from our path. We are leaving."

He spun his sword casually. "Now, I know your friends are vicious but you can't possibly think that they can protect you from all of us."

Efah closed her eyes for a moment, praying to her patron deity to protect them.

"The god of death is with me," she said, turning her stare on him. "I don't think that's a good sign for you all. If you don't fight us, you will be spared. If you try to hinder us in anyway, I will not be able to protect you from my girls."

The man sighed. "Capture them."

The guards surged forward and Nesi and Usa began their laughing cry. It echoed around the room, stealing the courage of several of the warriors. The others paused, but they still came. Her hyenas closed in tighter around her, moving in concert as they were attacked. From the spaces in between them, Efah watched as people were torn apart swiftly and efficiently. One peacekeeper tried to reach for her in a desperate dash between her familiars and, swifter than she could react, Nesi turned on them, biting them in the shoulder and throwing them away.

Their ball of death pushed its way farther into the room and between the fighting Efah got a glimpse of a long hallway. Doors opened briefly and she could see the way back into the city.

"That way!"

They ran down the hall, Nesi picking her up by the back of her shirt and placing her on her sister's back. Efah grabbed handfuls of Usa's fur just to stay on the swiftly running beast. The remaining unhurt warriors gave chase but were left behind quickly. Nesi took the lead and shouldered the doors open, running into the sunshine. Efah patted Usa on the shoulder.

"Keep going," she encouraged her. "We have to get out of the city."

The trio took to the streets of Ofolabaru to the horror of its citizens. They skidded around corners, barely keeping from knocking over street stalls and bounding over wagons. Horses and other beasts of burden shrieked and threw their riders. The guards at the main gates didn't know what to do as two huge hyenas bounded past them. Efah laid over on Usa as they took to the road out of the city. This was not the way to go about this. She looked to the winding road that led her here. These people were too embedded with the Ega. She needed to start with people she knew. Efah swallowed. As much as she didn't want to return there, it was time to go back to Garemba.

* * *

The treasury was much darker than Ashaki remembered. The torches seemed to burn lower and the accountants moved in hushed tones as if this were their temple and they were its dedicated priests. Ashaki chuckled. Priests to riches. The thought would horrify her uncle. She found an empty office with a good wide table for her to work. One of the accountants came in immediately. They bowed quickly and asked, "What may I do for you Great Dara?"

Ashaki took out her own book of tallies. "I need ink and reed. Then can you bring me the latest numbers for our gold, pearls, silver, and bronze. That will do for now."

She kept her dread in until the man was gone. Ashaki ran her hands over her short, curly hair, letting out a heavy sigh. Ten years. The Batubangi wouldn't be back for ten years. The Ega would be breathing down her neck for gold and that strutting ostrich and his forces had thrown their only source of it away. She sighed again. The other cities would soon clamor for their gold as well. Ashaki prayed that they had enough to cover this year's expenses. Once she saw to that, then she would worry about the next nine years.

Half a score of accountants came into the office, arms laden with books. Ashaki's eyes widened. One couldn't accuse them of not keeping good records. She thanked them as they set the books down and bowed out of the room. The head accountant bowed to her again.

"Is there anything else you need, Great Dara?"

"Uh, no," she responded, looking over the small pile of books in front of her. "I will fetch one of you if I need you."

He bowed and stepped out leaving Ashaki to her task. She opened the first book, seeing it was of the gold tallies. She quickly discovered, to her thanks, that the piles were divided by subject. So, gold first.

It was a bleak tally. Ashaki took her time and went through each book and shipment calculation. She combed through all of their expenditures. She didn't have to do this herself, but her father had made sure he knew all of the ins and outs of the city so she felt it was her duty to do so as well. Ashaki sat back after her double check. She hoped that the tallies of the other precious metals would be more hopeful.

Nsongo was the source of gold for the rest of the south and for the Ega empire. They had been for generations. Their exclusive trade with the batubangi had brought in riches from as far away as Wiluru. It had brought Nsongo to its prominence and rose its dara to Great Dara. But now, what else would they trade? Ashaki tried to run her mind over the possibilities as she turned to the other piles of books. Ofolobaru had its carved works that fetched a great price all over the rest of the Ega's empire. Amakari had the pearls the rest of the south loved, even the batubangi. They were the main producer of salt in the region and sent it off on ships to even more distant lands. Even the Lonik region, while it had no cities of note, produced the finest weapons from the steel in its rich mines.

But what did Nsongo have? Spices you could get anywhere? An overinflated sense of self-worth? Ashaki frowned and sat back as she pushed the last stack of books away. They had much now, but not enough to offset a decade without trade across the river. She ran her hands over her face. She supposed that if times were tough, they could melt down figurines and decorations to turn them into coin and bars. She ran a hand over her necklace that Lafosa had given her at their wedding. They could have people contribute jewelry if times became that hard.

She cursed, banging her hand on the table. On top of all this trouble, she had to consider the tax to the Ega. If only they would rescind it, or even lower it. That would make a difference because she knew that they wouldn't take any substitute for the gold that Nsongo "owed" them. She conducted a quick set of figures in her own book. If the tax could be lessened, they may just survive a little bit better over the next years. But there was only one man that could do that.

Ashaki frowned and rose from the table. She tried to leave the books as neatly as they'd been brought to her and found one of the accountants.

"Thank you for hosting me. I found what I needed."

The accountants bowed as she left and Ashaki traversed the halls of the treasury to the outside. She tried to force a better expression on her face as she began to walk the streets but one wouldn't come. She had to talk to . . . *him*. Ask a favor of him. Beg for mercy for her people. The very idea of doing so, to have to kiss up to some pampered northerner who hadn't even smelled battle made her sick.

He was holed up in the largest compound in the city besides her own. The noble family, cousins of her mother's, had been completely ousted, their servants taken to serve him. He'd barely left them with any of their belongings as they vacated the premises. Ashaki did her best to find decent lodgings for her distant relatives, but it was hard in the uproar after the war. The family ended up splitting up and staying with other relatives across the city.

She frowned as she stopped before the entry arc of the compound. Two Egan guards stood at attention, watching noble women as they walked quickly by. She cleared her throat loudly when they didn't notice her approach.

"I need to speak to Hotemkhar."

"His excellency is inside," one of the guards replied, waving her in like she was a commoner.

Ashaki held her head high as she entered, other Egan guards and servants about. Only the native Nsongans bowed to her as she passed and she was pleased to still have some respect in this place. She flagged down one of them to lead her to the pompous magistrate. He was in his rooms and Ashaki was hesitant to enter when she heard giggling coming from inside. The servant knocked for her, announcing her arrival. A beautiful servant girl, the classic bronze of the Ega and with their bright, heavy makeup, opened the door. "Please, enter, Great Dara."

Ashaki slid past her, not wanting to touch the foreign woman. The room, somehow, reeked of incense even with an open porch at one end of the room. Hotemkhar sat in one of the elaborately carved wooden chairs from Ofolobaru. Anger bristled through her. That chair had probably been in the family of this house for generations. Now it supported his posterior as one of his painted women massaged his shoulders. Another massaged his feet. Ashaki nearly gagged at the sight of his long, naked toes.

Hotemkhar reached down with his fan, tickling the girl at his feet under the chin.

"Tickle me again, A'amat, and I'll have to punish you." The woman giggled and Ashaki thought she would vomit. The magistrate finally turned his attention to her. "Great Dara," he said lazily, "to what do I owe the honor of your presence?"

Ashaki hoped he choked on his sarcasm. "I have been reviewing the treasury in light of our recent . . . trade disruption and I've come to ask something of you." The last words had to be torn from her tongue.

He glanced back at his shoulder massager and they shared a surprised look.

"Oh, you have come to ask something of me."

"Yes." She looked to his servant women. "Perhaps we could discuss matters of governance without your servants?"

Hotemkhar took a moment to melodramatically consider it. He waved the three women away with a flick of his fan. Ashaki sighed as they retreated into a side room. He slid his sandals back on and poured himself a drink.

"Now, what is it that is so important that you came out of your way to speak to me?"

Ashaki swallowed what was left of her pride. "I need to talk to you about the taxes for the next ten years."

Hotemkhar set his drink down sharply. "Ten years?"

"Yes, that is when the batubangi will return. We won't be receiving any more gold until then." *Thanks to you,* she wanted to add. "Is there any way we can perhaps exchange other goods -silver, bronze- instead of the gold."

He gave a little cough of a chuckle. "No, dara Ashaki. You will give us gold. We don't want your other little trinkets."

Ashaki bit her lip. She knew it wouldn't have worked but it was worth a try.

"Then . . . can we perhaps lower the amount some? We still need funds to pay for this year's expenses for the city. If you all could take a smaller amount-."

"Absolutely not," he laughed. "You think you're going to bargain us down? Exactly what leverage do you think you have to ask such a thing?"

"I have no leverage. I'm asking it of you. I know you have the power to do it. Or at least you have the authority to ask it of your capital. If you take the full amount . . . Nsongo may fall." She swallowed the feelings attached to that notion. "You've already caused our supply to be cut off. How do you think we'll be able to fulfill it anyway?"

Hotemkhar sat up in his chair.

"Are you saying that this is my fault? I'd watch my words carefully."

"It is your soldiers' fault," she ground out. "If they hadn't been so reckless the batubangi wouldn't have been offended and I don't blame them! This city is supposed to be a safe place for them and your-, the Egan soldiers made it very clear it wasn't."

The northerner eyed her and she was afraid that she'd gone too far. He shifted, crossing his legs and fanning himself. Ashaki's nose crinkled at the slight scent of his perfume.

"Well, you won't have to worry about your lack of gold from those jungle people much longer."

"What do you mean?"

He hesitated in a manner she didn't like. "We are crossing the river."

Ashaki's mouth hung open and she struggled for words.

"You can't do that."

"What's to stop us?" he snapped at her. "Some little antiquated agreement your ancestors made with them? We will enter their forest and we will find their mines and take them for all their worth." He stopped, suddenly smiling at her. "I may be able to think of a way for the tax to be reduced." He ran a pinky along the rim of his glass. "Contribute troops to the invasion and I'll consider an appropriate sum to reduce the tax."

"No." The answer came immediately.

"Oh ho? I thought this was something your people desperately needed. Are you sure you don't want to reconsider?"

Ashaki chewed on her lip. To violate their pact with the batubangi was going against generations of tradition. *You've already broken tradition and surrendered. What's another one broken?*

"I . . . will consider it," she finally replied. The words felt like poison.

"Don't consider too long. We'll be making plans soon."

He waved her off with his fan and it took everything in her not to leap across the distance and throttle him. She turned on her heel, knocking over one of his gaudy vases on her way out.

* * *

Izriamat threw out another handful of feed to the eager birds gathered in the courtyard. Sea birds had flown in to attempt to bully the doves and imported peacocks. She was proud as the palace fowl held their ground. She wondered if any of these were the same birds she remembered from before her wedding.

She looked to the railing at the edge of the courtyard and the city beyond. Ships were coming in from their long trading voyages and she wondered what trinkets would find their way to the palace. She thought she might have to take a trip down to the marketplace herself. Such a small pleasure was forbidden to her for so long. It would be nice to be amongst people, her people, again.

"Looking to the docks, I see."

Izriamat jumped at her mother's voice. She hid her embarrassment with a hand as the queen laughed at her.

"Good afternoon, mama," she chuckled as her mother took a seat beside her on the bench. "Yes, I was looking at the docks. I see some of the trading ships have returned."

"And you were thinking of picking up a few items yourself."

"That would be nice, but . . ." she trailed off, looking over the city again.

"But what?" her mother asked and took a handful of the feed to throw.

"But . . . I don't know. I haven't gone out with the people in so long."

Her mother patted her hand. "Then perhaps you should start again. There is no time like the present."

She laughed as her mother took the bag of feed, artfully throwing the rest out in a single arc of her arm.

"There. The birds are fed." She laughed again at the feeding frenzy that was ignited. She took her mother's hand as they went to arrange for their excursion into the city. Servants and guards were eager to accompany the queen and their beloved princess to the market. Izriamat nodded at the scores of servants that greeted them on the way out. It felt odd to be beloved after so long in a place where her presence was regarded with either barely masked disdain or fear. Her spirits instantly lifted.

The sun hid behind a patch of clouds as they exited the palace. Two servants trailed them, holding aloft a wide canopy for when the sun did return in all its might. The market nearly came to a stop when their small procession arrived. Izriamat smiled at being attacked at the myriad of smells and sights that she'd held so dear in her memories. Shoppers bowed deeply in respect as the queen and princess approached. Some made the sign of Yutuu, lips moving in quick prayers. Izriamat tried to greet as many as possible, a little flustered by the crowd. Her mother took it in stride as always, nodding to her subjects.

"Shall we look at jewelry, my daughter?" The queen gestured to a series of stalls ahead.

Izriamat could just make out the shine of green gems between the milling shoppers. Her eyes lit up. Green was her favorite color.

"Yes, let's," she replied with a smile.

They moved their way through the crowd to the stall. The merchant stood, mouth agape, when he realized who his next customers were. His wife, a stout woman with white ribbons wrapping her braids, maneuvered past him.

"Blessings unto our beloved queen and princess," she said, her multiple sets of dangling earrings clinking against each other. "How can we help you?"

Izriamat leaned over the table, admiring all of the items.

"You have beautiful pieces." She held in a giggle as the woman preened. She looked over the pieces in earnest, her eyes settling on a golden necklace with a large green sea glass pendant. Its shifting colors pulled her in. It captured every hue of her favorite color. She gave a little smile. All of her jewelry had been long discarded after her arrival in Metkara. She suddenly realized she had nothing from here. Izriamat chose several pieces, putting on the first necklace that had caught her attention.

She told one of their attendants to pay the merchants and turned to her mother.

"What do you think?" she asked, holding her hair to the side.

Her mother smiled, looping an arm in hers as they moved to the next stand.

"I think that it's good to see a true smile on your face."

Izriamat examined a pair of silver, foreign made earrings from the next merchants. "I suppose," she said absently.

"No, truly, my daughter. There is still such a sadness about you, but I'm glad to see it beginning to fall from you."

She thanked the merchant as she had these pur-
chased as well.

"I don't think I will ever be free of the stain of Metkara," she said lowering her voice. "Or . . . him."

There was a pause and her mother gave her arm a
loving squeeze.

"Have you been to the temple of Yutuu since you
came back to us?"

"No." She could barely speak the word. The idea of
going anywhere near her former temple was a weight on
her.

"Perhaps you should. I know your uncle would be
overjoyed to see you again."

Izriamat tried to ignore her mother's suggestion,
trying to focus on their shopping excursion. She ran her
hand over a series of bracelets.

"I don't know if I can, mother," she finally said quietly. She forced a smile on her face as the merchant greeted her, clearly surprised when she looked up from her
crafting.

"Of course, you can. I think you need to." Izriamat
didn't have to look at her mother to feel her insistent gaze.
"Let Yutuu speak to you."

"I don't think he would." She moved their path to
the middle of the walkway. "I am . . . a filthy creature
now."

Her mother stopped, grabbing her shoulders and
turning her to her. "Don't ever say that." She pulled her
into a fierce hug. "Never say that. You can't help what
happened to you."

Izriamat wrapped her arms around her mother, not
feeling the hug in her soul. She looked down the coast, in
the direction of the great temple of Yutuu. She didn't belong there. She didn't deserve to congregate with the other
priests and priestesses. She wasn't worthy to commune
with him anymore. Her mind ran back to the joy of serving
the temple under her uncle's tutelage. She'd run through
its halls since she was a girl and it felt as much her home

as the palace. What she would give to have never been severed from her service. She felt her longing weigh on her. What she would give to have never been sullied by that man, to have never produced fruit from his wicked seed. Then she felt something tug at her soul.

"Izriamat?"

Izriamat blinked heavily at her mother, lost. "Mother, I . . ." She looked back in the direction of her old temple. Her heart skipped a beat at the feeling of a moment ago. She looked around at their attendants, their guards, and their subjects, all staring at her, concerned. "I . . . I'm fine. I felt a little dizzy for a moment but I'm fine."

Her mother searched her face as only a mother could. "Are you sure? We can return to the palace."

"No, no," she began with a reassuring smile. "Let's continue shopping." She led her mother to the next stall keeping Yutuu's temple out of her thoughts.

CHAPTER FOURTEEN

Erenemo looked over the low table as his kitchen servants brought in food. The fattest fowl and calf had been prepared just for this special dinner. It was usually his wife's job to oversee such but today he needed her away so he could entertain. Members of the council were beginning to assemble in his compound's courtyard. He needed to give them a meal that they would remember, a meal that would speak to their souls and hopefully make their minds more pliable.

The last of the help exited, save one, his most trusted acolyte from the temple.

"Is that everything, Saidata?"

The lithe young man looked over the table again, his lips moving in tally. "Yes, master."

Erenemo sighed, thankful. "Then would you bring the council in please."

Saidata bowed to him with a smile and left the room. Erenemo shook his head. That young man was wasted in the priesthood. With a frame like that he should have become a spearman. His son could have easily whipped him into shape.

Erenemo brushed his thoughts aside as the four council members began to file into the room after his acolyte.

"Great elders of Nsongo," he greeted them merrily. "Welcome to my home."

"This is most irregular, Erenemo," the oldest woman said, but readily took a seat on the plushest looking cushion.

"What have you brought us here for?" another elder

with a bold geometric tattoo on his forehead asked.

Erenemo sat down with them, waving his hand dismissively at people he'd known most of his life.

"To the point as always, Iysha, Embalu," he chuckled to the two who'd spoken. He nodded to the last two elders, a man with three gold cuffs at the height of each ear and a woman who held her cup up to be filled. "Abemisi. Oshala."

Abemisi nodded in response. "It is good to break bread with you again." Oshala grunted.

"Please eat," Erenemo said to the council. "There's plenty so don't be shy." Embalu took no time commencing, his tattoo furrowing with his brow as he tasted the meats.

Oshala motioned to her cup, the wiry muscles in her thin arms still telling of her time in the military.

"You still haven't told us why we're here," she said as Saidata filled her wine again.

Erenemo filled his own plate with food. "I wanted to speak with you about the state of Nsongo which our current dara has brought us to." There were sounds of disapproval and shaking of heads. "The postponement of trade with the batubangi could cripple us. I for one do not want to see this city fall low and become nothing more than the basest whore of the northerners. We've already rolled over for them enough."

Iysha grunted as she adjusted her legs. "We've already become part of their blasted empire. What can we do about it now?" She cast him a pointed look as she piled on food.

"What Nsongo needs, my friends, is leadership. Real leadership like my brother, may he be honored among the ancestors, provided us." The council members chewed thoughtfully at him. "What we need is a new dara."

Abemisi snorted while Oshala gave a short laugh. Abemisi took a sip from his cup before speaking.

"Erenemo, we've chosen the dara-."

"No matter how some of us may feel about it now," Iysha muttered around a chicken leg.

"And there is nothing to be done about it. She is the

Great Dara. We are under the heel of the Ega bastards. That is that."

Erenemo fought down his scowl. These people had always been stubborn. So stubborn he would have been counted among them if Embalu wasn't holding on, tooth and nail, to this life. He took a small breath, remembering that he should be thankful that he didn't have to deal with the other three council members.

"There is a precedent," he said at last.

The elders looked to him, all of them suspicious. He motioned for Saidata to hand him a scroll. It took him so long to find this, days of pouring through the history of the daras of Nsongo. He felt a jolt of satisfaction as the scroll was placed in his palm. Saidata moved aside his plate so he could unfurl the ancient paper.

"The 27th dara, Obakisue, was removed from his position after being deemed unfit. He was a fearsome warrior but took an ax to the head. He survived but became erratic and unfocused." He tapped the scroll. "Surely we can all agree that Ashaki is unfit for office based on her shameful surrender and leadership."

The elders hesitated, looking around the table to each other. Oshala rubbed the back of her neck. Iysha settled her needling look on him again.

"That dara was unfit in the head," she said, still absentmindedly chewing. "This is not the case, Erenemo."

Embalu nodded, tattoo furrowing again as he finished off the last of his wine. "There is a difference between a bad dara and an unfit one."

"Look, Erenemo," Oshala said, wiping up the last of a bit of sauce with a piece of bread. "She shamed us all when she surrendered. Cowardly snot. My choice to elevate her to dara has stayed with me and I question if I did the right thing often. I wonder if there had been a better choice that we just didn't see. Or maybe they hadn't shown their merit yet." She paused, popping the bread into her mouth. "But as Abemisi said, what's done is done."

"A dara is only removed by death," Iysha chimed in. "She is still capable although not to our liking. There's nothing we can do."

Erenemo couldn't help the growl in his throat. "So, you're just going to sit and let her turn Nsongo, the Golden City, into a hovel? But I suppose it's easy when you only have a few years left on this earth."

The elders stopped, staring. Oshala put down her cup dangerously. Embalu pushed away his plate.

"The dinner was delicious, Erenemo. I think it's time for us to go." The elders at once stood up to go.

Erenemo cursed himself as they left the room. Saidata showed them out as he fumed. He wanted to blame them and their stubbornness, but he knew he'd been too eager. He'd been too hopeful. He should have known that his precedent was only slightly appropriate. It would take more than that to convince those old fools.

Saidata came back into the room timidly. "Master, is there anything I can do for you?" he asked coming closer.

Erenemo didn't answer at first, still caught up in his anger. Saidata knelt beside him.

"I will find a way." His acolyte boldly began to reach under his robes and Erenemo leaned back and let him. He needed a release. He grunted as Saidata leaned over, taking him in his mouth. Iysha had said that a dara could only be released by death. He felt a dark resolution settle in him. If that was the only way then his path was clear. He placed a hand on the back of Saidata's head, forcing him closer. Death was the answer.

* * *

Something wasn't right in the palace. Bakari couldn't put his finger on it. He leaned on the table across his papers and looked at the two men being held up by his guards. They'd been beaten and tortured by the Arakgu'un then dragged all the way to the palace before him. He took in their swollen, bleeding lips and bruised faces slowly, drinking in every detail. He let his gaze settle on the man to the left, a middle-aged merchant. This was the miscreant who'd yelled during his proclamation and the man on the right was his brother who'd tried to defend him when guards arrived at his house.

Bakari rested his chin in his hand and raised an eyebrow.

"Was it worth it?" he asked them. The merchant looked daggers back at him. His brother merely looked confused. Bakari looked to one of the guards. "Are their jaws broken?"

"No, my emperor."

He looked back to the two men. "Then speak. I didn't ask a question to be answered with silence." Hetsaf entered the room a set of scrolls tucked under an arm. Bakari's face lightened. "Brother, you've come just in time. I'm about to decide the fates of the dissenters."

The merchant spat at him, the emission landing with a loud wet plop on the floor.

"We will never go along with your insanity. Koleh be praised."

Bakari's frowned again. "Unrepentant to the end."

Hetsaf stepped forward. "Shall I, my emperor?"

"By all means."

His brother stepped to one of the guards who sported a large club for a weapon. Taking it off the man's belt, Hetsaf tested the weight. The convicted men stared warily at the chancellor of the empire. Hetsaf came behind the brother, who blubbered in terror, and gave one precise swing with the club. The wet crack echoed through the room and the man dropped, body twitching.

The dissenter took in his brother's body and stared at his emperor. "Koleh be -." His sentence was ended by Hetsaf. The chancellor handed the club back to the guard and came to Bakari's side, taking care not to step into the blood pooling on the floor.

Bakari chuckled as servants swooped in to begin cleaning up the mess. His guards quickly took the bodies away.

"What do you have for me?" he asked his brother as he set the scrolls on the table.

"I've made a list of the best days to begin travel for the Pilgrimage."

Bakari rubbed his chin. He'd forgotten all about it. "Already?"

"Yes, my emperor." Hetsaf began going through possible routes to take since this would be the first year they headed through the south. Bakari nodded as he spoke, not truly taking in the information. He was missing something.

"My emperor?" Hetsaf called. "You seem distracted."

Bakari looked out the window, thinking of the trip north. "Have we received word from Izriamat?"

"Um, no, my emperor."

"She should be on her way back now. Odd." He thought of her lithe body and full breasts. Surely, she missed their son by now. She had to be racing back to see him again. But then again, she hadn't seen her family since before their marriage. He could allow her more time. "If she hasn't already started the journey back, we'll retrieve her when we go to Wiluru."

"Of course, my emperor." Hetsaf paused studying him. "In our trip south, we will have to make trips to each of the principal cities. Since each of their economies are different, separate tallies of their goods will have to be made. We'll also have a better idea of what taxes to levy on them. We took a heavy amount of goods primarily from Nsongo at the end of the war. We may be able to garner even more from the other daras."

"Yes, Hetsaf," he said distractedly. His mind had been on Izriamat again. "Your expertise in these matters is invaluable. Who cares for my son now?"

Hetsaf looked confused for a moment. "I believe that one of your lesser wives has taken him in."

"Very good." Bakari rose, too unfocused to think of bureaucracy. He began heading toward the door. "I'll leave preparations for the trip to you."

"But you need to choose a date and route," Hetsaf called after him.

"The soonest one that leaves for the north."

He took to the halls of the palace, suddenly wanting nothing more than to see his only proper son. His attendants fell in behind him quickly, surprised by the sudden change in schedule. Bakari barely acknowledged the servants and courtiers that scrambled to get out of his way. The guards to the wing of that his lesser were housed in bowed dutifully and stepped aside. There was a wave of surprise as he strode through the wing.

The head servant of these quarters rushed up to him, bobbing up and down in several bows.

"My emperor," the portly man groveled. "We are honored to have you here. I am sure that several of your wives would be more than happy to have a visit from you today."

Bakari stopped at a junction of halls. "Who is taking care of my son?"

"That would be Neytiri, my emperor. She is right this way." The man bowed to him again and shuffled down a side hall.

Bakari looked about as children, his children ran about the halls. Their mothers pulled them back as he approached. He smiled at them trying to not instill a fear of him in them. There were several boys here and they made him think of Koletun again. Despite having different mothers, he could still see the resemblance in them. It was heartbreaking. He wondered if they mourned their brother at all.

The chief servant led him out to a small courtyard with a rain collection pool in the middle. A woman sat on one of the benches, humming a child's song. Bakari walked past the servant, coming beside his wife. He was surprised as he realized she nursed his son and an older baby that must have been her child. She looked up to him in shock then quickly dropped her head.

Bakari reached down, lifting her chin up. He took in her high cheekbones and thick lips. This one he remembered. She'd come from a family toward the coast and had been most eager to please him. He was glad to see he'd provided her with a child. "Neytiri," he said rolling her name around on his tongue.

"Yes, my . . . emperor." She gave him a small smile and he found himself returning it.

"I'm glad to see you've taken in my son while his mother is gone."

"I didn't feel that it was something that should be left to a servant." She winced as her son latched on harder. Neytiri smiled apologetically. "I'm sorry. He's starting to teethe."

Bakari smiled and reached down to let the baby grab his finger. "He's a big boy," he chuckled as the baby looked at him.

"The boys in my family usually are." She shifted the weight of the children. "Your son looks like he'll be tall like you, my emperor. He's such a good child. He's barely fussy and he nurses so well. It's been a joy to look after him."

Bakari took in the scene. She held the children expertly, looking at his son with a love that he'd never seen on Izriamat's face. However, his northern wife had always been cool. Being a doting mother may not be in her nature. He will have to spend time around more loving women as he grew older.

"Neytiri," he called, and she looked up to him with that adoring smile again. "Would you take care of him until his mother's return?"

"I would love to, my emperor."

"And would you take time to check up on him after her return? The Second Wife is not as affectionate as you. I want my son to have that."

She looked up; eyes wide. "I would be honored. I will do what I can to help her be more motherly. I haven't been a mother for long, but I will do what I can."

Bakari stroked her cheek. This one was a gem. "I'll see that you're rewarded for your care. I'll have new rooms provided for you."

She leaned into his hand. "I would do *anything* for you, my emperor." His son stopped nursing and began to coo quietly. "Would you like to hold him?"

Bakari suddenly realized he'd never held him before. "Yes . . . yes, I would."

Neytiri handed him off into Bakari's waiting arms. It had been so long since he'd held one of his children, since he held a son. He felt something lighten in his heart as he and the baby regarded each other.

"Please, my emperor, have a seat." Neytiri adjusted her growing boy again. "I'm sure he'll fall asleep soon."

He sat down beside her on the bench, taking in the peace of this courtyard. It seemed like a different world. He stroked his son's cheek with a finger and the little one yawned deeply.

"I'll be back to visit him often."

To his surprise, Neytiri placed a hand on his thigh. "I'd like that, my emperor."

*　*　*

Falee's Bay was cool when Yutuuan arrived with a refreshing breeze coming off the waters. The prince looked out to the horizon while his party rode down the road into the city. A storm was coming later, possibly a bad one. They would probably have to stay the night. He smiled. Falee's Bay wasn't the worst place by far to be stranded for an evening.

People moved aside quickly for the royal procession, bowing until they passed. The roads of the city were paved in expert designs of dark brown stones. Buildings rose up sharply once they were inside the city limits, bright white stucco like Wiluru. Prayer flags of every color waved from windows high and low. The sounds of life competed with the roar of the sea. Yutuuan smiled as he took it all in. He remembered having to take to port here over the years and he always had a wonderful time.

Guards from the governor found them mid-city, quickly escorting them to rest of the way. The governor's palace sat to the side of the city, rising up along the hill that marked the east side of Falee's Bay. He could already see the vast courtyards and fountains. A lovely place to stay and a welcome change from camping.

Yutuuan thanked the guards as they entered the palace's grounds, giving a special smile to one of the female guards who'd escorted them. To his amusement, she looked shocked and turned her attention aside, flustered. Their horses were taken and he was brought inside and immediately offered something to drink. The prince took it, surprised at the attentiveness of the servants. This was a wonderful example of great hospitality.

A couple swept into the waiting room, arm in arm, looking more than pleased to see him. Yutuuan smiled warmly. He hadn't seen the governor and governess in years, honestly, he barely remembered them, but they were distant family. A certain façade had to be kept up.

"Governor Iken. Governess Usadi. It is good to see you both again."

They both bowed in unison. "It's been too long, Prince Yutuuan," Iken said with a grin that showed all of his teeth.

"You've gotten even taller and more handsome," Usadi gushed over him. "Tell me, how is my cousin Izrata?"

Yutuuan chuckled. The governess was one of a handful of people left who could call his mother by name.

"Mother is well. By father's side as always."

"And how is the king?"

"My dear," Iken butted in, "I'm sure the prince would like to come in and rest himself from his journey. We can speak at lunch."

Usadi bowed to him. "I'm so sorry, Prince Yutuuan. I get so overjoyed when we have guests." She clapped her hands and servants appeared from the halls. "Take our dear prince to our finest guest rooms. See that his every need is met."

Yutuuan nodded to the happy couple as the servants came up to him. "I greatly look forward to lunch. I have important business to discuss with you all." The governing couple looked concerned for a moment but bowed to him again.

The rooms the servants brought him to were excellent, with a series of glass windows that looked over the sea. His belongings had already been placed inside and he changed from his traveling clothes. He sighed, taking a moment to sit on the large bed. The governor and governess seemed like amicable enough people. They were at least very welcoming. Yet, if he was honest with himself, he wasn't sure how his offer was going to be received. Governess Usadi and his mother had been very close when they were younger despite being second cousins. He hoped to use that familiarity as a way to persuade them to add Falee's Bay to his coalition. He hoped they were pragmatic enough to see the opportunity they had to regain their freedom.

Lunch came and Yutuuan was shown to a small veranda that lead out to an elevated courtyard. Diners had a view over the entire city from here. He put on a smile as Iken and Usadi took their seats. He sat just as servants began to fill the table with food. Usadi looked to him with her beaming smile.

"I hope you were able to rest yourself, Prince Yutuuan."

"I was. The room is beautiful. It makes me think of home."

"Wonderful! And speaking of home, we've heard rumors that your sister has returned."

Yutuuan nodded, taking a sip of the water he'd just been poured. That was a perfect segue.

"Yes, yes she has. The netkoleh allowed her to visit us."

"How generous of him," Iken said flatly.

"That actually brings me to why I came to speak with you." They looked up from their meals. "And it's a very sensitive topic," he added, glancing at the servants. Iken nodded and waved them all off.

"My goodness," Usadi said, clasping her bejeweled hands together, "what it is?"

"The netkoleh has declared that the empire is not to worship the gods anymore."

Iken choked on his drink and Usadi stared at him, mouth agape. Iken coughed deeply, hitting his chest.

"That can't be. You can't be serious."

"This comes from my sister's own lips. Eventually he will send people here or come here himself to have all the temples destroyed. All of the temples, even ours." He paused as Usadi took a drink of her wine to settle herself and Iken wiped his mouth.

The governor shook his head. "Surely your father won't stand for this?"

"He . . . he wants to reason with him. I don't think mother has made up her mind. They actually hadn't made an official stance before I left." He paused again. It wasn't any easier to say this time. "My siblings and I talked it over and we see that this will only lead to war. We all know that we won't abandon our faith. We haven't since the Ega came and we won't now."

The governing couple looked at each other in disbelief.

"I just can't believe the netkoleh would do something so reckless," Usadi breathed.

Yutuuan frowned. "The netkoleh was a selfish, uncaring man when I met him and my sister tells me that he's only gotten worse as the years have gone by." He breathed out, cooling his anger. "He won't listen to reason as my father still seems to think. We will only survive this by war and for war we will need forces. That's the reason for my traveling. If I can have the word of the seven major cities in Wiluru that they will commit forces if this comes to war, then I can show my father that we can succeed. We may even be able to win back our independence."

Usadi looked to her husband, an expression that must have held volumes that only he understood. Iken took a breath.

"This is . . . much to take in, Prince Yutuuan." He sipped from his cup, coughing again. "Has the king spoken anything of war?"

"No, but we have to be prepared. But are you prepared to bow to the outrageous demands of the Ega again?

Haven't we given them enough?" Yutuuan looked across the table but the governor and governess didn't seem completely convinced. "And my sister has no intention of returning to Metkara. I have no intention of letting her. This is a plan she believes in and hasn't she sacrificed more than the rest of us?"

Iken and Usadi looked between each other again. Usadi took a breath.

"If your sister believes that the netkoleh's action will bring war then that is something we will have to consider." She turned. "My husband?"

Iken took a moment, steepling his fingers before him. "Prince Yutuuan, you must understand that the might of Falee's Bay lies in its navy. We don't have many ground forces to speak of."

"I understand. However, we'll need every warrior if we're going to fight off the empire. Asfara has already committed to this so you are not alone in your decision."

They shared a look again. Iken tapped his fingers against his lips. "Then if it comes to war, Falee's Bay will be with you."

Yutuuan smiled brightly. "Thank you for your support. I and my siblings will not forget this." He raised his glass and the couple slowly followed suit. "Let us toast our alliance and the future freedom of Wiluru." The prince drank deeply. At least this meeting didn't cost him anything.

CHAPTER FIFTEEN

Walking through the forests leading to Garemba felt completely different. All of the usual fear and trepidation Efah had about traveling here seemed like far away memories. Garemba felt like a place full of possibilities to her now. Usa and Nesi walked calmly on either side, taking in the surroundings and moving stray branches out of her way. Above, a handful of vultures flew in and out of the thick branches and she knew *he* was with her.

Efah stopped as they rounded the bend in the path and saw the great decaying entryway to Garemba. She took in the weathered stone of the statues with the vines permeating their cracks. She felt the sensation in her spirit. Garemba was a dead city. She was supposed to be here. Efah took a breath, the realization weighing on her. This is where she should have started her mission. The people of the south would be revived.

She walked up to the ancient gates and Ayodele's guards gathered in her way, weapons ready and eyes fixed on her companions. The lead one, a burly man with a thick beard she'd seen before, took a step forward. His eyes darted to her for a moment.

"Haven't I seen you before?"

"Yes, but that life is over. I wish to enter Garemba." She put a calming hand on Usa whose fur was starting to rise.

"Okay," he started, unsure. "But you have to pay the toll . . . and your animals have to stay outside."

She looked over the men and could feel their fear. She actually didn't want this to come to a fight. A sensation touched her and she knew her god wasn't eager to take souls.

"I'm not paying the toll and Usa and Nesi will be coming into the city. I need to speak with Ayodele. Immediately."

The guards exchanged glances. The lead guard cleared his throat. "I don't think-."

He was interrupted when Nesi jumped forward, growling loudly. At the growl a small flock of vultures landed in the surrounding trees and on the statues behind the guards. Efah stepped forward, Usa protecting her other side.

"Move," she commanded the lead guard. He scrambled out of her way and the others followed suit. Efah smiled and nodded to them as they passed, pleased that they had no bravery to speak of. Sometimes fear kept you safer.

The inside of Garemba was just as inspiring and depressing as when she fled from it. People began shouting and screaming as she walked down the main way. She was sure she was a sight with her two large companions. They lost all of their aggressiveness once inside. If only people knew how loving and playful these two actually were. They picked their way carefully to one of the last reliable staircases. Ayodele would be in his usual spot on the second floor.

She didn't stop once she reached the long hallway leading out to his favorite veranda. The minions he had lounging outside called out in alarm when they approached. Efah ignored them, letting her hyenas make a path for her. She pushed open the carved doors and stepped out into the sunshine. Ayodele's people on the veranda were slow to catch on to what was happening. They'd clearly heard the shouts from inside but hadn't gotten the chance to prepare for danger. They froze at the sight of the giant hyenas calmly strolling towards them.

Ayodele lounged on his great couch again, caught in the midst of counting gold and other trinkets collected from the desperate people here. Efah looked around. Iyola was nowhere to be seen. She was glad. She didn't feel like dealing with any unnecessary aggression today. Efah fixed her eyes on Ayodele, looking past the underlings that had placed themselves in the way.

The want-to-be king's surprise turned to outrage.

"Who the hell are you?" he grounded out.

"Ayodele," she started, once again surprised by her own voice. "I know you don't remember me because you have so many who come through your city, but I am Efah Aboujale. I used to run with Kenta's band."

"What in the name of the abyss do you think you're doing? Bringing these . . . beasts into my city?" He quickly shut up the container of gold, shoving it to one of his minions to take away.

"I'm not here to take anything away from you. I've come to respectfully ask for a safe haven here in Garemba." She worried her lip, unsure of what to tell him. "I've run afoul of the dara of Ofosolo and need to find a better place to stay."

"And what of your animals?" Efah didn't miss him subtly picking up a sword. "Where did they come from?"

"They came from my god, Usharabi." The collection of gasps was satisfying.

For the first time since she'd come here, Ayodele looked worried.

"You can't say his name," he breathed, sounding like some child afraid of the dark.

Efah stood up straight, Usa nuzzling up to her. "He has chosen me to be his voice on this side. The people of the south will return to the old ways or they will feel the fires of rebirth along with the Ega."

Silence played across the expanse. Even the animals that usually chattered in the canopy went quiet. Ayodele's hand tightened on the handle of the sword. He frowned deeply.

"And how do we know that all this is true? You could have just found these freak monsters and called yourself some god's speaker." He snorted. "Nobody tells me what I'm going to do in my city. Get the fuck out of here." With his free hand, he snapped loudly, jarring his warriors back to attention.

"I wouldn't do this," she said lowly as the men started to advance. She looked up and saw the vultures starting to convene on the area. Nesi and Usa sat down, unconcerned. Efah pointed up to the birds in the over-hanging branches and out to the ones landing on the bro-ken railing of the veranda. "My girls have decided to let their brethren handle this and I don't think you want to go through that."

The minions lost their courage at the sight of the scores of vultures surrounding them. The birds stared pointedly at each of them and Efah felt as if the god of death himself was looking through their eyes. Perhaps he was because the minions began to step back, not wanting any trouble. Even Ayodele looked about his face slack with fear.

Efah turned her full attention to him. "So, can I stay?"

The faux king's mouth moved wordlessly. "Yes," he finally managed.

"Thank you. I will find my own room." Efah turned to leave and breathed a sigh of relief. She'd never been so glad to be protected before.

She instinctively started for the lower floor but paused and decided to explore the better cared for parts of the third floor where Ayodele and his people stayed. She and her hyenas turned down a side hall, terrifying the kept women and other underlings of Ayodele. She explored to their shrieks and screams until she finally came on a room big enough to hold all three of them comfortably. She had barely settled in when the door was thrown open.

Efah turned, shocked, as Iyola marched into the room, sword at the ready. The rage on her face was barely tempered by the sight of the large beasts that quickly turned on her. Efah put her hands on them as they started growling viciously. Iyola's eyes darted between them, her posture ready to fight.

"Who do you think you are?" she said between grit-ted teeth. She looked over Efah's face and scowled harder.

"I remember you. You're just some graverobber. You have some balls to think you can demand anything of Lord Ayodele."

Efah studied her sword. She had faith in her girls but she didn't want them to get hurt.

"Iyola," she began as a warning, "Usa and Nesi aren't above eating someone. They were sent to me by the god of death and they want nothing more than to ensure my protection."

Iyola considered the beasts again. "Even if they were sent to you, they're just beasts, flesh and blood, and they can still get hurt."

Laughter started to mingle with the hyenas' growls. They moved forward painfully slowly, as if they were stalking her even though she could see them. Iyola's sword started to lower and she took a step back. Nesi and Usa pressed in closer and Iyola looked past them to Efah.

"Call them off."

"Leave," Efah responded. Iyola took another step back as the hyenas moved close enough to strike. She stepped back again and fled the room. Efah released a breath. Nesi and Usa stayed in place for a few more moments then padded back to her as if nothing had happened. She smiled as they licked the sides of her face and she fought them off. Without them, she was defenseless. She thought of the last look Iyola gave her before she left the room. Iyola realized it too and that was a dangerous prospect.

* * *

Newa weaved through the thick traffic of Oxur. He was a fish swimming upstream against the throngs from three different trade routes all on their way to the capital. Yanu struggled to keep up and he had to stop more than once to find the young man in the throngs. He sidestepped a pair of oxen and their wagon, cursing the driver as his feet were nearly run over. He tried to make his way to the side of the wide street but traffic kept him firmly in the middle. He cursed this city, its people, and all the travelers. He'd never make it to the temple of Gu'un at this rate.

"Master," Yanu called. "What do you think the temple in this city will be like?"

"Hopefully receptive," he yelled back. "Now, keep up."

As they walked, the shadow of Koleh's temple passed over them. He looked up at the tall columns marking the entrance, Koleh's face backed by the sun carved into the top of each one. A long walkway cutting through a lush courtyard led to the main structure. He frowned. He never liked the rampant opulence of Koleh's priests. That's probably why he'd done so well in the Arakgu'un. A priest should be fully dedicated to his god, not looking to fatten his pockets on this side. A priest was sure to live richly in the second life. Riches here was just greed.

They walked for what seemed like hours. He wiped the sweat from his brow as they made it to an intersection and finally saw the unmistakable temple of Gu'un at the end of one of the streets. He smiled as they approached. This dead-end street held a couple of other temples as well and people came in and out of them freely. They avoided the stark, unadorned wall that was the front facade of Gu'un's temples. He made a beeline for its single dark opening, thankful when he was finally shielded from the unrelenting sun.

Another priest in richly dyed gray cotton made a sign of greeting when they came into the first great room. Newa returned his greeting, glad to be in a real, functioning temple after visiting so many country villages.

"Brother," he started, "can you guide me to your leader? I have news from the Hand."

The other priest's eyes widened. "Right away."

They cut through a series of side hallways and Newa took in the familiar smells with a smile. The temple of Gu'un should smell of shed blood and fear. His smile grew as he heard a distant scream. These people were true priests. The other arakgu'un stopped before a wide door, knocking firmly.

"Come," answered the gruff voice from inside.

Newa and his apprentice entered. He was taken aback by the leader's office. On one wall was the customary collection of weapons but these were far grander than even the ones the Hand owned. They looked to be worth a fortune. The desk he worked from was ornately carved and looked to be the work of the deep southerners. Newa took in their leader with growing wariness. The man was stout and tall, a build that told of thick, carved muscle when he was younger. But Newa knew he couldn't be fooled. This man still held great strength.

"My leader," the other priest said. "I have a brother with a message from the Hand."

The older man looked up, surprised. "Leave us," he instructed the priest.

Newa bowed to the temple leader as the door was closed. Yanu followed suite.

"Greetings from the capital, great leader."

The leader put down his work. "And what message has the Hand deemed us worthy of?"

Newa didn't like his tone. "This is a message for our sect only and it's very important that we keep it amongst ourselves until an official proclamation comes." The other man raised a wiry eyebrow. "The Netkoleh has declared that there are no gods."

"What!" The older man shot up from his seat. "What blasphemy is this?"

"The Netkoleh, now to be call the emperor, has declared that there are no gods and he will have them scrubbed from the empire. He will-."

"This is an abomination! How can he, of all the people on this earth, declare such? This can't stand!"

"Are you through?" Newa asked calmly. "Because there is more and I remind you this comes directly from the Hand of Gu'un, himself." The older man sat down, the red fading from his face. Newa waited a few more moments to make sure the man was paying attention. "The emperor wants us to work with him, however, we will not go along with his blasphemy. We will continue on our path of bringing wayward people back to the path of just living and dealing swift justice even if it means dealing with a heretical ruler. Our mission is more important."

The red returned to the leader's face but he didn't shout this time. "And what of the other sects?"

Newa shrugged. "They can decide how they wish to deal with this on their own. Our only concern is our mission."

"I . . . see." The leader sat back down. "And am I to tell my followers of this?"

"Yes. But this can go *no* farther than this temple. Not even to lovers and family."

The older man sat back in his chair, looking suddenly even older. "Very well." He lowered his head. "As the Hand guides, we shall follow."

Newa nodded and left the office. He glanced around quickly, taking in the decorations. He didn't like this temple. Not at all. Once outside he and Yanu quickly made their way back into the main fairway to find a travel house. He wasn't going to spend another night out on the road if he didn't have to. Sleeping in the dirt was a life he'd abandoned and he was loathed to return to any facet of it.

He paid extra for one of the better rooms and settled in easily. After dinner he meditated, letting the sound of his blades against the whet stone focus his thoughts. He ran Yanu through his daily exercises before they retired for bed. He wouldn't let the boy become rusty while they were on the road. Once his apprentice settled in, Newa laid down in his own bed. He fell into a dreamless sleep, the kind he preferred.

His breathing was cut off as something was pressed down on his face. Newa kicked and flailed instinctively as he awoke and the pressure on his face increased. He felt a set of hands grab one leg and another pair struggle with his hands. He calmed his panic, realizing someone was holding his pillow over his face. Envisioning the position of the person that must be over him, he kicked out for what he assumed was their stomach and was rewarded with a cry of pain and a thud on the floor.

He wrenched his head from beneath the pillow to see the darkened silhouettes of the three men. In the dim moonlight coming in from the window he could just make out the heavy necklace of Koleh swinging from one of their necks. Outraged, he brought his heel down on the hand of the man holding his other leg. Half free, Newa twisted violently, casting himself off of the bed and bringing the man holding his arms down with him. He wrenched an arm free, just as his legs were grabbed again, and grabbed one of his blades from underneath the bed.

The sickle shaped blade easily cut through the wrists of the man that held his arms, his fresh, warm blood splattering across Newa's face. The first man he'd kicked was back on his feet and rushing this way, the other man scrambling back to avoid the same fate as his bleeding brother. Newa rolled to his knees, blades out and ready. He heard the man behind him scrambling, probably seeking a way to stop the bleeding. The priest of Gu'un moved slowly to a vantage point that allowed him to keep his eyes on all of the men. He looked over to Yanu's bed but the boy was still in his bed, another priest just removing the pillow from his face. Anger flooded Newa's body. These priests would pay dearly for his apprentice's life.

"So, priests of Koleh?" he said with a wicked grin. "What grievance do you have with me?"

The men didn't move and their hesitation told Newa that they didn't come here for a true fight.

"Heretic," one of them ground out, the one that was smothering him. "Your blasphemous message will die with you. And we will send your body back to your leader as a warning."

Newa smiled wider. So, the priests of Gu'un must have talked to others. He had half a mind to go back and kill their leader for his disobedience against the Hand. The priests in front of him still hadn't made an aggressive move toward him. The one whose wrists he'd slashed finally lost enough strength to force him to collapse to the floor. The moonlight glinted off of Newa's blades as he shifted position. If they wanted out of this room, they would have to get past him and he would be glad when they lost their courage.

The one who'd held his legs broke first, running toward one of the windows instead of trying his chances against the blades of Gu'un. He gave a strangled cry as he fell two stories and there was an abrupt thud.

"Your turn," Newa said lowly to the last priest.

The man was a bundle of panic. He grabbed one of the room's stools, holding it high as he ran towards him. Newa was disgusted. The priests of Koleh were certainly not made for combat. The priest swung the stool down, aiming for his head. Newa swung up with one of his blades, catching one of the legs in its curve and pushing it aside. His other blade sunk into the soft flesh of the priest's neck, slicing from one ear to the other. Newa could see the man's mouth moving in the same disbelief he'd seen in all those who were suddenly about to die.

He let the man fall of his own accord as he surveyed the room. He cursed looking at the pooling blood around the room. Two dead priests of Koleh and his apprentice in his room. The proprietors knew his profession and knew he was from the capital. It wouldn't be a mystery what happened. He packed his belongings quickly. If these three were sent or came here of their own accord there may be more looking to take his head. Who knew how far the news of the emperor's decree had spread? He was confident in his abilities but he knew he couldn't fight off a whole city of angry priests, warriors or not.

Newa dressed and shrugged his pack on. He wiped the blood off on one of the priests' clothes, thanking Gu'un for the clean kill, placing the blades at the holders at his hip. He went to Yanu's body, wishing he could secure a proper funeral for him. He hoped that the proprietors would turn his body over to one of the temples, but there wasn't much that he could do but hope. Looking out the window he saw the last priest on the ground below. The man moved, groaning faintly. Taking out a smaller pair of knives, Newa tested the thickness of the mud brick of the travel house. Satisfied, he hopped onto the window sill and planted the knives firmly in the brick, using them to climb down to the street.

The injured priest looked up to him in confusion when he jumped down to the ground. Poor man probably hit his head as well as broke his legs. Unconcerned, Newa looked around the barely illuminated night, searching for more enemies. There wasn't a sound except for a cat chasing rats around a corner. He put up his small blades and ran down the street.

Three dead priests of Koleh was not something he had hoped to be responsible for. All the temples kept a healthy respect of each other. But now with his proclamation, he wasn't sure how things would play out. How would he be greeted in the next cities he visited if he chose to continue his mission at all or return to the capital? The questions swirled in his mind. He concentrated on his exit. Those questions would have to be answered once he was safely out of town.

* * *

There was no way around it. Ashaki had racked her mind for another solution to Hotemkhar's outrageous demand but she couldn't think of a single way to subvert it. She sighed as she laced up her sandals. They had to add troops to the invasion across the Bangi. The very thought made her throat tighten. The treaty had been in effect for all of known memory. Even before the trade deal was struck, it was understood that you didn't cross into the batubangi's territory. This was a travesty.

She wrapped her *abisi* around her waist, throwing the last few feet over her shoulder. The rich purples of the fabric were interrupted by gold thread designs. It was a nice accent to her outfit and she needed to dress nicely if she was going to speak with her war minister today. That woman was a stickler for appearances. The only advice the general had given her on her ascension was that a dara should appear as a dara. Ashaki wouldn't disappoint her today.

She walked out into the morning light taking in her city. It was peaceful and there wasn't an Egan soldier in sight. She knew that wouldn't last long so she enjoyed the moment while it lasted. People greeted her as they rushed about their morning duties, many on their way to the market or vendors rushing to set up their tables. Day servants bobbed their heads in greeting, not high enough in station to speak directly to her. She returned their nods with a smile. People like that were the building blocks of the city.

Ashaki walked along the streets that took her to the noble compounds. Flowering trees rose behind the tall outer walls, dropping their multicolored petals into the street. She paused before the great door of the compound of the line of Bilamba. Her heart stung looking at the familiar carvings of her in-laws' door. She hadn't visited in some time. Seeing the spots where she would court Lafosa, the tree that they would steal kisses under, still brought tears to her eyes. Ashaki hurried past it.

The compound of war minister Ngali sported wide double doors with swords carved into each one. She grabbed the gold-plated knocker, rapping on the door three loud times. She knew Ngali would be home. The woman was always up at the crack of dawn and with her first grandchild on the way she was sure to be in a place to be found when the news came. One of the doors was promptly opened, a well-dressed attendant staring wide eyed at her once they realized the Great Dara was before them.

The man bowed, stepping aside. Ashaki smiled kindly.

"Is war minister Ngali in her inner courtyard?"

"Yes, Great Dara. I can lead you there."

"Thank you," Ashaki responded, allowing him to take the lead.

Ashaki smiled when they reached the courtyard. Her war minister was already busy. Ngali held a wooden sword and was putting her youngest daughter through her paces.

"Surely you can beat your old, frail mother by now,"

the minister scoffed, parrying a slice.

The young woman scowled. "There is nothing frail about you, mama." She attempted to feint to the side, but Ngali was prepared and blocked, sweeping her immediately.

Ngali stepped to her with a chuckle. "You can't fear your opponent," she said reaching down to help her up. "No matter who they are. Understood?"

"Yes, mama." She looked over in surprise when she noticed Ashaki standing to the side.

Ngali looked over, raising a salt and pepper eyebrow. She nodded to her daughter and the young woman excused herself with a bow.

"Great Dara," she began. "You honor my home this morning."

"I am honored to be welcome in your home."

Ngali put her sword against a stool and picked up a cloth to wipe the sweat from her brow.

"Now, what business brings the Great Dara here instead of summoning me?"

Ashaki cleared her throat. Commanding the woman who'd been her vast superior until three years ago was still quite the task.

"We have a problem."

"Oh?"

Ashaki stepped closer to her trying to look as serious as possible. "The magistrate wants to send forces over the Bangi to find their gold mines."

"Arrogant bastard," she spat, throwing down her cloth. She folded her arms over her chest. "What does he hope to accomplish? Getting his men lost or cursed? What did you tell him?"

"I couldn't tell him anything. What they do with their own forces is their business." She sighed, not wanting to continue. "But he's made a request from me and I don't see any way to avoid it. He wants us to contribute warriors to their invasion."

Ngoli laughed sharply. "He's lost his mind. We won't." She looked to Ashaki, her face losing its mirth. "We won't, right?"

Ashaki sighed again. "I'd gone to him to see if our taxes could be reduced and this was his condition. I . . . have to submit to it." She could tell the war minister was swallowing a retort. "I have no choice, Ngali. I've tried for days to find a way around it but there isn't. If we can't pay the Ega less then Nsongo won't survive. I need you to help me choose the right people to send on this mission."

Ngali stared at her, eyes narrowed. "So, you're looking for people to sacrifice to the whims of the Ega."

"You know me better than that," she snapped. "I have never thrown anyone's life away that was under my command. How dare you? I came to you because I want good warriors to go. I want people who will have the best chance of coming back. I could have not involved you and chosen them myself but I respect your office and your wisdom enough to council you."

Ngali closed her eyes for a moment, taking in a breath. She bowed slowly; arms outstretched.

"Forgive me, my dara. A warrior's tongue is as sharp as their blade."

Ashaki studied her for a moment. These slights were beginning to take their toll.

"You may face me." She folded her arms as the war minister rose. "I want some of our best seasoned warriors to go with the Ega."

"How many?"

"Twenty to twenty-five. They'll get no more from us for now. I want them to make sure that if no one else survives, they all make it back. And I want them to tell us everything the Ega say or do while they're there. I want to know how often they take a shit. Everything."

Ngali nodded. "I already have several candidates in mind. Do they have a date for the invasion?"

"Not yet. I think they're still trying to gather their own forces. But I'll bother the peacock until he makes things clear." She gave her minister a wry smile.

Ngali bowed again. "Very well. Is there anything else you need from me, my dara?"

"No, Ngali. Thank you for your help. Send the list when you've written it." The war minister nodded and Ashaki made her way out.

She frowned, still angry at the insult. Ngali might have been leagues above her in rank before the war but she was the Great Dara now, despite how much she and every-one else might wish else-wise. A measure of respect was all she asked for.

CHAPTER SIXTEEN

Yutuuan was tired of traveling. It had been an unusually dry trip and his men and horses felt their stamina withering away under the sun. The prince sighed. But at least Tilizaa would be the last city he visited before heading home. He sighed again. Home. What he would give to already be home, to sleep in his bed and sink into the charms of Talekh. He smiled absentmindedly, thinking of her seductive smile. Even though his mission was important, going home would be the greatest reward.

The road wound its way around the side of large arid hills and the group could just make out olive groves carefully planted on the mounds ahead. A warm wind brought in the smell of the trees to him. It was sharply followed by the scent of smoke. Yutuuan snapped out of his slight daydreaming, glancing at Naret. The man shared his look of concern and then jutted his chin at the path ahead. Past the orchard thick, black smoke rose up from the hills. Yutuuan brought his horse to a run, his group following suite.

He raced through the twists and turns of the road, cresting a large hill before he could see the source of the smoke. A village spread out in the valley below, sprawling out to the sea. Screams reached him and he urged his horse into a harder run. Ships with flags he'd never seen before were at the docks. Several of the buildings were on fire and pandemonium ruled.

"Defend the village," he yelled behind him, taking out his sword.

He and his men rushed down into the small streets of the village. They were a small force but perhaps the element of surprise would help them against these attackers. Yutuuan rode up to the first one who was attempting to set another building on fire. He reared his horse up, stomping on the man on the way down. The man's head gave a sick crunch as Yutuuan rode over him. The next man went down in a single swing from his sword. He didn't realize the prince was on him until it was too late.

Yutuuan took a moment to assess his surroundings before continuing. The surprise of his soldier's attack had worked to their advantage but now these . . . enemies realized their danger. They were beginning to fight back and he saw that they were no mere pirates. These were soldiers. He spurred his horse forward, heading toward the nearest combatant. The man saw his approach and blocked his first swing. Yutuuan kicked for him, knocking the man off balance and giving him the chance to swing again. His sword caught the man in the side of the throat trailing a bright red arc of blood.

These attackers were fierce but his warriors were fiercer. Soon a horn sounded and the men began to retreat.

"Don't let them leave!" Yutuuan shouted at the top of his lungs. "Don't let them make it to their ships!"

He rode forward, hearing the thundering hoofbeats of the rest of his group. More of the attackers were cut down in the midst of their fleeing. Yutuuan heard the blood pumping in his ears as he pursued them to the docks. He sliced down two more men as they tried to climb up to their ships. Anger fueling him, he rode his horse up the gangplank, taking to cutting more of the enemy down. His horse suddenly bucked and he found himself thrown to the deck.

Yutuuan quickly rolled to his feet, his shoulder throbbing from the fall. Four of the enemy were on deck with him, swords out and ready. He recognized their people. They were from a country far to the east of Wiluru's influence. They saw a ship come into port in Wiluru every so often and they'd always been friendly. He looked up to the sail and the unfamiliar emblem on it. They'd never been hostile before.

He was relieved when six of his soldiers ran onto the ship. One of the strange enemies took this moment to lunge for him. Yutuuan parried his blow aside, bringing his sword around to stab the man in the stomach. The other three held onto their courage for a moment more, then one slowly put his sword down. The other two reluctantly followed suite.

"Restrain them," he ordered, looking over the docks and the other ship. The second sailing vessel had been taken over as well, the last of its occupants being cut down. He looked over the ships more carefully. He knew this type of vessel even though he'd never set foot on one. He'd wanted to see if some of their design could be incorporated into Wiluru's ships.

He turned back to the captives, who were now on their knees in the middle of the deck.

"Do you speak Wiluruan?" he asked them. The captives looked up at him with a mixture of defiance and confusion. "Does anyone speak Rahbahn?" he asked loudly so even the men on the dock could hear.

A thickly muscled woman jogged up to the deck. "I speak a little, my prince."

He nodded. "Ask them where they came from." She took a moment to think and then stumbled through her question. One of the men growled his answer back, spitting at her. She moved just in time to avoid it.

"What did he say?" Yutuuan asked, frowning.

"He called us a few names, but I caught that they're from Masharadi."

"Masharadi?" another of the soldiers asked. "I've heard of it. It's just a trading port."

Yutuuan propped his chin in his hand. Attacks from distant trading ports. All under an emblem he'd never seen before. He needed a good interpreter and soon. He looked around to his group. There were few injuries, thanks to Yutuu. His attention turned to the town. Several buildings were still on fire and were starting to spread.

"Get water," he shouted. "See if any of the townspeople need medical attention. And someone take word to Tilizaa of what happened."

His soldiers snapped into action, the servants of his party that had stayed back moving in to help the villagers. Yutuuan was about to join them when he was knocked back and a pain exploded in his right shoulder. He looked down curiously at the shaft of the arrow sticking out of him then looked ahead and saw the hatch from below decks closing quickly. His men threw it open as he went down to a knee, three of them yanking a man with a crossbow out. Yutuuan tried to focus, but the pain clouded his vision and he let himself succumb to it.

* * *

The evening had settled like ink on the city when Erenemo finally left the temple. An evening of communing with the gods and ancestors, searching for the right path for his plans left him slightly exhausted. He pinched the bridge of his nose, feeling the pressure building. He prayed he could just make it home and get to sleep without any other aggravations. Saidata walked beside him, lantern held up on a flexible rod. The city was quiet on this moonless night and he was grateful. The northern soldiers didn't seem inclined to harass the citizenry tonight. Perhaps they finally had lost interest in the tormenting of their usual targets. He frowned deeply. That would all change when he was in charge.

The thought of Ashaki's murder rose to the top again. His surety that she had to die hadn't left him since the dinner with the elders. They'd left him with no other choice. He'd wanted to do this legally but they showed him that wasn't an option if Nsongo was to be saved. Now, he just had to figure out how he would carry it out. He could be nowhere near it, couldn't let anything be traced back to him. So, he needed someone to carry out this plan for him. He was sure Saidata would do it. Eagerly even. But he wouldn't risk losing him. He had a promising future. No, he needed someone disposable.

Movement ahead of him in the street caught his attention. A figure froze then dashed into a side street. Erenemo paused. If someone was trying to evade detection, they were doing a horrible job of it. He moved forward slowly, Saidata following slightly behind. Erenemo stopped at the side street, looking down it. There weren't many places to hide and he didn't hear any retreating footsteps. He motioned for his acolyte to bring the lantern to the entrance of the street. A small head ducked behind a wagon parked to the side. Erenemo's eyes flew wide open. It couldn't be.

"Masola?" he called, unbelieving. There was no reply and he took a step into the street. "Masola," he called more firmly. "I saw you."

A moment passed and the dim figure of his greatniece emerged from behind the wagon. She hung her head solemnly, hands clasped as she came to him. He stared at her, his mind not grasping that she was out here in the night.

"What," he began, choosing the question he wanted to start with carefully, "are you doing out here?"

She started to tear up. "I sneaked out. I wanted to see someone and mama wouldn't let me. Please don't tell her."

Erenemo's mouth worked. "You came out to see who?" he hissed.

"A . . . friend."

"I'm sure." His disapproval was painted on his face. "This is very disappointing, Masola." He exaggerated his frown to drive his point home. He was sure she inherited this rebellious streak from her low born birth parents.

"Please don't tell mama," she begged again. "If she would just let me see him, I wouldn't have to sneak out."

Erenemo pinched the bridge of his nose again. This was because of some sweetheart in the city.

"So, who?"

"His name is Yambi." She folded her arms, looking aside with a pout. "Mama said he's too low." The vehemence that came with her statement surprised him.

"If your mother says he's too low for you, then he's too low. You do not see rats cavorting with lions, do you?"

"I don't care!" Erenemo was surprised again. "Mother always thinks she's right. She's not. She only cares about being the dara now, not what I want. And she's a horrible dara. She should have avenged mami."

Erenemo put a hand on his great-niece's shoulder. "And what else do you think she should have done?"

Masola wiped away tears with the back of her hand. "She should have never surrendered. Grandfather and mami and all my uncles died and she surrendered to those dogs. And now I can't even see a boy I like because she has to play at being dara."

"Being the dara is hard and she has a lot she has to consider."

"I don't care," she snapped back at him and he had to pull back a smile.

"Come along, Masola. We'll go to my compound for the night. Aunt Patya will make you some tea and milk." He put a comforting arm around her shoulders as they walked on. "I'll escort you back to your mother in the morning and you will have to face punishment." He almost chuckled at her scowl. "There's no way around it, but we can say that you wanted to visit and talk and we lost track of time. No need to tell her of your . . . misstep."

"You'd lie for me, Uncle?"

"While, yes, you deserve to be punished, this is a relatively small mistake. Just promise me you won't make such a mistake again. The city is terribly dangerous at night. Anything could have happened to you."

"Yes, Uncle."

Erenemo escorted her along the dark city streets, his attendant lighting the way. He had to smile, but not in affection. Masola was a foolish girl but her disdain of her mother may prove to be helpful. He gave up a small thanks to the ancestors.

*　*　*

Efah sat out in an area of the city where the roof had collapsed, letting in some much-needed sunshine. Monkeys played in the trees high above her, chattering amongst each other about the strange trio below them. Nesi had her head in her lap, loving the scratches behind her ears. Usa was curled up at her side, providing the perfect support. Efah smiled, watching the monkeys. She'd never been to this part of the city before but, then again, there was so much she hadn't seen and so much that was probably uninhabitable.

It had been peaceful in her time here. Ayodele and his minions were obviously still horrified of her. Iyola hadn't shown her face since that first encounter, probably at her master's command. Efah stretched, unsettling Nesi for a moment. She began scratching again as an apology. It was nice to have the people who'd robbed and terrorized her and so many others terrified. She just wished that the others in the city weren't terrified of her as well. Her travels through the city were still met with shrieks as they walked. People fled at the sight of her and her girls. She was sure the news of her being the voice of the god of death had spread throughout the entire city by now. Efah frowned. She had to find a way through to them.

A shadow moved at the corner of her eye. Efah casually looked over and the god of death walked leisurely by. She turned, following his path until he came to stop where the side of the building had collapsed, looking out over the cliffs leading to the jungle and the river below. Efah rose slowly, disturbing Nesi's nap, and walked to him. It was strange seeing him in daylight, seeing that sickly colored skin so clearly. She stopped just short of standing beside him, looking up to the feathered mantle and the side of his face.

"You've done well, Efah Aboujale, my messenger."

"Thank you, but I don't feel like I've done much."

He looked to her with those white eyes, pinning her

184

to the spot. "You have been a light in the darkness. If your message hasn't been received it is a burden they will have to carry. They will see your light eventually and realize that it's been sent to save them, not harm them."

Efah worried her lip. "What will happen to those that don't turn back to the old ways?"

He didn't answer her at first and she thought she might have offended him somehow.

"They will be caught up in the coming fire."

"Is it truly fire?" she asked. He'd told her so little she was starved for more.

"Death," he began slowly, "is considered the end of life for many. Yet, it can bring newness. To begin planting, you must clear the field. To find riches you must tear through the mountain. There will be fire, yes. There will be bloodshed, yes. And I fear that there are those that wish for this to happen as much as I wish for it to be avoided."

He looked out to the cliff again. "I take no glee in visiting death on the living. If it is necessary, then I am happy to bring peace. If not, then I wish for it to be avoided. I wish for none to come to me until it is their time."

"That is why you sent me," Efah said looking down in thought.

"Yes, you know the pain of watching those you love suffer and die. And you know the relief of knowing they will suffer no more. You, Efah Aboujale, understand."

She thought of her grandmother and brother, trembling and sweating underneath the terrible sickness that broke out when she was younger. She nodded. She did understand.

"I will do all I can to spread your message."

"I know that you will."

Nesi and Usa barked, catching her attention. A woman carrying a bundle timidly stepped out into the ruined hallway. Efah looked back to the god of death but he was gone. She took a step back then hurried back to where her hyenas reclined.

"They won't attack," she called out to the woman. "Did you need something?"

The woman took a few more cautious steps forward and Efah could see the exhaustion in her face.

"I heard that you're the woman who walks with death."

She exchanged looks with her companions. She hadn't heard of that one. "I am death's messenger."

"Then I need your help." She came forward, holding the bundle protectively to her chest. "My son. He's terribly ill."

Efah pet her hyenas on the head and came over to the woman. She presented the bundle in which a tiny boy was wrapped, breathing so shallow she could barely tell he was alive. She felt his forehead and it was cold. Efah shook her head. "I'm not a healer."

Tears began to gather in the woman's eyes. "I don't want you to heal him. He's not getting any better. I want you to end it. My husband still wants to look for a cure but I don't want him to drag on like this."

Efah moved her fingers down to the boy's chest. She could feel his little heart, beating slowly. Moreover, she could feel his life barely holding onto this body. The connection was so fragile it felt like it would break under her hand. He wouldn't survive this sickness.

"I . . . I will end it." Efah could feel his life between her fingers, a wisp of a sensation against her skin. It tried to float away like mist to the other side. Taking a breath, she grabbed the spot that still held on and plucked, severing it. The boy's chest rose one last time and settled, still.

The mother clutched him closely, sobs pouring from her. Efah put a hand on her shoulder, waiting until she could hear her above her grief.

"Go, cry, moan, scream. Do whatever it takes to grieve him for as long as it takes. He suffers no more."

"Thank you," she sobbed.

Efah gave her a long hug and watched as she returned into the rest of the city. She looked back to the cliff. Yes, she understood.

CHAPTER SEVENTEEN

Umakaal opened her eyes at the sound of sea birds playing loudly past her windows. She smiled as a most familiar pair of arms circled her torso and squeezed. Ladawi pressed herself closer, her breasts rubbing just under Umakaal's shoulder blades.

"Good morning," Umakaal said taking her hands in hers.

"Good morning," her lover replied, biting one of those shoulder blades.

Umakaal sucked in a breath. "Don't you have duties to return to?" she ground out.

"I am attending my princess like a good little attendant."

She turned awkwardly and wrapped her arms around Ladawi, kissing her.

"And you are a very good attendant, indeed." They both giggled as they continued kissing until the sunlight came in through the windows. Umakaal sighed heavily. "I have to go."

Ladawi frowned. "I wish you weren't head of the palace guard. You never get to rest."

"Well, one day I will have enough time to spend every waking moment with you." She rolled out of bed to collect her clothes.

Her attendant turned on her stomach languidly, showing no intentions of getting up yet.

"And what about when you marry?"

"You will be part of my household and I'll still spend every night with you and keep my husband around for when I want children." She shrugged on her tunic and pants, searching her room for where she threw her belt last night. "And we'll raise my children together and they'll be our children."

Ladawi laughed. "And maybe I'll use your husband too and we'll have more children!" She hopped up on her knees on the bed, excited. "We'll have a hoard of children!"

Umakaal couldn't help herself and rushed back to the bed, tackling Ladawi down. "Yes," she said kissing her nose. "A hoard of children." She kissed her deeply. "I love you."

Ladawi reached up, moving the braids from her face. "I love you too."

The princess took a deep breath, staring into her lover's eyes. Every morning was getting harder. She pushed herself up quickly, getting dressed, but sneaking one last kiss before leaving the room.

Umakaal rushed down the hallway, half running to make it to the barracks of the palace guard. It wasn't required that she be there for the morning changing of the guard but it was something that she wanted to be present for. She wouldn't be the leader in name only like so many of her family. She wanted to be a true leader and inspiration to her subordinates. Being late wasn't exactly inspiring.

"Good morning, commander," her armorer greeted her as she rounded the last corner.

"Good morning, Ikaaten." She hurried into the changing room with an apologetic smile.

He already had her breastplate in hand, ready to help her.

"The change hasn't begun yet. If we hurry, you'll just make it."

Umakaal winced and stood still as he adjusted her armor. "Sorry. I was . . . busy this morning."

"I'm sure," he said with a smirk. "You and your brother have similar personalities."

"Hey!" She didn't appreciate the slight. "I'm am *not nearly* as bad as my brother."

Ikaaten shrugged as his deft fingers worked at the

lacing of her bracers.

"Well, at least you show up in the mornings."

She snorted and helped tie the other bracer while he worked on her greaves. A servant came to the door, looking hurried. Umakaal looked up, raising an eyebrow.

"Is there something you need?"

The servant bowed. "Your father wishes to speak with you, princess."

She and Ikaaten shared a glance. "Yes, I'll be there right away. Is he in the council room?"

"Yes, princess."

She nodded and finished with her armor. She grabbed her sword from the wall, securing its scabbard in her belt.

"Let Captain Taautan know that I'll be with the guard as soon as possible and to oversee things for me in the meantime," she said to Ikaaten. Her armorer nodded.

The halls were busier than when she'd run down from her room. She nodded curtly to people who greeted her as she walked back to the more important areas of the palace. She grabbed her stomach as it groaned. Breakfast would have been a good idea this morning. Just as she was about to turn down the hall that lead to the council room, she saw her sister coming her way, a concerned look on her face as well.

"Morning, sister," she called out.

Izriamat smiled back and gave her a hug the moment she reached her.

"Good morning. Did father summon you too?"

"He did. What do you think this could be about?"

Her sister looked down the hall. "I hope that we're not going to try to negotiate with the netkoleh."

"I hope so." She took a deep breath. "Then let's go. We won't find out standing out here."

Umakaal smiled as Izriamat took her hand and they walked to the council room. The room was nearly empty when they entered, save her father sitting at his seat at the head of the meeting area. Their mother was there too, sitting at her place to the side. She looked disappointed when she looked up at them, but Umakaal's focus fell quickly on their father. She'd never seen such a look of anger on him before. She glanced up at her sister and they approached their parents.

Izriamat gave her hand a squeeze before taking the lead. "You summoned us, father?"

The king held up a folded piece of paper before him. "This morning I received a letter from the governor of Falee's Bay telling me that my son is going around the whole of Wiluru and forming a war committee behind my back. He lied to my face when he told me of his trip's purpose. You two lied to me. You knew what he was doing!"

"Father," Umakaal started, "it's not as bad as you think."

Their father threw the letter aside, suddenly looking very old and defeated.

"Not as bad as I think," he said lowly. "What am I supposed to think when my own children are conspiring against me?" The princesses were left without an answer. "I said that we would try to speak with the netkoleh. That is the decision that I've come to. How dare you think that you can subvert my authority."

"We are not trying to undermine you, father," Umakaal pleaded. "Yutuuan went to see if the governors he chose would be ready for war, not to declare war."

"War will come, father," Izriamat added calmly. "I'm sorry, but it will."

Their mother put a hand on his as he struggled with his anger.

"We will always try peace first," she said sternly.

"And when it fails?" Umakaal asked. "What are we going to do then? Izriamat doesn't want to go back and you know good and damn well that he will send forces to collect her. Are you going to let them prance in and take her?"

"Watch your tongue," her father snapped.

Izriamat stood up straighter. "Even if I weren't here, what do you plan to do about his decree? He won't be dissuaded from his decision. Once he has set his mind to an idea there is no wavering. We can't abandon our faith and the gods that set us here."

Their mother stepped in again. "We won't abandon the gods. That goes without saying, but that doesn't excuse your . . . deceitful actions."

"But you wouldn't listen!" Umakaal looked over to her sister at the outburst. Her fists were balled at her side, her eyes closed tightly. "You wouldn't listen," she reiterated. "I have lived there. I have suffered under him for seven years and you think you know him better than me! He is a monster and he will seek to crush us if we don't bend to his whims. That is how he is!" She yelled so loudly that her voice was shrill.

Umakaal put an arm around her sister. She felt her trembling.

"Father, it was the only way that we could see forward. We didn't do this out of hatred of you, but out of love for our country."

Their father deflated, sinking lower into his low backed chair. Their mother looked up to him. He took a deep breath.

"Leave us," he said weakly. "I will make a final decision on this situation when your brother returns."

"But father," Umakaal started.

"That is all," he said, finality in his tone.

The princesses turned to leave, Umakaal still with a supportive arm around her sister. They stopped once outside the room. Umakaal turned to Izriamat expecting to see her crying but her sister's face was tight with anger.

"Are you alright?" she asked her.

"I'm fine. I hope Yutuuan's mission was successful. I see now that we'll have to force father's hand." She looked back to the doors and moved a little farther away. "If a coalition is formed then he'll have no choice but to think about war planning."

"You know he'll still want to try to negotiate."

Izriamat frowned deeper. "He can still negotiate and when it fails, we'll be ready."

It was Umakaal's turn to glance back at the council doors. Worry fluttered through her.

"We'll have to be ready."

* * *

The palace of Metkara was abuzz with activity. The day for the start of the Pilgrimage was looming ever closer and there was much for Bakari to oversee. The city itself was quiet and he was thankful that Hetsaf had taken up locating any other dissenters and having them brought to the Arakgu'un. The assassin priests themselves had been invaluable in rounding up those who were conspiring against him and ushering them on from this life. He smirked as servants brought clothing to him to be approved for his travels. It was good to know that there were those who'd carry out his word without question.

Arkoleh stood beside him, surveying his clothing with him. He smiled at her as she shook her head at an ensemble made of southern fabrics.

"We should have you in only the most Egan wear," she said firmly.

He chuckled. "I'll be so sad to leave you behind, my dearest wife."

Arkoleh looked to him, blinking in confusion. "I'm . . . not coming with you?"

Bakari waved the servants off for a moment. He took her hands in his.

"I'm afraid not. I need you here." She didn't say anything at first and he was afraid she was angry with him.

"My love, my first love, I need someone here that I can trust. Remember my glorious vision." He took her out of the room and into a nearby arcade. "Remember how you will be my right hand. I need you to oversee the capital. Everything flows from here."

She looked away from him. "You have Hetsaf."

"Hetsaf isn't you." He cupped her chin, turning her back to him. "He is . . . talented. But he is a good follower. You are a leader, my love. He needs someone like you to guide his hand."

She finally smiled at him. "But I'll miss you terribly."

"You'll just have to be strong." He took her hand, leading her back into the room. "Also, I need you to look after my second son while I'm away. He's under the care of Neytiri and she's done an excellent job."

"Who is that?" she asked, stopping.

Bakari looked to her sharply, pulling her along.

"Neytiri is one of my lesser wives." He frowned at her rolling her eyes. "Look in on him. I've moved her to better rooms and she'll be looking into his care after Izriamat's return as well."

Arkoleh paused, lips pursed. "I will."

"Good."

He waved for the servants to return to their duties. He caught sight of his brother entering in the midst of the tempest of preparations. Hetsaf bowed curtly before them.

"Emperor, empress, I've concluded the inspection of your horse and lodgings for the trip. Everything is in order."

Bakari clapped his brother on the shoulder. "You've come at a perfect time. I've told Arkoleh that she will remain behind to oversee things in the capital, and I need you to uplift her. Be as valuable to her as you are to me."

"You're leaving her in charge here?" Hetsaf asked slowly.

"Yes, she is my right hand."

His brother paused, then nodded. "Very well." He turned his attention to Arkoleh. "My empress, I will do all I can to ensure your word is treated as law." He turned back to Bakari and the emperor couldn't help but wonder about the look in his eye. "My emperor, may I speak with you. It is a . . . personal matter."

Bakari chuckled and turned to his wife giving her a kiss on the cheek. "Let us have a moment, my love."

"Of course." She nodded with a smile at her brother through marriage.

Hetsaf waited until Arkoleh had completely left the room, and then waited a few moments more before speaking again.

"My emperor, I have . . . concerns about your plan for the capital."

Bakari frowned, curious. "What sort of concerns?"

"About the empress." He glanced back the way she left. "Are you sure she's fit for this?"

Bakari felt his temper rise. "Of course, she is fit to lead. She is my wife. She is my Great Royal Wife. There is no one better suited to lead this empire in my stead than her."

Hetsaf looked down, screwing up his mouth in thought.

"And what of the Second Wife? She seems like more of a level head than the Great Royal Wife."

Bakari grabbed the front of Hetsaf's robes so quickly he didn't realize he had the man until he jerked him close.

"Watch your mouth. You are my lesser, brother or not."

"Of course, my emperor," Hetsaf said calmly. "I meant no insult." Bakari released his hold, still looking daggers at his chancellor. "However, they are women. Some may not be as . . . receptive to their leadership as you would like."

"Would that include you?" It infuriated him to think his most loyal servant would harbor such feelings.

"I am only a chancellor. I will serve them as I serve you."

"Good." He straightened his clothes back up. "Now, is there anything else?"

Hetsaf bowed deeply to him. "No, my emperor. All is prepared for your departure in the morning."

Bakari waved him off and he watched his chancellor walk off. "Hetsaf," he called before the man could leave the room. Hetsaf stopped, taking a moment before he turned around. "If you have any other opinions, I hope you'll keep them to yourself." His brother nodded and left, but Bakari didn't miss the tight look on his face before he departed. He hoped his brother would remember his place in all this.

* * *

Tekhamun's long shadow proceeded him into town like a specter announcing his arrival. The people of Ketum gave him a wide berth, looking down their noses as they passed. He didn't miss any of it. Their disdain, their scorn ran off of him like summer rains. He knew that he must look haggard to them, but his mission was more important than appearances. They would understand it soon enough and if they didn't, they would pass away.

He stopped in the square of the town, not quite sure which way to turn, which way to begin spreading his message. He thought of the temple of his order and wondered if the blasphemous priest had been here already. His fingers twitched at the thought. What if that man had poisoned his brethren already? This wouldn't stand. Tekhamun mouthed a prayer to Gu'un for guidance and searched the city for the temple.

He entered it timidly, then had to remind himself of his great and holy mission. He'd never been in a temple so large before. This building could easily house a dozen of his. He looked around in awe until he nearly bumped into another priest.

"Good afternoon . . . brother," the tall, thin man said, looking him over.

Tekhamun bobbed his head. "Good afternoon."

"Is there something I can help you with?"

He licked dry lips. "I bring you greetings from the tiny village of Arakush. I'm afraid I've come to bring you dire news but good news as well."

The priest's eyebrows arched. "Follow me." He fell in step behind the man, walking into a back room that served as the kitchen. Five other men gathered, beginning preparation of the evening meal. Tekhamun took in the aromas greedily and his stomach responded.

"Are you hungry, brother?" the man asked, leading him to the long table in the middle of the room.

"I . . . yes." He placed a hand to his stomach. His food had run out the day before his arrival and he hadn't had the chance to replenish his supplies.

The other priests set out a plate, handing over bits of food that had been finished or didn't need cooking. The man who'd brought him in turned to the other brothers.

"This is one of our brethren from the temple in . . . Arakush, was it?" Tekhamun nodded, beginning to eat. "He says that he has important news."

"Do you now?" asked an older man across from him, plucking feathers from a bird. His hair was pure black, even though his face sported a host of lines. "My name is Itkarmen. I'm the leader of this humble temple. What may we call you, brother?"

"Tekhamun," he said after he swallowed a mouthful. "And yes, I have horrible news. A priest from the capital came to my temple telling me that the netkoleh has committed the greatest of blasphemies. He has thrown off the gods and wants the empire to do the same."

The other priests exchanged looks as they continued their tasks.

"This priest," Tekhamun continued, "told me that the Hand has decided to go along with this. He says that we will go along with this abomination while continuing our sacred mission. I say that is an abomination in itself."

The priest that brought him in gave a cough. "That is disturbing news. Are you sure of this, brother?"

"I'm certain of it. His name was Newa. I will never forget that name or face. He was the barer of perverse news and I will see him pay for it."

Looks were exchanged again. Their leader set down the fowl.

"Is there anything else that we should know?"

Tekhamun finished off the last of his food with a smile. "Oh, yes, absolutely. You see, brothers, I have received a vision from our great lord Gu'un. He appeared to me in a dream, telling me that this blasphemy cannot go on. He plunged his blades into me, cutting away all unbelief and doubt within me and leaving me pure for his purpose."

"And what would that purpose be?" Itkarmen

asked.

"To cleave away the nonbelievers." He looked down, smiling, as he thought about how freeing it was to cut down those who would not hear the message of Gu'un. "I have already done so. My village was full of them, laughing, disbelieving baboons who would happily turn their backs on their gods if it meant their continued prosperity. That's why I've come to your temple." He looked around the table at the other priests. "I want you to join me. I've seen a glorious future where Gu'un will usher in a new era of prosperity. I will lead us to it."

The others didn't answer him at first. Then, Itkarmen stood and came beside Tekhamun.

"Thank you for your words, brother." He placed a hand on his shoulder and there was something about it that Tekhamun didn't like. "We will take your words under consideration."

"What is there to consider?" Tekhamun looked up to him with genuine confusion. Had his words not been clear?

The priest who'd lead him deeper in the temple brought him to his feet, the man's hand firm on his arm.

"Let me lead you out now that you've finished eating."

Tekhamun moved along, confused as he was ushered out of the kitchen and back into the temple. The leader and the other priest held his arms in such a way that he couldn't twist and get to his weapons. They threw him back into the street, Tekhamun stumbling and falling into the dust. Without another word, they turned and receded into the darkness.

Tekhamun lay there, mouth agape, staring back at the temple. His own brethren rejected him. They rejected the message of Gu'un. He scowled as he stood, dusting off his robes. They were no better than the other blasphemers. They would be cleaved as well. He turned, retracing his steps to the main square. People milled about even as the sun was starting to recede behind the buildings. He stepped up on the lip of the fountain that brought most people here.

"People of Ketum," he shouted, arms wide. Some stopped to look at him while many continued on their way. "Come! Heed the call of Gu'un. The capital and the netkoleh himself wishes to make us all blasphemers and force us away from our rightful worship of the gods. I, Tekhamun, have been chosen by Gu'un to put a stop to this. Join me and we will cleave the nonbelievers from this land like wheat in the field. We will cut down all those who would give in to the poisonous decree from the capital and live in the renewed favor of the gods!"

His shout echoed off the surrounding walls. He breathed in deeply, trying to calm himself. People stared at him, some looking concerned, most just sharing a disbelieving expression. Tekhamun's face fell as he heard a few derisive chuckles. More started to laugh and whisper as they went by. He felt his face get hot. He couldn't believe that there would be so many here as well. How could they so easily reject Gu'un's chosen messenger? He pulled his curved blades from their holders, spinning them into a fighting position. Blood would have to be spilled here as well.

Tekhamun jumped from the fountain into the crowd, running up on a man who was gossiping jovially with a friend. He cut the man's throat cleanly, the blood spurting into the friend's face. The screaming started then. Tekhamun ignored them, moving on to the nearest target. Four more people went down before he met any opposition. Someone grabbed his wrist from behind, trying to pull him away from a woman. Tekhamun turned, stabbing the interloper in the stomach. The man released his wrist and was rewarded with a stab in the neck.

The square was in utter chaos. Tekhamun looked around and there was no one immediately around him. The crowd was moving away, forcing people to bottleneck down other streets. Through the throngs he saw men, what the town must consider law enforcement, moving towards him. Other men pushed through carrying weapons. Tekhamun made a quick count and realized there were a few too many for even him to fight.

He rushed down the street he saw the fewest oppos-
ing people in, shoving his way through the crowd and using their terror as a cover. Screams deafened him and he
couldn't tell if his oppressors were still giving chase so he
assumed they were. He twisted down several streets getting lost deeper in the city. Another turn led him to a dead
end. He heard shouts along the street behind him and he
ducked behind a pile of discarded boxes until they passed.
Across the narrow street he saw an alley and a small side
door.

Taking a glance around the boxes to make sure the
way was clear he sprinted across, making his way in the
forgotten door. Tekhamun found himself in an abandoned
storeroom. Dust flew up at his arrival and he stifled his
coughs. A couple of rats scurried by, squeaking their pro-
tests at the intruder. He brought his hand over his mouth
to muffle his breathing. Moments passed and he could still
hear the distant uproar he'd caused. Occasionally he heard
people running and shouting as they ran by on the nearby
street. Still, he waited.

The moon was high in the night sky when he dared
to open the door again. He crept out into the evening,
moving with practiced silence. If he couldn't work in the
open, then he would do so by night. Tekhamun moved
slowly through the streets, looking for an appropriate
place to start his work.

He spun around as he felt someone approaching
behind him. A young man brought his hands up immediately at the curved blade pointed in his face. Tekhamun
studied him for a moment. He was no threat.

"What do you want?" he hissed at him.

A handful of other young people came out into the
open, but still sticking to the sides of the small street. "Are
you the killer the peacekeepers are looking for?" the first
man asked with a smile.

"I'm no killer. I am a servant of Gu'un."

"All right," he added hesitantly. "Then why'd you
start killing people in the square?"

"They would not listen to my message."

"And that message is?"

Tekhamun hesitated. He didn't like the calm nature of this man.

"The netkoleh wants us to abandon the gods and I won't let that happen. Gu'un has shown me that people will either stay true in their beliefs or they will be cleaved away." He watched as the young group glanced at each other. "You didn't answer my question. What do you want?"

"We wanted to find you. People say you put down twenty folks in just a minute. We had to meet a man who could do that."

"It... was only five."

"But still, we wanted to find you because... we wanted to learn from you."

Tekhamun was taken aback as the rest of the group nodded. His blade dropped a little. Students had never been a concern of his or even a dream. He looked about the group taking in what details he could in the dim moonlight.

"If I were to take on students, they would have to be fervent believers. Gu'un has spoken directly to me, anointed me and I can't pass any teachings onto nonbelievers."

The young man's smile disappeared and he took on a solemn look. "We can understand that completely. We swear that we'll be your most diligent students and will follow the gods' will."

Tekhamun considered them again. They all looked eager to begin. A feeling he was unfamiliar with swelled up in his heart. Was this happiness? They may be a small group but could they be the first in a wave of true believers? He nodded.

"Then come. We'll begin your lessons in the true path of Gu'un tonight."

CHAPTER EIGHTEEN

Garemba could be so quiet and today was one of those days. It was days like this that it felt like all of the pain, trauma, and sadness that came with the people who fled here leeched into the air killing any chance at happiness for the day. Efah walked through the ground floor of the city carefully, not wanting to scare anyone unnecessarily with her beasts. People still cowered from them, but she noticed how some began to whisper as they passed. She saw the woman whose child she helped pass at a distance and, while she was still in mourning, there was a certain burden lifted from her. Nesi seemed to sense her feelings and rubbed up against her. Efah scratched her head then Usa leaned in for her turn. She happily obliged her.

Efah looked about, studying the city for the first time since coming here. While she was with Kanta's band, she'd wanted to do nothing else but sleep and eat peacefully when she was here. Perhaps be able to get a bath. She'd no interest in what the ancient city actually looked like. She placed a hand on a massive column, running her fingers across the leaves of vines that snaked up its height. It was still solid, a few cracks yes, but solid and sturdy. She began to study more of the structure and saw quite a few other columns that looked in good repair as well. She took a deep breath, letting the humid air fill her lungs. This was a dead city, but parts of its skeleton were still strong and maybe other parts could be repaired. She breathed out. Perhaps, this city could live again.

"Excuse me, miss?"

Efah turned around at the small voice. A teenaged

girl stood ten feet away from her. She was small with a frame that spoke of too many missed meals. Efah smiled at her. In another life, this was her.

"Yes?" she asked, as kind as she could.

"You . . . you are the woman who walks with death?"

"Yes, I am. What's your name?"

The girl looked shocked that she was asked such a question.

"Kima."

"My name is Efah. I'm glad to meet you."

"Glad to meet you too." Every word was an awkward dribble. The girl rubbed an arm. "Can I ask you a question?"

Efah's eyebrows shot up. No one had tried to speak with her since she came here, save Ayodele and Iyola. This was a nice change.

"Yes, please."

"Why did you come to Garemba? Is it cuz we're all gonna die?"

Efah could see the tears threatening to form in the girl's eyes. "No, no. It's nothing like that. I came here because this is where the god of death sent me. You see, he's given me a mission." Efah took a couple of steps towards the girl, wanting to put a little distance between herself and the hyenas. "Do you know the old gods, the ones our people worshiped before the Ega came?"

Kima rubbed her arm again. "I don't know all of them."

"That's fine." Efah paused. "I can teach you. He wanted me to tell everyone to worship the old gods, the real gods of our people. He wants us to do it in our way, not theirs. If we don't, well, terrible things will happen."

Kima took a step closer. "What sort of terrible things?" she asked, her little voice squeaking.

"I . . . don't know for sure. There's something terrible coming. But I do know that if we come back to our true ways, it will protect us."

"Are you sure?"

Efah smiled. "About that I'm sure." She moved over

to the top of a small set of stairs leading into the main courtyard of the city. "Would you like to learn about the old gods?" Efah sat down and patted the spot beside her.

Kima hesitated at first but slowly walked over, keeping a stern eye on the hyenas. Once she was beside her, Efah began telling the girl the stories her mother told her as a child. She was amazed and saddened that clearly, Kima had never heard the tales before. After a while, others stopped what they were doing, moving closer to hear. A few others came to the bottom of the steps, their children sitting down before her to listen in. Before she knew it, a small crowd gathered at the steps, aptly listening into the tales of the gods of their ancestors.

At the back of the crowd Efah saw one disgusted face. One of Ayodele's men stalked the edge of the crowd, scowling intently at her. Efah ignored him and continued with her stories. When she finished the crowd stayed, some coming closer. She looked up to them as Kima ran over to what must be family. They were a tired looking group. One, who sported a bruise on her cheek stood in front of them.

"Lady of death," she called timidly.

"I'm not a lady," Efah responded.

She nodded. "We were wondering . . . if we could stay with you." She glanced back at the rest of her group. "We work for Ayodele and his warriors as . . . as bed warmers. We want to be free."

Efah blinked. She wanted to take them all in. She looked over the young men and women before her. They all looked no older than she was. Usa and Nesi padded up to her, Nesi rubbing a cheek against hers.

"I can't protect you, not truly. I can't be everywhere at once." She thought back to Iyola's threat. "But if you wish to stay with me, then I will do all I can."

A young man came forward. "Are you death's bride?" he asked quietly.

"I am just his messenger."

She looked up and saw Iyola entering the courtyard from deeper in the city. Behind her a handful of men followed. The warlord's right hand saw the group talking and made a beeline toward them. Efah ushered the group behind her. Usa took up a position in front while Nesi stood at the top of the stairs. Efah stood, making it very clear that she saw them coming.

"Those people need to come with us, graverobber," Iyola shouted from a position well out of Usa's reach.

"They've come to me for protection. They won't be used by your people anymore."

Iyola unsheathed her sword, growling. "They belong to us."

Usa jumped forward, her growl drowning out Iyola. Efah came down the stairs. "They are a free people. They belong to no one and now they are under the protection of the god of death." She placed a hand on her companion's back. "Or do you wish to tempt death today, Iyola?"

Efah did her best to keep her heart in check. For a moment it looked like Iyola was ready to try her luck against the hyena. Instead, she sheathed her sword roughly, turning on her heel and leading the other warriors back the way they came. Efah released a breath and forced a smile onto her face. She turned back to the people that had so bravely sought her out.

"Come with me," she said, climbing the stairs again. "I know of a few places that people haven't taken over yet. We'll make our place there and I swear I'll do everything in my power to protect you." Efah raised a prayer to death, hoping to keep her vow.

* * *

Hotemkhar's peaceful morning was pierced by shouting. He was sitting in an inner office looking over correspondence from the capital. As he began reading them, his face settled deeper and deeper into a scowl. First, his request for more troops had been approved but the meager amount they'd committed wouldn't be here for another three months. He resisted the temptation to crumple up that letter and set it aside. Didn't they realize what he was trying to accomplish for the empire? If they could hold the mines, they would control the wealth of the world. Didn't they want that?

The shouts drifted in the high windows of the office, distant at first so he ignored them. He looked over the next letter and his face dropped from the frown. It was time for the Pilgrimage. The netkoleh would be coming to the south personally. He swallowed. The netkoleh was coming and the gold trade was cut off. He shook his head. No, not cut off. Delayed. He looked over the date that it would start and the estimated date of his arrival in the south. It was plenty of time to take over the jungle people's mines.

The shouting grew louder and Hotemkhar slammed down his scrolls down.

"What is that racket?" He stormed to the door, throwing it open and focusing his anger on the servant waiting outside. "Find whoever is making that noise and stop them. They're disturbing my work."

The servant nodded and started to move when an army messenger ran around the corner.

"Magistrate," he shouted coming to a stop before him.

"What is the meaning of this?" Hotemkhar roared. "You've disturbed my household with your howling."

"Commander Tutamen needs to speak with you immediately."

Hotemkhar bristled at the messenger's stern tone. "Concerning what?" he sneered at the man.

"The Bangi," he replied and said no more.

"I will be along shortly."

"The commander said to tell you he meant immediately."

Hotemkhar scowled at him, but the messenger regarded him flatly. "Fine," he finally spat out. "Lead the way."

The messenger nodded and turned around, leading him off in a quick pace that the magistrate had to take long strides to keep up with. He barked for one of his attendants to accompany him, the slender man jumping at his orders. He was knocked into an even fouler mood as they walked into the muggy heat of Nsongo and he was angry that they hadn't had the time to fetch a canopy to keep the damnable sun off of him.

Hotemkhar scowled at everyone and everything by the time they reached the compound of the commander. He pushed his way past the messenger when they reached the room Tutamen was occupying.

"I am not one of your subordinates, Tutamen," he growled.

The messenger came in behind him. "Uh, Magistrate Hotemkhar," he announced without effort.

The commander looked past Hotemkhar. "Thank you, Imhoten. That will be all."

"What is it that you want so badly?" Hotemkhar snapped.

"We have a new kink in our plans." The commander stepped over to a nearby table. On it was a large basket covered with a thick cloth. He pulled off the cloth revealing a pile of ten severed heads.

"These were fished out of the river this morning."

Hotemkhar's hand shot over his nose and mouth. The men's faces were frozen in terror, their eyes staring pointedly.

"Are people killing our soldiers? Are the Nsongans retaliating for the gold trade?"

"These," he said looking at the basket studiously, "are the scouts I sent into forest. Their heads were ripped off. You can tell by the neck." He pointed out the shredded, decaying flesh and Hotemkhar thought he may retch. "This was the entire scouting force." Tutamen looked up to him, his face turning angrier than the usual impassive expression. "I don't know what those people have in that forest, but it is formidable. We need reinforcements. Have you heard anything from the capital?"

"They should be here in three months."

"Good. We-."

"That's too late." Hotemkhar moved to a far side of the room, hoping the smell wouldn't reach him there.

"The Pilgrimage is coming. The netkoleh should be here in six months and I fully plan to have the mines secure by then. We have to."

Tutamen raised an eyebrow. "We should wait."

"We can't wait. Or would you like to tell the netkoleh to his face that we lost the gold trade because *your men* were too enthusiastic in their interrogations?" He waited for a rebuttal and was thankful that the commander had none. "Then you agree with me now that we must go ahead with the invasion?" Tutamen nodded. "I've already spoken with the dara and she's granting us troops to bolster our numbers."

"In exchange for what?" Tutamen asked, narrowing his eyes.

"That is not your concern. You just get your men together as soon as possible. Such an insult cannot go unanswered." He swallowed, tasting bile. "Now, I'm leaving this putrid smelling room. I hope you can begin preparing for your task today."

Tutamen took a deep breath. "I'll begin assembling a force immediately."

"Good."

Hotemkhar turned on his heel, heading as fast as he could outside. He gasped in the fresh air, thanking Urast for her clear skies. He didn't know how the commander could stand to be in that room, breathing that air and looking into those cold eyes. Hotemkhar shook the thought from his head, drawing himself back up. His servant stood meekly behind him.

"Let us return to the compound."

They set back out onto the streets of Nsongo, thankfully in the less crowded noble walkways. Nsongans quickly moved aside as he walked, as they should. One pedestrian caught his attention and he turned his nose up at the pompous high priest. The old man nodded to him as he came closer.

"Good morning," he said, a certain mirth in his voice.

Hotemkhar didn't appreciate it at all. "Good morning," he answered, not pausing.

"I heard about the . . . incident at the river this morning."

The magistrate spun around, his servant nearly colliding with him.

"How do you know?"

"The gossip from the riverside runs through this town like rivulets after a rain. It doesn't appear that your plan is working." There was a small tug to the priest's lips.

"Keep your opinion to yourself, priest."

The priest looked completely serious, all mirth melting away. "You were told to stay away from the other side of the river. Your people got what they deserved for their conceit."

Hotemkhar leaned back, shocked at this lowly, heathen priest's gall. "What is your name, priest? I never learned it."

"Erenemo of the line of Yundasha."

"I will remember that."

The priest turned to walk on. "You should."

Hotemkhar watched him, mouth moving in shock. These people thought too highly of themselves. He turned violently around. After they subdued the jungle people and secured the mines then he would turn his focus on Nsongo. It was time for them to learn their place.

*   *   *

Yutuuan concentrated on his previous injuries in duty to distract himself from the bumps in the road. How long had it been? Six, seven years since he'd been slashed across the chest by a pirate off of Hauila Island? Then there was the time he'd been stabbed in the arm by a smuggler three years ago. That one had hurt for what seemed like ages. But this, this hurt worse. A bad jolt rocked the wagon he rode in, knocking his head against the side. The servant who drove it apologized profusely but Yutuuan waved them off with his good arm.

He pressed that hand against his wounded shoulder, hoping a bit of pressure would alleviate the pain. They'd told him the arrow had made a clean wound, or as clean a wound as a crossbow bolt could make. He smiled wryly. He didn't know how the knowledge of a nice, clean hole in his shoulder was supposed to make him feel better. Another bump and the pain shot through him again. He hoped the healers in Tilizaa had better remedies than the ones in the fishing village. This was agony.

To his relief, the call came from the front of their procession that Tilizaa was near. Yutuuan sighed. His shoulder wasn't the only reason he was eager to make it to Wiluru's easternmost city. The governor had to be filled in on the entire situation. He cursed the attackers. They were already preparing for war coming from the south and now there was some threat to their eastern coast. Now, he had to take time and mend before continuing his mission. He planned to be back in Wiluru in the next month or so. His recovery would delay their trip for weeks.

The governor's sentries were waiting for them at the gates of Tilizaa, saluting him, their commander stepping forward.

"Your majesty," he said bowing curtly. "The governor is waiting your arrival. We're glad to see you're recovering from your injury."

"Thank you," he said, nodding. "I thank the governor for her hospitality."

People hailed him as they passed through the city. Yutuuan waved, wanting nothing more than to have a comfy bed to lay across, wine to drink, and whatever medicines or invocations the healers worked on him. He rested against the side of the wagon as they passed under the arched doorway of the governor's manor. He climbed down from the wagon, refusing his doting attendant's assistance.

"It's my shoulder that's injured, not my legs," he quipped.

Servants came to quickly sweep him inside, taking him to a room. Healers were already waiting for him, three purple robed priestesses. He smiled, thankful, at the women who took immediately to redressing his wound. He winced as they applied a salve that cooled and burned at the same time. As they worked some sort of healing over him, their mouths moving in near silent chants, the door opened. A tall, regal looking woman came in and stopped, waiting with hands clasped until the priestesses were done. Yutuuan took in her high cheekbones and bow shaped mouth. She must have been quite the beauty in her heyday.

The priestesses finished, helping him put his shirt back on. He thanked them, relieved that his pain was nearly gone and turned his attention to the woman who must be the governor.

"Governor Liitaraza, I'm sorry to come to your city in such a sorry state."

She smiled kindly, bowing. "I'm happy that you reached us in good time." She took a seat nearby. "Was it pirates that you battled in Wassu? Your letter said it was an unknown force."

Yutuuan readjusted himself on the bed. "We're still not quite sure who they were. I know they were from farther up the eastern coast, but I've never seen the symbol on their sails before. The name of the place they're from is just a fishing village from what I understand."

The governor tapped her chin. "We have a few residents who have connections to their lands, merchants and sailors who've brought home eastern wives. We'll ask them if they may know of anything."

"You have to fortify the city, governor. And spread word to your other towns and villages."

She chuckled. "My prince, we may be on the outskirts of Wiluru, but we aren't hapless bumpkins. I will make sure my people are protected." Yutuuan felt a bit silly as she winked at him. "But you rest and recover. Tilizaa is a city of renewal and I pray the goddess Ruta leaves you feeling renewed." She smiled and left him.

Yutuuan carefully laid back in the bed, letting the sounds of the manor lull him to sleep. He fell into a peaceful slumber until the sounds of alarm reached him. The prince jolted up in bed, immediately grabbing his injured shoulder as it shot a pain through his chest. He threw off the covers, rushing out of bed and to the door. He stumbled for the handle in the dark, finally throwing it open. Many of his men rushed past, dressing for battle. He grabbed one, the man surprised to see his commander.

"What's going on?"

"More ships have arrived at the docks," the soldier said rushed. "They're attacking the city."

"Then be on your way." Yutuuan released him and the man saluted before carrying on. He rushed to the main areas of the manor, looking about for the head of his guard. He saw him just outside, standing in the middle of the main courtyard, barking orders and shrugging on his armor.

Yutuuan made his way out there. Naret saw him coming and shook his head vigorously.

"No, no, no. Prince Yutuuan you should go back to bed."

"What's the current situation?" he asked, ignoring the admonishment.

Naret breathed out, hard. "Six ships entered the harbor just before moonrise. Their soldiers were well into the city before an alarm could be sounded. Some citizens were killed and there are reports of some being pulled off to their ships, but we haven't had the chance to investigate." He tied on his sword belt, checking that his weapon was secure. Naret looked Yutuuan in the eyes firmly. "We will turn these bastards back. I swear it."

Yutuuan nodded and clasped forearms with the man before he took off into the city with the majority of his guard. He found himself standing in an empty courtyard, nursing an injured shoulder. He'd never felt more useless.

"You there," he called out to a Tilizaan servant who'd been helping the guard get ready. The rushed over to him, bowing. "Where is the governor?"

"She's out in the city, helping evacuate."

"Then bring me a horse."

"I'm sorry, your majesty?"

"Bring me a horse and a sword." Yutuuan looked through the gate to the city. "I will not sit here like some frightened child while people are in danger."

The servant bowed, scurrying off to fulfill his prince's orders. By the time he was ready to go, the sounds of terror were floating up to the manor. Yutuuan let them fuel his anger and focus his mind. He climbed onto the horse with difficulty, ignoring the little nagging voice saying this was a bad idea, and rode out. He took to the streets looking down to the docks with fury. Fires were starting to burn brightly in the night and he knew that each one was someone's life destroyed.

He spurred his horse on, yelling at people just coming outside to leave the city and head for the hills. People dropped what they were doing immediately, grabbing family members and fleeing. He rode down a street lined with the homes of nobility. Lights were on inside the homes and he could tell that they were hoping to ride this out.

"This is Prince Yutuuan," he shouted. "You have to leave the city while you still have time. Do not take anything with you. Items can be replaced." A few shutters cracked open to see who the speaker was. "Don't hesitate! Gather your household and take to the hills. The governor is ushering the city to safety."

People began to run out of their homes, terrified, Yutuuan urging them in the right direction. A pair of women screamed and he turned to see a pair of the attackers running down the street toward them. The prince urged his horse into a run, bowling one of the men down before they could react. He unsheathed his sword with his good arm, the weight feeling heavy in his left hand. He brought it down awkwardly into the man's shoulder, missing his mark completely. He took the moment the man reacted in pain to bring the sword down again, striking him cleanly in the side of the head. The enemy fell and Yutuuan made his horse rear up, bringing heavy hooves down on him.

Yutuuan looked behind him and was satisfied that the nobles were well on their way. He took a few deep breaths and rode to the next streets shouting the evacuation order. The moon was nearly across the sky when he caught up with the governor. She looked over surprised as he rode up.

"Prince Yutuuan, what are you doing out of the manor?"

"I thought I could be of use." He attempted a roguish smile, but gave up. He was exhausted. "When they told me you were evacuating the city, I thought I could at least help save the citizens."

"Thank you," she said watching another group hurry past Tilizaa's gates. "Have you heard anything from the battle?"

Yutuuan looked back to the city. "I haven't. I suppose they're all still engaged with the enemy."

Litiraza cursed, spitting on the ground. "My mother always told me I should have picked up the sword," she muttered looking to the city as well. "I have never felt so useless."

"We do what we can," Yutuuan responded. He counted the distant fires and was thankful that they hadn't multiplied. "For now, it looks like our job is done and we let those who can fight do so." She nodded. Yutuuan sighed, adjusting his sling. He would have to accept a few more days of uselessness.

CHAPTER NINETEEN

Newa woke in a nest of tall grass, for the first time in ages, unsure of his surroundings. He sat up slowly, in case of enemies, taking in the early morning sky and the wide, rolling plains. His memory came back to him. He was traveling. The road lay not far from him and he could see a wagon making its way over a hill in the distance.

He lay back down in the grass, contemplating his next move. There was another city less than a day's walk from here. He'd probably reach it before mid-morning. He could find the next temple, give them the message, and move on quickly. Hesitation gnawed at his insides. But how would this temple receive it? What if they turned as violent as the temple of Koleh in the last city? A handful of sun priests was one thing but fighting his way through a force from his own sect was another altogether. Yet if he abandoned his mission? He'd already lost his apprentice. He didn't want to think of the shame of returning after such a defeat.

The sun rose high enough to be a nuisance and Newa finally pushed himself to his feet. There was only one option and that was forward. He checked his weapons and started out on the road. The next city was thankfully not as crowded as the last. He easily weaved his way through the light morning traffic, cutting in between travelers and wagons. A priestess of the temple of Ula, in her dusty blue dyed robes swept the entryway. He nodded to her in passing, at least giving respect to another follower of the night. She scowled at him in return. He was taken aback. He knew he looked a bit travel worn but their temples had an understanding. He moved on quickly, wanting to get his meeting at the temple over with.

As he neared the plain entrance of Gu'un's temple, something turned in his chest. He felt eyes on him. Newa looked around, searching for the source of his unease. There was no one he could tell that was paying him any attention with the exception of one young man who stood at the temple of Koleh. Newa stopped his pace, staring back in defiance. Shaken, the young man turned and receded into the temple.

Newa looked up to the temple of Gu'un, a wariness settling on him. He should feel at ease entering into the domain of his god, but the feeling wouldn't abate. He entered cautiously taking in every detail of the temple. The actual area of worship was large enough to fit a score of people although he doubted that many had ever assembled here. The side walls were covered in ancient weapons from floor to ceiling. Newa looked to the altar and its richly stained stone. It made him feel a little better that this was such an old temple but not by much.

"Can I help you?"

Newa looked to his right and saw a priest coming from a door leading to the rear of the building. He made a sign of greeting, the priest doing the same.

"Yes," he began slowly. "I need to speak to your leader. I have a message from the Hand."

The priest's eyebrows shot up. "Follow me and I will take you to him."

Newa took a step and stopped. No. "I would prefer if he would speak to me before the altar."

"Very well." The priest gave him a studious look and returned to the back.

The uneasy feeling grew solid in Newa as he waited. It was an odd request but he felt he couldn't go back there. Not alone. Soon enough, another man stepped through the doorway. He was an unassuming man with a crooked nose and a scar that ran through his top lip. This man had been a fighter before his service Newa guessed. He bowed in respect.

"Greetings from the capital, brother."

"Greetings unto you. Now, what message does the Hand have for us?"

There was a tone to his question that seemed like this man didn't like him already. Newa lowered his voice.

"The Hand sent me to tell the other temples of the netkoleh's decree. He wishes to erase the gods from this land." He stopped to gauge the man's reaction.

"And what does the Hand plan to do about this?" the leader asked almost indignantly.

"He plans on playing along. We still fulfill our duty to both our god and our leader."

Newa saw the man's hand going subtly to an extra fold in his robe's skirts. He tensed his body against a possible attack.

"I never knew the Hand would be so selfish," the leader said, his crooked nose wrinkling. "Our temple would never participate in such blasphemy."

"This is an order from your Hand," Newa replied, his eyes flicking to a shadow that passed the outside door. "He is the man that Gu'un has chosen to lead us. You have no choice in the matter."

"Obviously, he has chosen to work in a way that will bring him more glory and not Gu'un. Therefore, we need a new hand."

Newa saw the man's hand close around something and he began backing up. "You do realize this will mark your temple as an enemy."

"With the other temples that feel like we do, we will survive this." He brought out a long dagger, one of the ones with grooves to channel blood. "You will not."

Newa's eye shot open. The other temple must have sent word. He took off toward the door, unsheathing one of his curved blades. The door outside was blocked before he reached it as a priest stood, blocking the way. This one held a sickle. Newa glanced behind him before he reached the man, to see the distance between him and the leader. He only had a few moments to react. He went low, slicing for the priest at the door's legs. The man brought his sickle down to block and parry and Newa allowed him, planting a foot into the man's crotch.

He twisted to the side as the leader was on him. The dagger stabbed in for his side and Newa jumped back, bumping into one of the walls of weapons. The leader stabbed in for him again and Newa dropped his blade to catch the man's arm by wrapping his around the forearm. Newa immediately struck the underside of his elbow, forcing it up with a satisfying pop. He was repaid by a punch to the face. He shook his head, regaining his senses in time to dodge the second blow. He kicked at the man's knee, taking a punch to the ribs.

The priest at the door had enough time to recover from his debilitating blow and charged in, trying to hook one of Newa's legs. Newa moved aside, grabbing a weapon from the wall. He was delighted to realize it was a cleaver. He was good with cleavers. He began to swing at the pair of priests, keeping them from the wall. He kept his swings wild to keep them off balance and to stop them from finding a rhythm in his attacks.

He feigned a stab, making the leader jump back to avoid it and immediately slashed him across the stomach. The other priest called out for more of his brethren to come. Newa kicked him in the knee, bringing him down. He quickly moved to put him in the way of the attack of the leader. A quick chop down and he'd cut halfway into the neck of the lower priest. Newa didn't spare another moment and ran.

Now he was sure why he'd had such an icy reception from the other priests he'd seen. He took a glance back and saw a mob of armed priests pouring out after him. Newa steadied his breath for a long run and made his way through the twists and turns out of town. A brick was thrown by his head and he looked to see a priestess hurrying to find another one. Newa increased his speed. Other shouts came and he realized people were telling the other priests where he was. He cursed them all.

Newa burst out of town, taking off into the thick grasses. He glanced back again and saw the throwing knife sail into his arm. He didn't miss a step but kept up his pace. When the grass was thick enough, he crouched down in it, moving as quickly as he could from the mob hunting him. They were closing the distance faster than he would like and he prayed that this wouldn't come to a fight, but he'd fight until the end if it did. A wind started up and Newa took this chance to move quicker, the swaying grass concealing where he parted their stalks.

The shouts of the priests died down but he knew they hadn't given up their chase. If anything, his sect worked better in silence. He risked a moment of stillness, listening. The sounds of them running through the grass was a good distance away. They'd spread out to find him. Good. If he did have to make this a fight, he could take them out one by one. Newa pressed on.

The chase continued into the afternoon until he reached the end of the grass. He stopped, looking at the scrub lands before him. The sounds of the mob were still moving, but he could barely hear them over his thundering heart. He couldn't just run out there. He'd be completely open and he was exhausted. He looked behind him, even though the grass obstructed his view. But they had to be exhausted too. He pulled back into the grass fully and waited.

Silence soon passed. The sounds of their approach stopped uncomfortably close to him. He wasn't quite sure how many still followed, but he knew he had to attack or die. The wind started again and he glimpsed the top of one of the priest's heads. Newa began to creep that way. He surged forward, taking out his other curved blade, quickly hamstringing the man. He cursed as the man cried out and he stabbed him in the throat on the way down.

Newa took off into the grass again as he heard the others running over. The wind blew with more force and he was afforded a glimpse of another priest. He ran that way, quickly coming up behind him and pulling him into the grass as he killed him. All movement stopped as they realized he was fighting back. Agonizing moments later, he heard the whisper of steps in the grass. Newa crept to-wards the edge of the grass, matching his steps with that of another priest. The wind revealed another priest to him and he threw a small knife for his throat before taking off for the scrub lands.

Newa used what energy he had left to push himself further. Soon he realized he didn't hear the sounds of a chase but he didn't dare look back this time. He rounded a boulder standing sentry in the plains, dropping to his knees but still holding up his blades in case he was attacked. He waited for what seemed like an eternity, sweat pouring in rivulets down his body. There was no sound of pursuit and he chanced a glance around the boulder. Relief washed over him as the landscape was empty. He laid his head back, breathing heavily.

After he regained some of his strength, he took out his map, trying to plot out where he was and how he would get back to the capital or at least to a city he knew would be safe. He tried to estimate how long he'd been chased and how much distance he could have made off road, but his time in the grass had disoriented him. Newa laid his head back again, the realization painful. He was lost.

* * *

Today had been a fine day. Izriamat watched the flags of various houses blowing in the strong wind. She breathed in the salty air wanting to remember this scent for as long as she lived. There would be a storm this afternoon. She could tell by the way the clouds congregated on the horizon. It would probably be one of the last of the season before the drearier weather crawled in on them. A smile crept onto her face. Now would be the perfect time for a walk.

She reached the streets of Wiluru in no time, her steps light without the weight of the capital. Her mission was a heavy one, but she would still enjoy every single moment she had left. Who knew when she'd be able to visit her homeland again? Izriamat pushed away the encroaching sadness. She would only have joy in Wiluru.

People greeted her happily as she walked through

the streets. A tiny pang of guilt and shame lanced through her as many still called her priestess. She assured them that she was no longer in Yutuu's service, but it changed nothing. After a few tries she gave up. An older woman went to her knees, asking for a blessing. Before she could catch herself, she placed her hand on the woman's forehead, reciting the words. She gave the woman a smile despite the feeling creeping up within her. She felt like a fraud. A disbeliever simply making the motions. Izriamat quickly excused herself and moved on.

She walked through the market, taking in the sights of her childhood, the goods from across the sea and the fresh catches of the fishermen. She made her way along the docks, admiring the ships of the navy. Sailors called out praises and wishes of long life as she passed. She waved at them, chuckling at their enthusiasm.

She stopped, suddenly remembering in what path she stood. She looked ahead as it wound down through the rock to a natural set of caves in the shore. Her breathing quickened. She hadn't meant to come here, not back to the temple of Yutuu. She didn't belong here. She wasn't worthy to set foot in such a holy place ever again. But still, a longing to walk in the spot where Wiluru was founded again pulled at her. She took one hesitant step forward. She just wanted to see it again. If only to beg of Yutuu's forgiveness.

One step turned to two and then she was walking down the familiar stairs again. She ran her hand down the smooth wall, memories flooding her. She had been so shy when her mother and father first dedicated her to the temple. She was so small. She'd just learned to read, and her mother explained it was her duty as first born to serve Yutuu. She hadn't understood but she soon learned to love her place here. She loved every moment of her service and thought it would never end. Yet . . . it was stolen from her.

Izriamat felt a shiver run through her as she placed a foot in the deep cave that was the first chamber of the temple. This was where most came to pay their respects. Only the clergy would go to the deepest chamber. She

looked longingly to the stairs that led to the inner sanc-
tum, where her ancestor met Yutuu and began their kingdom.

"You look as if you desire something," came a voice
from behind her.

Izriamat turned and tears immediately sprang in
her eyes at the sight of the old priest.

"Uncle Munabis," she said, throwing her arms
around him.

He chuckled, giving her a squeeze. "I had heard of
your return. I hoped to see you."

"I . . . I wasn't sure about coming here." Her eyes
trailed to the stairs again. "After all that has happened, I'm
not sure I should be here."

He searched her face and she fought the desire to
turn away.

"Are you concerned about your marriage?"

"He forced me to break my vows. I have even
birthed his child."

"But did you break your vows in your heart?" he
asked, a hand on her shoulder.

Izriamat wiped tears away. "I don't know anymore."

He motioned towards the inner chamber. "Then
perhaps you should let Yutuu decide. The chamber is empty at the moment. Go down and speak to him yourself."

"But, uncle-," she protested.

"Go."

She smiled, defeated, and hugged him again.
"Thank you."

Izriamat approached the stairs, leaving her sandals
beside the entryway. The stone was cool beneath her feet
and rubbed smooth by the sea and generations of clergy.
The chamber opened directly out to sea and was only ac-
cessible during low tide. She took in the familiar sight of
the high domed ceiling, her heart fluttering. She felt frozen
on the last stair, but her longing pushed her forward. She
wanted to feel as she did before just as much as she wanted to run from this place and never return.

The sand was a cold, thin layer between her and the

stone. The waves lapped hungrily at the seaward opening, eager to reclaim this space. Izriamat took a deep breath, taking in the scene before she knelt down in the middle of the room. She lowered her head to the floor, facing the sea and the source of their life and livelihood. For moments, words escaped her.

"Dearest Yutuu," she began and faltered again. What was she to say?

"Dearest Yutuu . . ." Tears began to form. "Please forgive me. I am not worthy."

A wave crashed against her face. She sat up in a panic, sputtering. The sea rushed in around her, already swirling around her knees. No, this wasn't right. The tide wasn't due to come in for hours. Izriamat stood as the water rose up to her knees. She waded through the waters, trying futilely to reach the stairs, but the waves were too quick. The room was flooded before she'd even managed to make any headway. The waters rose still, higher than she'd ever known them to. She was tumbling underwater in an instant, her scream sucking in saltwater.

Izriamat struggled as water poured into her throat, filling her lungs. She felt it fill every part of her and then she heard a voice.

Daughter of the line of Olemni. My priestess. Do not despair. You are no further from my fold than any of my other children.

She calmed her struggle at the realization that she wasn't dying.

You have kept your faith in the true path for your people through trials that many would have folded under. For this you are blessed and favored in my sight.

It is time for the line of Olemni to be great again and it shall through you. Stand tall and lead your people to their rightful place. Stand tall and lead your people to a new era in greatness. Stand tall against the heretics of the south. You will be remembered not just as my highest priestess but as the rightful queen you were meant to be.

Izriamat woke on the floor of the chamber, coughing up water and soaked. She struggled to sit up, feeling her braids drag themselves out of the sand. People were rushing in calling her name, but she couldn't react to them. Her eyes were fixed to the sea. Hands helped her to her feet, her legs barely holding her up. The feeling of Yutuu's words washing over her wouldn't leave. It permeated every fiber of her body.

She looked over and saw her uncle with her right arm over his shoulders. His words finally reached her ears.

"Izriamat, are you alright? What happened?"

"Yutuu spoke to me." She smiled weakly. "He spoke to me."

He looked to the other priest who helped her walk. "That is good. I knew that he would still accept you."

A laugh escaped her as tears ran down her face, mixing in with the water still clinging to it.

"He said I was blessed and favored."

"Then so shall it be, niece."

Izriamat laughed and let them escort her out if the chamber. She let her mind linger on the physical connection she felt with her god now. She could never let go of this. She would fight anyone that tried to take it away from her.

* * *

"You have a visitor, my dara."

Ashaki looked up from her reading at the servant's call. "Who is it, Umala?"

The young woman bowed. "Councilmember Oshala."

The dara put her book down, sitting up in her chair.

"Please, bring her in. And bring us something to drink."

Umala bowed again and stepped out. Ashaki was surprised to be getting a visit from one of the councils. They didn't seem to want to be bothered with anything unless it was an important, official matter. She paused, dread settling on her. Oshala was especially loathed to deal with frivolity. This couldn't be good.

Umala ushered in the elderly warrior, Oshala refusing help over the low threshold. Ashaki stood, bowing to her elder.

"Councilmember Oshala," she said warmly. "What a pleasure to have you in my home."

"A pleasure to be welcomed here, Great Dara," she replied, taking a seat gingerly across from her.

"Is your knee bothering you today?" Ashaki asked, noticing the councilmember's movements. "You can take my seat. It's far more comfortable."

"My wife has doted on me enough for today. I don't need you too." She readjusted her position slightly and folded her hands in her lap. "I won't take up much of your time today, but I thought I'd get to you before the rest of the council starts to pester you." She sighed. "You need to choose an abodara."

Ashaki froze. This wasn't a conversation she thought was coming but it wasn't one she was looking forward to.

"An abodara?"

"Yes." She delightfully took the drink Umala offered her. "There were those that wanted to pressure you soon after your ascension, but they were swiftly reminded that your year of mourning wasn't over. However, it has been two years since. There's been talk. So, I came here to give you the suggestion to head them off."

Ashaki took her drink, staring into the clear liquid. She hadn't even given any thought into a successor.

"Do you have anyone in mind?" she asked hollowly.

Oshala waved her hand in front of her. "Oh no. That is not up to me. You served our land. You know people who would make good leaders when the time comes. This decision is up to you." She took a sip from her drink. "Did . . . you have anyone in mind?"

Ashaki frowned, hesitating. She didn't want to show how little thought she'd given to this.

"Well," she began slowly, "there is my cousin." The sharp, dismissive sound that came from the older warrior was far harsher than she felt about him.

Oshala straightened her expression. "Forgive me, Great Dara. I meant no slight to your family. He is a good leader on the field, but a dara . . ." Her eyes wandered aside as she trailed off.

"He was only the first person that came to mind," Ashaki said, waving her hand as if waving away the thought. She paused again, staring into her drink. "I will be sure to give this great thought, councilmember. You and the rest of the council can rest knowing that I will choose the best abodara for the future of Nsongo."

Oshala nodded, her face pulling into a relaxed smile.

"We know you will." She pushed herself up to her feet. Ashaki stood, rushing over to help but the retired general shooed her away. "These old legs just get stiff sometimes." She looked up to Ashaki with a firm gaze. "We look forward to your decision."

Ashaki swallowed and nodded. Umala quickly came up to escort the councilmember out. The dara returned to her seat heavily. She couldn't believe that she already had to consider choosing her successor. She couldn't believe she hadn't already chosen a successor. She sighed, deflating. Was she truly fit for this role?

She told Umala on her return to fetch something to write with. With all that was going on she needed to get at least this important but simple task out of the way. There had to be several worthy candidates from which to choose. Umala set paper, pen, and ink down on the small table nearby. Ashaki immediately began scribbling down names.

Yes, there was her cousin. That would at least preserve the daraship in the same lineage. It wasn't a direct line but at least it would be the same family. He was a good commander. He hadn't risen to third in line for war minister without some talent. But outside of battle, he hadn't shown any sort of leadership qualities. He was out and she was sure everyone would be relieved.

There was also the highly regarded line of Oshala. Ngali had continued her mother's incredible service record and it looked like her eldest daughter would have done the same. Had she not fallen to the Ega. The second daughter was a good warrior and Ashaki had worked alongside her several times during the war. She was a serious woman and her subordinates looked up to her. She had an innate way of inspiring people. Ashaki tapped her chin. And she was always looking for a way to distinguish herself from the legacy of her older sister. She would be a good candidate, but at twenty-seven she was a little old for an abodara. She would still consider her.

There was also the son of Godoama, the second in command. Ashaki smiled thinking of the skilled young warrior. She'd been at the blood-bonding ceremony when Godoama and his husband made the boy their family. He'd let loose a wail that scared the priestess when she pricked his tiny arm. He'd grown up into a good young man. Disciplined. Levelheaded. He would have been an asset in the war. She added him to the list.

"Mother."

Ashaki looked up at Masola hesitating at the entryway to the room.

"Sola," she said smiling. "What is it, heart of my heart?"

Her daughter held her head up confidently and walked over, almost standing at attention when she reached her side. Ashaki had to hold in a chuckle.

"Mother, would it be alright if I were to go into the market this afternoon? I would take my attendants with me."

Ashaki raised an eyebrow. Asking was a nice change. "Yes, of course. I don't see why not."

"Thank you, mother." Masola took half a step away, then paused. "What are you doing?"

"I have to choose an abodara," she sighed. "I'm trying to get a list of names to whittle down."

"I'm not on there."

Ashaki looked up, surprised. Her daughter's face was honest. "Sola, I have a lot to consider."

"But I'm your daughter. Why wouldn't you consider me? Just like grandfather chose uncle Ofaru."

"This isn't something I can just . . . hand out," Ashaki stammered. "You've never even shown interest in what I do."

"But I could. I could." She screwed up her face, fists balling. "You weren't even going to put me on that list, were you?"

Ashaki took a deep breath. She prayed to the ancestors and the gods that the rest of these moody, insolent years would pass by quickly.

"No."

Masola looked ready to cry. "It just proves you've forgotten all about me." She turned on her heel and ran from the room.

"Sola, you come back here immediately!" Ashaki called her name again, but her daughter was gone. She slammed a fist down on the table, rattling the container of ink. She took a few deep breaths and pushed the desire to run after her daughter. If she caught her, she wasn't sure she could hold back her anger. Finally, after several minutes, she returned to her list, cursing the egah, their gods, and every circumstance that led them to this moment.

CHAPTER TWENTY

It was too damned early in the morning for this. Hotemkhar hid his sprawling yawn with his fan and looked over the people gathered by the river. A score of boats were floating from the docks of Nsongo, ready to be filled with soldiers. He shielded his eyes against the low morning sun taking in the sight with only a modicum of satisfaction. He was glad that commander Tutamen was able to assemble an early invasion force so quickly. He was also surprised to see the Nsongans had gathered an impressive looking group of warriors. He was sure the dara would slide them a gaggle of fodder warriors. He nodded, impressed. This looked like all would be successful. He yawned again. But did it have to start at such an hour of the morning?

He snapped for his attendant to follow him, strolling down the docks, looking more closely at the warriors who were chosen for Nsongo. They appeared to be good, sturdy soldiers, even the women they had among them. He looked to one old woman who seemed to be giving orders to them as they prepared. His eyebrows raised. He'd seen this woman before but couldn't place his finger on it. She happened to catch his approach and turned to quickly whisper something sternly to one of the men.

Hotemkhar rushed over wanting to know what his approach had spawned.

"You there, old woman," he called.

The Nsongan soldiers all turned their eyes on him, their hate obvious. Hotemkhar scowled back. He would not be intimidated by these people. The woman turned slowly to him, a hand on her hip. She cocked one gray streaked eyebrow at him instead of a proper answer.

"I'm not familiar with your name."

"I'm war minister Ngali, magistrate." She shifted her weight, keeping that hand firmly on her hip.

"What were you telling that guard when you saw me coming?"

"I was giving him his last instructions."

She didn't elaborate and Hotemkhar's eyes narrowed.

"Which were?" he asked after a moment.

"Between a commander and her warrior."

He released a breath between clenched teeth. He snapped his attention to the warrior she'd spoken to.

"What did she tell you?"

The man smiled pleasantly. "To keep my warriors safe."

"Barabi will be the field commander for our warriors," Ngali cut in. "You can be sure your people will have good, experienced allies in this heinous act."

Hotemkhar ground his teeth. He had half a mind to back hand this old woman for her insolence. "Your opinion of the actions of the Ega are not your concern and you should keep them to yourself."

She nodded curtly. "I'll try to remember that. It's hard, being an old woman and all." There was a snicker from one of the warriors, but they were lost in the assembly.

Hotemkhar stared at her for a moment longer, then turned on his heel. He marched to where Tutamen was talking to a small gathering of the head soldiers for their side.

"Commander," he said as formally as possible.

Tutahmen's shoulders slumped for a moment. He dismissed all the soldiers but one, a slightly short man with light bronze skin. Tutamen rolled his gaze toward his magistrate.

"Yes?"

Hotemkhar came closer to the man than he would normally want to. "I think the Nsongans are conspiring against us."

"Have you just thought of that?" The commander looked over to the add-ons. "They are probably trying to figure a way out of this."

"And what do you plan to do about it?"

"Make sure our men succeed." He put a hand on the young man's shoulder that stood by him. "Magistrate, allow me to introduce field commander Turo. Turo distinguished himself in the last battles of the war and has been an asset to the army since the occupation."

The young man bowed curtly. "A pleasure to meet you, magistrate."

Hotemkhar waved his fan absentmindedly. "Yes, a pleasure." He looked back to Tutamen. "I'm glad you have one of your favorite soldiers in charge. How is that supposed to make me feel better about Nsongan treachery?"

Tutamen gave a slow blink. "Because his orders are to kill anyone who goes against the mission or his orders. The Nsongans will be no problem. They're outnumbered and outmatched. If anything, we'll put them up front to use as shields if it comes to combat." He blinked again. "Does that settle your fears?"

Hotemkhar seethed again. He had to figure out a way to make this man show him respect.

"Yes," he spat.

"Once we've located one of their villages, our men will occupy it and learn where the mines are. Once we do that, we can bring in heavier numbers to invade." Tutamen looked to him, flatly. "I hope you'll have secured our reinforcements by then."

"How dare you question my capabilities," Hotemkhar hissed.

"Do you? I need to know so I can have a proper timetable planned."

"When I receive confirmation from Metkara I'll be sure to inform you."

"Very good. Is there anything else, magistrate?"

Hotemkhar hated the way he slurred his title. "No. That's all."

The commander returned to his men, thoroughly ignoring him. Hotemkhar stepped away to a place where he could properly oversee the sendoff. He noticed that the dara had come to watch as well. He took a small bit of pleasure at the displeasure painted across her face. It was for the best. The south was part of the glorious empire now. They should get used to contributing to the betterment of it. They'd already had three years. It was more than enough time to accept their defeat.

The soldiers climbed onto their small boats, both forces looking solemn. They rowed slowly against the river's current, ending up a little farther down the riverbank on the opposite side. Hotemkhar held his breath as they began to depart the boats and enter the forest. The last of the warriors disappeared into the jungle and he breathed again. He cursed himself for thinking the worst. Vague threats shouldn't be heeded, and his soldiers would prevail over some primitive little jungle people. He stared at the other shore intensely then smiled at last. Their victory would be his glory.

* * *

Yutuuan had long given up on sleep and rose with the sun. Last night had been taxing, exhausting even, but he was still ready to learn the truth of what was going on. Last night had been a true attack. He was loathed to use the word invasion yet, but it gnawed at the back of his mind like a persistent flea. He heard the noise outside as the people of the city were being ushered back home. It seemed like most would return to houses untouched by the enemy, but he didn't want to think of those who lived closer to the docks. He washed and dressed, his shoulder protesting with every movement. A sigh escaped him. He was going to pay for his heroics last night. It was worth the price. Extending his injury was a far less price to pay than losing any more of his people's lives.

The governor's manor was nearly deserted, but those he did see hurried along in their tasks. He came to the main entry room and saw the governor giving orders to soldiers and servants. The bags under her eyes spoke of a sleepless night for her as well. She nodded and gave a weak smile when she saw him approaching.

"Good morning," she said managing a short bow.

"Good morning," he responded. "My attempt at catching a small nap was futile. Did anything else happen last night?"

"No, thankfully." She chuckled. "My servants tried to usher me to sleep, too. Little good it did." She struggled to stifle a yawn. "I've been told that all but one of their ships were taken. The last managed to sail off before the end of the battle. The city guard have gathered the prisoners in a building at the docks."

"Perfect," Yutuuan said, smiling. "I was thinking of having a little chat with our new enemies. Would you care to join me?"

To his surprise, she gave him a flirtatious smile.

"Now, now, my prince. I'm a little old to be charmed away from my duties." He blinked, surprised and he was sure her small chuckle was at his expense. "Perhaps another time."

"Uh, yes." He nodded to her and turned to leave the manor. He shook his head against the embarrassment of being caught off guard. It was unbecoming.

The docks were still hazy in the first rays of sunlight. Smoke lingered in the air causing him to cough a bit as he arrived. Soldiers were still working diligently to clean up from the attack. The bodies of Wiluruan fallen had been taken away early this morning and waited for a proper funeral. Now the unpleasant task of clearing the dead of the enemy was left and few seemed enthusiastic. He greeted the soldiers that were a part of his party as he passed, feeling guilty that he wasn't helping. He stopped more than a few times to see if people had a chance for food and rest, sending them off if they'd said no. He tried to assist in the cleanup but was refused. He sighed heavily. Then he'd just supervise.

A soldier jogged up to him, saluting sharply.

"Your majesty, Naret and the head of Tilizaa's guard are about to start questioning prisoners. If you follow me, I'll take you to the building."

"Lead the way." Yutuuan followed the soldier around a corner to a large building that had been touched on one side by last night's fires. It looked to be a storage house, more than large enough to serve as a makeshift prison. He stepped inside and everyone stopped, saluting. Yutuuan nodded back at them then turned his attention to the captives.

Tied up with arms behind their backs, the group looked pitiful. They were wounded but not anything grievous. Yutuuan walked down the line of them. Hate filled eyes stared back, some bloody, some missing. He passed and then came back to one man. He was dressed better than the rest, the thick, richly patterned fabric blood-stained but still beautiful. Something noblewomen would have paid a pretty penny for. Yutuuan smiled darkly.

"Is this their captain?" he asked, still focused on the man.

"From what we can tell," answered Naret.

"We found an interpreter," commented the head of Tilizaa's guard.

Yutuuan looked back at the merchant coming forward. There was a nervousness about him and a hint of shame as he looked to the prisoners.

"What's your name, merchant?" Yutuuan asked, trying to sound as friendly as possible considering the circumstances.

"Zalim, your majesty," he answered lowering his head.

"How long have you lived in Tilizaa, Zalim?"

"Ten years this spring."

"And did you have regular contact with your people when they came to port?"

The man looked up. "I have a cousin that works on a ship. We would speak when he came but . . . I haven't heard from him in nearly a year and a half." He looked to the captives kneeling on the floor. "We haven't seen a ship from home in that long."

Yutuuan stopped, thinking. Rahbahn ships were infrequent but to not see one in over a year. That was suspicious.

"Ask them what country or kingdom they come from."

Zalim nodded and began speaking to a few of the captives. The first two didn't want to talk, turning their heads from him. He came to the captain and asked again. The captain looked him in his eye and answered. Yutuuan looked over to Zalim when he hesitated to translate. Zalim glanced to him.

"He says he won't speak to a foreigner's dog."

"Tell him he can talk now, or we can start carving him."

Zalim translated again. The captain laughed, looking up to Yutuuan. He began speaking quickly, his tone dangerous. Zalim's face went slack. He spoke to him again and the captain spat out his answer. Zalim shook his head, eyes wide and confused.

"What is it?" Naret asked from the other side of him.

Zalim swallowed. "He says he is not afraid of torture. He will gladly walk to the other side and enter the halls of his ancestors a proud warrior." He licked his lips. "He says . . . you will fall to the empire of Fahzi. They will take your cities one by one until you are under heel. Your families will be divided up as slaves and there will be no one left to mourn your broken bodies."

Yutuuan looked to the interpreter. "What did you ask him?"

"I asked him of my city, Masharadi, what had become of it."

"And?" Yutuuan prodded.

"He says it is a glorious city, ready to birth forth the soldiers of the empire." Zalim shook his head. "That is not what I left." He licked his lips again. "May I go? We have a newborn and my wife will need help with the other children."

"Of course." He watched the man leave then turned his attention back to the captain. The man smiled up at him, confident even in his defeat.

"Naret," he called. His bodyguard was by his side immediately. "Send word to the fleet at Falee's Bay. Have them bring no less than five ships here. We need them patrolling our eastern coast as soon as possible."

"Right away, your majesty."

The head of his warriors took to his task immediately. Yutuuan turned to the head of Tilizaa's guard.

"I would like to see that these men get fed." The guard looked shocked. "We need them ready to tell us everything we need to know about their Fahzi empire."

* * *

Erenemo shrugged on the plain robes borrowed from a servant's husband. He wrapped the muted *abisi* around his waist, noting how much more it took to wrap around his stomach than the last time he wore one. He gave a twisted smile as he used the rest to come over his shoulders and head. Such was proof of an always full belly. He checked over his outfit, making sure that there were no distinguishing features that could out him, and exited through the temple's rear door.

He kept his head down, the cloth of the abisi pulled low to obscure most of his face. There were few people out on the streets now as the day was winding down. Only the barest of light from sunset pierced through the city streets and it was hard to see. He'd considered bringing a lamp but was afraid of someone recognizing him. Instead, he waited until a night of the full moon to make his late trek into the city. Already, it was shining down on the walkways, like a beacon from heaven. Erenemo nodded in satisfaction. If he could make this quick and avoid detection, this would be a most blessed night.

He walked past the shops and homes of artisans. He could hear their families readying for dinner, laughing and communing with each other after a hard day's work. Once past the artisans, the streets narrowed and Erenemo put a hand to the knife he'd tucked away in his *abisi* in case of danger. He may not have been a warrior, but he had grown up in the household of one. He'd be damned if he would be brought down by a mere thief.

A woman whistled curtly at him from the door of an old compound. He glanced over and saw her, gowns entirely too small, pulling on every curve. He wrinkled his nose at the prostitute, holding up his hand as a rebuke as he passed. She laughed and turned her attention to the next passerby. Erenemo was starting to feel a bit claustrophobic when he reached what he thought might be his destination. He stopped in front of a low building with a thick, old-fashioned thatched roof. The building itself looked old but kept up for the most part. He hesitated before the door, painted the stark black and green of an herbalist.

Unsure of what to do, he pushed on the door. It gave easily under his hand and he entered the darkness. His eyes took a moment to adjust, but he realized it wasn't complete darkness but just dimly lit. He placed a hand on the handle of his dagger and stepped in further, closing the door behind him. The room was wide with a maze of shelves that held clay jars of every size. A pair of lamps sat on a table near the back of the room and he could make out several mortars and pestles.

"Hello," he called out. No one seemed to be about which sparked his anger. The time of this meeting had been chosen by them.

"Hello," he repeated curtly.

"Patience. I heard you," replied a voice from somewhere.

Erenemo searched the room for the source and finally saw movement from what he realized was a small doorway. The woman who came out had a head full of braids that were pulled up into a messy ball. She wore a leather apron that had a host of dark, multicolored stains on it. Her fingertips were stained as well. Something about this woman unsettled him and it wasn't just her occupation. He approached carefully as she stood at her worktable.

"Are you the herbalist, Unazimali?"

"You came all this way to my shop after setting up a meeting with me and you're not sure?" Her laugh grated on his mood. "Yes, I'm Unazimali. What can I do for you tonight, great priest Erenemo?"

He dared come farther in the shop, wanting to get farther away from the door in case anyone may be eavesdropping. "I need a poison and I was directed to you."

She raised an eyebrow, looking him up and down. "A poison?" she asked as she began taking down jars from her shelves. "What sort of threat are we dealing with?"

"A great threat."

Unazimali weaved around her shop, picking up jars and inspecting their contents, sniffing at some, and putting them away. "That doesn't tell me much." She returned a few of the jars to her worktable. "Is it beast or man? Are we looking to bring them low . . . or kill them?" She fixed him with a pointed stare as she waited for an answer.

"I just need a potent poison, herbalist."

She chuckled and blinked at him slowly. "The need determines the poison, *priest*. Man, or beast?"

"Man. And I want them dead."

The herbalist began pulling ingredients and placing them in a series of bowls. Some were just dried herbs. Some were items he wasn't sure he recognized. She smiled at his reaction when one of the items was a small, dried lizard.

"Will you be placing this in their food? Perhaps in some of their oils or salves?"

Erenemo paused. He'd been so focused on procuring the poison that he hadn't thought about the delivery of it.

"I would like to put it in their drink."

She nodded. "Something that won't be found in the bottom of a cup." She set aside a few of the ingredients, replacing them with a few others from the shelf behind her. "Will you need an antidote, just in case?" she asked looking up as she began to grind a strange looking collection of stems.

"No," he answered firmly.

"Good to know you're committed."

Erenemo watched her for a moment, impressed by her quick decisive work.

"You seem to have done this many times."

"Why do you think you were sent to me?" she chuckled. "Do you think we herbalists make our living by just healing? Why do you think bodies turn up without a wound on them, eh?" She laughed. "How do you think people are suddenly free of no longer wanted partners? Come now. Don't be so naive."

He frowned at being called naive. But he hadn't given thought to how much a poisoner's talents would be needed in a city like this. If he became the new dara, or at least steer the new one, such services may be needed more than once. He could think of a few whose deaths, peaceful and in their sleep, wouldn't be questioned. He watched her swiftly adding more ingredients. He also liked how she didn't ask too many questions. But one of his own remained.

"Unazimali," he called. She didn't look up but sounded her attention. "How can I be sure that you won't tell others of this?"

The look she gave him reminded him of his wife when he said something foolish.

"How would that benefit me?"

He nodded. "I may need your talents again."

"Good. I love repeat customers." She gave the new mixture one last stir and poured it into a tiny container, barely bigger than his thumb. "This should serve your needs. Mix it in with their drink, make sure it's completely dissolved, or it may be tasted, and they will leave this world quickly."

"How quickly?"

"It depends on how much you give them. Half the box, they will last hours. The entire mixture will be near immediate."

He nodded, taking it when she offered it. He quickly

tucked it into his *abisi,* secure and out of sight. He took off three of his iron bracelets and handed them over. Unazimali grinned as she examined the weight.

"That should be more than enough payment."

"More than enough," she said bobbing her head. "Thank you, great priest."

Erenemo turned, leaving the shop cautiously. He made sure his disguise was secure before making his way back home. The poison was a pleasant weight at his waist. He placed a hand over the tiny container, a satisfied smile coming to his face. This was the first half of a better future for Nsongo and himself.

CHAPTER TWENTY-ONE

Efah knew her peace in Garemba was destined to end at some time and she had felt it coming for a few days. Her new charges were a wonderful group and they'd settled into their new lives and surroundings well. Efah wished she had someplace to take them that wasn't the city they'd been through so much in but at least there was some semblance of peace in this part of the city. They were in one of the most eastern areas, near where she'd talked to her deity. It was nice and quiet. They'd even discovered rooms that were virtually untouched because of the rubble blocking the entryways. Together they'd worked to clear a path and now shared a row of what looked like old storage rooms.

Over the past few days a few others came to ask for protection as well. Efah was still reluctant since it was only Nesi and Usa standing between them and Ayodele's people. She accepted them anyway, wanting to believe that with her they could find rest.

Efah sat out in a large room with a collapsed roof watching a trio of children playing with a ball someone had cobbled together from odds and ends. It was amazing to her how quickly children could forget their troubles. It was as if this city was the safest place in the world to them right now. A sharp bark from Usa caught her attention and she saw her hyena just outside of a doorway. She told the kids she'd be right back and walked over.

Usa seemed angry as she approached her.

"What's the matter?" she asked suddenly worried. Usa moved off a bit and Efah could hear the sound of scrambling as she came into the next room. Vultures perched on window ledges, looking down and shuffling back and forth. She turned her attention to what seemed to be capturing theirs. A man lay on the floor, bloodied and mangled. Efah took a step further and recognized him as one of the main guards that would be at the gate into the city. This wasn't her hyenas' work. The body would have been worse. There were torn holes all over his body. Beak sized holes. She glanced up at the vultures. They seemed unashamed as they looked back at her.

"Did he try to sneak in here?" she asked, and she felt confirmation in Usa's stare. "Get rid of his body. Then join your sister and look for more. If they try to attack anyone . . . kill them." Usa gave a short bark and padded off.

Efah breathed a sigh of relief as she turned back to the kids and their game. The peace lasted a few hours longer before it was broken by screams. She jumped up from her seat, running inside where she and her people had taken refuge. People ran towards her and behind them Efah could see warriors who were minions of Ayodele. She ushered her charges behind her, coming forward to stand between them.

"What do you want here?" she asked forcefully.

The woman in charge sneered at her. "Your animals aren't here to protect you now. Those people are coming with us."

Efah's heart raced. She tried to keep up a brave face but who knew where Usa and Nesi were.

"You'll never take them," she said as confidently as she could. Her declaration was met with chuckles. They started to advance and Efah took a step back. She called for her hyenas, her voice echoing around the hall. The attackers laughed at her desperation.

Then the sound of wings filled the hall. Everyone looked around trying to find the source of the noise. From every room, vultures poured out, swarming over the attackers. Efah scrambled back and the hallway was filled with blood curdling screams. The vultures flew faster than she thought birds of their size could and blood soon began to pool at the bottom of their swarm. The screams began to fall away one by one, the flock taking off after a pair of warriors that fled down the hallway.

"Stop," Efah commanded and the vultures immediately broke free, flying away into the city. She walked toward them as they continued to limp away. Usa and Nesi bounded down the hall blocking the way. Their mouths were already bloody. They must have taken care of more warriors trying to sneak in. Efah moved closer and the men struggled to focus on one target. Her hyenas ushered them toward her.

"Did Iyola send you or did Ayodele himself?" she asked.

"Ayodele," one of the men slurred out, his lip torn.

"But it was Iyola's idea," the other blurted out.

"Thank you." Efah stepped up to him, placing her hand to his chest. She could feel his life pulsing under her fingers, erratic but still strong. He would make it through this attack, although scarred. She took the ribbon of his life between her fingers, plucking it like a stubborn weed in a field. The man dropped, eyes staring vacantly down the hallway. "Nesi, Usa, let the other pass."

Her hyenas stepped aside, the man trembling.

"Go," Efah told him. "Go to Ayodele and tell him what happened." The man turned and ran as best as he could. Efah walked calmly behind him, side stepping the blood on the floor.

"Stay here," she called behind her to her people. "The vultures will protect you."

She followed the injured warrior to the third floor, Usa and Nesi flanking her. They found Ayodele in one of his rooms, feasting on a roasted warthog while so many of the city's residents were near starving. The warrior collapsed into the room, half crawling his way to his master. Ayodele stood immediately.

"What happened to you?"

Efah entered soon after him, her hyenas pushing open the door farther. "You sent your warriors after a protected people. I allowed this one to keep his life."

"Iyola!" Ayodele inched away from the table, his

eyes darting about the room. Efah didn't know if he was
looking for a weapon or another way out but neither was to
be found.

Efah stared at the man that had made the lives of so
many so difficult. "I know that attacking me and my people wasn't your idea. I know you have enough sense not to
anger the chosen of death. Your warrior told me that it was
Iyola's idea."

"Yes," he stammered, eyes darting between the hyenas who were perfectly silent. "It was all Iyola's idea."

As if summoned, the woman appeared in the doorway behind them. She stopped just shy of Efah's beasts;
sword already drawn. Taking in the scene, she launched
into an attack trying to slice down Nesi, but Usa was too
quick. The hyena lunged forward, catching Iyola at the elbow and jerking her forward. Ayodele's chief minion
screamed as teeth sunk into her arm. She tried to swing
with her sword arm but Usa jerked her again, the bones of
her forearm snapping.

Efah frowned at her, all her hate focused on this one
woman.

"Stop moving and you'll keep at least one arm."

Reluctant tears began to flow from her eyes, but the
second in command remained still. Efah turned so she
could look back and forth at them.

"There will be peace in this city," she said with finality. "You will leave the people who've come to me alone
and if any more decide to come they will be under my protection. Send any more troops and you will receive a pile of
meat in return, if I feel so generous." She pinned down
Ayodele with her eyes. "I won't say this again."

Ayodele nodded vigorously. "I swear it. We won't
bother you again."

"Good." She turned to Iyola. The woman looked at
her with the focus brought on by pure hate. Efah took a
breath. She would still be a problem.

"Take it," she said to Usa. The hyena closed her jaw,
freeing the majority of Iyola's arm from her body. Iyola fell
to the floor clutching the spurting stump. Usa crunched

twice and swallowed it.

Efah scratched Usa on the neck, looking one last time at the both of them. The fear on Ayodele's face and the abject pain Iyola was in gave her a satisfaction like no other. They should know the terror that they've instilled in others. She hoped that they heeded the lesson. A repeat of it would only lead to death.

* * *

Bakari coughed at the road dust kicked up by their arrival. The city of Djelebe rose before them in the plains and he'd never been so happy to see civilization before. The beginning of the Pilgrimage had been unusually dry with an unrelenting sun. It was baking his entourage and he grew tired of the monotony of the road between cities. One night the schedule had them making camp outside of a town and Bakari decided to stay in his tent rather than suffer the hospitality of some flea ridden leader's home. To have a proper city to dwell in was welcome.

He breathed out against the heat. The spread of the proclamations seemed to be going well. As he took stock of the country's riches, his guards and the fifteen agents of the Arakgu'un Hetsaf sent with him swept through the city, taking down the temples. They made sure his word was carried out swiftly and there were none who dared oppose him.

If only Arkoleh could be here to watch this new era swept in. And Izriamat. His mind swept to his northern queen and a frown settled on his face. There still hadn't been any word of when she would be returning. They had yet to run into her traveling retinue. He could understand her taking some time visiting her family. He was sure she must miss them greatly, but she knew that he needed her. He thought he'd made it clear that they had a mission to carry out and she was an integral part of it. There was no way she'd forgotten. And his son needed his mother. This was very odd behavior indeed.

His heart rejoiced when they reached Djelebe's

gates. The great entrance to the scholarly city creaked open and Bakari studied the carvings of them carefully. If there were any depictions of the gods, they would have to be destroyed. He stopped his horse, scrutinizing them. Thankfully, they were just of old kings. The gates would be spared.

Inside, a great cheer rose from the crowd gathered to greet him. He smiled, taking it in. He saw the infamous scholars crowded near the streets leading to the great university of Djelebe. His father had been sent to learn there as a young man and he'd deemed it unnecessary for Bakari to do so. He often wondered what secrets he might have learned if he'd attended. Still, he didn't envy the scholar's life cooped up in dusty libraries, nose down in books. He could think of far better ways to spend his time.

His entourage moved down the streets slowly, the party that would be spending their time in the city having to bottleneck to get into the deeper parts. Finally, they reached the residence of Djelebe's governor. The king and a large group were gathered outside to meet them. Bakari took in the balding man with humor. Time had moved in on the man and not kindly. He turned his gaze to who obviously had to be his wives and children. They were plain woman but, being a scholar, he probably chose them for their intellect or something of the sort. His children were definitely his. Each one, from the eldest son to the youngest girl, had some distinct aspect of his face. One girl unfortunately so.

"Welcome to Djelebe, netkoleh," the governor said bowing deeply. His people followed suit. "We hope your journey here was a good one."

Bakari dismounted his horse. "It was dry and hot, Governor Mgobe. Something to clear all of this dust from my throat would be nice."

Mgobe quickly ordered two of his people to fetch something to drink. "Please, netkoleh-."

"Emperor," Bakari corrected. "You all will call me emperor." He looked around the people still gathered along the streets. "I am the netkoleh no more," he said, raising his voice. He turned to face them. "The gods are dead to us and we will no longer worship them. Prepare yourselves to live in a new age where man will decide his own fate. Be prepared to have your own victories sung and recorded in history and not attributed to the favor of some non-existent celestial force. I, your emperor, welcome you to the age of man!"

Bakari waited for the crowd's reaction and was met with silence. His temper flared for a moment, but he remembered that his people needed to be pushed forward.

"I understand you may be confused, perhaps even hurt at my words. When my son died, I entered a state of confusion as well. I asked myself over and over why the gods would allow him to die. I asked them over and over again why they would do so. My questions were met with silence. A stark, overbearing silence. That, my people, is when I realized that they were not there to answer me, and we are on our own on this earth.

"It will be frightening at first, to walk on your own. But you will come to know the satisfaction of tasting the fruits of your own labor and knowing your life has been your own." He turned back to the governor, leaving the crowd to take in his words. "Can we get out of this blasted sun?"

The man's mouth moved like a fish. "Yes, net-, my emperor."

Thankfully, he regained his composure and led Bakari and his immediate attendants and guards inside the building.

Bakari looked around the structure. Everything looked exactly the same as his last trip here. This palace, this city never changed. It was the same plain, mudbrick walls and ugly geometric decorations he'd first seen in his youth. But this place was ancient. They had their own ways. They'd been allowed to keep their customs and culture by his long dead ancestor that conquered them. He gave the surroundings another disapproving look. Perhaps it was time for that to end.

The king led him to a large meeting room. In it were

their typical low tables with cushions surrounding them for seating. Mgobe bowed to him again and servants flocked to the table he would be seated at, setting down glass cups and containers of drink. The king motioned to the plushest pile of cushions.

"Please, emperor, have a seat."

Bakari took his place, wishing he didn't have to sit so low. One would think there would be at least one chair in this city so he wouldn't be level with everyone. He took in the king's nervousness as he drank the beer offered him. It was good, better than he remembered.

"I'm sure my proclamation came as a shock," he said as the man's family was seated nearby.

Mgobe held his cup nervously, twisting it back and forth. "Yes, it is. And you are right. It is a frightening prospect." The man glanced up at him, too fast for Bakari to read his face. "Will we have to abandon *all* of the gods?"

"All of them."

The king was quiet for a moment and Bakari didn't like it.

"Even our own?"

Bakari rocked his cup back and forth. "Did I not say all?"

"Yes, you did," Mgobe nodded. "I'm sorry, emperor. I just wanted to be clear."

"While we're here I will see that the cleaning of your temples is begun, and the priesthood dismantled." One of the wives, began coughing on her drink, the others trying to help. Bakari threw a look of contempt their way.

"My accountants will begin the tallying of your storehouses today. My plan is to make this pilgrimage swift so that we can free the entire empire from the shackles of the gods."

Mgobe finally sipped from his drink. "Will you be going through the library?"

Bakari tilted his head. "Should I?"

"Not if you don't want to, emperor. It is books on sciences, math, and history. Nothing concerning religion except to chronicle points in the past."

Something about the way he spoke bothered Bakari.

"Tomorrow we will go there." He paused. "And I will go through your university while I am here. I wish to know what's being taught to my people."

Mgobe lowered his head for a moment. "Very well, emperor." The king put an obviously forced smile on. "But please, for now enjoy the hospitality of Djelebe." Bakari nodded and allowed them to feast his arrival, never taking his attention away from the nervous man across from him.

* * *

Arkoleh watched her daughters play in the court-yard, thankful for an afternoon with them. Today's game was tag and her second youngest was currently the chaser. She laughed as her eldest deftly evaded her sister's reach. Their laughs echoed off the high walls, fading into the open air. Her youngest soon ran over to her, eyes wide with crocodile tears.

"Mama," she said, her still chubby hands wrinkling her skirts. "Sisters are too fast. My legs too little."

Arkoleh stroked her thick braids as her little one buried her face in her lap.

"You will get faster in time, my shooting star." She raised the little girl's chin. "And if they are too fast, you will have to wait like the cobra from our story and strike." Arkoleh shot her hand out, ticking her daughter behind the ear.

Her daughter put her head back down, moving her mother's hand to her hair.

"I miss Kolehtun," she said quietly. "He was fast-est."

Arkoleh bit her lip. "I miss him too." She stroked her hair, fighting back tears. "Yes, he was the fastest. He loved playing chase with you girls. I know he loved you all very much."

She sat, quietly stoking her daughter's hair, watching as her other children's game somehow turned into a tickling match and they all fell exhausted to the ground.

Arkoleh gave a sad smile. Her daughters were such a joy, but even they couldn't fill this hole still in her heart. Her youngest ran back off to join her sisters, happy again. She had to wonder if anything would.

A servant hurried to her, bowing lowly. "My empress, the chancellor says that he wishes to speak with you. He is in the north facing meeting room."

Arkoleh frowned. "Tell him I will be along shortly." She stood, sad to leave her girls. "Daughters," she called, and they looked up from their pile on the floor. "I have to attend to business." They all rushed up to hug her. Arkoleh smiled, surprised as her eldest was nearly at her shoulder. She was going to be tall like her father.

"I love you all."

She untangled herself from her children and walked to the appointed meeting room. She frowned again as she found Hetsaf at a series of windows overlooking the great lake. His hands were clasped behind his back. He stood like this room belonged to him and all that lay before him.

"You needed to speak with me," she called, trying her best to sound as authoritative as possible.

He turned smoothly and bowed to her. "My empress."

"Well," she began, coming closer, "what is so important? I was with my children."

"And I apologize for that, but we have urgent matters to attend to. There is a rebellion on the northwest side of the city." He turned back to the windows, pointing to an area just to the farthest left. "I've already sent extra city guard to subdue it, but it has taken some time."

Arkoleh couldn't hide the shock on her face. "A rebellion? What are they rebelling for?"

Hetsaf raised an eyebrow when he looked back to her. "They don't want to follow the emperor's orders. They're demanding that the temples be reinstated."

"Well, that won't happen." She worried her lip. "How far has it spread?"

"Not far although it has consumed most of the district. I'm hoping to have it put down by the afternoon."

Arkoleh nodded. "Very good. Is there anything else?"

Hetsaf stared at her. "What are your commands, empress?"

"My commands?"

"Yes, your commands." He didn't speak for a moment. "Do you wish for me to send more guards to the district? What will you want done with the prisoners if you want any prisoners taken at all? Your commands?"

Arkoleh faltered. She hadn't thought of such things. She'd assumed that all would be peaceful while her husband was gone. Hetsaf was staring at her with that damned impassive face of his. It felt like he was judging her every movement.

"Send more guards. If we can have the rebellion put down as soon as possible, that would be good." She paused. "Anyone taken alive should be executed. We . . . we should make a point."

Hetsaf nodded and bowed. "Very well, empress."

He paused before he turned to leave, and an ugly anger rose up.

"Do you have something else to say, Hetsaf?" she snapped.

Once again, he paused before turning back to her. His eyes slid to the side as he was obviously thinking.

"You could stand to be more decisive, empress."

Arkoleh narrowed her eyes. That wasn't what he wanted to say.

"You doubt me," she said scowling.

"I do not." His face was still a blank slate. "The emperor has deemed you worthy to rule in his stead and I will fulfill my duty to him by carrying out your orders."

She seethed. There wasn't a single part of his statement that said that he had any loyalty toward her. Did he think she would be fine with that, that she would have missed that?

"I am the empress," she said, temper rising. "I am my husband's voice while he is gone. You will obey me just as you would obey him. Do you understand, Hetsaf?"

"You are just his wife," he said lowly.

Arkoleh struck him before she realized it. He blinked as his head was turned. She ignored the immediate burning in her palm and mustered her courage.

"You are a servant. A servant! You are a tool that serves this empire. Remember it because there are many others who would *love* to take your place." He straightened his posture, looking at her with a hate in his eyes. "Now go and follow your empress's commands."

He bowed lowly, a full and proper bow this time. "Yes, empress." He left the room without any hesitation.

Arkoleh brought her hand up to blow on it. She would be respected, damn it. If he thought less of her then he'd best keep it to himself from now on and just do his duty. She wouldn't stand for any more insolence from a man she only half liked in the first place. She shook her hand out and started back to the courtyard with her daughters. She needed the comfort of their presence again.

CHAPTER TWENTY-TWO

Yutuuan sat, tapping the end of the reed against his chin. His attempts at writing this letter home had been fruitless. Word had been sent about the attacks yesterday, but he didn't know how he would word that he wouldn't be returning any time soon. He dipped his reed back in the ink. He apologized for not being there for some time, but he was sure that they would hold to their plan and convince their father to go against the netkoleh. Umakaal would have to act as the voice of the royal family of Wiluru in his stead. He nodded as the words became easier. He knew she had the fire to do it.

He called for one of the manor servants as he signed and sealed his letter.

"See that this is sent off to the capital immediately." They bowed and set off for their task.

Yutuuan stretched and immediately crumpled in pain. He cradled his slinged arm and smiled through it. Another session with the healers and the pain had been less but it was still fiercely there. They told him he'd have a hole through his shoulder blade for the rest of his life and his sword arm would probably never be the same. They could only see with time and more healing. He supposed that he should be thankful that he was alive. The bolt could have hit a hand's width over, and he wouldn't be here. With his good hand he made a sign of thanks to Yutuu for the bad shots in the world.

"Prince Yutuuan." He looked up to see the governor standing in the doorway. "I pray I'm not disturbing you."

"No, not at all," he replied. "Just making myself miserable by forgetting my injury."

She chuckled, entering and taking a seat across the table from him.

"I can see if the healers can come again today."

"No, I don't want to bother them. They're busy enough from the last attack." He smiled brighter to try and throw off her concerned expression.

"How are the townspeople holding up? I've been caught up in orders and sending messages for the past few days."

She sighed. "They're terrified, understandably. We lost a few who were caught up in the initial attack. But the healers have been able to save so many. They've been working so hard. I need to make quite the donation to the temple."

"I think we need to serve the temple for a time after all they've done."

She laughed and Yutuuan found himself smiling in earnest. He checked himself before she looked at him again.

"You may be right. I think you would look quite fetching in a priestess's robes." She winked and he was caught off guard again.

He cleared his throat. "How has the increase in defense gone?"

"I pray reinforcements get here soon, because between you and me, we're stretched thin. I've had to send members of our city guard to the other towns and villages along the coast. I pray the Rahbahn don't attack again anytime soon." She played with a bit of fading paint on the table. "I'm not sure we'll make it."

"We'll make it. We'll fight until the enemy has turn tail and sailed off."

She looked at him flatly. "Prince Yutuuan, you have one good arm right now."

"And I'll just have to learn to use it."

"Absolutely not." He winced at her tone. "How will I look my king and queen in the eyes knowing I let their only son go off into battle injured? No. No, that's not happening."

He sighed. "Ah, well. I tried."

She chuckled again. "But you've been so cooped up in this room, would you care to take a ride to inspect the city's defenses. As the leader of our military, I'd love your input."

He stood up from the table. "I would be glad to, governor Liitaraza."

Yutuuan moved to put on his outer long duster and she moved to help him. He was surprised at the care she took to mind his injured shoulder. She stepped in front of him to fasten the top button and he found himself taking in the streaks of white in her dark braids, like lightning was captured in her hair. She looked up at him and he noticed what a clear, deep brown her eyes were, a deep brown a man could get lost in.

"Are you ready?" she asked with a sly smile.

Yutuuan stopped himself. "Yes, absolutely."

They took to the streets of Tilizaa, a handful of guards with them. The city was still so deathly quiet compared to when he'd first arrived, and it pained him to see it so. It was such a stark contrast. The signs of life were still there, little bits of normal life trying to creep back into the everyday. Instead of setting up at the town's market, food merchants were going door to door. The baker was back at work and Yutuuan smiled at the scent of what must have been the last loaves of the day. He had to make sure these people could get back to a normal life.

They made their way to the docks, soldiers saluting them as they passed. Yutuuan was impressed. In just a short amount of time the governor had put together a decent defense against the invaders. Most of the piers had been rendered impassable. Great wooden spikes salvaged from buildings ruined in the attack, rose from the water, cutting off any ship. A pair of Tilizaa's own ships now patrolled the waters constantly, looking out for incoming vessels. If they managed to make it to the docks, she'd made sure the other of the city's ships were completely manned with both her mariners and city guard.

"This is impressive, governor." He nodded as he

looked over the side of the dock. More spikes were hidden just under the surface so a ship couldn't see them.

"Perhaps we can get some of the citizens to help clear them out once reinforcements arrive."

The governor opened her mouth to reply but was cut off by the call of alarm. They both looked out to the sea where the patrol ships were moving into an attack formation. Liitaraza shouted to the man giving the alarm.

"What's going on?"

"They signaled that they saw three ships approaching," he shouted back. "Enemy sails."

"Shit," Yutuuan spat out. This Fahzi empire moved quickly. The governor began barking orders to her people while he searched for his.

"Governor, I'll gather my soldiers to the docks in case . . ." He looked to the ships that were their only defense. "Well, in case." She nodded and hurried off.

It didn't take much time for all of the able-bodied warriors to be gathered at the docks. They watched as three ships, far larger than they expected, sailed into view. Yutuuan sucked in a breath. Those ships were at least as large as their warships. The dwarfed the patrol vessels of Tilizaa. Each had to hold at least 60 sailors. If they made it to shore . . . He didn't want to think of it.

Naret cursed beside him. "They're bold enough to attack in midday."

"Let's hope it's just hubris and not tactical surety."

The sea battle began, the larger ships surrounding the two patrol ships. The ship that the governor kept in reserve set sail and was doing its best to join its sisters in battle. The Rahbahn kept a steady distance around the Tilizaa's vessels and Yutuuan thought he began to see tiny points of light. He rubbed his eyes, thinking he'd been staring too hard, but they were still there and were multiplying. He recoiled as the two Wiluruan ships ignited in a fearsome blaze. Finished with them, the warships turned and began approaching the city.

The entire crowd at the docks watched in horror as the patrol ships burned and sunk quickly into the waters.

The last of Tilizaa's vessels sailed to intercept. The lead enemy ship didn't move to avoid them and crashed into them, sending planks of wood and sailors flying.

"Ready for battle," Yutuuan shouted to keep his forces focused. "Find us some magicians! Ready the healers! This will be bloody! And someone get me a sword!"

"No," Naret said, glaring at him. "You need to stay back. Get somewhere high so you can see the battlefield and give orders."

Yutuuan glared right back at his guard commander, but the man was right. He reluctantly nodded and moved off to find a better vantage point. He managed to climb on top of a low building that gave him direct sight of nearly the entire docks. There was even a chimney to hide behind in case the enemy tried to snipe him. Now, all they had to do was wait.

He watched, blood beginning to pound, as the warships came as closer, close enough for him to see people beginning to assemble along the side of each ship. "They're readying to fire!" he yelled out. "Ready defenses."

He cursed that none of the military's magicians were stationed here. He had only a few in his traveling group and none of them were battle hardened. He watched as the defenders of Tilizaa gathered to counter the foreign magics. A series of fireballs began launching from the nearest enemy vessel as it came into port. The city's magicians cast as well, hitting some of the fireballs with their own. Unfortunately, some sailed over them, striking in the city. The ship pulled in closer and he faintly heard their calls of alarm at the spikes rising up from the waters, but it was too late for them to avoid disaster.

The warship crashed into the spikes, their approach coming to a stop. Yutuuan couldn't tell if any major damage had been done to the hull, but at least they were stranded here. The other ships quickly course corrected, setting anchor away from the docks. They began to send out smaller ships, filled with men. Naret yelled out for the magicians to focus on the stranded ship and they turned their spells on them immediately.

Yutuuan called to the soldiers below with his estimates of how many men were approaching on the boats. He hated playing lookout but any advantage they could get was necessary. The stranded ship dropped ropes, sailors quickly dropping down as their magicians tried to cover them. Several were taken out by spells, but the majority reached the dock. He and Naret gave the call to attack at the same time, he keeping his eye on the boats approaching. They would be here soon, but if they could make it through this first wave before their comrades arrive, they might win the day.

He worried as he saw a second wave of boats dropped from the far away warships. Then the ocean winds carried a sound he never thought he'd be so thankful to hear. The call of a Wiluruan war horn carried above the noise of battle. Four warships sailed around a curve in the coast. They turned, making a line for the enemy vessels. A call went up from Tilizaa's forces and Yutuuan felt the morale rise. They'd make it after all.

The moment they were in range, the Wiluruan ships set their magicians to firing. While some launched fire at the enemy's sails others focused to turn the sea against them. Yutuuan cheered as the soldiers on the docks below him found a new energy to fight. The Rahbahn were distracted at first by the turn in events but suddenly remembered they were in the midst of the enemy. The small ships that were still in the water were conflicted to which front to go to. Some tried to return to their warships in the midst of the battle. Some still approached the dock. His soldiers were ready.

The battle raged on with casualties on both sides. The enemy warships were eventually run off, one trailing smoke as she sailed. The stranded vessel fought to the last man, leaving their forces in the smaller boats to be picked off easily. There were no prisoners this time. He breathed a sigh of relief as the victory cry spread among all the soldiers.

Yutuuan's attention turned to the Wiluruan ships close enough to send out their own landing ships. They'd

arrived just in time. The Fahzi empire was attacking swiftly. Far too swiftly for a long-range voyage. He started making his way off the roof. They still had too little
information about them to properly counter such a threat.
That would have to change. For the sake of Wiluru.

* * *

Turo walked through the jungle carefully. He knew
he'd have to lead his men in a second scouting mission
since it was hard to gain any information from dead men.
He shuddered at the thought of the heads of the scouts so
callously tossed into the river for them to find. Those were
good men, proud soldiers of the empire. They deserved
better. They deserved to be avenged and he would make
sure they were.

The sun reached higher in the sky as they marched
on, methodically mapping out their path so they'd have an
easier time coming back. Brush was cleared, making a
path for their return as well. Turo watched the Nsongans
carefully. They did their best to not disturb the forest and
he curled his lip at their cowardly mannerisms. It was just
a forest. Nothing more. The jungle people had attacked
their men and they had to be repaid for it.

Turo and his men ducked as birds they'd only become familiar with since coming south darted back and
forth above them. There were strange, loud calls in the distance from an animal that he couldn't even fathom. Monkeys swung overhead, chattering noisily. He glanced back
and was annoyed to see the Nsongans unbothered by the
life around them. The noise was nearly deafening. Insects
as big as his hand flew by his face and he struggled to keep
calm. He prayed that they'd find one of the villages soon so
that they could return to a proper city.

The light from the mostly obscured sun began to
dim and he finally called for a stop. "We'll make camp
here," he shouted for the whole group to hear. Immediately his men began to cut down smaller trees to clear a space,
some setting about the task of collecting dry branches for

their fires. Turo looked to the Nsongans who didn't seem sure of their task.

"Are you not going to make camp?" he taunted.

The man who was their leader turned to him. "We will make our camp in our own time, in our own way. But we thank you for being so concerned."

Turo scowled truly looking over the Nsongan group. Ten women were among their number and their leader was one of those womanish-men. It was disgraceful. They moved methodically through the bush, not cutting down a thing and making their individual spaces between the brush. He rolled his eyes and went back to overseeing his camp. The forest grew quieter as night fell but nothing unusual happened. There was a small alarm as a man had an insect with more legs than any of the Ega had seen crawl into his bedroll. Another woke in the night beset by beetles. Finally, the evening was quiet.

The rising light of dawn woke Turo and he shivered as he awoke. He looked around and others were waking as well. The sentries post, however, were all staring intently into the forest. He could tell by their postures that they were on edge.

"What's wrong?" he asked, quickly getting up.

The sentry nearest him glanced over. "A few minutes ago, the forest went completely silent. Animals were starting to wake and make their noise again, then nothing."

Turo woke the men nearest him, whispering for them to do the same. He grabbed his sword, looking around the jungle. They were right. It was silent as a tomb. He looked up to the canopy and only the barest light was filtering down as if the sun were too frightened to rise. He raised his hand, making a motion for his men to tighten ranks. The Nsongans followed suit and took out swords and spears.

Turo heard his heart beat against the unnatural silence, a lone drum. He forced himself to breathe slow and measured to fight against his body's instinct to panic. He scanned the surrounding forest slowly, looking for any clue of what was going on. His search was rewarded by a ghostly shadow streaking by between distant trees. He heard some of his men react and quickly called them back to attention. A few more shadows passed in the distance and then stillness.

The nervousness of the group hung like fog in the air. Turo readjusted his grip on his sword, his palm beginning to sweat. Now shadows began to flit by overhead, blinking out the weak light. He looked up in time to see nothing but the fluttering of dislodged leaves. His heart began to pound despite his best efforts. The shadows were getting closer and Turo didn't like that he couldn't tell if it was one beast or several that stalked the forest just out of sight.

A rustling sound to his right caught everyone's attention and all eyes swung that way. Turo knew he saw the hide of some kind of beast moving away from camp. Then, a loud, heavy thump sounded in front of him. He whipped his head around to come face to face with a huge creature that was from his worst nightmares. It stood three heads taller than him, with long, lanky limbs and shaggy gray fur. Turo quickly took note of the long curving claws on its hands and feet. It looked like it was smiling at him, its teeth shinning like well-polished blades. Dark eyes caught the light.

"Get ready," he called, then realized they were surrounded by the beasts. None were as large as the one before him, but they all looked ready to dive into his group. Turo steeled himself. These must have been the beasts that tore the heads off the scouts. They didn't move a muscle at first and he wondered if he should call for the attack.

"You," the beast in front of him said languidly, "were told not to come here." Turo's mouth worked, amazed that the creature could manage a human tongue. "You were warned by the heads of your first invaders. You do not belong here."

He was about to respond when the Nsongan leader stepped up beside him, kneeling before the creature.

"Oh, great beast," he said humbly, laying his arms

out wide before him. "I and my kind have respected your forest for ages. We were forced to come here and be a part of this violation. Please forgive my warriors."

Turo's eye went wide. "You traitorous bastard! You'd turn on us so easily."

The Nsongan leader said nothing but remained on the ground before the creature. Turo looked to the beast who tilted its massive head down, considering the man. He tensed, sensing that this was the moment. It raised a hook clawed hand, gesturing toward the Nsongans.

"You all may have a head start. Make it to the river and you will live."

The leader rose and turned to run in one smooth movement. He glanced behind him in time to see the other Nsongans abandoning them as well, running at full speed the way they came. A trio of his men tried to follow but were blocked by one of the beasts. He turned his full attention towards the creature, its blade toothed grin closer.

"As for you," it said in an almost purr, "we will feast."

Turo called for the attack.

*   *   *

Erenemo grimaced as a berry hit him in the cheek. He looked to his wife with a crooked smile. Patya looked back to him innocently.

"Your aim is off," he chuckled. "You used to be better at this."

She grabbed another berry from the bowl beside her and took aim again.

"Just hold still," she said holding one eye closed. Erenemo chuckled. "I said hold still."

He did what he was told, holding his mouth wide. When two people wanted the same food but were too lazy to cross the room, you had to come up with creative ways.

The next one landed in his mouth and he gave her a slow clap as he chewed. She scowled at him and threw another. Erenemo moved and caught it anyway, smiling triumphantly. His wife rolled her eyes and returned to her task. He picked his book back up, rereading an old tale that he loved from his youth.

He frowned as he heard his and his wife's name called down the hall. Patya looked up, confused, just as Masola came into the room looking upset.

"My sweetest," she said, beckoning the girl into her arms. "What's troubling you so?"

"Mother is awful," Masola said hugging her great-aunt.

Patya clicked her tongue. "You must never speak like that. She is your mother and the only parent you have left."

Erenemo rose from his seat, coming by his wife's side. "Now why would you say something like that?"

"Mother is trying to choose the abodara and she isn't choosing me. She won't even consider it."

Patya looked up to him, concerned. He gave a small sigh.

"Your mother has a lot to consider. Perhaps she's still narrowing her choices."

"No," Masola snapped. "I spoke to her twice."

Patya held her at arms' length, looking at her sternly. Masola wouldn't meet her eyes.

"You will speak to us with respect, Sola."

Erenemo put a hand on his wife's shoulder. "Masola, walk with me." He guided his great niece out of the room, giving Patya a reassuring look over his shoulder. Once they were away from the room, he spoke again.

"Masola, is this really what's troubling you?"

"Yes," the girl replied emphatically. She paused. "No. Maybe. I don't know."

He held in his frustrated sigh. "Masola," he prodded when she didn't continue.

She glanced up at him. "I am mad that she didn't even think about putting me on the list. I'm her daughter."

Erenemo stopped himself from rolling his eyes. There was no good reason for her to be considered for abodara. She was selfish and lazy. Her mothers had spoiled her, and she showed no interest in a path for her future. He briefly reconsidered his plans. Perhaps there was someone else that would be able to get close enough to Ashaki to deliver the poison. However, he wasn't sure of how loyal her servants were and a sudden stranger in their ranks would be questioned. No, he was left with this girl.

"Yes," he began patiently, "you are her daughter but the daraship isn't always passed down directly. Our family has been favored. This is the first time that it has been kept in one family for so long."

"But why wouldn't she want to keep that going?" Masola frowned deeply.

He swallowed his retort with difficulty. "That is true. One does have to think of legacy." He looked to her, making his expression as concerned as possible. "But it doesn't seem like this is all that's bothering you."

The girl sighed. "I've barely seen her since she became dara. I know there's stuff I want to do but . . . when I want to spend time with her, she's out in the city or busy with meetings. Things just aren't the same and I hate it." She hit her fist against the wall. "She could make time for me. She's the dara. She can do whatever she wants."

Erenemo saw his way in. He paused as if lost in thought.

"You're right." She looked up to him, shocked. "Your mother needs to spend more time with you. She has been working far too hard as the dara." The words tasted foul in his mouth. "She should be more focused on you, her only daughter. When Ofemu was young, your aunt Patya would drop whatever she was doing to attend to his needs. She was a great mother. In becoming the dara, I think your mother has forgotten what that means."

Masola looked even more dejected. "It's like she's forgotten all about me sometimes."

Brat, he thought. "Forgetting your child. That is the worst thing a parent can do." He paused, faux thinking again. "Perhaps she should be taught a lesson." Erenemo took in her confused face. "Come with me."

He led her to his office. After shutting the doors and

dramatically making sure no one was listening, he went to the shelf where the innocent looking little box was kept.

"Sometimes even adults need to be punished. I'm sure you understand this by now." He made a show of searching the shelves for what he wanted. He turned with the box in hand. "Your mother has cast you aside for her new role so it would only be fitting that you teach her a little lesson."

Masola eyed the box. "What is that?"

"This," he said holding it up, "is a little something that will make your mother just a bit sick for an evening. Perhaps if she sees what a loving and caring daughter you truly are during that time, she will realize how neglectful she's been. I'm sure she'll even reconsider not having you on the list for abodara."

He handed the box over to Masola carefully. She stared at it, unsurety still in her eyes.

"How do I use it?"

"You have to put it in her drink. And just half the box. Just half. We only want to make her sick. Do you understand?"

"I understand." She moved to open the box and he stopped her. "How sick will this make her?"

"Sick enough that she'll need someone to care for her." His niece twisted her mouth. "If you don't want to do it, I can understand. But if your mother's already making the list then she's sure to pick her abodara soon. You need a chance to show her what a good daughter you are and show her she needs to spend more time with you."

He was pleased when Masola's face turned determined. She stood.

"Thank you, uncle."

Erenemo came and placed a fatherly hand on her shoulder. "Remember. Even children can sometimes teach their parents things." He began to tell her about a time when Ofamu proved to them that he was able to perform several tasks by himself. By the end of the tale, she seemed far more confident about her task. He sent her on with a smile that dropped the moment she left.

"Was that Masola leaving?" he heard his wife ask behind him.

He brought the smile back up. "Yes, she's headed back home."

"And, how was she?"

"Better. I explained that her mother has much on her mind, and she shouldn't be concerned with if she would be abodara or not. She should hope that her mother chooses the best person."

Patya nodded, looping an arm around his waist as they returned to their sitting room.

"Good. I'm afraid that girl has been deeply troubled since losing her mother."

"She has," he said putting his arm around her shoulders. "But I think, in time, things will get better."

CHAPTER TWENTY-THREE

Tekhamun was growing antsy. His new followers had made him wait until nightfall to go out in this new city and he was ready to make his voice known. Karatel came up beside him, an eager smile on his face. The young man had been helpful since their first meeting even though Tekhamun didn't completely approve of his tactics at times. The room they were in was a basement, a storeroom holding various provisions for the travel house above them.

"Is it night yet?"

"The sun just went down," Karatel replied. "We can go soon enough, master."

Tekhamun nodded. He glanced around the room at his small band of followers. They were a useful lot, eager to learn the arts of the arakgu'un. In their travel from the last city, he'd learned that they were a group of thieves looking for a better life. He could think of no better life than serving Gu'un. It had been the best decision of his life and he swore to his god that he would be the master his followers, no, his acolytes deserved.

Moon, a woman with a whited-out eye, looked up to him and Karatel.

"Can we go now? I'm starting to feel cagey." Takhamun liked that one. She was the only one that seemed to have any sort of religion before coming into his fold.

"We should go," Tekhamun said. "We want to take full advantage of the night."

Karatel lowered his head to him. "Yes, master."

Tekhamun led the way out of the basement and through the back door of the travel house. His eyes took a moment to adjust to the low light of sundown that seemed far brighter than the lamp light of their hideaway. This city was thick and close, with narrow streets through most of it. The alleyway they stood in was barely an arm's span wide and full of discarded items and trash. He looked up one way and saw a man settling down to sleep. It was littered with discarded people as well.

"Master," called a slender young woman. He looked over at Pta, the one he'd learned was involved with Karatel. "We thought we could begin spreading your message with the poor of the city. They might be more ready to hear you. Rich people want to keep their lives just the way it is."

Tekhamun nodded. She was right. He'd been ignored so far by the upright citizens he'd talked to. Those who had nowhere else to turn might be more accepting. He looked up and saw the sliver of the moon in the purple sky rising like the sickle of Gu'un himself. Growing confidence filled his heart. He would reach out to those under the sickle moon and if they were the only ones to survive the cleaving, then so be it.

"Let's go," he said looking back to his acolytes. "We will find the people of the night, those who are also shunned, and bring them into the fold."

Karatel lowered his head, smiling. "Yes, master. I believe I know where to look."

Tekhamun allowed his main follower to take the lead. Their path took them down other alleys and behind buildings that he didn't like the feel of. Soon they found themselves looking at a dead end, boxed in by three two-story buildings. Tekhamun turned as he felt the approach of another group. His acolytes turned as well to face the darkly dressed people. He looked them over carefully. They looked like another assembly of thieves. There were six of them, all male.

"You've come to the wrong part of the city," their leader slurred. "This is our territory and we don't like outsiders."

Tekhamun stepped in between his group and theirs. "You're thieves?" he asked.

"Killers too," the man replied with a sneer.

"Good." Tekhamun smiled. "I am Tekhamun. I'm a priest of Gu'un and his chosen warrior. He wishes to see the unbelievers and the blasphemers of this world cut down. Join me, join my cause and you will find yourselves greatly rewarded."

The other thieves looked at each other and broke out laughing. Tekhamun seethed. His hands went to his long daggers, but Karatel put a hand on his arm.

"Maybe I can speak to them, master." The priest considered it for a moment, the desire to deal with these ruffians still burning in him. He finally nodded.

Karatel took a step forward. "You shouldn't be laughing. This is a great man, an incredibly dangerous man. He's a priest of the Arakgu'un and he's taken us in as his students. We've learned to become even deadlier." He glanced to Tekhamun. "All to bring about Gu'un's vision."

Their leader snorted derisively. "All for Gu'un's vision," he said mockingly.

Tekhamun rushed forward, bringing up his dagger and slashing the man's throat in one motion. He immediately turned his attention to the rest of the group who was caught in shock.

"I will not stand for mocking Gu'un's name. Those who won't go along with his plan will be cleaved. Those who seek his just path will be spared. Which will you be?" He looked each of them in the eye. "Running is not an option."

A tall one near the back looked between him and Karatel. "Did he teach you to kill like that?" he asked the other man.

Karatel glanced at his master. "He's started too. And he's promised to make us members in time."

"Then I'll join you."

The rest of the group voiced their surrender to Gu'un's vision one by one. Tekhamun nodded. They may not be the eager converts his acolytes were, but their hearts would change with time. He knew it. Karatel looked up to him.

"Do you want to keep looking for others to convert?"

A pride welled within him. "Yes."

"Maybe, since we have more people now, we may try to convert some people with more, uh, power than just us thieves."

Tekhamun considered him for a moment. "Show me what you mean."

Karatel lowered his head. He led them out of the alley, walking past the newest members with a small smirk. Their group moved quickly in the growing darkness. The number of people out in the streets were thinning, making traveling easier. Karatel turned down street after street, making it clear that he'd been to this city before. Tekhamun wondered what other secrets his acolytes held.

They stopped beside a large house in a better kept side of town. This one was an impressive three stories tall. Set away from the street and with a wall to keep pedestrians from seeing inside, it was obviously the home of a very comfortable family.

"Why are we here?" he asked Karatel.

"Because, master," the acolyte whispered back, "we all need to eat and after you talk to them, they might convert to your vision *and* contribute to our group."

Tekhamun frowned. He hadn't thought of how they were supposed to provide for themselves, especially if their numbers grew. He'd figured that Gu'un would lead them to what they needed. Tekhamun stopped, looking up at the sickle moon, then at his newest followers, then finally at Karatel. It appeared that his god had.

He nodded to his chief acolyte and they found their way to the alley that led behind the house. Just as they were coming up, a servant opened a back door, whistling as he tossed kitchen scraps onto the ground. A slew of cats from the alley descended on it, delightfully tearing apart the meat and fighting with each other over portions. Pta rushed from behind him, taking out a knife. She ran up on the man before he noticed her and pressed the blade to his throat. She pressed a finger to her smiling lips for him to be silent then signaled for the rest of the group to come in.

Tekhamun ran inside the house, immediately disgusted by the tasteless opulence. He moved through the kitchen, hearing voices in a nearby room. Slinking through a small adjoining room, he caught a glimpse of the dining room ahead where the family was having their evening meal. They laughed and told stories of their day. He scowled deeply. Like so many, they made no thanks to the gods as they recounted their good fortunes. These were the main types of people that Gu'un wanted him to convert.

Tired of skulking, he entered the dining room. The wife and two daughters shrieked at the sudden appearance of a stranger. The father shot up from his seat, calling for servants or guards. Tekhamun didn't care.

"I am Tekhamun of the arakgu'un." The wife started to cry at the mention of his sect. "I am the chosen of Gu'un and his messenger. The netkoleh wishes to take us away from the worship of the gods into a new blasphemous era. If you join me and my cause, we will rise up against him and all those who would support his blasphemy to bring the empire back to righteousness. If not . . ." He took out his daggers, spinning them once. "Those who won't come to the side of the gods will be cleaved away. What do you say?"

"Get out of my house," the husband shouted. "You . . . madman."

Tekhamun seethed at the insult. He signaled for his acolytes to come forward. They came in quickly, surrounding the family. Karatel stood behind the wife, his dagger pressed gently against her cheek. Pta stood behind one of the daughters. Moon grabbed a handful of the son's hair, fixing her one good eye on the father.

"So, will you join the right path," she began, twisting her hand in the young man's hair, "or will you all be part of the ones we cut away?"

Tekhamun smiled at the fright in the father's eyes as he watched his family being threatened. This was the fear he was taught you'd see in a man's eyes just as he realized the weight of his sins. This was the fear of a man who was just about to repent.

"Swear to us that you won't let anyone in your household succumb to the blasphemy that's spreading."

The father swallowed. "I swear. I swear I won't even let a servant fall to it."

"And swear that you'll help our cause as needed."

"Anything you want."

"Good. Release them." His acolytes stepped back from the family, retreating into the small room behind him. "I will check in on you to make sure you haven't gone back on your word." After one long look at the family, he returned to his followers. They moved back into the kitchen and he saw the other followers raiding the storeroom. At first, he disapproved of their thievery, but if they were going to continue their mission, they had to be fed.

"Take what we can."

Sacks were found and loaded with food that would keep for a few days. His acolytes also took a number of valuable belongings to fund their ranks later. Pleased, Tekhamun led them back into the night. He found himself torn as they moved back into less affluent areas. Did they spend the remainder of the night convincing the lower people to join them or bringing the well off to heel? He watched his people as they delightfully broke into their bounty. It didn't matter. Little by little, the ranks of the true followers of Gu'un would grow and they would take back this country from its corrupted leadership.

* * *

Newa threw himself at the pond, nearly drowning himself as he plunged his head down at the water. He drank heartily for nothing in his life had tasted sweeter. The nearby cows looked to him curiously and he ignored them as he took in his fill. Thirst satisfied, Newa sat back on his knees, wiping the water from his mouth. His water skin had run out two days ago and this was the first pond he'd seen in nearly three. He thought he was headed vaguely south. Why was the south so dry?

Newa dropped to the ground, spreading his tired legs out. A cow wandered near, curious about the pond's new inhabitant and he was too satisfied to wave it off. He looked to the small village just at the top of a nearby hill with trepidation. He'd been avoiding towns since his last run in with the priests of his order. One night, he'd ventured to get close to a village and heard talk of a priest that was being hunted. He slinked back into the night, deciding to stick to the wilderness until they'd called off their hunt.

But he needed food, proper food. The lowly rats and small birds he'd caught on his trek had only given him so much sustenance. He wanted meat and bread. He wanted beer and Wiluruan wines. He looked to the village again. A chance had to be taken eventually.

Newa pushed himself to his feet. He moved lowly, staying in between the cows until he reached the other side of their herd. A farmhouse sat nearby. Laundry lay on the wooden fence, drying in the afternoon sun. He looked at his own robes with a frown. He was obviously a part of the Arakgu'un. Perhaps it was time for a disguise. Newa crept up to the fence, looking around for any of its residents. Snatching a few items down, he hurried back to the protection of the cow herd, changing quickly. He made a makeshift sack out of his old robes to carry his weapons and stood up. He stepped to the water to get a look at himself. It had been years since he'd been out of the robes of the priesthood. It was almost like looking at another person.

Newa's stomach growled loudly, startling the cows around him. The scent of meat, probably fowl, wafted to him on the light breeze. He clutched a hand to his stomach, still debating on heading into the main part of the village. But where else would he find food around here? He walked toward the cluster of houses on the hill, not sure how he was going to do this. He was a priest and assassin. He wasn't a thief. The smell of the cooking food blew harder. He would just have to learn today.

It was easy to find the house that the smell was coming from. They had an outside kitchen and there were a number of hens cooking over a fire. His stomach twisted again. Someone came outside and he ducked behind a series of wide bushes. He watched through the thick branches as they carefully attended to the meal and return inside. Newa looked around to make sure there was no one else about. All activity seemed to be going on inside or in the front of the houses. It was now or never.

He darted out from the bushes, taking cover behind two more before jumping the low fence. He rushed toward the fire, keeping a low profile. He took one more quick glance around to be sure no one was there. Wrapping his hand in part of his robes, he reached for one of the hens. Holding his prize close, he stood and felt a cold blade at the side of his neck.

"We don't take kindly to thieves here," rumbled the deep voice.

Newa put his hands up, still clutching the chicken and turned slowly around. The man in front of him was a wall of intimidation. He was jet black skin and taut muscles. His eyes held a fierceness that Newa hadn't seen in some time.

"I meant no harm," he said, paying close attention to the wide, long blade at his throat.

"No harm except to take food from my people." The man opened his mouth to say something else, but Newa's stomach growled loudly. He studied the priest. "How long has it been since you had a meal?"

"A good meal? Days." Newa hoped this man had some pity. He didn't wish to harm a man trying to just protect what was his. "I've been lost for about a week. I've only had small birds and rats." The man didn't look convinced. "I have some money. If you'll just let me reach into my sack, I can get it for you. I'll pay whatever price you name."

A few tense moments passed, then the man took the blade away from Newa's neck.

"Have the bird. You look like you need it more."

"Thank you," Newa said, nodding. He turned to leave, wanting to get out of this awkward situation.

"Did you want something to drink?"

He stopped, considering. "Yes," he conceded.

The man pointed to a stool in the corner. "Have a seat. I'll be back."

Newa took the seat, waiting for the man to return inside his house before tearing into the hen. He licked up the juices running down his fingers eagerly, not wanting anything to get past him. The meat was tender and juicy and everything he'd hoped it would be. He didn't even care that he was burning his fingers and tongue ripping into it.

The man returned, offering him a wooden cup filled with a strange frothy white liquid. Newa looked up quizzically.

"Kovo, made earlier this year." Newa took it, sipping then drinking fully.

"Take it easy. That will have you flat on your ass."

Newa slowed his drinking. "What's your name?" the man asked, returning to his cooking.

"Newa," he managed to get out between chews.

"You're from farther north with a name like that. My name is Isomen." He turned the hens again, taking a couple off of the fire. "What happened that left you lost, Newa?"

The priest paused, taking a moment to lick his fingertips. "I was run out of town by a gang of men."

"Really? Did you owe them money?"

Newa scowled. Nosey country people. "No, they wanted me to go along with something I didn't want to."

Isomen nodded. "One has to stick to their principles. What good are you without something to believe in?" Newa didn't say anything but finished off the hen. "Are they still chasing you? Is that what brought you farther south?"

"Yes," he answered cautiously. He moved his sack of weapons closer with one of his feet.

"Are you going to head back north? I could tell you how to get to the main road."

Newa took a long drink, finishing off the last of the kovo. The priests were probably spreading the tale of his message far and wide among the cities here. They'd definitely taken the main roads to do so. That route was out.

His sect wouldn't hesitate to search in smaller town, villages, and even the wilderness if they were determined to find him. He needed someplace to hide until they gave up their chase.

"Is heading back north out?" Isomen asked, cutting into his thoughts.

"Yes," Newa answered slowly.

Isomen nodded thoughtfully, taking the last hens from the fire.

"Those men may still be looking for you. Perhaps you should travel farther south for a while. Wait until they've lost their lust for your blood." He chuckled. "You may find a better place there. Who knows what fate may bring?"

You may find a better place there. Newa looked at him. Something about his words struck Newa in the chest.

"You sound as if you know something."

Isomen looked surprised. He tapped his chin in thought. "There are . . . stories," he said hesitantly. "There's supposed to be some sort of city of thieves in the jungle far south. I don't know if it's real, but people sure love the story. More kovo?"

Newa nodded, deep in thought as Isomen refilled his cup. He couldn't head back north not just yet. Yes, he was sure he was being hunted, but his mission had also been a failure. He wasn't sure if he could show his face in his temple knowing that he'd failed his directive so spectacularly. Who'd known the other temples would be so disobedient? Who knew they'd work with the other temples so readily? He sighed, taking a sip. No, he needed to lay low.

Newa stood, handing Isomen back the cup. "Thank you for the meal," he said, nodding his head to him.

"You're welcome. I hope fate leads you to better times."

Newa nodded again and jumped his fence. With a wave he checked the position of the sun and started walking south.

* * *

Arkoleh lounged in bed, her mind running across her husband and what he may be doing at the moment. It was late in the morning, far later than she usually stayed in bed, but she couldn't bring herself to get up just yet. Bakari had invaded her dreams, the young Royal Son she'd grown up with. She dreamed of them coupling passionately on the front steps of the palace, the crowds cheering on their lovemaking. She shook her head at the ridiculous shamelessness of her dream-self. Only in the mind could such take place.

Arkoleh turned over, making herself rise. Her head swam the moment she stood to her feet and she sat back down.

"Water," she called out and moments later, two servants came, one holding a pitcher, the other an ornate glass. Arkoleh took a drink and felt her stomach twist. She grimaced at the uneasy feeling. She beckoned the servants near to help her stand. She rose slowly this time. The dizziness didn't return but her stomach still felt uneasy.

"Is breakfast ready?"

"Yes, empress," they answered meekly. "Are you well today? Do we need to fetch the physician?"

"No. I think I'll be fine once I eat."

She allowed them to escort her to her dining room, the smell of the foods on the table turning her stomach. Arkoleh pressed her fingers to her mouth, willing the feeling to abate. She sat down heavily in a chair, staring at the meal in disgust. Taking a breath, she made herself gather a plate, eating down as much as she could before the smell affected her. She was starting to enjoy it when her stomach lurched and she vomited to the side. Arkoleh held on tightly as her body heaved repeatedly, not stopping even when there was nothing left in her.

More servants rushed over. One offered her water when she'd finished and a dish to spit it in. Another brought a cloth for her to clean her mouth. Arkoleh held the cloth to her mouth as her servants rushed to clean up her mess. She grimaced as the smell of the remaining food threatened to send her into another heaving fit.

"I have to leave this room," she said standing.

Arkoleh fled back to her bedroom, sitting heavily on the bed. She placed a hand to her stomach as it still churned. She could barely remember a time when she'd felt this sick. The last time she'd felt this way was when she was carrying Koletun. Arkoleh gasped. She quickly thought to her last moon days and realized it was before Bakari had left for the Pilgrimage. Tears formed in her eyes.

Her servants flocked to her as she broke down in tears. The questions of was she alright and if they could do anything for her washed over her. She finally looked up to them, smiling.

"A seed has been planted." She cried through their congratulations and cries of joy. Arkoleh stood, slowly, and rushed from the room. She had to tell her girls that they were going to welcome another sibling into the world. She quickened to a jog, laughing and crying as she moved through the halls. *Let it be a boy.* She hoped with a fierceness that it was a boy. She needed a boy. This empire needed her to have a son.

Arkoleh stopped when she saw someone who wasn't a servant walking down the hall of Izriamat's wing. She backtracked just in time to see them go into the second empress's bedroom. Arkoleh moved quickly to the door they'd left open. Humming floated out and she had to know who would be so bold as to enter here. She slipped in the room, wanting to catch them in the middle of whatever their plan was. Curiously, by the bed, Arkoleh saw a woman holding a baby, pulling a cover up to her.

"Who are you?" Arkoleh demanded. "What are you doing in the empress's rooms?" The woman jumped, spinning around. Arkoleh looked to the baby, recognizing him immediately. "Why do you have the second son?"

The woman bowed as best as she could, bouncing the boy who looked like he was about to cry.

"Empress," she said breathlessly. "I am Nitiri. I'm

one of our emperor's lesser wives."

"What are you doing with the second son?" she demanded, coming closer. "Why isn't he with his nanny?"

The woman jumped again. "I volunteered to take him. I have a son who is only a year old. I would have no difficulties caring for him and nursing him. I thought he needed a mother to care for him, not just a servant." Nitiri took a half step back. "Our emperor has declared me his caretaker."

Arkoleh looked this younger woman up and down. He could see why her husband would give her favor. She scowled. And this girl already had a son. How many other contenders for the throne were waiting in his wing of pleasure?

"And what were you doing in the empress's bedroom? Pretending? Imagining?"

"My empress, I only came to find something that may still have his mother's scent on it. I thought it may help him sleep at night."

Arkoleh walked to her, catching the woman's chin in her hand. She turned her head side to side, looking over her features.

"How long have you been in my husband's service?"

"Three years, my empress."

The woman looked terrified of her, improving Arkoleh's mood considerably. She released her, picking up the cover up that the lesser wife had been looking at.

"This will do," she said handing it to her.

"Thank you, empress." Nitiri brought it up to the boy, stroking his cheek with it.

Arkoleh looked at the baby, her husband's other son, with disdain. He already favored Bakari so much. She'd never held such hatred for a child in her life. He smiled at her, not knowing what he represented to her. This tiny child would inherit everything that her Koletun should have. She thought of the small life just starting to grow inside her. Hopefully not.

"Empress, are you all right? You look pale?"

She slid her eyes to this woman. "I am fine." She

eyed them both again. "You may go."

Nitiri bowed and quickly swished her way out of the room. Arkoleh watched them leave then sat down heavily on the bed, hand clutched to her stomach. She scowled at the thought of that full figure barely hidden by that woman's dress. In her three years as a wife, Bakari may have visited her two, maybe three times? The fact that she'd already given him a son burned deep inside Arkoleh. Her mind returned to her son's funeral and the host of children from his other women. So many sons. So many chances for her to be pushed aside and another woman risen. The thought terrified her.

She put a hand to her stomach again. *If you are there,* she thought, *please let this one be a son.*

CHAPTER TWENTY-FOUR

Turo sliced for the horrid creature in front of him, trying to open its stomach. The thing jumped back out of his reach, grinning with those blade sharp teeth. He heard the shouts and war cries of his other soldiers behind him as the other creatures fought back against them. The large one in front of him rushed forward, faster than he'd expected, bringing down one of its hands to claw at him. Turo tried to bring his sword up to block, but the force nearly knocked him down. Its long claws reached over his blade, still managing to cut into the skin of his hand. The bones of his sword arm tingled from the blow, but he struggled to fend the creature off.

A strangled cry came from behind him and he cursed the Nsongans. Such cowardice. If they made it back, he would be sure to find them and reward them for abandoning the mission. Turo spared a fleeting glance behind him. He didn't see the men that were immediately to his left. Panic began to grow when he realized he heard far less of his men fighting. He bit his lip as he still pushed against the creature in front of him. It was barely moving. It could have brought its other hand around at any time and finished him off, but it hadn't. It was toying with him.

He sneered at it.

"Retreat!"

Turo gave one last push with his sword, turning as he broke into a run. He almost stopped at the scene before him. Only half of the force he'd come with were left. The rest were scattered about in pieces. A few of the monsters had pulled back and held some of the captured men, drinking the blood from them or stripping meat from their bones. He pushed at the closest man in front of him, forcing him to run.

"Move, you bastards! Retreat!"

His force broke ranks, fleeing back the way they came. Turo didn't bother glancing behind him. At first, he heard nothing but his blood pounding and their flight through the underbrush. Then, he heard the creatures give chase. He heard the sounds of their running behind them. He heard the distinctive sounds of them taking to the trees. Ahead of him, a man was pulled into the forest. His high-pitched screams filled the air, echoing off trees. Then there was a resounding crunch and he stopped. Turo allowed his fear to push him on faster.

They continued, his men glancing about the forest fearfully.

"Keep your eyes ahead," he barked, his fear taking some of the authority from his voice.

A man at the front of the group shrieked when something was tossed down to him. The contingent came to a crashing halt, soldiers falling over one another. Turo pushed his way through, urging them to keep going but they were a cluster of confusion. He made his way up front to find the man holding a severed spine. Turo quickly struck it from his hands and punched him.

"Keep running," he commanded, pulling the man along. He took the lead, bringing them back to their breakneck speed. He didn't care if they ran until their bones snapped. They had to reach the river.

Another man screamed behind him and Turo shut his ears to the horrible sounds coming from the jungle. They had to focus. Something dropped onto his shoulder with a wet sound and he jumped at the sight of intestines. Swallowing his own scream, he knocked it away. He had to concentrate on the path.

The sound of pursuit stopped after a while and Turo realized his men were beginning to slow down.

"Don't let them fool you. They want our fear. Keep running."

They ran for what seemed like hours, Turo only allowing them to slow down enough to save their stamina. He couldn't tell exactly how much time had passed. The sun had yet to fully pierce the canopy and the odd fog still lingered. He was sure it had to be at least mid-morning. He finally called for a halt and his men dropped to the ground, exhausted. Turo hunched over, hands on his knees, desperately trying to catch his breath. The forest around them was quiet, but he could hear a few birds calling. He swallowed, attempting to quench his dry throat. Had they made it far enough away?

He looked around, just to be sure they were still on the path they'd cut through the forest. Relief washed over him. He sunk to the ground, all his strength fading. This was worse than he'd thought they'd encounter. He thought that perhaps the jungle people were more fearsome warriors than they'd given them credit for. Who would have thought they'd have monsters defending them? Surely, they were summoned by magic. He'd hate to think that such creatures were here naturally. And if they were natural, what other sorts of abominations were lurking here? He worked to steady his breathing. Even he could admit that was a terrifying prospect. They would need an army to make it through here.

He called for them to keep moving, pulling himself to his feet with difficulty. His legs felt like iron as he led them in a jog. Before he knew it, he heard a familiar sound. He called for another stop, listening carefully. It was the unmistakable sound of the Bangi. He was just about to give the signal to move out when he realized he heard no other sounds. Turo took his sword out, his heart thundering again. He turned, surveying the surrounding forest. His men did the same, terror reflected on their faces.

In a flash, one of the creatures rushed past him, before he could react, taking the soldier closest to him. The man screamed as he was dragged off by a shoulder. Turo recoiled as man after man was attacked, some taken into the forest, some attacked from above and pulled into the branches. One man was crushed as one of the creatures landed on him. Turo turned and ran. He could hear the creatures feasting behind him, the screams of his men punctuating the sounds of chewing and slurping. He tripped over a root, barely catching himself, and scrambled to regain his balance. They were still chasing him. He knew they were.

Turo burst out of the jungle to the river's shore. He stopped, realizing the boats were gone. He dared look behind him and the pack of creatures were running for him, teeth and claws bloody. Turo ran to the waters and jumped in. His limbs protested every stroke. His heart and lungs felt as if they would burst. Turo pushed himself against the current, keeping the goal of Nsongo in his vision. A group of fishermen tying up their boat saw him and a pair jumped into the water to reach him. They made it to his side just as his limbs were starting to give out.

Turo was pulled to dry land, spitting out water. He still tried to climb onto shore himself, scrambling to get away from the river. His eyes frantically searched the other shore, sure the creatures would be assembled to chase him even here. He watched the waters, waiting for them to emerge, but nothing came. His heart wouldn't stop pounding. He kept watching the other side even as soldiers came and pulled him into the city. The creatures would come for him. He knew it.

* * *

Garemba didn't hear the attack coming. Efah walked along the outskirts of the eastern side of the city, the far more populated side. Her band had always headed west where they'd be harassed less, especially when they'd made a good haul. Here she found strange empty sections that had been reclaimed by the forest. Large rectangles, thirty strides long were marked off by stones embedded in the ground. She and Usa wandered through them, winding between lesser children of the great towering trees outside the city. Nesi was looking about in other parts of the city to keep watch.

The people who'd camped out here watched her
with curiosity. It was obvious that many of them hadn't
had the chance to see her yet and she was sure Usa was
quite an impressive sight. She made sure to keep her distance to not frighten anyone. She may have made allies in
this treacherous place, but she knew the rumors that still
floated about her. The fact that she'd cowed Ayodele and
taken Iyloa's arm must have made its way through every
floor by now. She wasn't sure if that would endear or push
away more people but only time would tell.

Efah stopped as she saw the heart shaped leaves of
a familiar plant growing up out of the ground. It was hidden between two trees and she could see how it would be
easy to miss. She stopped, reaching for it, pulling and digging with her other hand. In a moment she'd pulled a fat
yam from the ground. Efah looked past it into the space
between the trees and saw more leaves jutting up here and
there. She took a moment to look around the area again. It
was so organized, she didn't realize why she didn't see it
before. It must have been a sort of garden.

She stood, walking faster through the marked areas.
Soon she saw a cluster of sad looking millet hanging onto
life at the forest edge of its area. Efah's face pulled into the
brightest smile. Surely, there were some farmers among
the people here. If they could manage to clear these small
fields, they could plant. They would be able to start feeding
the people here.

Efah made her way inside, taking care over the rubble in the hallways. She glanced back to the trees that were
trying to spread into the city. If there were carpenters, they
may be able to take the wood from the felled trees and use
them to strengthen the city. Perhaps they could even find a
way, or someone who knew a way, to repair the stone of
the walls. Efah grinned wider. The city could be a home for
so many again. She reached the main courtyard, watching
as people bathed and washed clothes in the large pool.
They would have to find better water too. She was sure
they would find a way.

Nesi's bark brought her out of her thoughts. Usa

barked in response to her sister. Efah looked to the entrance of the inner city and saw her other companion running up with one of the guards. She ran up to meet them. Worry set in her as she took in the man. He was out of breath and radiated unease.

"What happened?" she asked calmly.

"There are soldiers coming," he panted. "Some people saw them as they were on their way here, so I got sent to scout." He took a moment for a deep breath. "It looked like a huge group of soldiers from Ofolabaru. They're coming this way, into the forest."

Efah's breath caught. "How long until you think they'll get here?"

"Maybe half an hour."

"How many were there?"

"I don't know. Maybe one hundred."

She bit her lip. She stepped out of the way. "Go tell Ayodele."

The guard took off and she looked around at all the people going about their business, not knowing they'd soon be under attack. She patted Nesi's back and the hyena lowered so she could climb on.

"Everyone," she shouted. People looked up at her curiously, but she had their attention. "There are soldiers on their way from Ofolabaru. I need everyone who knows how to fight to find a weapon. Everyone else needs to hide deep within the city. Spread the word. I need all the fighters to meet back here."

People scrambled at her announcement, some hesitating. She turned her attention to a woman who seemed unsure about running.

"Can you fight?" she asked her.

"Yes, but. I haven't since the war."

"Then find a weapon." Efah looked around to the others who hesitated. "We need everyone who can fight. The soldiers aren't here to talk."

She turned Nesi to the entrance and rode out into the outer courtyard. The guards scrambled to form some kind of defense, breaking off parts of the great doors to make a barrier. She did a quick count of the men at the gate and her heart sunk. There were too few. With Ayodele's people and any fighters that might volunteer from the refugees, Garemba would barely scrape up enough people to combat Ofolabaru's forces. And these were trained soldiers against people who'd made the best of their circumstances. She said a prayer to the god of death that he would visit their enemy's soldiers more than Garemba's fighters.

"Have they made it yet?" came Ayodele's booming voice as he and his people burst into the sunshine. He shrunk a bit when he saw her but continued on to get closer to the doorway.

"Not yet," she replied for the men, who still feared the 'ruler of Garemba.' Efah looked over the fighters he'd brought with him and it was just as she'd feared. They were nothing more than a small group of enforcers, barely half of the force approaching. "I've tried to gather fighters from the people who live here, and they should be coming back to the inner courtyard now." She looked to him with a tired disdain. "Do you have any extra weapons?"

"For who?" he asked. "Not for the riff raff in here?"

Nesi and Usa turned toward him before she could instruct them.

"Some of those people are soldiers from the war. We need them. There are one hundred soldiers from Ofolabaru out there and they'll be here any minute. If they break through . . . when they break through our defense, we need everybody who can fight to do it."

Ayodele turned the thought over in his head, his mouth twisting.

"Kamba," he said to the man nearest him, "take three people with you and get the swords from Iyola's rooms." He looked to her as they ran off. "The other fighters will have weapons," he said like an insolent child.

Efah narrowed her eyes at him. She opened her mouth to make a retort but was cut off by a strangled cry from the top of the wall. One of the guards fell from the great height, striking the ground with a sick thud. Efah immediately noticed the arrow rising from his chest.

"They're here," another guard called right before he was shot down from the wall as well.

She looked to Ayodele who was staring at the gates, terror in his eyes.

"Well," she shouted at him. "Lead your warriors."

He began barking orders to fortify the makeshift door and find some good archers. Efah rode back to the second courtyard to see how many, if any, fighters had assembled. To her relief, nearly thirty people were gathered. They looked frightened and some of them seemed to have seen better days, but they were willing.

"This isn't going to be easy," she said trying to muster her own courage. "There are a hundred of them. Just pray they don't break the barrier too quickly." Ayodele's people soon returned with armfuls of weapons, wrapped up in cloth. The volunteer fighters took them and she was glad to see that many of these must have been trained during the war.

Efah sat back in shock when she saw Iyola making her way into the courtyard. Her missing arm was still bandaged, but she held her sword in her right. She gave Efah a scathing glance, cutting through the group assembled.

"Are you sure you're ready to do-."

"I don't need your pity," Iyola snapped back. "I still have one good arm and can outfight anyone you've put together." She made her way to the outer yard.

Efah nodded, at least admiring her determination. "We will stay at the entryway to the inner courtyard," she called out to her volunteers. "And we pray." The gaggle of shouts from outside let her know it needed to be an immediate prayer. She positioned Usa and Nesi at the doorway leading out and waited.

She knew the wood of those ancient doors would only hold for so long. The sounds of shoving and then chopping floated to them. She watched, her heart racing, as Ayodele's people struggled to add more to the barrier. A panicked cry went up as the first ax made its way through the thick wood. Once the hole was clear, arrows flew through taking down two warriors. Another moment and the attack on the doorway ceased.

"Give us the girl," she faintly heard from the other side. "The seer with the beasts."

All eyes in the outer courtyard turned to her. Ayodele looked quite ready to give in to their request. The look on Iyola's face said that if she could throw her over the wall she would. Efah swallowed. A force had been sent just for her. Anger welled up at the death of the warriors they'd already killed to get to her. They would be repaid for their callousness.

Efah turned to the warriors gathered behind her.

"I know you know who I am." Several nodded while others didn't seem to want to acknowledge it. "The god of death led me to this city to protect the people here. Believe in me and we can throw back these people."

The soldier on the other side shouted again. "Give us the seer and we will leave your city alone."

"Lies," Efah hissed. She looked back to the volunteers, praying that somehow their hearts would be swayed. None of them fled.

One man, an older man missing a few fingers on one of his hands, stepped forward.

"Ofolabaru has wanted to find Garemba for ages and take it out. They won't just stop at just taking you. I'm with you, lady of death."

Efah worked to keep the smile from her face as the others decided to stay with her as well. She returned her attention to the titanic doorway of the city of thieves. She rode Nesi to the middle of the courtyard, sitting as upright as she could. On the walls, vultures began to gather. She began to feel the soldiers on the other side of the wall, the rhythm of their heartbeats running along her skin. Efah turned her gaze to Ayodele.

"Let them in."

* * *

Umakaal didn't want anything to distract her this afternoon. She concentrated to ignore the warm sun on her skin and the refreshing breeze coming in. The captain of the Luumawa was running over the daily routine of her ship and she had to stay focused. When Yutuuan became king, she'd take over as head of the military. She'd already outshone his tenure as guard captain. She'd outshine him in this too.

"I would love it if you were able to come with us to sea, princess," Captain Netkala said, smiling. "Real knowledge is only gained by doing."

Umakaal smiled back, panicking as she realized she hadn't heard the last things the captain said.

"I'd love to come out too, but unfortunately, an afternoon seems like all the time I can spare." She looked around the ship with longing. Her brother commanded from a ship much like this. It would be nice to call something like this home for a few months. "Once I've gotten the hang of the guard, I'll be sure to take you up on the offer."

"Excellent, princess." She clapped her hands together. "So, are there any questions I can answer for you before we get into more detail with the running of a ship?"

Umakaal's smile twitched. "How many ships are there in the fleet at the moment?"

"Two hundred and thirty-seven," the captain answered proudly. "Nearly one hundred and twenty of them are usaans, sixty are alsaans, and the rest are scouting vessels."

Umakaal looked up to the tall sails of the huge alsaan warship Netkala commanded. "Well, the Luumawa is beautiful."

"Thank you, princess. We'd be honored if you were to have it become your command vessel."

The princess had to stifle a laugh. She wondered why the captain was so eager to mentor her.

"I will, of course, consider it, captain."

They began to walk to head below decks when a servant from the palace ran onto the ship. Captain Netkala looked insulted.

"What is the meaning of this?" she barked.

The servant bowed before Umakaal. "Princess, your sister wishes for you to return to the palace. A letter has arrived from the prince."

Umakaal's eyes saucered. She turned to the captain. "I'm so sorry. I have to leave."

"Yes, of course. We can continue another time."

She nodded to the captain and hurried back to the palace. Izriamat was in her rooms, pacing.

"Sister," she called, coming in. "You look like something's wrong."

Izriamat looked up to her, brow creased. "Close the door," she whispered.

Umakaal did as she was told and crossed the room. "What happened?" Her heart started to race as her mind began constructing terrible scenarios.

"He's not coming back. At least not for some time." Izriamat took a deep breath. "And we just received word that *he* will be here in less than two weeks' time."

Umakaal snatched the letter from her sister, pouring over the lines. She clutched it to her heart when she was done. Her brother was injured and trapped fighting against some unknown kingdom. They needed all the forces they could muster against the coming war with the Ega. They couldn't afford to divide them.

"What are we going to do?" she asked her sister.

Izriamat stopped, looking out her windows. She didn't answer and Umakaal stepped closer, putting a hand on her shoulder.

"We will continue on without him, just as he said in his letter. He has faith in us. We should as well."

Umakaal crossed her arms, biting on a nail. "We'd have to bar the netkoleh from entering the city."

"Don't you head the guard? Ensure that they're closed that day."

"The palace guard isn't the city guard, Izri. I don't have the authority, even as princess."

Izriamat looked out the windows again and Umakaal didn't like these far away looks her sister was having lately.

"We need to speak to the head of the city's forces. We need them on our side. They'll be our first defense if . . . *he* decides to try something that day." Izriamat looked down at her. "I can't rule out that he wouldn't even with the meager forces he'll be traveling with."

"And what about father? He's still furious with us." Her sister nodded sagely. "He'll be looking for any other sort of 'betrayal' from us."

"Then we'll have to be even more careful." A sea bird landed in the window and Izriamat held her hand out. It climbed into it as docile as any pet. She nuzzled it against her cheek.

"Father will come to understand in time."

Umakaal watched, frozen as her sister released the bird back to the window. "Sister, what is going on with you?"

"What do you mean?" she asked, smiling.

"It's like you haven't been here. You've been some-where else, at least your mind has been."

Her sister paused again, hand to her chin. "Did I tell you I finally returned to the temple?" Umakaal shook her head. "I spoke to Yutuu. I heard his voice, felt his pres-ence. He told me that I was never lost to him." She opened her mouth to say something else but stopped. "My place here has been restored."

Umakaal frowned. She wanted to be happy for her sister, but she didn't like that small pause as she was talk-ing.

"So, will you go back to being a priestess?"

Izriamat laughed. "If you mean will I go back to serving at the temple, no I won't, but I never stopped being one of his priestesses. He showed me that my place is here." She pulled her into an embrace that Umakaal was reluctant to return. "Don't worry. I won't leave you in any of this."

Umakaal gave a weak laugh. She finally hugged her sister tightly.

"Well, send a few more prayers for me too. We're going to need all the gods to get us through this."

"They're already with us."

Umakaal stepped back from her, looking her sister over. "I should probably head on. I still have a lot to learn about the military. And I'll be talking to the city guard commander tomorrow." She began to head toward the door.

"Good," Izriamat replied. "I'll speak with uncle Munabis for his advice."

"Do you think you can trust him not to speak?"

"I'm sure."

Umakaal hesitated. Her sister looked so confident. "Very well," she said, nodding. "I'll see you later."

"Very good, my little Uma."

She turned and left her sister's room, her face settling into a frown. Her sister was holding onto something and Izriamat wasn't one to keep secrets. She felt like she should just leave it alone. Izriamat seemed so happy now, so at peace. It was a complete reversal from when she first arrived. Umakaal chewed on her nail again. She had to let it go. Her brother had charged them with making sure those gates were closed when the netkoleh arrived. She had far bigger things to think about.

CHAPTER TWENTY-FIVE

Ashaki cursed under her breath as the field commander from the excursion left her office. She would have never imagined there were such horrors lurking in that forest. Who would have thought the batubangi would have vicious creatures at their command? She'd underestimated them greatly and that may cost them. Now the batubangi knew they'd broken their treaty completely. She hung her head down, running her hands over her short hair. Perhaps the creatures' compassion toward her warriors meant that the batubangi would show them some consideration to their circumstance. She cursed again. Who knew?

Leaning back in her chair, her eyes rested on the list of candidates for abodara. She scowled at it. That list had haunted her for days. She thought she'd finally narrowed it down to three possible people. They were all excellent leaders. None were related to her and she didn't care. Maybe this was just the end of the line of Yundasha's rulership.

Ashaki sighed deeply, her body deflating. Her life had become a constant string of keeping disasters in check or at least attempting to. She wasn't very sure she had. The war had been disastrous. So many passed on to the ancestors. She hadn't wanted her first command as dara to be surrender but she wanted something to be left of the south. It was her surrender that had ensured survivors, but it still felt like her greatest shame.

The tribute had gone horribly thanks to those damned Egan bastards. She cursed Hotemkhar again. She found herself doing that at least once a day now. Thanks to him and his soldiers' violence, she may be the dara that oversaw the fall of Nsongo. The thought pierced her heart and she struggled to push it away. No. She wouldn't. She'd make a way. There was no other choice.

"Uma," she called to her attendant.

The young man stepped into the room bowing.

"Yes, my dara."

"Would you please bring my dinner in here? I think I'm going to work a little longer."

He smiled. "Of course, my dara."

As he went off to secure her food, Ashaki turned back to her list of candidates. She would need to speak with them individually of course, gauge their reactions to possibly being the abodara. She was pretty sure she was going to choose the war minister's daughter. That would delight Ngali and her husband. Ashaki rolled her eyes. That would put councilmember Oshala over the moon. At least she knew the old woman would vote in favor of that decision.

Uma returned with a tray holding her dinner. Ashaki smiled as the scents crossed the room. Her stomach rudely announced how hungry she was.

"You also have a visitor," Uma said as he set the dishes down before her.

Ashaki looked up to see her daughter standing shyly at the side of the door. She raised an eyebrow. Masola had been a ghost in the compound since their last argument. She'd only seen her daughter in passing and when she did have a moment, they would only exchange a handful of words.

"Good evening, Sola," she said with a half-smile.

Masola nodded to the attendant as he left and came into the room, stopping short of her desk.

"Good evening, mother," she said rubbing an arm. "Can I spend time with you while you eat? I didn't want to disturb your work."

Ashaki's face went slack. Was she actually being polite?

"Please," she said motioning to a nearby stool. "Did you want something to eat?"

Masola brought the stool to the side of the desk.

"No, I'm not quite hungry yet." She leaned against it as Ashaki took her first bites. She found the piece of paper with the list of candidates. "You still haven't chosen an abodara," she commented.

Ashaki prepared herself against another outburst. "No, I haven't."

"Well, at least you've narrowed it down from the last time I saw the list." She looked off. "That's good."

Ashaki turned a small smile towards her daughter.

"I'm sorry it couldn't be you, my heart. Nsongo needs someone who's a true leader."

"It's alright," she snapped. She glanced over sheepishly. "Mother," she added softer.

"Are you sure?" Ashaki moved to be in her line of sight. "It looks like you're still angry about it. It's alright if you are."

"I'm fine," she sighed. Ashaki nodded, leaving the subject be. She grabbed for the pitcher of kovo to fill her cup but Masola grabbed it before she could. "I'll do that for you."

Ashaki smiled and held out her cup. "Thank you very much, Sola." She took a deep drink after Masola filled it, letting the fire of the kovo coat her throat.

"Can I drink some?" Masola asked coming to stand at her side like some kind of servant.

"Absolutely not." Ashaki laughed. "You'll be throwing up in the corner at one sip."

"I'm not a child," she said, frowning.

Ashaki put another bite of meat in her mouth. "Fine." She held out her cup. "One sip."

Masola looked at the cup warily and Ashaki nearly laughed. She took the cup, sniffing it first, then slowly raised it to her lips. She sipped and promptly spit it back in the cup. "It burns!"

Ashaki sucked her teeth. "That's my cup! Go pour it outside." She sucked her teeth at her again as she sulked out of the room. "I told you it wasn't for you," she called after her. She chuckled as she kept eating. Masola soon returned and refilled her cup. Ashaki watched as she looked into the filled cup, swirling its contents thoughtfully.

"You better not think of taking another sip."

"Ew, no." Masola thrust the cup back at her and Ashaki took it thankfully.

They were quiet for a time while she ate, Masola watching her every so often. Ashaki was sure she had something to say but was far too prideful to come out with it. She kept eating. Her daughter would speak when she was ready.

"I enjoy spending time like this, Sola." She downed the last of her kovo, licking her lips to get the last drop.

"It would be nice if you had more time to spend with me."

"You never seem to be where I can find you." She pinned her daughter with a look.

Masola rolled her eyes. "Well, I'll spend more time around the compound." She set the pitcher down and started to walk toward the door. "Maybe."

Ashaki smiled. "Maybe I'll find you." Masola grumbled something and left.

She chuckled, finishing her dinner. Her stomach full and satisfied, Ashaki looked back to the list. She was glad that Masola had come to terms with not being chosen. Perhaps, finally, her daughter was starting to grow up. She called for Uma to take away the remnants of her meal.

"I'll be retiring for the evening." She took the list of candidates from her desk and walked down the halls.

She decided to spend the evening with a good tale from her childhood. She took down the old book, brought by merchants from the north, about a king's daughter who was chosen to be sacrificed to a dragon. She'd always imagined herself as the hero, ready to save the daughter and take her as a wife. She smiled sadly as she read over it again. At least she had her fanciful tale for a little while.

Ashaki frowned as a pain started in her stomach. She tried getting up, but another shot of pain forced her back down. She felt as if she needed to throw up. She pushed herself to her feet, but the sudden burning pain grew, sending her to the floor. Ashaki curled into a ball as she vomited, her dinner and blood splashing on the floor. She tried to call out but vomited again, harder. The room started to lose definition. Ashaki reached a hand out, attempting to claw her way to the door. Tears began to fall from her eyes. The pain erased all thoughts from her mind. She convulsed as she vomited again, the blood dark and viscous. The room began to go dim. Ashaki called for her daughter one last time.

* * *

There was an incessant knock at Erenemo's door. He heard it but it was just an unpleasant sound in his dreams. When his name was finally called, he pulled himself out of the deep sleep he was in. He blinked in the darkness, trying to come back to his senses. The knocking was at his bedroom door, steady and insistent.

"Lord Erenemo," his servant said from the hall.

The priest rose from his bed, pulling on a robe. Rubbing the sleep from his eyes he opened the door.

"What is it?" he grunted, squinting from the lamp the man held. This had better be important. It was too late at night for any sort of foolishness.

"Your great niece Masola is here. She's crying and won't tell me why she wants to speak to you."

Sleep left Erenemo completely. "Where is she?"

"She's in the common room."

He nodded. "I'll take care of this."

Erenemo let the servant lead him to the room and dismissed him for the evening. Masola was at the far side of the room. She paced back and forth in the lamplight; face soaked with tears. Every so many steps she stopped talking to herself to dissolve into unintelligible sobs. He worked to look concerned.

"Masola, what's the matter child?"

The girl looked up to him, eyes bloodshot.

"Uncle." She cried uncontrollably for a moment, struggling to speak. "Mama . . . mama's dead."

He came closer, placing his hands on her shoulders and looking her in the eyes.

"What do you mean, your mother's dead?"

She wiped her nose on the hem of her shirt. "I did just like you told me." She fell into a short series of hiccups. "I went to check up on her later to see if she was sick. She was on the floor. There was blood everywhere."

Erenemo wanted to smile. Relief washed over him, and he struggled to keep his expression. He looked at the girl in horror.

"That can't be. She was just supposed to fall ill." He paused as if realization dawned on him. "You must have used too much."

Masola began to sob again. "No, no. I did just like you said, uncle. Just half of the container. I put it in her kovo so she wouldn't notice it. I swear I only used half."

"You must have measured wrong, Masola. This is horrible." He looked off as she sobbed and snorted. After a moment he looked to her sorrowfully. "You killed your mother."

She covered her mouth, thankfully muffling her wail. She fell to her knees trying to breathe.

"By the gods, I killed her." She looked up to him. "What am I going to do?"

Erenemo shook his head. "You have to leave, Masola."

"What?"

"You killed your mother. You killed your dara. Do you know what will happen to you?" She stared at him, the thought slowly settling in. He came to her, helping her to her feet. "You have to go. Leave now and go far away. As far away from Nsongo as you can."

"But-," she protested.

"You need to leave now before anyone realizes it was you. That is the only way I can save your life, my niece." Picking up one of the lamps, he quickly escorted her out of the room and to the front of his compound. "Please leave this city, Masola," he said opening the door. "Save yourself."

She stepped out into the darkness of the city, turning around to look at him with her swollen eyes. Tearfully, she nodded and ran off. Erenemo watched her until she disappeared into the night, then closed the door behind him. He carefully made his way down the halls as silently as he could. He didn't want to wake anyone else up.

He sat down heavily on his bed when he returned to his bedroom. He released the grin he'd been holding in all this time. Ashaki was finally gone. Nsongo was rid of its most incompetent dara. They were free to choose a new one who might be able to throw off the shackles of the Ega and return the south to the height of its glory. He removed his robe, settling in under his cover. With a smile on his face, Erenemo fell back into a deep sleep.

* * *

The soldiers of Ofolabaru moved back as Efah approached the cleared doorway of Garemba. Usa and Nesi growled lowly, the sound punctuated by sporadic laughs. Efah looked to the leader. Her eyebrows lifted. The peacekeeper who tried to stop her escape was leading this force. His facial scars were healed over but still pink and painful looking. His mouth twitched into a frown.

"Come with us, seer," he spat out. "You are outnumbered. We're ready for you and your beasts this time."

She glanced back to the fighters who'd pledged themselves to her. "I won't surrender to you and your dara. If you want to take me, it will be my cold, dead corpse." She managed a smirk. "I don't think death is ready for me yet. However, he can be ready for you." She looked up to the walls and the vultures that still gathered.

The peacekeeper studied the vultures, his face tight.

"Your creatures won't be able to protect you from all of us."

"If you're so sure of yourself, attack. I know we have the god of death on our side. Who do you have?"

He grimaced at her question. "Attack her," he shouted.

The forces of Ofolabaru approached, spreading out from their tight, three lined formation. They had their swords out, moving toward her cautiously. Efah felt their fear through the rapid beating of their hearts. Her hyenas began to laugh, making the men pause. Efah frowned. She was tired of their hesitation.

"Let's go," she whispered to her hyenas.

The three of them surged forward. The cries of her fighters sounded behind her, filling her with pride. Usa jumped onto one of the warriors, cracking his head between her jaws and ripping it free. Nesi charged another, clamping onto her arm. She swung the woman around, hitting three more soldiers before tossing the woman away. Her fighters ran forward to engage the soldiers.

With the first wave cleared, the dara's peacekeeper came to meet her. Eyes full of hate, he approached quickly and cautiously. He'd already had a taste of fighting her hyenas before. Efah was sure he didn't want another.

"What is your name, peacekeeper?"

"Ala of the house of Inamu." He leveled a spear at her. Nesi began laughing at him.

Efah nodded. "Ala of house Inamu, I hope you've settled your debts with the gods. You're going to meet them today."

He growled and began stabbing at Nesi. Her hyena deftly hopped and maneuvered out of the way, laughing increasingly louder. Another soldier came to help him, slashing at her leg. Nesi evaded them both. Efah called to the vultures that were watching the battle, shouting for them to help her fighters. They dove from the wall, attacking the enemy soldiers' heads. Eyes were pecked out and faces raked with talons. Her fighters took every opportunity to finish off what the birds started.

Ala began stabbing at her, spittle foaming at the side of his scarred mouth. She held on as her hyena moved to keep her safe. The other soldier assisting him tried to feint to the side and attack, but Nesi swept a paw forward, hitting him in the chest. Another soldier came in from the other side, stabbing Nesi in the shoulder. Her beast turned on him, her motion pulling the spear from his hands and she bit into his face.

Efah reached down for the spear, working to remove it while Nesi backed away from the peacekeeper. Ala was moving slowly forward, spear poised and ready. She took a moment to glance around. While she had her standoff, her fighters were surrounded. They battled ferociously with the help of the vultures. Usa was a force by herself, a small pile of dead Ofolobaruans laid at her feet. Yet, ahead of her there were still scores of soldiers ready to take their chance. The path kept them bottlenecked, thankfully, but as soon as one soldier went down another came to take his place.

Efah wrenched the spear from Nesi's shoulder, turning it to wield it. Ala smiled.

"Do you even know how to use that?"

Efah smiled back at him, tired of his presence. "Yes. The pointy end goes into the other warrior." Nesi lunged at him, catching him off guard. He was forced to scramble back. This gave Nesi the opportunity to continue snapping at him, trying to get a good bite on him. He caught his footing, stabbing past Nesi's last bite to get to Efah. Efah swung her spear to counter. To their surprise, her desperate move knocked his lunge high, leaving him open. Nesi bit, jaw wide, to encompass his rib cage. The first bite didn't crush him so Nesi bit again, his chest collapsing under the force.

Efah watched as his expression turned confused until his face went slack. A silvery wisp detached itself from his body, dissipating into the air. Satisfied with his extinction, she urged Nesi back into battle.

* * *

Newa faced the jungle, shifting back and forth on his feet. The information he'd gotten on this city of thieves was sketchy, and he was hesitant to follow it. Several people in the last city he'd left seemed to know about it. It even had a name: Garemba. It was supposed to be the lost city of some long dead king, almost a fairy tale. He looked up and down the road at the wall of trees not yet touched by man. Then, he looked to the barely noticeable path in front of him. While he didn't like the idea of spending more time just out in the wilderness, he felt compelled to continue.

He took his first step into the jungle. As the forest closed in around him, there was a strange feeling settling in on him. Newa tried to ignore it, but it was something that had nagged at him since he started on his journey to find this hidden city. It felt like something was guiding his path here. He prayed it was Gu'un, but he couldn't think of what his god would want him to do this far south in a city of thieves. These people didn't even believe in Gu'un. They still had their odd host of ancient gods or ancestors or whatever confused religion they believed in. But this would be a place no one would look for him so he would be a resident of the far end of the south until he could be sure he was no longer being hunted.

Newa slowed down his steps after he tripped over a root for the third time. Cursing, he untangled his foot, slapping at bugs as he rose to carry on. The path before him was faint but even though he was a child of the city, he could tell where repeated traffic had worn the world down. Just as dirt or brick would have been worn smooth, the ground was laid bare. Plants wouldn't want to grow in a spot that they would surely be trod upon.

Overhead, monkeys swung by him, hooting and calling. Newa stared, amazed. He'd never seen them outside of cages or not with traveling entertainers. He saw a beautiful white plumed bird fly by and suddenly realized where those expensive, sought after feathers came from. He kept watching the bird's flight until he heard the sound of fighting. He stopped, listening carefully. It was far off but there was no doubt to the sound of swords meeting.

He moved along the path as quickly as he could without falling, curious as to the source of the din. He was surprised as his path merged into another and then what must be a main path. This one was wider, enough for two people to walk down together. Newa picked up speed, urgency coming to him. He turned around corner after corner until he reached a long, straight length of the path. Ahead of him, a force gathered outside a massive wall built into the jungle itself. It was obvious by the roar that a vicious fight was happening at the gates.

Newa paused, ready to fight but his mind questioning him at the same time. These forces looked to be from the city he'd just left. He wondered why they were attacking some fabled city deep in the jungle. Newa looked up to the massive walls that may hold his salvation for a time. He made his decision. They stood between him and his goal, so they had to be removed.

He took out his fighting blades, crossing them in front of himself in supplication to Gu'un. The soldiers at the rear of the contingent didn't even notice his approach. The noise of the battle covered up what little noise his footsteps caused. Newa ran in between their loose formation, turning and slicing as he stepped. Four of the soldiers went down before he was seen. The next line turned at the sound of their comrades dropping, shouting at the discovery of a new enemy. Newa ran up to the nearest one, stabbing him in the stomach up to the hilt. He forced the man between him and the other soldiers, using him as a shield. Newa struck out at another soldier, cutting this one across the face. The man reared back in pain, getting in the way of a woman trying to spear him. Newa took that moment to kick the slowly dying man off his blade, sending him staggering into his fellow soldiers.

He ran forward, keeping low to slice at the thighs and calves of more soldiers. More of them turned around to see what the commotion was, leaving Newa surrounded and excited. He couldn't help the smile on his face. He had no true stake in this fight, but he couldn't ignore the feeling that he needed to be in this fight. This was his fight. He spun and cut a pair of sword wielders down. He ducked low under a stab from a spear, rushing in to open their stomach.

He felt lighter on his feet than he'd ever felt skulking about the city or working on the unrepentant in his confession room. The grin wouldn't leave his face as he cut down soldier after soldier. He knew in his heart that these people needed to be cut down. He barely noticed the main fighting had gotten close to him until he heard a loud growl near him. He cut down the last of the soldiers near him and turned to see what was happening.

Newa's jaw dropped at the sight of the woman atop the massive hyena. Her beast took one last bite of an enemy, throwing the body aside as it chewed. Another beast ran up, laughing and taking down a few more of the last soldiers as it caught up to its twin. Newa couldn't take his eyes from the sight of them. Death clung to her and the air around her. Death rose up behind her and he gasped at the great figure standing up. He was clothed just as the temple murals depicted him. His arms were decorated with bejeweled gold bands. On his head was the vulture feathered headdress that came down, covering his shoulders. The symbol of death was tattooed across his bare chest. Newa dropped to one knee before her, lowering his head. He felt the hyenas come closer, sniffing about him. He tried to keep still under the scrutiny.

"Who are you?" she asked, and the authority of her voice rippled across Newa's skin.

"I am Newa." He dared to look up and saw her considering him from atop her beast.

She tilted her head. "You are a servant of Ikombe, the Twin Blade, the Sword of Death."

Newa was about to say no, when the depiction of his god came to mind.

"Yes."

She didn't speak for a moment, turning her head slightly to the side as if she were listening to someone.

"Ikombe has always been the servant of Death. Your people chose to rise him up to an equal."

Newa looked up to this woman, so small and unassuming, yet with a power and presence that pressed down on him. He felt tears form in his eyes. He felt the truth in her words.

"My lady, as a servant of Gu'un, I am here to serve you." He lowered his head again.

He was fearful when he heard nothing at first. Then, he was licked up the side of his face. She gave him a small smile when he looked up again.

"Then, welcome to Garemba. I'm happy to have you here."

CHAPTER TWENTY-SIX

Today was the day. Bakari took a deep breath, catching the slight sent of the ocean on the breeze. The low mountains of Wiluru rose before them in the distance. He was utterly relieved that their trek north was almost over. From the city of Wiluru, they would travel to the other major cities and then head back south by sea. And on his trip south he would finally have his beloved Izriamat with him.

He smiled, thinking of possessing his second wife in his arms and bed again. Getting her back at the end of these months of travel had been the only thing helping him endure the repeated drudgery of the Pilgrimage. Yes, he needed to personally oversee the tallies of his empire's riches but after the sixteenth town it became an exercise in boredom. The taxes collected would be considerable this year. The abundant rains over the first part of the year had brought a boon to their farmers and the grain harvest was exceptional. That combined with the fabrics and paper produced would fill many of Metkara's storehouses. He smiled. Already the age of man was proving fruitful.

Bakari's smile disappeared as the procession slowed to a stop. Murmurs of confusion spread from the front and he grew annoyed. They were so close to Wiluru, the mountains towered over them now. He could feel the energy of the city.

"What's going on?" he demanded.

His closest guard lifted up in his saddle to try to see ahead.

"I'll go see," he said breaking from the line and riding ahead.

Bakari released his reins, crossing his arms. If this

was not a serious matter, he'd flay someone alive. His guard rode back after several minutes, concern plastered across his face. Bakari frowned.

"Well, what is it?"

The guard hesitated. "The gates. They're closed."

"What do you mean they're closed?"

"The gates into the city are closed. They won't open them."

Bakari broke from his place in the procession, pushing past attendants and their horses. He kicked his steed into a run, anger starting to spread through his veins. He pulled to a stop as he reached the front, looking up at the tall and very closed gates. His face burned. He turned his attention to the men riding at the front of the procession.

"Do they not know who we are?" he shouted.

The men all jumped at his tone. The head of them bobbed his head.

"We tried to explain to them in case the message of your arrival didn't make it. They said they were told not to open them to you."

"What?!" His shout echoed off of the walls. Bakari turned his searing gaze on the men at the top of the wall.

"Do you know who I am? Your emperor stands before you."

A young woman in armor came to the middle of the gates, looking down on him. He could see her sneer from where he stood. There was something about her that reminded him of Izriamat.

"We know why you're here, *emperor*," she said. He seethed at the way she said his title. "We won't let you spread your abominable message here."

There were sounds of agreement from the other guards near her and he thought about how he'd see them all punished.

"Woman, you will open these doors immediately!"

"No," came a familiar voice.

Bakari turned his attention to the new speaker. His anger faded. It was Izriamat.

* * *

Izriamat felt change in the air the moment she awoke. After taking a few moments of prayer and reflection she sat by the window, staring out toward the sea. Today was the day her husband was to arrive at the gates. She still felt sick at the thought of him. She was sure he thought his trip here would be a peaceful one. He'd conduct his counts, collect her, and they'd be on their way. She couldn't help a chuckle. He had no idea how much his plans were about to go awry.

Umakaal had done an incredible job talking to the city guards and bringing them to their side. Some were a little hesitant to oppose the netkoleh but once she'd brought in the perspective that they could be risking their position on the other side; most were eager to become conspirators. The captain was on board with the plan the moment he was told what their ruler planned to do. He was a very faithful man.

Izriamat was impressed at her sister's gift of persuasion. People lent an ear to her readily and her easy, cheerful personality drew them close. Their brother was charming, a fact known far and wide, but it seemed their little sister was the real people person. She would make an impressive military leader when she finally ascended. Izriamat was sure of it.

A strong breeze pressed through her windows, caressing her face. She looked from the sea to the cityscape. She couldn't see the wall from her rooms but she knew her attention was being drawn there. He was on his way. Izriamat took her breakfast, calm despite her feelings about the creature that would soon be approaching their gates. Today was going to be the start of a new history for Wiluru. She knew it. She felt it in her soul. She would have no fear today because Yutuu was going to restore his people.

She finished her food and dressed for the day, taking to the city. Her attendants asked if they were going to the market. When she told them of their true destination, their faces fell one after another. Izriamat stifled a chuckle. The wall wasn't the most enjoyable spot in the city but today it was the most important.

People greeted her warmly as she made her way along. Many asked for blessings and she was more than happy to oblige. Izriamat had to blink away tears as she did so. It felt so wonderful to be back about Yutuu's work and being among her people. She didn't realize how much she'd missed it.

She approached the wall slowly, seeing guards rushing to get to the gates. Her skin tingled under the tense feeling in the air. She began to climb the stairs to the top of the wall. Guards scrambled, shocked, to stand aside for Wiluru's eldest princess. As she ascended the last of the stairs, she could hear shouting coming from the other side of the gates and her heart skipped a beat. That was the unmistakable voice of her husband. She watched as Umakaal shouted back at him, proud as her sister stared down at him unafraid.

"Woman, you will open these doors immediately!" came his petulant cry.

"No," Izriamat replied loudly, her mood souring at the sight of him.

Umakaal looked to her, eyes wide.

"Sister, what are you doing here?" she hissed.

"I'm doing what's right."

Izriamat stared down at the man who had been the source of her every woe for seven years. She saw him turn black with his rage as if he were burning up from the inside. She saw his people aflame, burning to bodies of ash that slowly fell apart in the wind. She knew the fire, the destruction led back to the heart of the empire where it burned away its rotten core.

She blinked, the vision clearing. Umakaal put a hand on her shoulder.

"Are you alright?"

Izriamat nodded. "I'm fine." She looked back to the tiny shape that was her husband. His face was a deep maroon as he yelled up to them.

"Bakari," she called down to him, savoring the collective gasp at her using his birth name. "Your plan to make Wiluru part of your godless empire will only end in ruin and ash."

"How dare you?!" he roared.

"Turn your people around and do not return to our gates again."

His mouth worked furiously. "You are my wife! You will open those gates and stop this foolishness. Your disobedience won't go unpunished, Izriamat."

Izriamat looked down her nose at him. *A petulant child,* she thought, watching his rant. He was nothing more than a petulant child that had never been told no.

"Yutuu has severed any bond I may have had with you. I am restored to my proper place here."

"You have a son!"

"He has severed those bonds as well. Now, leave. There is nothing more to discuss." She waited patiently as he absorbed her words. Her sister and the other guards at the wall stared, but nothing could waver her resolve. Yutuu had made it clear. It was her place to lead and she would fulfill her duty to her utmost abilities.

"You have doomed your lands, wife," he said, spitting out the last word. "I will return with an army, a host of soldiers from all corners of the empire. We will run through Wiluru and burn it to the ground. We will burn every building, every ship, every temple. We will take all that it has to offer to strengthen the rest of the empire. Wiluru will be just a whisper of the past, a tale of a city that dared to disobey its emperor.

"And you, you I will deal with myself and drag you back to your proper place."

Izriamat turned from the wall and began making her way to the stairs. Umakaal caught her arm.

"Why did you provoke him so?"

"Provoking him was the best thing I could have ever done." She motioned to the guards, who were quickly talking among themselves. "We outed his plan for the empire and forced him to show his true nature. The tale of the netkoleh's threats will be exaggerated through the city ten-fold by morning." She pinned her sister with a stare. "This is what we wanted. We want to fight his blasphemy. Yutu-uan put his trust in us to see this through without him. Please don't tell me your courage is giving out now."

Umakaal released her, shaking her head.

"My courage has never given out," she said firmly.

"Good." Izriamat looked up to the guards whose attention was starting to turn toward them.

"Now go and be with the guard. They'll need your courage as well." Her sister paused, then turned to return to her place at the wall. Izriamat began descending the stairs, looking out over the city as she did so. A cool breeze caressed her face, sweeping away any uncertainty she had left. For her people, this was the only way forward.

*   *   *

Bakari stared at the wall as if his sheer will would open the gates. He could feel the stares of the guards looking down on him from atop the wall and the gaze of that impudent woman who'd first defied him. He felt the expectant stares of his people, felt their chatter crawling over his skin. His anger smoldered just beneath the surface of his body. Wiluru had turned him away. They'd openly defied him. His wife had openly defied him.

Bakari's face melted into the deepest of frowns. He would make Izriamat pay for this humiliation. Her utter disrespect was unfathomable. He didn't know what had gotten into her, what ideas her family had put in her head, but he would make sure she remembered her place for the rest of her life.

He turned his horse, walking it away from the city. The group parted for him in confusion, but scrambled to fall into their proper places around him. He didn't speak; he couldn't. His anger had stolen every word. Silence fell on his entourage as they left Wiluru and he was glad of it. There was only the sound of the horses until they'd made camp for the night.

Bakari walked off from the group as they worked to erect tents. He stared out to the landscape, watching as the grasslands of the heart of the empire encroached on the arid climate of Wiluru. Footsteps approached and after a moment he heard the voice of the head of his guard.

"Do you have any orders, my emperor?"

"Yes, send word to Metkara. Tell them to gather the army."

"What about the rest of the Pilgrimage?"

Bakari rounded on the man. "Fuck the Pilgrimage!" he said, back handing him. His head guard took the blow, lowering his head as he recovered. "Do you think I'm worried about taxes when the north has rebelled? Send the message to gather the army, as many men as they can muster. Tell them to send word to the outer cities if they have to. I want a force that will crush Wiluru."

"Yes, my emperor."

The man bowed and quickly walked away, leaving Bakari to his thoughts again. He watched the thick grass being blown by the wind, moving in waves toward the north. A grim determination settled on him. His ancestors had subdued proud Wiluru in the past. It appeared that he would have to subdue her again.

CHAPTER TWENTY-SEVEN

Sept'ha burned her finger on the oven again. She cursed, sticking the throbbing digit in her mouth. That's what she deserved for trying to eavesdrop instead of paying attention to dinner. She focused on taking out the large loaf of bread, trying not to listen but it wasn't as if her family was being quiet. Her brother, Imhoten, was on another one of his speeches about the evils of the empire and how the emperor and all that joined in his heretical crusade would be judged by the gods. She was looking forward to her parents' response today.

Imhoten had been nearly insufferable since his return from studying at the temple of Nemamun. Now that he was no longer on his way to becoming a priest he sat around the house, railing against the emperor during the day, drinking at night, and becoming a drain on their parents' money and food. His talks with mother often led to her taking refuge in her room. His conversations with father often led to a knock to the side of the head. Unfortunately, that often left Sept'ha to listen to his religious ramblings. She sighed, checking on the lamb roasting in the oven. The big brother that she'd once known and loved was gone, replaced by a pompous lush. He should be glad mother and father could take him back in after the temples of Metkara were closed. Many priests had found themselves on the street.

The conversation from inside grew louder and Sept'ha prayed the neighbors couldn't hear. It sounded as if father had taken on admonishing Imhoten this time. As she brought out the lamb and the cooked vegetables, she heard shouts of 'keeping thoughts to himself' and 'getting us all in trouble with the guard.' Sept'ha brought the dish inside hoping that dinner would stifle any more arguing. Her mother brought out a pitcher of beer, setting it down on the table with a sigh. Her father and brother stopped their current discussion, staring each other down as they sat for the meal.

Thankful for silence, Sept'ha brought out the rest of the food. Her brother made a show of saying a prayer over it, thanking the gods for their bounty even in the midst of such blasphemous times.

Their father slammed his cup down, its contents sloshing around.

"Damn it boy, if you don't stop all of that blasphemy talk! Do you want to see all of us taken off?"

Imhoten sniffed, indignantly. "I cannot lie about the truth of the matter, father."

"For the last time, keep it to yourself."

Their father's tone quelled any retort her brother had. Dinner was held in silence until he bit into his leg of lamb.

"This meat is a bit tough, sister. Are you sure it's a lamb?"

The ungrateful nature of his voice irked her. "It's the best we could afford. Maybe if . . ." She stopped herself before she said something she might regret.

"Maybe what?" her brother asked, eying her. "Go on. Say it."

Sept'ha balled her fists in her lap. "Maybe if you got off your pompous ass and got a job, we could afford better."

Father chuckled and Imhoten's face reddened in response. "I will not take insult or advice from someone who's waiting for father to choose the best man to lay them on their back."

Sept'ha punched him by the time she rose from her chair. Imhoten was knocked back, enough to make him topple over. Her breath was heavy, her fists balled and ready to punch him again.

"Sept'ha," her father called. "Leave him be."

She wanted to obey her father, but she spit on her brother instead. Her parents called after her as she left the room heading for the door outside. Her anger felt too large to be contained in their house. She needed air and distance from that creature. She stomped through the dimming streets of the city, the heat of the day finally abating.

Father should have let her find work. But he said he wouldn't let any of the women in his life toil as long as he had an able body. It was ridiculous. She was a good baker and cook, she was sure she could find work in some noble's house. She could take in laundry. She could be an accountant. She could find someone to take her in as an apprentice. If her father would just see some reason, they wouldn't be as strained as they were. Maybe things wouldn't be so bad.

She paused in her walk, taking a deep breath. This was silly, storming around the district when it was almost night. There was nothing to be had out here that would fix any of her troubles. Sept'ha started to turn but stopped. She looked up into the dark entrance of the local temple of Met. It stood as a ghost along the street, its doorway marred by the chisels that had taken away all of the inscriptions. The goddess no longer looked down from the top of the entrance, her ruby eyes boring into all that entered. Sept'ha had never been in the temple of the war goddess but she'd heard about the incredible interior. All inside was supposed to inspire warriors to fight for their empire to the fullest.

But all of that had been removed by the city guard now, carted off to the emperor's storehouses more than likely. Sept'ha stepped closer, trying to peer deeper into the near black interior. Only a little light poured in from the skylights but she could tell that the entire place had been stripped. She looked around, licking her lips. Surely, in their haste to erase the goddess's presence, they hadn't taken everything. Perhaps there was something left, something to salvage. Even a small trinket from the temple, more than likely made of gold or silver, would fetch a good price to the right buyer. It would probably fetch even more from some secret religious zealot.

Sept'ha looked around again, making sure no one was around, and stepped inside. She stifled a cough from the dust that still lingered from the desecration of the images and statues. Piles of rubble littered the floor, proof of the damage. Sept'ha began trying to move some of it, hoping to find some kind of trinket to sell. Nearly anything would do. She made her way all the way to the altar, or at least, where the altar had been. Only the stone slab that supported it remained, all of the gold carted off. She carefully inspected the floor around it. The dim light made it even harder to see but she was determined to make money for her family.

She froze at the sound of growling coming from behind her. She slowly lifted up, expecting to see a feral dog that had wandered its way in. She stopped again when she saw not a dog, but a leopard in the dim light. Its eyes glowed and were locked on her. She didn't dare move. Leopards made their way into the city seldomly, but they were usually met with an angry mob. Only she would have the luck to pick through the temple that it had made its home.

"I just want to go home," she said in a sing-song voice. "Please let me by, pretty kitten."

"He won't hurt you," came a sudden voice from the side.

Sept'ha jumped, looking over. A tall woman stood beside the altar, clad in layer on layer of the most luxurious sheer fabric. She reached a muscled arm out to the leopard and it ceased its growling to pad over to her. Sept'ha took in her beautifully braided hair and chiseled face. Her eyes widened. She dropped to a knee, lowering her head.

"Praise be to Met," she said, her heart racing.

"Look up to me." Sept'ha did as she was told and found herself lost in the goddess's golden eyes. "You have the spirit of a fighter, a woman after my own heart. Had this been another time you could have been a commander of soldiers." Met tilted her head, a small smile coming to her lips. "There still may be time. You may not command troops directly but you will command them from afar. I need a hand in this world, a true follower to go forward and lay out my desires. You, Sept'ha, daughter of Kama, are the one I choose."

Sept'ha struggled to respond. "What would you have me do, great Met?"

"You will be a support to the netkoleh. Lend him your insight and advice. Help him strive toward his goals."

"But, the netkoleh destroyed the temples. He doesn't believe in you anymore."

Met smiled down at her. "His disbelief is irrelevant to his purpose. Help him."

Sept'ha lowered her head again. "I will, great goddess." She felt the warm hand of Met on her chin and the goddess lifted her face up.

"Do not worry, my chosen. Now is a time to rejoice." Met smiled brightly, her leopard rubbing against her leg.

"War is coming."

ABOUT THE AUTHOR

Sarah A. Macklin is a writer born and raised just outside of Columbia, South Carolina. An avid reader as a child, it was only natural that she soon turned to crafting her own tales. When not writing, you can find her making art, sewing, or creating her own recipes. She is blessed to live with her equally dorky husband and two quick witted daughters.

We hope you enjoyed The Royal Heretic by Sarah Macklin. For more exciting Sword and Soul adventures and the Best of the Black Fantastic, visit us at
www.mvmediaatl.com